THE BOSS PROBLEM

A SINGLE-DAD, WORKPLACE ROMANCE

NEW YORK OFFICE BILLIONAIRES
BOOK 2

MEG GARNET

Copyright © 2024 by MEG GARNET
All rights reserved.

Visit my website at www.meggarnet.com
Cover Designer: Qamber Designs
Editor: Jovana Shirley, Unforeseen Editing, www.unforeseenediting.com

No part of this book may be reproduced or transmitted in any form or by any means, electronic or mechanical, including photocopying, recording, or by any information storage and retrieval system without the written permission of the author, except for the use of brief quotations in a book review.

This book is a work of fiction. Names, characters, places, and incidents either are products of the author's imagination or are used fictitiously. Any resemblance to actual persons, living or dead, events, or locales is entirely coincidental.

❦ Created with Vellum

1

CHLOE

The name on the coffee cup—*Chloe*—was mine, but the check marks on the label were right next to *decaf* and *cappuccino*. Under notes, someone had scribbled *dry*.

It had been sitting for the longest time on the counter of The Jumpy Bean—a café on my way to my fiancé, Bruce's, house.

The problem was that while I *was* Chloe, it was not the drink that I'd ordered via the app. But then again, it was seven in the morning, and mistakes could be made at this ungodly hour.

I'd been here for fifteen minutes now, I realized after checking my phone for the time. Since I was planning on eloping with Bruce in two hours, I was in a bit of a hurry. I'd already gotten a flat white for Bruce.

If only my drink would show up.

Setting my phone and Bruce's freshly dry-cleaned suit down on the counter, I grabbed the cup marked Chloe and walked up to the cashier, whose nametag read 'Mia'.

It took two attempts to get Mia to look at me. When she

did, she froze while I acknowledged that a woman in a white wedding dress at a café was bound to get some jaws dropping.

It wasn't too expensive, I wanted to say about my wedding dress, realizing that anyone's first concern would be about getting coffee on the dress. You could drop coffee on it and pop into a dry cleaner for a quick wash, and it would be as good as new.

Initially, I hadn't been too happy about getting my dress from the clearance section of David's Bridal, but now, I could agree that a cheap wedding dress had its perks.

But something else struck me.

Mia wasn't staring at me.

What could be more astounding than a bride in white lace and frills, tempting fate by getting coffee first?

A quick check confirmed that there was a hulking man behind me, a man Mia was ogling. A man who seemed to fill out the space quite comfortably and whose physique quite justified the ogling.

The man didn't look at us, but someone in the line behind him coughed, reminding Mia and me of our manners.

"Can I help you?" Mia asked finally, tearing her eyes away from the man behind me.

I had to resist looking over my shoulder at the man who seemed to command so much attention. When you were almost married, as I was, second looks at other men were not in the cards.

I forced myself to think about the problem at hand and held my drink out. "This cup has my name on it, but it isn't the drink I ordered via the app. But because it's been sitting there for over ten minutes now, I suspect it could be mine. But I asked for an Americano, not a cappuccino," I said, placing the cup on the counter as I registered that Mia was now giving me a pointed glare while also trying to keep a smile on her face and look approachable.

"Sorry about that," Mia said, reaching for a cup. "I'll get the right drink going for you now."

The man behind me cleared his throat, which I knew was an indication of me taking too much time, so I thanked Mia and turned around.

The man I saw had two fine eyebrows on a dimpled face with eyes that were deep brown. His gaze met mine, and I realized he was definitely irritated.

The dimple disappeared, and he spoke. "Excuse me, are you done?" he asked, sounding annoyed.

I had stepped aside and was not blocking his path to Mia or the counter, but he'd still insisted on asking me this question, which was something I'd seen irritable people do.

"Yes, of course," I said. "I can't spend more than twenty minutes here because I plan to get married to my fiancé this morning, and I need to be at court in under an hour. So, yes, I am done."

There was a sudden silence as the man's eyes lingered on my face for a moment longer than was necessary. His gaze rested on me, as though he actually saw me and saw something he liked.

"I was hoping the wedding dress you're wearing was for a costume party instead." His voice was wry as he continued to gaze at me, and his lips had a mocking smile.

I realized he was joking. Of course he knew I was headed to a wedding. Why was I announcing it to everyone when my dress was already doing it for me?

"No, it's not," I replied curtly, but he was already speaking to Mia and placing his order for an Americano.

I pressed my lips together, unsure what to make of him.

Unfortunately, he was the kind of guy that women found attractive, so I bet he was the kind of guy who had success in flirting with other women. He had short brown hair that was cut very well, a kind of windswept look to him even if the look implied that he had just stepped out of a hair salon, which couldn't be true really since it was only a little after seven in the morning.

I turned to go, heading to the counter where my Americano was ready.

Just as I went for the coffee cup, the handsome man swooped in.

He reached in front of me for the cup. "Ah, *my* coffee. Thank you."

Startled, I territorially put my hand on the lid of the cup while he held fast to the cup. Sure, he had broad shoulders, but that didn't change the fact that he was unmistakably condescending. And it irritated me.

"Wait, no! That's mine. I paid for it," I said, even though Mia hadn't written any name on the cup.

The man raised a cocky eyebrow, his charcoal suit not showing a single crease while he stepped forward. "*You* paid for it? Darling, you're mistaken. I always get my coffee here, and I know when it is mine."

His hand touched my fingers, and the touch felt like fire on my skin. My first instinct told me to yank my hand away —I had no business feeling tingly feelings today, of all days, with another man—before I realized he'd run off with my coffee if he had the chance.

Thank goodness he was a jerk. Those nerves in my stomach would disappear soon.

My voice trembling, I protested, "Look, I work really hard at my job just to afford this. It's been a rough morning, and I need that caffeine boost."

Leaning in, the beautiful man smirked, a look that only made him seem more irritatingly handsome. "Rough morning? I doubt your definition of rough matches mine. I practically own this place."

My eyes narrowed. I'd had enough.

"Listen, dude," I said firmly, "I don't care if you're a millionaire or the king of coffee. That cup is mine."

He smirked, leaning casually against the counter. "Well, darling, I—"

Before he could finish, I pulled the cup toward me. His hand slipped over mine, our hands collided, and hot coffee spilled onto the counter.

The barista looked up from the espresso machine, alarmed. "Whoa, folks! Easy there!"

Ignoring him, I stared at the man. "I won't back down," I said, my voice determined. "Not today."

He wiped some of the coffee off his cuff before he looked at me, his intense expression unreadable. His gaze roved my face before he spoke slowly. "You're quite the feisty one, aren't you?"

I grabbed the now-free cup, my knuckles white. "Yes, and unlucky for you, today just happens to be my day."

I clutched the cup to me just as he reached for it, grasping at the space where the cup was. Feeling victorious, I placed my two drinks into a cardboard tray, and picking up my drink and Bruce's suit, I headed toward the door.

At the door, I paused and turned around for a last look at the coffeehouse man before I pushed the door open.

"Someone had to put him in his place," I muttered.

He had turned around, and he was looking in my direction. Our gazes met, and for an instant, it was as if the air around me had charged up. I felt the intensity of his gaze pulling me in until, flustered, I turned away. But not before I had this odd, out-of-place thought.

He is totally the kind of guy I'd be attracted to if I wasn't in love already. And if he wasn't a jerk.

I walked out of the café and into the early September morning sun. I shook off all thoughts of the jerk as I looked around.

New York in the fall was beautiful if you asked me. New York at any time of the year was beautiful. Some people complained about the tourists, but I still loved the variety of people you met here.

Like the skateboard guy who showed up at our apartment daily, selling apples to fund his next movie. I didn't like the premise of his movie—too violent—but I still bought his apples every day because dreams must be encouraged. If you didn't stand up for another person's dreams, how could you stand up for your own?

I didn't have too many dreams at the moment. Getting married was one that was coming true soon. I figured I'd sort out the rest of my life later.

My regular day had three main priorities—taking care of my wheelchair-bound brother, Henry; working as an admin assistant in Mindwell Inc.; and spending time with Bruce.

Today, I wouldn't be able to get to the *working as an admin assistant* part of my day and would barely spend time with Henry. Thankfully, Bruce lived not too far from here, and I couldn't wait to surprise him with the cup of coffee.

I wasn't going to let Bruce see me in my wedding dress, but I did want to hand over the tux at his doorstep. I wanted to see him before we met at the courthouse.

My court wedding was in a few hours—nothing fancy,

just a simple ceremony. But it felt meaningful, like the start of something new. I felt the anticipation rise in my chest.

"Excuse me," a less familiar voice called out from behind me.

I turned around and saw those brown eyes again. It was the same man from the café.

For an instant, I felt worried. Had he followed me out here to argue with me? But I noticed he had a smile on his face. A charming smile.

The fact that he'd followed me out onto the sidewalk ought to be mildly startling. Instead, I felt a sense of weakening in my knees as I continued to gaze at him.

"You left something behind at the café," he said.

I looked at his hands, which I noticed were really broad, before I saw my phone in one of them.

My heartbeat picked up at the thought that I'd almost lost my phone. I couldn't afford another phone.

Setting the tray of coffee drinks and Bruce's suit down on a nearby café table, I turned to him. I stared at my phone in his large hand, feeling immediately guilty for the way I'd behaved with him. He *was* nice if he could care enough to return the phone to me after our little fight.

"Isn't this yours?" he asked, his voice like velvet.

My heart swelled as I nodded and reached for it. "Thank you," I said, noticing the phone light up. I was getting a call, and it was my brother, Henry. My stomach immediately knotted in worry.

"But first," the man said with an undeniably triumphant look as he held on to the phone, "I'll need the cup of coffee."

My jaw dropped. "Are you serious?" I demanded, feeling instantly angry. All thoughts of me feeling guilty for my behavior went out the window. *How dare he?*

He held the phone out of my reach. "I am if you want

this back," he said, holding it up just as Henry's phone call ended.

Shit.

Henry would call again, I was sure, and he would only be more agitated the next time.

"Damn. Must have been an important call," the man teased.

I almost wanted to fling my cup of coffee on him in frustration. The complete jerk. The café would've made him another cup. He was really going to make me give up my coffee on my wedding day just to score a point over me?

My phone buzzed again. This time, it was a message, probably from Henry.

I closed my eyes, feeling exhaustion and helplessness wash over me. "Take it," I said hollowly, shoving the cup into his outstretched hand as I took the phone.

I didn't miss the jubilant grin on the man's chiseled face as I gave up.

"I hope you rot in hell," I said, grabbing my phone from him at last.

When I looked up, he was smiling at me again. Strange. I'd said nothing to warrant a smile.

"I figured you'd probably need it for your elopement," he said, his voice deep. "I'm Sean, by the way."

I'd temporarily forgotten that I was planning to run away with someone else. I could still feel the touch of his fingers on mine as he handed the phone over, and his eyes were locked with mine in what felt like a very strong handhold. As though we'd known each other before and we were only just meeting again now.

"Well, Sean, you can fuck right off," I said, bristling.

"There was a call on your phone just now," Sean said

unnecessarily. He had barely gotten the words out when the phone began to ring again.

I glared at him before I looked at the phone. It was a call from Henry. A knot started to form in my stomach as I answered. I turned away as I did, aware that Sean was still around. Was he going to gloat over my loss by drinking my coffee in front of me?

"Chloe," Henry said, his voice sounding worried over the phone. "Where are you?"

I inhaled. "Not yet at the courthouse, Henry. Is something wrong?" I asked, trying to keep my voice light, but something felt off.

Henry was going to be one of our witnesses for the wedding, and he'd be coming over directly from our apartment.

There was a pause on the other end. Then his voice, strained, came through. "Chloe, I... had a little accident."

My heart sank. "What happened?"

"I was leaning too far forward, trying to get a glass from the table when I fell," he said with a half-hearted laugh. "It's nothing serious, just banged up my shoulder a bit."

I closed my eyes, letting the words sink in. Henry had been in a wheelchair since the accident, and the thought of him being hurt made my stomach twist. "Are you sure you're okay?"

"Yeah, I'm fine," he said quickly, but I could hear the pain in his voice. "I don't want to mess up your day. You've got the wedding and everything."

I glanced at the time. The courthouse ceremony was a couple of hours away. I was so close to being married. But I couldn't stop picturing Henry, hurt and alone.

"No," I said, already knowing what I had to do. "I'm coming back."

"Chloe, don't be ridiculous. I'll be fine."

"Nonsense," I said. "Nothing is more important to me than making sure you're okay."

He let out a long sigh, and I could hear the guilt in his voice. "I didn't mean to pull you away from your big day."

"You're not pulling me away," I corrected. "I'm pulling myself away. We'll just reschedule. It's a courthouse, not Buckingham Palace."

There was a pause on the other end.

Then, softer this time, he said, "Thanks, Chloe."

"Always," I replied.

I hung up. The dress, the ceremony—it could all wait. Henry couldn't. Besides, I didn't want to go through the ceremony without Henry.

When I looked up, Sean was still looking back at me. He hadn't touched the coffee. "Is everything okay?"

I turned my back to him, determined to ignore him, even as I felt hopelessly vulnerable. I needed to make another call.

Bruce was not going to like this.

A minute later, when I got Bruce on the line and explained that I needed to reschedule—without mentioning Henry—Bruce snapped, "What do you mean, you need to reschedule? We're getting married, for heaven's sake!"

"I'm sorry," I fumbled, wishing I had a better alternative.

"It's because of Henry, isn't it?" Bruce fumed over the phone. "What reason did he have this time? Wait. You know what? I don't even want to know," he huffed out. I could hear him pacing his room. "Chloe, you've got to realize it's unhealthy, the way you and Henry are codependent."

"It isn't."

There was a strange silence over the phone.

"You don't get it, do you?" He sounded bitter. "If I asked

you to choose between me and Henry, how would you answer, Chloe?"

I inhaled sharply. "You can't ask me that," I said immediately.

"It's time I did, and I have my answer. I'm tired of coming second in your life, Chloe, and I can't spend our married life being second to Henry. I can't marry you, Chloe. I won't marry a woman who is destined to have a miserable shell of a life."

His words hit me like a brick to my stomach.

"Bruce—" I began, my voice shaking, but he hung up.

I looked down at the layers of white lace and satin on me and felt the ground collapse beneath me.

My knees gave way, but before I could hit the sidewalk, Sean caught me, stabilizing me with his arm while my wobbly legs slowly regained strength.

"You look pale," Sean said while I felt like I'd forgotten how to breathe.

I came up for air at last, gasping as though I'd recently surfaced from an icy-cold lake.

I stared at my phone, still in my hand, as though it were a joke. I forgot about my coffee fight. I forgot about scoring a point over the strangely handsome man.

"Bruce," I breathed out, my voice half sobbing, half urgent as I leaned against him. My fingers caught the edge of the cup, and the Americano toppled over me.

Sean cursed, pulling me away from the spill, but it was too late. His shirt got some of the drink, causing a big brown splotch to appear on his suit, while my white dress got the rest of the Americano.

I stared at the mess hollowly while Sean's hands gripped my arms and pulled me a step back. I stumbled, and while I didn't entirely fall, I ended up leaning into his side. For a minute, all time stopped as he held me, his grip tightening around my arms. He felt strong.

Strong and safe, I thought, trying to stand up.

Bruce's rejection stung more than it should have because he took down Henry with me. Henry, who still suffered from that horrible accident on his way back from his friend's house, ten years ago, all because of me. He'd pushed me out of the way when a car swerved to avoid a squirrel and hit him instead.

Sean held me, arms steady on mine. This time, he was looking at me—really looking at me—and I was looking back, stupidly searching for some explanation about what was happening to my perfectly ordered life. Those dark brown irises softened while he returned the gaze, eyes darting over each angle of my face, as though he was searching for something too.

Nothing. I had nothing. All I could think of was that Henry was waiting for me and I had broken Bruce's heart. I'd had to choose between breaking Bruce's heart or Henry's, and I had known which one I could live with.

I hate my life.

I rubbed the trail of salty water away from my cheeks, but my eyes easily made more to replace it. Something in my expression and something to do with tears on my cheeks made his expression harden.

"I know people cry on their wedding day, but I don't think it's supposed to look like this. Did he …" He didn't complete his sentence.

"Yes," I replied. I hung my head, remembering my joy earlier in the café about how well this week had been going for me.

I looked at the man's clean-shaven face and his set jaw.

This was an unexpectedly long time to spend in a stranger's arms, but it didn't feel awkward at all.

"Shit," I muttered and sat down on the ground.

The first person to know I was jilted was a complete stranger.

"I'm not getting married after all," I managed to say.

The look on Sean's face was one of incredulity. "You need to tell *him* to go to hell."

I said nothing, and Sean sat down next to me. He was silent for a bit.

When he spoke, his voice was dry. "I don't see the point in weddings myself, but I can realize what an utter fool he is for breaking it off when all you asked was if you could reschedule. A man isn't fit to marry a woman if that's his response to your request. He's an asshole, a bloody bastard, and I hope he lives to rue this day."

I turned away, ashamed at the burning sensation in my eyes. It wasn't completely Bruce's fault, but Sean didn't know the entire picture. I didn't want to burst into tears in front of Sean, but I was also incapable of responding to him.

There had been clues. Small, nagging ones that showed he didn't value my brother as much as he should have. Instances where he constantly questioned my choices. Like when, in a fit of anger, he'd demanded to know if I was going to spend our married life ferrying my grown-up brother to his college classes. Or the time he'd complained about Henry's increasing medical bills that I'd been paying out of my own wallet.

"Thank you," I said, unable to tell this man that I'd pushed those red flags under the carpet, hoping to God that I was overthinking things.

I hadn't wanted to doubt the one good thing in my life. I'd resolutely believed Bruce was the missing piece that would make our home a family. Our home that included Henry, my twenty-three-year-old brother, who was all grown up, but was wheelchair-bound because of my negligence.

Until a year ago, when I'd started dating Bruce, Henry was all I'd had in this world. Our mother had passed when we were little, and Dad was left with the responsibility of taking care of eight-year-old me and three-year-old Henry. When Henry got into an accident at the age of thirteen, unknown to me, Dad was close to his breaking point.

Some time later, when I quietly told Dad about my acceptance into Juilliard's Dance Division, it turned out to be the last straw. He knew what that meant. I'd possibly live in the dorm, and he'd be left alone with Henry, caring for him. But instead of talking it out with me and trying to find a way to share the care for Henry, Dad left.

I was eighteen, and I'd become Henry's caretaker.

Financially, medically, and emotionally for the past ten years.

Henry still didn't know why Dad had left. I'd led him to believe Dad had left because I'd asked for college money while the truth was tangled up in something much worse. Every time Henry brought it up, guilt gnawed at me, but I forced myself to stay quiet. He didn't need to carry that burden—it was mine alone to bear.

"He said I was destined to have a miserable shell of a life," I said, covering my face with my hands. "How could he talk like that? As though he despised me?" I asked, my voice breaking. "And why did he want to get married at all if he had such a bad opinion of me? Who does that?"

"A good many people—that's who," he said, his voice angry. "When I found my ex cheating on me, she told me that she had long suspected I was cheating on her and wanted to give me a taste of my own medicine—only I *wasn't* cheating on her. That was the end of our relationship."

Something about recalling that memory shook Sean because he looked broken for a moment.

Only for a moment because that memory seemed to decide things for Sean.

His jaw set, he picked up my phone and handed it to me. "Get your fiancé on the line and call him out about the way he spoke to you just now."

I stared at this man and my phone, feeling very lost.

"Listen," Sean said, "you're in charge of this situation. What do *you* want to do?"

Those words stirred something in me. *I am in charge.* Without thinking, I scrolled to Bruce's number and hit Call.

When Bruce answered, I spoke, my voice hard, even as it shook. "Bruce, just so you know, that was no way to speak to me. How *dare* you suggest I'm destined to have a miserable life forever? How could you speak like that to a woman you were minutes away from getting married to?" I asked, bristling.

The heavy breathing from the other end of the line paused. "Well, mark my words, Chloe. You'll see for yourself."

"You deserve to go to hell." My voice broke, my lips trembling with rage.

Sean took the phone from my shaking fingers and put it to his ear.

When he spoke, his voice was rough and angry. "What your fiancée forgot to add, scumbag, is that she deserves someone who shows up on her wedding day without calling her names first. Oh, and I agree with her. Go to hell."

He hung up and tossed the phone to me.

"I'd block him if I were you," Sean said, getting up and

helping me up. "Get over him and move on. And develop a better taste in men. You—" He paused and looked at me. "I don't know your name."

I smiled at him through my blurry eyes. "It's Woman Who Hates Bruce."

He smiled back. "Well, Woman Who Hates Bruce, can I get you a cab?"

I nodded and rubbed my cheeks before Sean produced a napkin out of nowhere. I took it and dabbed my face. "I never thought I'd say this to you, but thank you."

He chuckled. "I never thought I'd hear you say that to me either." He looked at the suit I'd placed on the outdoor café table. "Say, what's in this?"

I cast a glance at it. "Bruce's favorite suit, for the elopement. I picked it up from the dry cleaner earlier."

Sean reached for the other cup of coffee on the table. The flat white I'd gotten for Bruce.

"Pity the coffee is cold now," he said, removing the plastic wrap and holding the suit out to me. "Go on. I think it's your turn to ruin his clothes now."

2

SEAN

Six Weeks Later

Sunday's *Business Globe* was spread out on the glass-topped oak table, and I stared at the article on the second page. It was a small one, and it briefly read, *Lead Capital Group to buy disgraced Mindwell Inc. in a surprise move that shocks many.*

In terms of scandalous headlines, really, it wasn't. The two class action lawsuits against the company were listed at the very bottom of the article, and they were the real scandal. Mindwell had hidden details of emissions from their manufacturing of computer chips, and now that it was found out, the CEO, Gary Chalk, wanted to bolt. All things considered, my partners and I had bought it for a good price. The company had potential. The question was, was I the one to turn their fate around?

Desmond, Alex, and Jonah—my partners at Lead Capital—seemed to think so. I had my doubts, but I welcomed the challenge. Anything to keep me busy while I dealt with a very inconvenient truth at home—my seven-year-old son actively disliked me.

My phone beeped with a text message from my ex-wife. Helen had traveled to Australia for a month-long vacation with her boyfriend, Matt, and was due back next week.

Helen: *I'm shopping for gifts for Lucas before I land in New York. Any suggestions?*

Helen and I shared joint custody of Lucas, for whom I'd gladly give up making surprise deals that shocked many. I wanted his admiration and attention the way I used to look up to my dad when I was seven. But Lucas was a closed book around me, and I knew nothing about his likes or dislikes. He hated me.

Sean: *I think I saw him playing with an old set of Mr. and Mrs. Potato Head in his room. Perhaps you could buy him a newer one?*

I didn't ask her how she liked Australia. We'd gone there for our honeymoon eight years ago, and reminders about that time were just painful.

Her response came swiftly.

Helen: *From what I remember, he hates lovey-dovey things. Are you sure he's playing with those toys?*

She was right. I'd seen him hold Mr. Potato Head on his first day with me, but now that I forced myself to think of it, I'd probably seen it in the trash the next day.

Helen: *I was wondering if he had a new toy obsession, but it looks like he hasn't developed one so soon. I think I'll fall back on his favorite Spider-Man toys. How about this one?*

Every day in the past three weeks of living with Lucas had been a lesson in how little I knew him. How little quality time I had spent with him all these years. I bit back the urge to curse myself and instead looked at the picture of the toy Spider-Man she'd sent me.

Sean: *Sure, you could buy that. You know him the best.*

I felt a pang of envy as I admitted the truth.

From the rows of figurines in the background of the picture, I realized that she was at Paddy's Markets, the famous shopping marketplace I'd taken her to during our honeymoon. Was she taking Matt to every place we'd been together? What next, the Bondi to Coogee Walk and a ferry to Watsons Bay for one of their many seafood restaurants?

There was no response from Helen. In the silence, as I stared at her message, my assistant, Amelia, peeked into the office.

"Everyone's assembled in the Orion conference hall," she said, eyes darting between me and the door, as though she wanted to make a run for it before I gave her another disagreeable task to do.

I turned my phone off and set it in my pocket. Recently, I'd registered just how little emotion I felt when I saw Helen's photos, and it struck me as a grave reminder of the effects of love.

Love was just a false high. There was always a low that followed.

I had seen that with my dad and mom. Dad had been head over heels for Mom, but somehow, it wasn't enough for her. After Mom cheated on Dad and left us, it had been incredibly lonely—not to mention disheartening—to live with a father who was depressed and silent.

I'd lived through the low myself. When Helen revenge-cheated on me after accusing me of having an affair when I was simply overworking, I was hit with a divorce. In short, I was a mess. After Helen had left, taking Lucas with her, I never entertained thoughts of falling in love again. Love happened only once, and when it was done, all that was left was bitterness and a child who hated you.

"Is everything okay?"

I looked up to find Amelia gazing at me in concern. I'd never confided in anyone about my pain of losing out on time with my son. After the divorce, he spent most of his time with his mom. He was so unhappy to spend time with me in my home—the home he'd grown up in—that I voluntarily gave him more opportunities to stay with his mom instead. Opportunities Lucas would grab without hesitation. Now, I was left with a stinging regret for all those times and a child who was as emotionally distant from me as possible. It hurt.

No one could understand this.

I drew in a deep breath and shook my head.

"All good," I said gruffly, but Amelia's worried face reminded me of my job here.

"Everyone in the conference room? Good. That wasn't so hard, was it?" I asked, fixing my tie and walking around the table to stand next to my assistant. "I assume no one bit your head off in the process?"

"They're worried," she said in barely a whisper. "They think this merger means that some jobs are going to go."

"Well, they aren't wrong," I said with a frown.

When Mindwell Inc. had merged with Tassater Inc.—the company I ran—we had duplicate teams. Two marketing teams, two analytics teams. It was a mess for sure. Layoffs were inevitable.

"But my job is to build the best tech company in the e-marketplace business, and I'll make sure the best of the teams stays on."

"There are two executive assistants for the CEO," Amelia said, lowering her voice even more and giving me a pointed look. "Mindwell Inc.'s CEO has an executive assistant, too, who is waiting in the same conference room as the others.

So, do I wait to see who you think is the best, or should I leave right away?" she asked in a shaky voice. When I didn't answer her, she disappeared out the door, looking miserable.

I stared at her retreating figure until the hallway outside was quiet, without the usual bustle of chairs and papers from Amelia's desk right outside. No doubt, getting the two companies to sit down together in a single room had been too much for her, or she would never have harbored thoughts of me replacing her.

Skittish.

An image of a beautiful, curly-haired blonde in a wedding dress came to my mind. She'd trusted me. She wasn't skittish. She didn't apologize when she spilled that coffee on me and didn't cower in fear, like Jeremy from accounting had when he spilled his latte over me. Very few people messed up and then calmly looked at me like she did. Forget calm. She'd been happy. Laughing, until that bastard of a fiancé had given up on her.

I walked out of the door and shut it behind me. I took a deep breath and walked to the elevator. I needed to stop thinking about that blonde woman every day. Had she gotten over the breakup? How was she doing now? Was she able to laugh again? Jesus. What was with my brain and these questions?

I'd never see her again, and thank goodness for that. A woman who kept popping into my mind when we hadn't even exchanged names wasn't a good woman to have in my vicinity.

I spotted Amelia's empty desk just as the elevator doors closed and heaved a sigh. I'd see about this new executive assistant—the one who still insisted on hanging around even though her CEO had been given the boot. I wasn't going to let Amelia go, skittish or not. She was loyal, even if she was a little too dramatic for me, and I always favored loyalty. Helen had cheated on me within two years of our marriage, whereas Amelia had been my assistant for five years now.

Loyalty was a quality that was missing in people today. I'd realized that years ago, after Helen's vindictive attempt. And as evidenced by Gary Chalk's executive assistant, it seemed, if he or she hadn't followed their CEO out.

I got out of the elevator on the first floor and walked to the Orion conference hall. Amelia had composed herself and was waiting outside the conference hall for me. Her hand was on her belly, and I could see that she was tired. She had another three months to go before the baby got here, and she didn't need more stress.

"What's the name of the other assistant?" I asked, stopping in front of her before walking through the door, where I could hear the voices falling silent.

"Chloe Nichols," Amelia said in a muted voice. "She's the one by the window."

I didn't turn to look at the woman by the window. I looked at Amelia's nervous eyes before I said, "Tell Edith from HR that we can let Chloe go. Make sure the compensation isn't too bad."

Amelia nodded, looking relieved. "I will. Thank you."

"Have her out of here by the next hour," I muttered as she stepped into the conference room while I made a quick detour to the restroom, completely forgetting to look at the woman by the window.

3

CHLOE

It was almost ten in the morning, and despite the two cups of coffee I'd downed so far, I still didn't feel the jolt of energy that everyone around me seemed to reflect.

I stared at the cardboard box at my feet. It was a box of things from my desk at the old office. I'd lugged it from my old workplace to the Tassater building, in the desperate hope that this would be my new workplace.

For the past two days, ever since the takeover of Mindwell Inc. had been finalized, I'd been a nervous ball of fear. Gary Chalk, the now-ex-CEO of Mindwell, had met the board of Tassater Inc. many times. As Gary's assistant, I'd facilitated that. Now, with Gary gone and no further instructions to me, I was waiting to find out what the fate of my administrative assistant job was going to be. I didn't miss Gary. I was relieved to not be working for him anymore. If only not working for Gary meant that I was working for someone better.

"I heard he's, like, a god of good looks. Like a Greek god." A raven-haired woman next to me giggled.

"You mean our new CEO?" the woman next to her whispered back.

"Yes. I heard he owns properties in Lake Como in Italy and Monaco and a superyacht that can hold fifty people. He's the richest man on this side of town, but he never dates. The paparazzi has never caught him with a woman, and they've tried their darned best."

Ah, Sean Tassater, the new CEO of Mindwell.

I hadn't met the man, and it looked like I'd missed out. How *did* he look?

The whispers continued to my right.

"Are you saying he's one of those guys who is perennially single?"

"Ever since his divorce, yes. Sigh. He is droolworthy."

The only man whose good looks had left a lasting impression on me was my coffeehouse savior. I remembered him all right. I had no trouble thinking of him as I went to bed at night, imagining him holding me like he'd done back then. In fact, I needed to stop thinking about the tall man who had been capable of making me feel butterflies in my stomach on my wedding day. Because this was all I'd permit myself to do when it came to men henceforth—daydream.

I knew Sean was just a man who had helped me get a cab. Not someone who could understand a woman's inability to process the barrage of emotions that hit her when she was dumped on her wedding day. That man didn't exist.

Bruce had broken up with me in a brusque, emotionless manner that was not unlike the way my dad had left me and Henry back when I was eighteen. I had sobbed my heart out for nights back then, and I'd cried my eyes out every night last month before I decided I was done dating. Just like I had stopped believing in fairy tales back when I was eighteen.

This much was obvious to me now—I couldn't be a responsible carer for my sibling *and* have love.

I checked my watch and realized it was about the time when Henry, my twenty-three-year-old brother, should be taking his medicine. I needed to give him a call to remind him, but I didn't want to risk missing the beginning of today's meeting.

Ever since the car accident, Henry had been confined to his wheelchair. He had good upper-body strength and minimal lower-body strength. He pulled himself in and out of his wheelchair when he needed to get to bed or had to use the bathroom. Most days were good. Some days, however, the pain got the better of him, and those days, he was emotionally and physically shut down, staying in bed for prolonged periods. I felt terrible on those days, bits of my guilt quietly creeping up on me.

It's my fault he's wheelchair-bound, remember?

We had been walking back home that night, and I was wrapped up in my own thoughts, dreaming about a future at The Juilliard School. Henry saw the car before I even heard it. The roar of the engine was drowned out by the thoughts buzzing in my head, excitement blurring my focus.

The car swerved to avoid a squirrel crossing the road, and the driver lost control. I was directly in its path.

Then, in one swift move, Henry shoved me aside, intervening at the last possible moment. I hit the ground, my back scraping against the rough bushes, the scent of crushed leaves filling my nose. The deafening screech of tires ripped through the air, but I was untouched. When I looked up with the metallic taste of panic rising in my throat, Henry was on the pavement, gasping in pain. The coppery smell of blood hung in the air.

He hadn't been lucky.

He had taken the hit.

He had taken the danger meant for me.

If I'd noticed the car first, he wouldn't have suffered. If I'd pulled him out of the way with me, he would have been spared.

If, if, and more ifs.

What remained was that I'd been foolish, and Henry had paid for it.

The only way I could assuage my guilt on those days was to give up something else I wanted to do for myself and spend time with Henry instead. Make him laugh, reduce his pain.

Lately, I'd noticed a correlation between his good days and staying on top of his meds, and I was hopeful he could have fewer bad times, going forward.

Just as I was thinking this, my phone began to buzz with a call. I took a quick glance around me before checking the caller. It was Henry.

Sean Tassater, the man who had taken over Mindwell Inc., was running late for this meeting, so I took my chance and answered the phone call.

"Hi, Chloe." Henry's voice, calm and confident, rang through clearly. "Are you busy?"

"Not at all," I answered, forcing my voice to sound cheerful and happy.

I was always happy to speak to Henry. Even if in the midst of all my sisterly love, there was a thread of perpetual guilt, mixed with financial frustration. Guilt because Henry had saved my life, at a horrible cost to himself. Financial frustration because so much of what he needed—like therapy, better medicines—was constrained by my lack of funds.

"You know, I'm always grateful that you're never busy whenever I call you," Henry said after a moment's silence, like he was musing out loud. "Even when you're at work."

"Isn't that a good thing?" I asked, though I didn't like the direction this conversation was about to take. "Say, Henry, did you—"

"Don't ask me if I've taken my medicines," he groaned.

I exhaled just as I noticed a flurry of activity outside the room. Sean Tassater had probably arrived—and with him, the fate of my job.

"Anyway," Henry continued, "I just called to ask how you're doing. I know mergers are pretty scary for the employees, and there's a lot of uncertainty associated with it. Are you okay?"

I made a noise of disbelief. "Of course I'm fine. You don't need to worry about my job. I just spoke with the HR at Tassater Inc. They're finding a new job for me here, I promise. You have nothing to fear."

It was a blatant lie, but along with the fear of losing my job, I seemed to have lost my mind. I was now making promises I shouldn't. For all I knew, this meeting could end with me getting laid off. A pit of fear expanded in my stomach, and I swallowed and tried to focus on something else.

Henry wanted to sign up for the student education association. The fees weren't covered by his partial scholarship, and I knew I could afford it ... if I had a paycheck to rely on.

When it came to college classes, Henry thrived in clubs where he got to teach. It challenged him and fulfilled his desire to be more to the people around him, to help more.

"You should sign up for the student club like you wanted to," I said.

In the silence on the line, I could almost hear the wheels in his brain whirling with excitement.

"Are you sure?" he asked, but the lilt in his voice was back. He was excited now. Already planning the presentation slides for the upcoming class. "It costs two grand," he reminded me.

Henry's undergrad classes in the nearby community college were the one thing he looked forward to. They gave him a life outside of home. The classes gave him hope that he could have a career, just like everyone else around him. I wanted that for him.

"Easy-peasy," I said with a laugh just as I noticed the air in the room stiffening. Someone important was about to walk in. I turned my attention back to the phone. "Now, I need to hang up," I said quietly. "I'll pick you up in the evening, after your classes, Henry. And remember—"

"All right, all right. I'll take my medicines," he said in a much happier voice before hanging up.

I stared at the picture of Henry on my phone before pocketing it. Shit. I needed to make sure I could keep my job. Any job that would help me be the responsible, repentant elder sibling, determined to make amends for abandoning her brother that one night.

To my right, I heard two women resume speaking.

"He's at the door. The one and only Mr. Tassater."

The other woman sighed and muttered under her breath, "God, if I'm going to be fired, I'd take it from a guy like him."

I looked quizzically at the two women just as someone tapped me on my left shoulder. A young woman with auburn hair and a beautiful blue sweater that I would totally kill to borrow was standing next to me. She was breathing a bit fast, and going by the looks of it, she was pregnant.

"I'm Amelia Miller," she said in a whisper. "Executive assistant to Mr. Tassater," she added.

"Oh! The assistant? Hey, would you know if it's a mass layoff today?" I whispered back as the people around us turned to us at the mention of the L-word. "Or are we keeping our jobs?"

"This is hardly the place to be discussing that," she said with a small frown at me. "Now, if you would please follow me."

I picked up my box, and we slipped out of the conference room quietly. There was no man at the door, but I briefly saw a trace of a navy-blue suit head into the restrooms down the hallway.

I followed Amelia, who was walking slowly in the opposite direction in a well-lit, high-ceilinged hallway.

She glanced down at the brown cardboard box in my hands and simply said, "I've reserved meeting room 5A for you."

"Just me?" I clarified as we walked, and Amelia nodded.

My heart sank.

It is as bad as I feared.

They were definitely firing me. Couldn't they have waited until the end of the day at least? This was turning out to be a horrible morning. I turned to see the room she was pointing to and found it was occupied by a forty-something woman with short black hair and red-rimmed spectacles, looking stern.

This did not bode well for me.

My mouth went dry as I considered the possibilities. Were they really firing me in the midst of a conference meeting? Was this so that the others wouldn't know?

My fingers twitched, and I wished I didn't have to hear the words I knew were coming. Henry was going to be so disappointed.

Before I walked in, I heard a noise down the hallway behind us. For a fleeting second, I saw someone walk out of another room, and it was as though I'd seen a ghost. My heart caught in my mouth, and I froze, just as Amelia stood in front of me, blocking my view.

"This way, please, Ms. Nichols," she said firmly.

4

CHLOE

Unable to ignore Amelia, I walked into the room. My mouth went dry as I went in alone, Amelia disappearing back the way we had come.

A large, rectangular table occupied the room, and the woman sitting at it looked up.

Seeing me, she smiled, if only stiffly, and shook my hand. "I'm Edith Simons, the head of HR at Tassater Inc. Please take a seat," she said, pointing at the chair across from her.

I took a deep breath as I set my box to my left and sat down. An image of Henry flashed across my mind as she began to speak.

"Now, this isn't going to be an easy conversation to have, Ms. Nichols," Edith began, looking deeply apologetic.

"You're firing me, aren't you?" I asked, feeling hopelessness wash over me.

I was using the monthly payment plan for Henry's tuition, and this month might be Henry's last month of classes.

"I knew Gary Chalk very briefly, but in that time, I realized how useful you were to him. I wish we had a position open that would fit your experience, but we don't. So, unfortunately, we will have to let you go—"

Why would you praise me then?

I remembered what the man in the coffeehouse had told me. The one with the straight back and broad shoulders. The one whose suit fit him so well that it had probably been tailor-made for him, sheen and all. *"You're in charge of this situation. What do you want to do?"*

"Isn't there any other job I could do?" I began, putting up some fight. "Some other role at Tassater? I looked at the job openings online, and there was an open position available for an administrative assistant."

Edith pushed her glasses down to look at me clearly. "I remember that position. Unfortunately, that position requires someone with the experience of one year." She double-checked her notes. "You have eight years of experience, Ms. Nichols."

Eight? The years had certainly flown by while I was trying to get through the days.

"Which means you will find a job commensurate with your experience very easily—"

A new job. In a new company. I hated anything to do with the word *new*. Getting used to the idea of Lead Capital Group and Tassater Inc. had been hard enough, but going out into the job market and interviewing? I'd rather go on three blind dates with snake-eating sociopaths.

"In this job market?" I had to suppress my urge to laugh, but I did come across as bitter. "Three newspapers today announced that the US is in an economic slump. I'm not an economist, but that doesn't look good for executive assistants with experience. Everyone else at my level has moved on to being a program manager or upped their skills somewhere. My brother did ask me to do a Project Management certification to prove I knew project management, but I thought my money was better spent on his undergrad classes."

She pushed a folder toward me, not to be swayed. "In this packet, you'll find a breakdown of your severance package. You'll notice that Tassater has been very generous with—"

The door of the small room flung open before she could complete her sentence, and the two of us looked up.

"Mr. Tassater," Edith exclaimed.

All concerns about Henry or my job fled my mind because the man I saw in front of me—the man who was very clearly looking back at me too—was in fact the man I had met at the café over six weeks ago.

The man I let see me in my tears, in shambles, after the groom ditched me on my wedding day.

The man who held me after I spilled an entire cup of coffee on his shirt.

The man who called Bruce a jackass and an interminable number of names, each one more vehement than the last.

The man who'd told me I deserved better.

The CEO of Tassater Inc.

5

CHLOE

The navy-blue suit Sean wore shone under the overhead lights, and his shoes made a crisp sound, all business and measured footsteps, as he walked up to us, his gaze fixed on me.

I shut my eyes, feeling a flutter in my stomach. *He* was the ghost from the hallway moments ago. A ghost who was —I gulped—very, very real.

With the way he filled out his muscular six-foot frame well, he came across as someone who handled his power with integrity.

With his crisp haircut that showed off his fine jaw, he indicated that he was a man who took care of himself.

With the ease with which he moved, he radiated a surety I rarely felt in life.

And me? Well, I was done for.

Edith's eyes darted nervously between me and the man while I was too shocked to speak.

"I didn't expect you here," Edith breathed out to Sean, her voice sounding shaky as she stood up.

"Edith," he said, turning to her briefly before his eyes darted back to me.

It wasn't the first time he had looked at me with suspicion, but I didn't have the will to protest. My legs seemed to tremble under his piercing gaze.

Why are you so handsome? It makes it harder for me to hate you for letting me go.

He finally turned his gaze back to Edith. "Can I get a moment with her alone, Edith?"

I saw her eyes widen, but she bit her lip, probably holding back a question that had risen to the tip of her tongue. Then, a resolute expression came over her, and she nodded. If she was surprised by his request, she didn't let on.

"It's fine," I said while Edith turned to me apologetically.

Of all the meetings you'd hate to have drawn out, the one where you were being fired was at the absolute top of the list.

But here we were. I was the impossible people-pleaser. I didn't stand a chance in life if I went about trying to make everyone else happy, but I couldn't bring myself to behave in any other way.

"I'll be back as soon as I can," she said, and I pushed my chair back to make room for her to leave.

Edith, in her hurry and nervous confusion on her way out, fumbled. Her stiletto heel caught the tip of my buckled flat shoes and pierced it, stabbing my toes. At the intense pain, I gasped, clasping my hand to my mouth, just as Edith's heel came off. She slipped, catching herself just in time.

Tears of pain pricked the edges of my eyes, and I was vaguely aware of Sean's hand on my arm.

"Are you okay?" he asked while Edith apologized profusely, looking flustered.

"I'm really sorry," she repeated, hopping on one foot as she picked up the broken heel.

I pressed my lips together and nodded dumbly, not trusting myself to speak.

I really was having a great day.

The door fell shut after Edith, with a backward look at me, stepped outside.

Then, it was just Sean and me in the room. He took his hand off my arm and edged closer, all six feet of him, his gaze roving my face, as though he couldn't believe it either.

"Are you really okay?" he asked, his gaze dropping to my foot.

I pulled my foot out of my shoe and noticed there was no blood, thankfully. It still hurt, but I could deal with that. I'd just limp back home in my broken shoe.

"I'm fine," I said.

"You have tears in your eyes," he pointed out.

I took a second glance at him. "That seems to happen every time we meet," I muttered.

That set him off all right. I'd reminded him of our first meeting, and it looked like he did not have warm memories of it, like I did.

"What the hell are you doing here?" he demanded.

Anyone would have wanted to shrink back at that tone. I didn't blame Edith for beating a hasty retreat either. But I just remembered how he'd held me that day outside the café. The vile names he'd called Bruce. And I wasn't scared of him.

Intimidated? A little, yes, but not scared.

I stood up instantly, trying to ignore the throbbing pain in my foot.

"*You're* Sean Tassater?" I asked in return, and for a second, he stared at my boldness.

"Yes. Who are you, and why are you here?"

My mouth fell open as I stared at him.

How had I not seen him before? I'd thought I'd met most of the people in the venture capital company that had bought Mindwell. All three of them. Was there a fourth partner? The one who would actually step into Gary Chalk's shoes? No wonder he could walk in and demand to speak to me. No wonder Edith, the HR lead, had just given in to his demands.

I needed a second to think because things weren't adding up. I sat back down in my seat, taking the weight off my aching foot. I hated myself just a little bit. I hated myself for the dreams I'd had of him, for painting him as a nice, kind soul. The sort of guy who reached protectively for your hand while you crossed the road together.

Going by the irritation in his eyes and the clenched jaw, Sean Tassater was not the hand-holding kind of guy. I could see his fingers curl into a fist as though he wanted to punch the nearest wall.

He had been so nice when I met him before, but *this* was how he was at work.

"I'm Gary Chalk's executive assistant. Well, I was at least," I said. "Chloe Nichols."

When I said that, he groaned and turned away, running his hand through his hair once in frustration.

What did I do wrong?

"Mr. Chalk left quite abruptly," I explained. "And he didn't give me any instructions before he took off. I've been feeling quite invisible until Ms. Simons acknowledged me and my presence even if she really was discussing my severance package."

He looked at me as though he had an even angrier retort on his lips when something stopped him.

"Is that yours?" he demanded when he saw the cardboard box next to me.

I nodded. "These are all my things," I said, hesitating.

It wasn't much. My favorite notepad, gifted to me by Henry; a new pen, something Henry and I had purchased at the hospital gift shop during his last appointment; and Henry's daily schedule. I used to have a photo of Bruce and me, but I'd thrown it away since the breakup.

Mr. Tassater shut his mouth, and with a vexed look at me, he cursed under his breath. His gaze fell on the paper detailing the severance package I was to receive—two weeks' pay and references—and then back at me.

"You can't work here," he said instantly. Far too instantly for my liking. "Excuse me," he said, striding toward the door where Edith waited just outside.

I saw the woman's eyes widen with fear as he approached.

6

SEAN

My frustration with Edith and, more importantly, Gary Chalk was on my mind as I walked out of that room. If only Gary Chalk had taken care of Chloe. Taken her along with him to his next venture perhaps. Or even—and I hated myself for even entertaining the thought—fired her before the acquisition, then I wouldn't need to sort out this mess.

But all thoughts about Gary disappeared when my gaze stayed on her through the glass window in the wall. She was sitting by the table again. She had gotten a haircut in the six weeks since we'd met. Her hair was short now, and it suited her even more. She was darn pretty all right. She had azure-blue eyes, flecked with gold, and a sprinkling of freckles on her nose. Even those eyes hadn't dulled in the aftermath of discussing the termination of her employment.

She was surveying the termination papers in front of her with a vulnerable look on her face. A look that stirred something primal in me. A damn frustrating desire to protect something or someone.

I shook my head. *No, no, no.*

I'd had a moment of weakness at the café six weeks ago. Telling her personal details about my failed relationship and laying bare one of my bigger wounds. In hindsight, it was more than embarrassing. I didn't want a woman at work who had seen me be weak and emotional. I'd shared personal details with Chloe, things an employee shouldn't really be privy to, and it couldn't be a professional relationship when she knew the exact words my ex had said to me.

I threw my shoulders back, reminding myself of how unmoved I'd been at various points in my life. My first failed business venture, my dad's death, and my divorce. I wasn't one to be swayed by the trivial trembling of a woman's lips. I hadn't been swayed in the past, and I wasn't about to start now. Even with lips as red as full-bodied wine. Mom had taught me emotions were worthless, and it was the only thing I'd learned from her.

I found Edith waiting for me, and aware that her office was just down the hallway, I asked, "Can we step into your office?"

She nodded with obvious reluctance, and hobbling on her broken pump, she led the way. In a minute, I entered Edith's office, where she reached for the gym bag in the corner, from which she dug out sneakers. While she swapped shoes, I looked around.

The rest of her office was decorated simply with a potted azalea on the floor and a single purple orchid on her table. It was sparse—exactly how I'd encouraged all my employees to keep their offices. No unnecessary family photographs or memorabilia to distract them.

Edith was a model employee, and I ought to cut her some slack even if she did often—sometimes rightfully—bring up her concerns about my personal life interfering with my professional one.

Like picking up Lucas from his games or school, which was sometimes a last-minute request from Helen. I'd had to scramble during meetings to call the nanny, delaying our meetings in the process.

Her shoes finally on, she gestured for me to take a seat. The last time I had been here, I'd brought up a request—reasonable, I was sure—of hiring a company mascot. I'd wanted a tiger—fierce but loyal—to represent our company, but Edith had quietly fought back on that, citing resource issues, and suggested getting a parrot instead. Needless to say, I had not appreciated it or given her the go-ahead. This time, I didn't wait to let her speak.

"Before we fire Chloe, I wanted to ask you one last time, isn't there any other job we can find her? Dave Walker, our CFO, I bet he could use an assistant."

"Blake Jones and Martin Shepherd," Edith responded with an impassive face.

When I gave her a look of confusion, she explained, "Those are Dave's current assistants."

"What about—"

"She's got two assistants already," Edith interrupted.

I frowned and leaned forward, my hands on her desk. "You don't know who I was going to ask about."

"Was it, by any chance, Kelly Townsend, our COO?"

"No—" I began in swift rebuttal even though Edith was right. Damn it, was I really so predictable? "Okay, yes, I meant her."

Edith eyed me carefully. "You're the one with only one executive assistant. I've been trying to get you to accept an administrative assistant forever."

"Nope. I already have an assistant, thank you." I knew Edith's plan.

The admin assistant would double up as my personal

assistant, and I hated letting anyone into the details of my personal life.

I shoved my hands in the pockets of my pants in frustration. I cursed myself silently. Why did I have to let this inconsequential, jilted bride change my mind?

"Surely, there has to be someone else who needs an assistant."

Edith cleared her throat. "Amelia spoke to me earlier today and told me that she's been advised bed rest."

I raised my eyebrows at her. "Amelia didn't mention anything to me," I said, thinking back to our interaction.

Amelia had definitely been hasty with me today.

"She's expecting a baby, as you know, and she needs to spend the rest of the three months of her pregnancy in bed. She's reluctant to do so, because she's worried about her job. I told Amelia that her job is safe—"

"Damn right it is. She's good," I growled.

"And that she can work from home, if needed, as long as she's comfortable. But we'll need to hire a temporary assistant to handle things in the office."

"A temporary assistant?" I asked, hands off the table as I considered this.

"Until Amelia is back," Edith added with a hopeful look on her face.

My hands balled into fists as I considered that infuriating option. Chloe would work for me for the next three months and perhaps another three months while Amelia began her maternity leave.

Could I handle seeing Chloe at work?

I'd have to forget about that image of Chloe in her wedding dress for six months if we were to have any sort of professional relationship.

I'd have to stash that image away, only to be retrieved half a year later.

God, I couldn't handle that. I liked that image, like a child fixated on a toy that held no sad memories. I wanted that image to remind me of my one good day. Most people always held their true selves from me, oftentimes being fake —less often being overly eager to say the appropriate thing and coming off as trying too hard. But Chloe had been raw, honest, and open, confiding in me.

Back at the café, she'd looked breathtaking, and I had the selfish thought that she shouldn't be marrying any man. She ought to be single. Ten minutes later, voilà. Only, I didn't have the heart to ask her for her number, given what her fucked-up fiancé had done to her. I would find her later, I decided. Haunt that café perhaps. Well, I'd haunted it a few times with no luck.

And now, she was here, exactly where I didn't want her to be. Employee number 2560.

I wanted her working some job in our basement perhaps. To not have her out of a job and possibly on the streets, but, God, I sure as hell didn't want her working for me.

I ran my hand through my hair, feeling frustrated that my moment of kindness had backfired on me. This was why I didn't do nice.

This is what you get for being nice, Sean.

Unless she voluntarily left early. Assistants had done that. Women had done that.

If I could temporarily make her life miserable, she would quit. By then, I'd have found her another job on another floor in this building. One that involved no interaction with me.

I turned to Edith. My hand went down to my side.

"Edith, I think you've just convinced me. Let's hire her as my admin assistant."

Edith narrowed her eyes. "Are you sure?"

I waved her concerns aside. "It'll all work out. I really ought to listen to you more, Edith," I said, waggling a finger at her as I stood up.

7

SEAN

I stepped out of Edith's office and began walking down the hallway, back to the tiny conference room where Chloe was waiting. In the distance, I could see the receptionist for this floor stiffening at my presence as he nervously adjusted the contents of his desk.

Most employees usually froze at my sight or said ridiculous, bumbling words. I preferred the former, finding my solace in silence.

After Mom had left when I was eight, extended silences at home had become what I was used to, growing up. It was also probably the reason why Lucas and I didn't get along. I simply didn't talk much. And I didn't know how to be around people who talked a lot. Like Lucas with his impossible *why* questions whenever I saw him with his nanny, Anne.

I finally entered the room and saw Chloe. Her pale skin flushed when I walked over, and she stood up when I came to a stop in front of her.

Ignoring the vanilla-tinged smell she carried about her, I opened my mouth. "Edith and I spoke, and it turns out that there's one job we can offer you," I told her gruffly, not feeling too pleased.

Her gaze was fixed on my face, and I could see the emotions flickering in those eyes. Hope, yearning, and perhaps a hint of desperation too.

"You'll be working as my assistant. A temporary one, mind you, while my current assistant is away for the next six months."

"An assistant?" Chloe asked.

Her cheeks were red, but she continued to meet my gaze steadily. We were standing a foot away from each other, her chest rising and falling as she breathed rapidly, as though she had run a marathon in the past hour. I couldn't blame her. One did not get fired and rehired in the span of a few hours.

"Yes. It involves getting me a lot of coffee," I said dryly, deciding to scare her off the job right away.

"Well, I've been an admin assistant for the past eight years, so that would be no problem. Besides, I love coffee. I was at a café on my supposed wedding day too, if you recall."

She bit her lip as soon as the words were out of her mouth and pressed her lips together. "Sorry," she said immediately, looking mortified. "I won't bring that up again."

"That would be the right thing to do," I said, clamping my jaw shut.

The image of her in a wedding dress at the café was not one I wanted crossing my mind right now. She had looked beautiful. Heck, she still looked pretty right now.

We stared at each other in silence, my mind playing out many impossible scenarios now that she was so close. None of which I'd entertain, of course. Even the one with her and me at the rooftop pool, where she was in a bikini that dipped low between her breasts, sitting by the water's edge. I'd pull her to me, her soft body flush against mine, while I took her lips in mine—

No, no, no. I coughed and turned away, fixing my mouth into a thin line. Which begged the question, *What the fuck am I doing, commencing a working relationship with such a woman?*

I felt Chloe's eyes on me and turned reluctantly.

"So, if I accept, you'll be my new boss?" Chloe asked, picking up her box and following me out as I tried to put some distance between us.

I turned around to face her. "Yes. That's the only position we have available, unfortunately." I paused, squaring my shoulders. I could make this easy. "No one's forcing you to take it. It's a job that requires far less experience than you—"

"I'll take it," she said breathlessly, finishing her sentence even before I finished mine.

Darn. The enthusiasm with which she spoke lit up those pretty azure eyes, and they were sparkling now. Didn't she know my reputation for being tough?

"Is something wrong?" she asked, her eyes reflecting some concern.

Yes, there's a hell of a lot wrong, I thought, feeling irritated. *I'm attracted to you when I shouldn't be, but my body isn't getting the memo. I've built you up in my fantasies as a mesmerizing woman, and I'm afraid that working with you will ruin it. I wanted to have you fired, but I only got closer to you instead. These are some of the things that are wrong, and there's not a damn thing I can do about it.*

We stood in front of each other, silent and unmoving. I

felt a strange sensation, almost like a warning for the days coming up.

"I'm not called a monster of a boss for nothing, Chloe," I said at last, an unfamiliar emotion creeping up on me. *What have I gotten myself into?*

"I've dealt with a lot of monsters," she responded, scanning my face, as though searching for a sign of one.

Has she found it?

"So, I'll take my chances."

8

CHLOE

The morning of my first day of work began before dawn.

I opened my eyes to see the morning light seeping through the faded curtains. I stretched, my fingers grazing the old headboard, and rose from my ancient bed—a solid find from the estate sale of a rich, old family.

I was making my bed, looking out the window, when I noticed that the apartment's trash bins were still out on the street. Crossing over to read the schedule on the wall by my bed, I saw that it was Greg Clemson's turn to bring in the trash bins.

Our apartment building, The Halcyon, had a scheduled rotation for different residents to bring the bins in from the street. Most days, it worked like clockwork. But Greg—a new resident—I noticed, struggled to leave his home for days on end and would forget to get the bins. Whenever it was his turn, usually, one of the neighbors would pound on his door to yell at him to do his share, which disturbed Greg even more.

I thought back to how Sean had given me one more

chance last Friday. A chance that gave me one more attempt at believing we lived in a fairer world than it really was. Everyone deserved that chance. Pulling on my jacket, I stepped out into the early morning chill and brought the bins back to the trash room.

Dusting my hands off, I walked back indoors. I washed my hands, ready to start my day. I got dressed for work, searching through my closet for something appropriate to wear. Every few months, I'd go through my closet and donate the clothes I no longer wore, except for the faded black pancake tutu hanging on the right, the one that held memories of my good days of dancing. I didn't have the heart to give that one away.

My first task of the day was to email Henry's doctor to thank him for the new prescription for an off-brand medicine and let him know it was going well. I'd visited the pharmacy two days ago and realized I didn't have the spare $397 for Henry's pain medicines. The medicines meant that Henry could go longer without a need to visit the occupational therapist, and the doctor had reluctantly given us a cheaper one, which Henry had started taking last night.

My second email was to Mr. Tassater, and I paused when I began the email, wondering what I was going to say.

This is the café guy, I reminded myself. The one who'd been with me when my world with Bruce fell apart. I couldn't believe I was working for him.

My eyes fluttered shut, and I felt my face go warm at the memory. How firmly he'd held me when I almost collapsed onto the ground. I'd seen traces of that last Friday too. He'd held my hand when Edith accidentally stubbed my toe and I was in pain.

I'd been so distracted by everything—losing my job and seeing Sean again—that I hadn't had time to consider what

I felt about working for him. On one hand, I felt grateful to him for how kind he'd been to me on both occasions. On the other hand, I wanted to steer as clear of him as I possibly could. Because I found that I did agree with the two women from the conference hall after all. Sean did look like a Greek god.

A shiver went down my neck as I remembered how I'd briefly felt the air crackle with chemistry when he looked at me. How my heart had lurched in my chest, as though I'd been searching desperately for the past six weeks for a second look at the man who had once comforted me. To prove to myself that he wasn't just a figment of my imagination.

Well, I'd soon be not too many feet away from him once I reached work.

My face felt warm, and I took a few deep breaths. It didn't matter how close Sean would be. I'd once abandoned Henry when he needed me, and karma, being the reliable bitch it was, had shown me exactly what it felt like to be abandoned—not once, but twice. First by Dad walking out and then by Bruce. There wasn't going to be a next time because I didn't trust myself to survive a third one. Where yet another man asked me to choose between him and Henry and my inevitable answer.

After taking a few deep breaths and exhaling slowly, I completed my email to Sean, letting him know that I was looking forward to working with him and thanking him for the opportunity.

I spent the next fifteen minutes at my desk, reading about Sean Tassater's professional life—and stoutly ignoring his personal one—and his start in investing before he partnered with three other men at the Lead Capital Group, which took off. One detail stood out about Sean.

While all the partners at Lead Capital had become incredibly wealthy, what set Sean apart from the others was the nonprofit he'd started. With it, he emphasized giving back to the local community and had credited his childhood friend with helping him come up with the idea.

The flutter that had been taking place in my heart now spread to my stomach, and I shut my computer. I didn't need more reasons to admire him.

Instead, I turned my attention to my notes from a late-night call with Amelia. I'd need an hour to get Mr. Tassater's morning schedule ready, which meant I ought to be getting ready right now.

A knock on my bedroom door broke me out of my thoughts.

"The dishwasher is broken again," a sleepy-looking Henry announced when I opened the door.

I followed him through the corridor and into the kitchen, a sinking feeling settling in me. This was not the start I'd wanted for the first day of my new job.

We lived in an apartment where the sink would often overflow with wastewater due to plumbing issues and rodents would occasionally make their way in. We put up with it all because we were close to Henry's college. But every so often, we'd have an unusual expense or setback, and I'd find myself wishing I made more money to afford a better place, that we weren't living paycheck to paycheck. Like unexpected college expenses or broken appliances.

This was why I'd put up with working for Sean even if I'd have to calm my racing heart down a few hundred times a day. I needed him to keep me employed. I'd get immune to his good looks over time, I was sure.

"Let me see," I announced and reached for the dishwasher door.

Henry rolled back as I pulled out the trays and inspected the dishes.

"They are still dirty, so it's a plumbing issue," Henry said, getting on the phone with our landlord.

I nodded, pulling an apron on before I took some of the dirty dishes out of the dishwasher. I needed to get a few of these cleaned before I left so that Henry had some dishes to use for the rest of the day. I glanced at the clock, my heart skipping a beat when I realized how close I was cutting it on my very first day.

"You know what this reminds me of?" I asked, piling the dirty plates in the sink, determined not to let this ruin my morning.

Henry grinned. "That scene from The Break-up?"

We laughed as I handed him a clean plate, and he placed it in one of the drawers.

"I want you to *want* to do the dishes," I said, sounding almost like Jennifer Aniston from the movie.

Henry threw up his hands. "Why would anyone *want* to do the dishes?" he asked, in a perfect imitation of Vince Vaughn's character, Gary.

Henry snort-laughed as I tossed one of the clean plates to him, and he caught it midair before rolling over to place it in the drawer.

"You always loved that movie so much," he said. "You'd watch it every weekend. I wrote it off as a teenage thing, but you kept doing that for over a year."

"Well, I remember you had the biggest obsession with Ariel from *The Little Mermaid* that year! You'd ask to go to every theater that showed that movie and watch everything related to mermaids when you got back home—"

Henry rolled his eyes. "It wasn't about the mermaids—"

"It was about Julie, I know," I said, and we both shared a knowing grin.

Henry had had the biggest crush on his classmate that year when he was eight, and he loved everything she loved. So, we had to watch *The Little Mermaid* over and over again so that he could impress Julie. It had worked.

"You guys ended up being good friends, even after that phase," I mused, remembering how Julie would come over every so often. She had since moved out to Colorado, but they were still in touch.

I cleaned the last of the plates, and after I set the plate in the drying rack, Henry held a towel out for me to wipe my hands. Drying my hands, I took my apron off and checked the time, realizing that I could still catch my train if I raced down the street.

"We've grown out of those obsessions, haven't we?" Henry muttered as he wheeled himself out of the kitchen and into the living room.

"You mean, crushes and movie obsessions?" I asked as I turned the lights off in the kitchen and got ready to pick up my workbag and purse.

He nodded. "Not movie obsessions. God knows I still have those. But crushes, lovers, partners, and things like that."

I laughed, even as a cold, clammy feeling caught up to me. "Yep, that's not happening again," I said.

He nodded.

"The Nichols siblings stick together," he said, his voice tender but serious. "No one else gets us, Chloe. No one else would understand what it means to be abandoned the way we were. I mean, you were eighteen, but still a child when it happened." He shrugged. "I don't get how Dad could just leave us like that," he said, his voice sounding broken. "How does someone walk away from their family and not look back, Chloe?"

He extended his arms around us, and I looked at our childhood apartment. The one that still held fading memories of Mom, but stronger memories of Dad. Mom couldn't help it; she'd passed away ages ago, when I was barely eight, and Dad ... well, his abandonment after Henry's accident was a scar that I would carry around for the rest of my life. In the end, both our parents had left us.

"I'm not going to add to those sad memories, Henry," I said in a soft voice.

I knew Henry's deepest worries even if he never voiced them. One did not just bounce back from losing use of their legs and subsequently their father in the span of months. The trauma of it all—physical, mental, and emotional—had taken a toll on Henry, and I knew it would be a long time before I could afford a psychiatrist to help Henry with his emotions. Until then, we would manage. I wouldn't leave Henry—ever.

It was the thing I'd been so grateful to Bruce for—that he wanted to move in with us. Look where that had gotten me. Jilted after being quite close to the symbolic altar.

So, I gave Henry a smile and leaned over for a hug. "I won't leave, I promise. The Nichols siblings stick together," I echoed. And ruffling his hair, I hugged him tight before letting go. "See you in the evening, Prince Eric. I've got to get to work and meet my new, mean boss."

He waved as I crossed the hall and prepared myself for the crowded streets to the subway station.

"And by the way, I always pictured myself as Sebastian!" he called out before I stepped out the front door.

9

SEAN

Monday morning dawned unnecessarily bright and clear, and when I woke up, I did so with a groan.

I was aware that I was as hard as a brick. I groaned and ran my hands over my face. I'd had a very erotic dream involving Chloe, and I'd enjoyed every minute of it.

Chloe had been in bed with me, her head thrown back, and her white blouse was open at the buttons, exposing her perfect tits. Her breasts, round and full, were in my hands as she moaned while I took one nipple in my mouth—tasting her, licking her—while my hand pinched her other. My cock was ready, and slowly, very slowly, I nudged her thighs apart. She was so wet, moisture pooling when I reached for her clit, and I felt a sense of triumph.

She wanted me too.

And then I had woken up.

I felt an odd emotion. Something like a sense of frustration because my dream wasn't done yet before another thought hit me.

Chloe can't be mine. But I'm going to see her every weekday for the next six months.

When I registered that, there were no further questions. I knew exactly why I was ticked off about it. And I knew exactly how to make myself feel better.

Going to the bathroom to take care of it, I ended my feverish dream with a quick shower, damn sure that this strange dream would never happen again. What the hell was my mind doing? I never had sexual dreams about women I hadn't slept with.

Chloe is just like everyone else, I reminded myself as I got dressed and walked into my kitchen for some coffee.

I didn't need yet another woman to prove Dad's words right.

When I had been younger, Mom had had an affair. When she got pregnant, she had to do a paternity test, which told Dad everything he needed to know. The child was determined not to be Dad's, and Mom walked out on us and moved in with her new man.

In the days after, Dad constantly reiterated to me that loyalty was nonexistent in today's world.

I didn't believe him.

I married Helen, and unfortunately, in two years, she'd proven Dad right—loyalty didn't exist anymore.

It was six a.m., and as the espresso machine ground the beans, I checked that Lucas was still asleep. He still had half an hour of sleep left before it was time to wake up for school. His face was small, peaceful, and I lingered by his bed for a minute, wishing he could look quite the same when he was with me.

I exited his room quietly and picked up my cup of espresso. I sat down at the long dining table and looked through the messages on my phone. I found one from my ex-wife and another one from my half-sister. A woman I'd met once, at Dad's funeral—Erin. Mom's other child. I had no plans of ever talking to her, so I ignored her text and scrolled to Helen's.

Helen: *Something's come up. Call me.*

I downed my espresso and went back to make a second one, steeling myself before I had to speak with her.

Second cup of espresso done, I called her. She answered on the fifth ring, just as I was wondering if I should hang up.

"Hello?" she said, sounding breathless. "Thank goodness you called. I have some exciting news."

I waited. She had never needed me to speak much.

"He proposed!"

I closed my eyes for a second. I had known she would get married soon, but this was even sooner than I'd expected.

"Congratulations," I said, my voice dry. "I hope you've made a better choice this time."

"Oh, Sean," she said, sounding upset. "I'm sorry. I—"

"It's okay," I cut her off.

She had been very apologetic once she realized I never cheated on her. And promised to be faithful, going forward. But we both knew that she wasn't happy with me. I worked long hours during our short marriage since it had been the start of Lead Capital Group, and I was in meetings with my business partners and clients more often than I was at home with her. I'd told her that it would get better with time, but she had assumed something entirely different about my absence.

"We're better off this way. Really. But I have work to get to, and you wanted to speak to me about something?"

"Yes. Lucas."

I sighed.

"Matt and I want to spend more time here. We're planning to have our wedding here in six months, and I need to scout more locations for the perfect venue. And since our work lets us log on remotely—"

"How much more time?" I asked, cutting her short.

I didn't need to know everything about her itinerary. She never understood the pain I'd felt upon learning about her sordid affair. And she continued to behave like we could still be friends. I wished she would stop trying.

She hesitated. "Another month?"

I screwed my eyes shut because I knew what this meant for Lucas. I loved having my son here, but the feeling wasn't mutual.

"I am more than happy for Lucas to be here, but I doubt he feels the same. He misses you."

"Please, Sean? Make it up to him by buying him something nice."

What could I buy?

"Moana figurines perhaps?" I asked.

"He's into Spider-Man," she corrected me.

I drew in a deep breath. Damn it. She was right. How had I forgotten?

"All right. I'll try to make him happy. You know I haven't seen him smile at me even once?"

The line cut off.

I stopped and cursed when I realized she had hung up. Of course she would have no solutions to my problems with Lucas. Why would I burden her with that expectation? No one knew how to help my son and me get along.

Setting my phone down on the polished oak table, I shoved my hands into my pockets furiously.

I wished she had told Lucas the news herself. He always did better with her.

The sound of footsteps broke me out of my memories. Wearing his blue Spider-Man pajamas, which his mom had purchased, and looking bleary-eyed, Lucas walked in. Had I been so busy that I didn't realize his obsession with Spider-Man? His brown hair was tousled, his eyes suspicious as he regarded me, and his mouth was set in a stubborn line.

"Hey, Lucas. You're up early," I said easily as I came close to him.

He retreated behind the couch, and I froze. It was obvious he wanted me as far from him as possible, and I could respect that, even if it hurt.

Besides, how soon did I have to break the news to him? If I told him the truth right now, it would ruin his entire day at school.

He eyed the phone on the counter. "Did I hear you talking to Mom?"

I nodded.

"Is she bringing me a Spidey toy when she arrives tonight?"

I inhaled and mentally reminded myself to buy him all the Spider-Man toys one might find in New York.

"She will—I'm sure of it," I told him and watched his rebellious face relax for a second. "But she won't be coming tonight, Lucas. Her flight—"

His face fell, and before I could reach out to him and tell him I'd make up for it in—oh, I didn't know—as many ways as I could, he ran back to his room and slammed the door on me. I heard the door lock as I approached and hung my head.

"Lucas," I said, standing outside his door and wondering how I could soften the blow. "It'll be fine," I said, wishing I knew what else to say instead. "I'm here. I'll be with you."

"I don't want you," Lucas called back. "I hate you."

My phone rang again, and for a split second, I had this unbelievable hope that it was Helen, calling to tell me she had changed her mind and would come back soon.

But it was just a call from Anne, our nanny, letting me know she was on her way.

I hung up, and abandoned Lucas's room after knocking on it a few more times.

Why do you hate me, Lucas?

Anne would make sure Lucas ate something and got to school on time. But even she had no luck getting Lucas to soften up to me.

When she came in, I spoke with her briefly, letting her know about Lucas's mood. With a nod, she indicated to me that she would handle him—my cue to leave. Lucas would never step out of his room until I left the apartment.

I sighed, and with some relief that I was already dressed, I grabbed my wallet and stopped in front of Lucas's door, calling, "Bye, Lucas. Have a good day."

I heard him kick something in response, and I leaned my head against the door, feeling frustrated. I considered how ridiculous it sounded, saying goodbye through a closed door. I wanted to say *I love you*, but I knew it would only anger him more because he didn't believe I loved him.

How could I not love my son?

When I stepped into the elevator, I felt some relief at getting back in control. Thinking about work, clients, and meetings—situations where I could be in charge. Being with my son made me powerless, and I hated that.

Do I really not love my son? Is Lucas right in hating me?

There were a lot of people who hated me, and I was fine with that. But if Lucas hated me, it would mean I was no different from my mother. A woman who had made no effort to earn my love after leaving us. And I didn't want to become my mom.

I closed my eyes for a split second and thought of Chloe Nichols, the only person who didn't seem to fear me or hate me. Her memory calmed me down as the elevator descended.

How was it that the beautiful bride I'd seen weeks ago was now my very much unmarried assistant?

I recalled seeing her at work last Friday—in her black skirt and gray blouse, her lips parting with shock when she first set eyes on me. My gaze had lingered on her lips—very kissable, but not by me, of course—and on her clear eyes. Clear blue, but confused.

My eyes flew open when I realized what I was doing. I was savoring my memory of her, and savoring any memory of a woman was a red flag. After my divorce with Helen, one-night stands and flings were the only things I permitted myself to engage in. I'd let the months pass into years, never attempting to build a relationship at all. I wasn't going to give another woman a chance to tell me I was bad at relationships—I already knew it. I had no relationship with my son and had ruined what I had with Helen. Who was I to ask for another chance at them?

Chloe was bad for me.

I opened my phone for a distraction, and no sooner had I checked my email than I found one from Chloe. It was a simple note that said she was glad for the opportunity to work for me and that she was always open to feedback. In her email, she included a P.S. noting that she'd bring chocolate chip cookies to the break room once she got to the office.

I groaned. Being around a woman that I could now bet everyone—including my grim HR—would fall in love with was going to be infuriating. I didn't want her working for me.

Remembering my decision from last Friday to get her rehired into a different position, I checked my phone for potential jobs while Chris drove. He had been with me for ten years, and he could sense my mood and knew when to comment on the traffic or the weather and when to stay silent. I was grateful for his silence today.

For ten minutes, I searched, until I finally found one job that could work. It required zero work experience, she would be on the first floor, but the pay was even lower than what she would make as my assistant. The last bit wasn't ideal, but I needed to act fast before this job was filled.

If I could just make her life miserable enough to get her to quit, I'd be in control again.

10

SEAN

My morning at work started like any other day. When the elevator pinged, I stepped in, noticing that quite a few of my employees were already here. The elevator was moderately full, but the crowd shuffled backward, making space for me. I gave them a stiff nod and got in, noticing someone simultaneously pressing the button for my floor.

A man to my left nervously began to speak. Going by his badge, he was a junior analyst, and he stammered, "Mr. Tassater, I've followed your career since the days of the garage start-up ..." He trailed off, looking sheepish, when I raised an eyebrow.

I wasn't ready for small talk so early in the day, not when my morning had been so rough and Chloe simply wouldn't leave my mind. Thankfully, people got off soon on the lower floors, and I was alone for the elevator's last bit of ascent to my floor.

When I got off on the thirty-fifth floor, I walked up to my assistant's desk and found Chloe already seated at Amelia's desk.

I did a double take even though I'd been mentally thinking about her on my ride here. She looked unnecessarily lovely. Her short blonde hair was held back from her face with a few clips, and she was dressed in a chic blue skirt and white blouse that reminded me of her curves underneath. I caught myself right away and reined in my thoughts before they brought to mind my dream from last night.

She looked up at me, her expression telling me her thoughts were innocent, while mine had been painfully wicked. I cursed myself mentally. She met my gaze without a flinch, suggesting to me that, somehow, my frowns and bad mood hadn't scared her. Yet.

"You're here," I grunted. I looked at her foot. "Is your leg better?" I asked before regretting that question already. Why did I care?

She was wearing sensible flats, and her face looked cheerier, less pained than she'd been last Friday.

She nodded, looking pleased that I remembered. "Thank you. I'm much better. I rested my leg—"

"I don't need the details," I said, interrupting her, and her cheeks went red.

I didn't want to imagine more scenes of her at her home, tending to her leg. I didn't want to feel more sympathetic to her, not when I'd decided that she should move out of here—soon.

"Of course," she added.

My gaze went to her white blouse, eerily similar to what she'd been wearing—or not wearing—in my early morning dream.

Feeling frustrated at the direction my thoughts were going in, I told Chloe, "I didn't want you as my assistant." As though that would help my body decide to hate her too. "HR forced my hand."

My blood rushed to my groin nevertheless, and I had no way of fixing that.

Chloe nodded, looking unperturbed, as though I'd just told her I disliked decaf lattes. "After all, they are the powers that run this organization."

I really did a double take at that. "Excuse me?" I asked, puffing up my chest and just about refraining from beating my fists like Tarzan. This woman thought I didn't have any say in how things ran here? "They *aren't* the powers that be."

Chloe was nodding with an expression of extreme understanding. "HR is extremely powerful. They make or break a company," she said.

"No, the CEO runs a company," I added, feeling foolish as soon as I uttered the words.

Chloe didn't seem to have heard. "Edith Simons in HR is a force to be reckoned with. I admire her."

She ought to be admiring me.

"I know it's your first day here, Chloe, but I need you to know that I don't tolerate assistants who slack off."

I was frustrated with myself, and I was taking it out on her. It was a dick move, even for me.

She stood up and nodded, affording me a view of her slim waist. Just the right size for me to put my arm around and ...

Damn it. I was doing it again.

I needed her gone, and I needed her gone quickly if I couldn't take her praising someone as innocent as HR.

"I know it's your first day here, and you haven't gotten the hang of my schedule yet. But tomorrow, I need you to have my breakfast on my desk by now and my nine a.m. meeting notes printed out and ready for me," I said, rambling to stall any thoughts I might have of pulling her to me.

She glanced through the open doors to my office, and I followed her gaze. Waiting for me on my desk was my breakfast—a grande cup of coffee that looked to be from my preferred store and a protein shake—as well as a stack of papers next to the keyboard, which I now guessed were the damn meeting notes I'd just berated her about.

"It had better be Columbian roast," I muttered as I looked at the coffee, finding that I couldn't find much to criticize even if I set my mind to it.

"It is," she added brightly. "And I've printed your meeting notes for the nine a.m. meeting with the C-suite team, as well as the eleven a.m. one with Horace Stafford from Wheeler Inc. I'll get your afternoon meeting notes typed up before your one p.m., and I booked a table for you at Slate for your lunch in case Horace Stafford decides to join you. Will you be needing anything else?"

I swallowed. "You missed my mid-morning coffee," I snapped at her. "I need a cup of Ethiopian roast at exactly ten ten. Not a minute sooner or later. If it's too soon, I end up needing to use the restroom in the middle of my meeting, and I'll hold you responsible for that. If it's too late, then I'm still too sleepy and cloudy-headed to be functional in my eleven a.m. meeting."

Her eyes widened, and she nodded. "Ten ten a.m. I'll remember," she said, her voice as smooth as butter.

I turned and strode into my office. If she was determined not to be fired, I was equally determined not to keep her for more than a week. I just didn't know how. Yet.

Ten minutes into reading my emails, I got an email from our production head, John Keene. I was due to meet him at three p.m., and he wrote to thank me for having the meeting early so that he could get to his son's baseball game at five p.m.

That gave me an idea. I walked up to the door and yanked it open, determined that I'd finally found a task that would make Chloe's confidence wilt. She would definitely be ready to accept any other job I'd offer her.

"I need you to change my meeting with John Keene from three p.m. to five p.m.," I told her as she held out the printout of my presentation slides for my next meeting. I took them from her reluctantly, half grateful and half resentful that she was doing a good job so far.

John Keene would never agree to a meeting with me at five p.m.

11

CHLOE

Eight hours later, when it was fifteen minutes before five p.m., I breathlessly rushed back to my desk, feeling nervous. I'd done something. Something big or something stupid—I couldn't say which. But there would be consequences. Of that I was sure. Especially with a man like Sean, who, for some unfathomable reason, was out to make my life difficult. I knew he was unhappy with the way I'd been assigned to him.

I didn't want to be around him either, but he hadn't taken into account a very stubborn sister who would do anything to help her brother pay for his college classes. So, I'd gone back and forth with John Keene's assistant to wrangle a meeting with him at five p.m., coming up with more and more creative solutions with each call, only to get turned down. But years and years of learning ballet had taught me one thing—resilience. I had been forced to give up ballet, but resilience? That part stubbornly refused to leave me. I knew everyone had a weak spot, and it wouldn't be too long before I found Mr. Keene's.

I walked up to Mr. Tassater's door a few minutes later

and knocked. When given permission, I walked in. He leaned back in his chair, surrounded by whiteboards. The start-up team had just taken their seats across from him, nervous but ready to present a new tech app feature. He ignored the three of them and looked at me with an expression that said he was ready to gloat at my failure.

I didn't give him a chance.

"Mr. Keene will meet you in the conference room in ten minutes," I announced. "At five p.m."

I wasn't prepared for how handsome Sean looked when he got caught completely off guard.

"You did what?" he asked, leaning forward on his desk and looking at me like he didn't believe his ears.

The other three people followed his gaze and looked back at me too. Sean's jaw cramped shut as his intense brown eyes met mine, searching me in disbelief.

My breath hitched, and I barely managed to nod. "The meeting with Mr. Keene has been rescheduled to five p.m., like you requested."

He grunted and stood up, his expression hard as he walked with me out of the office, ignoring the three stunned people who sat with their computers opened to their pitch.

"He'll be back in ten minutes," I assured them, realizing that Sean had been so sure of my failure that he set up another appointment himself for five p.m.

I led him down the corridor to the conference room.

The air around us was tense as Sean and I stood outside, observing Mr. Keene in the room. He was on a phone call, standing with his back to us. But he was very much undeniably *there*.

Sean looked at me for a long moment, seeming to struggle for words for a bit. "Well," Sean said finally, letting his guard down, "how did you manage to convince him?"

I considered how much I wanted to tell him. My palms were sweating as I prepared myself to drop the bombshell. "His assistant did have a huge list of reasons why Mr. Keene couldn't make it," I admitted. "The biggest one of which was that he needed to get to his son's baseball game at five p.m."

I stopped speaking, and I could see that Sean, while trying to feign disinterest, was hanging on to my every word.

"I called the coach and changed the time of the game to six thirty p.m.," I said at last, my words coming out breathy.

There. Now, for the repercussions.

It was the slowest head turn I'd seen in ages.

Sean met my gaze evenly. "How did you get the coach to do that?"

"The Tassater Foundation made a sizable donation to Mr. Keene's son's baseball team to help purchase new helmets and uniforms," I said, unable to keep a small smile from unfolding on my lips.

Sean's shoulders sagged just a little. "Should I ask how much?"

"You shouldn't," I said, "But it was twenty-five thousand dollars."

"Twenty-five thou—" he began, enraged, just as Mr. Keene turned around, spotting us, and hung up his phone.

"Mr. Tassater, I really must thank your nonprofit for the generous donation," John Keene said, walking up to Sean and holding a hand out.

Sean swallowed before he shook hands with the man and gave me a small look. It was an *oh, yeah? Let's see about this* kind of look, as though he finally realized that I wouldn't fall for his tricks so easily.

I had been very brazen, but it was worth it to remind Sean that anytime he challenged me, his nonprofit was going to be very generous.

I watched as Sean gave me a devilish smile over his shoulder before joining Mr. Keene in the conference room. It was a smile that said, *I'll see your move and raise you one of my own.*

Oh, he was enjoying this game all right. And the stakes were high.

My pulse began to race, and I turned on my heel, my head light and spinning. I knew Sean wasn't going to give in easily, and that twenty-five thousand could very well get me fired. But he wouldn't fire me just like that.

Nope, he was going to lay a trap and watch me fall in, if it was the last thing he did.

12

CHLOE

That night, I came back home, tired and hungry, to a quiet house. When I opened the front door and called out to Henry, I heard nothing in response. Assuming he was asleep, I set my handbag down on our secondhand brown couch from Goodwill.

"Henry, I'm making you your favorite dinner," I called, setting the chicken on the table. I'd bought it at Whole Foods on my way home from work as a treat to celebrate my first day at work. "How does lemon chicken sound for dinner?" I called as I opened the fridge.

I didn't hear any response, which wasn't too unusual since Henry sometimes took a late evening nap on days when he had early morning classes.

After washing the chicken and turning the oven on, I started to prepare the chicken. When it was done, I put it in the oven before walking over to Henry's room to check on him.

When I knocked and pushed the door open, I saw Henry lying on his bed, asleep, but pale.

Something seemed off, so I bolted in and felt his forehead.

"Henry," I said, shaking him awake as I realized he was running a fever.

Damn it. Two days ago, when Henry's doctor had changed some of his pain medications, he had warned me of a side effect that involved fever. It was uncommon, he'd said, but it could happen.

"You're running a fever, Henry," I said as he opened his eyes and looked at me faintly before shutting them again. "How long have you had it?" I asked.

I rushed to the kitchen and ran a towel under the tap before going back to Henry's room. I dabbed his forehead and face, leaving it on his forehead to bring his temperature down before I got the Tylenol from the cabinet.

"Here, sit up," I said, helping him up.

He was not strong enough to use the bedrails to pull himself up like he normally could. I reached for the bottle of water he always kept in his room and held him while he took a sip and swallowed a pill.

Once done, Henry lay back down with my help. "I tried calling you, but your phone was switched off," he said, head on the pillow but looking more awake and distressed. "Why would you turn your phone off, Chloe?"

Oh crap. I slapped my forehead with the palm of my hand. "My phone ran out of battery on the way here," I said, remembering I'd been listening to an audiobook on the subway. "When did the fever start?"

"It started a few hours ago. I felt hot and cold at the same time. I thought I'd be fine if I took a nap."

I picked up Henry's phone from the bedside table and made a call, pacing the room as I held it to my ear. It was around seven at night, so I was trying to reach the after-hours nurse line at Henry's doctor's office. When I finally got to speak to a nurse, I gave her Henry's information and his temperature. Minutes later, when I hung up, I looked at Henry, who had heard the entire conversation.

"Tylenol was the right thing to do," I said, sitting back down. "But we need to check with the doctor tomorrow to diagnose why this happened."

"That was scary," he said weakly from the bed, and I nodded.

I was glad I had come home at a reasonable time and that my work didn't involve overtime.

Something told me we needed to go back to the older medicines, $397 be damned. I'd find a way to make more, but Henry didn't have to suffer.

I set my phone to charge and made myself comfortable on a chair next to Henry's bed, intending to stay here and monitor him. But for some strange reason, I felt myself getting drowsy.

It was the smoke alarm that woke the two of us up later. The smell of burned chicken had reached the room, and I hurried out to the kitchen, noticing that the oven had been running for over an hour and smoke had filled the entire kitchen.

Coughing, I turned the oven off, which I'd accidentally set to 450 degrees Fahrenheit, before I took the chicken out. I dropped it in the sink with a heavy heart, berating myself for spending fifteen dollars on it. I opened the windows and front door and waited a few minutes for the alarm to turn off before I went back to check on Henry.

"Is everything okay?" he asked, looking worried as he sat up.

I nodded as I recognized he had managed to do that on his own this time before reaching for the thermometer.

"We're going to have instant noodles for dinner," I said, holding the device to his forehead.

His temperature was back down to 98 degrees Fahrenheit, and I breathed a sigh of relief.

"Noodles is fine," he said, closing his eyes again. "But I'm not really hungry. Just stay by my side, Chloe. Don't leave."

I held his hand in mine. "I'm not going anywhere, Henry."

In a minute, he had dozed off again. Getting ready to spend the night by his side, I sat down when I heard a beep on my phone with a text.

Sean: *Chloe, I need twenty unique Spider-Man figurines to be delivered to my office before I leave for home at nine. Let's see if you're up to the task, Woman Who Hates Bruce.*

I stared at the text. It was eight at night, so there was no way I needed to do this and particularly not when I had an hour to get this done. But it confirmed what I had suspected all along.

Chloe: *In an hour? That's impossible.*

Sean: *There is no such thing as impossible. Impossible is just an excuse for people who are too scared.*

Sean was certainly not giving up on his attempts to fire me. I looked at Henry, whose color seemed to have returned to his face, and placed a hand on his forehead. It was cool, and while I wet the hand towel again and wiped his face once more, I was drawn back to the phone as a new text came in.

Sean: *Is this task too difficult for you, Chloe?*

I gulped. So, this was his trap. I needed to run this errand, or I knew I could kiss goodbye any dreams I had of going back to Henry's old and trusted medicines.

Henry's temperature was normal now, and it would stay

normal for a few hours at least. By the looks of it, he was in deep sleep and would probably sleep through the night.

I knew one eclectic shop near Times Square that would have Marvel characters and be open at this hour, but would they have twenty *different* Spider-Mans?

I scooted out of my chair. The only way to find out was to get out there. If I was quick, I could finish my task, keep my job, and be back before Henry comprehended I was gone. Writing a quick reply to Sean that I'd do it, I raced to the door, grabbing my purse on the way.

If Sean was determined to fire me, I was even more determined to not be fired. I could still save my job.

13

CHLOE

Does Sean have a Spider-Man craze at his age? I wondered as I got into a cab after letting the driver know I was in a hurry.

It seemed unreasonable to want twenty figurines, but I had been familiar with a CEO who wanted miniature figures of an entire baseball team lined up on his table each morning. It wasn't too odd.

My first stop was a quaint comic-book store, tucked away in a corner of Times Square. As I entered, the familiar scent of ink and paper enveloped me. I approached the store clerk, describing what I wanted.

The clerk assisted me, leading me through rows of comic books, action figures, and collectibles. Time ticked away quietly, and soon, I found a few rare editions and classic Spider-Man figurines, bringing my count up to ten. I raced to the checkout counter, knowing that I was far from the twenty figurines I needed.

Leaving the comic-book store, I found a second yellow cab and got in, determined to finish soon and get back to Henry.

Next, I stopped by a bustling toy store in East Village. As I weaved through the maze of tourists in the shop, I scoured the store's shelves, finding Spider-Man in various poses and costumes. I paid for three pieces I'd found, but I still had twenty minutes and seven figurines to go.

Whipping out my phone, I located more specialty toy stores around me. I visited three other shops, negotiating with shop owners and even getting one of them to make a call to some of his friends' shops to find out if they had any more toys in stock.

When I got my twentieth figurine, I emerged triumphantly from the last store, a bag brimming with Spider-Man figurines slung over my shoulder. I hailed another cab, directing the driver to Sean's office. The city skyline sparkled as we drove through the streets, and I checked my phone in case I got any calls from Henry. There were none, and I breathed easy, knowing that he was sleeping through the night.

As I sat in my fourth cab for the night, I stared at the bags next to me on my seat, brimming with expensive Spider-Man treasures.

Since I'd joined Sean's company so recently, they hadn't issued me a company card yet. I was using my personal card, and every time I'd swiped it for another expensive Spider-Man toy, my heart had almost stopped.

I would be lying if I said I'd never once wished I could trade places with someone more carefree for a day. Some days, the desire to escape the weight of caring for Henry was so strong that I would Google Dad's name in desperation, wondering if he was nearby, and when I found nothing, I'd empty a bottle of wine. In the morning, self-hatred would creep in, and I'd make up for my previous day's thoughts by doing something extra special for Henry.

When I got to the Tassater building on the Upper East Side, I thanked my cab driver and got out and raced up the steps and inside the building. I waved to Charles, the security guard by the desk, and he waved back.

"You're a hard worker, Ms. Nichols," Charles said as I ran across the lobby to the elevators. "Let me know if you need me to find you a cab for your ride back."

"Thanks, Charles," I said, warming up to him as I got into the first elevator that opened. "You can call me Chloe. And I'll take the subway back tonight, but I'll let you know if that ever changes."

"Take care, Chloe," he said with a smile before the elevator doors shut.

The building was eerily quiet, a complete opposite to the bustle that pervaded this place in the daytime.

My head was a frenzy of thoughts as the elevator rode up, and I hoped I could drop the bag off at Sean's office and leave right away. Hopefully without running into the man who had sent me on this fool's errand.

It wasn't the empty corridor I met when the doors opened on the thirty-fifth floor, but Mr. Tassater himself.

14

CHLOE

"You're late," was all he said when I walked out of the elevator and into the corridor. "I gave you an hour, and you took ninety minutes."

I stopped a few feet from him and checked the time, cursing under my breath. He was right, the jerk.

I held the toy bags out, breathless and despairing. "Well, if you want to fire me now, go ahead. I have been cursing you all hour *and a half* anyway, and I have a few more swear words up my sleeve," I said, barely refraining from putting my hands on my knees and drawing deep breaths while he took the bags from my hands.

His gaze drifted to the bag and then back up at me. "Curses? For twenty Spider-Man figurines?" He seemed truly surprised.

"Yes, you oblivious jerk," I said, straightening up. "You know what I've been through to get this for you? I visited ten shops and spent eight hundred fifty-seven dollars, and I almost had a tussle with two tourists to get one of these figurines before they could. You'd better reimburse me for this—and fast."

I paused, taking a breath, but my rage didn't dissipate. I was in no way done with him yet. "And since I assume I'm fired, I'm going to go ahead and ask, what does a grown man need these for, anyway? Is there a Spider-Man fetish I don't know about?"

The elevator doors opened behind me, and a boy rushed out.

"Lucas, slow down," Sean said sharply, his eyes tracking the boy who raced toward him.

A young boy, not more than seven, ran past me. He had brown hair, a small face, and a downturn to the edges of his lips.

Sean's eyes were on me when I turned to him in surprise, and I could sense that he was evaluating my reaction.

What is a kid doing on this floor?

The boy's eyes took in Sean in a rebellious question.

"Where is Mom?" he demanded. "What time is her plane landing?"

A young woman, quiet and subdued, walked up the steps, breathless. Her gaze went to Lucas, and she said faintly, "There you are," before leaning against the wall to catch her breath.

Lucas paid her no attention, and I assumed she was his nanny.

Sean closed his eyes for a second, presumably steeling himself, before he took a step toward the boy. To my surprise, the boy immediately took a step back, distancing himself from Sean.

The look on Sean's face was one of defeat when he finally spoke. "I'm sorry, Lucas, I didn't tell you earlier. I didn't want to ruin your day. But Mom's not getting here for another month, son."

Son.

Sean had a son.

I'd never expected that. I'd read up about his professional life, but stayed well away from other details. With wealthy men, you were better off not knowing, and I hadn't wanted to taint my professional relationship with tidbits about his salacious affairs.

My attention went to the bag in his hands, and suddenly, the toys made sense. As I looked closer at Lucas, I saw he had the same straight hair that flopped over his forehead, that same upturned nose, and the same frown. They were father and son.

Lucas stomped on the floor and shouted, "You're lying. I want to speak to Mom right now. Call her!"

Where was his mom? Why wasn't anyone able to call her?

Sean attempted to soften his voice and knelt down to look in his son's eye. "Lucas, I'll call Mom later. Here, why don't you see what I got for you—Spider-Man fig—"

The boy wasn't paying any attention to his dad. His eyes drifted to the open office door and with a yell, he shouted, "I'm calling her right now from your phone," and ran for the door.

Sean and the nanny followed him inside while I was reeling with the realization that Sean was married and had a family.

I hadn't looked into his personal life, but I had noticed the lack of a ring and assumed that he was unmarried.

Wishing I could stop the train of thoughts in my head, I turned to give Sean some space. He was having a hard time with his son, and my presence was only making it tougher for him. I was familiar with hard times.

There had been a lot of emotional meltdowns while Henry tried to come to terms with his new way of living, and in these situations, I knew that strangers were a pain at best. Ten years later, he had long-term disability, and I had become well versed with pain management.

I reached the elevator and got in, pressing the button for the lobby when I heard another shout. Lucas ran out of Sean's office, Sean and his nanny on his heels. He outran them easily, getting into the elevator with me just before the doors shut, almost hurting himself in the process.

My heart raced at the close call as the elevator started moving down.

"Hey, are you okay?" I asked, kneeling down to look at him at eye level.

He looked visibly distressed, and tears were welling up in his eyes.

"Well, that was clearly a silly question for me to ask," I said in a lighter voice as I fake smacked myself on the forehead with my palm. "You have every right to be upset because your dad wasn't honest with you. Ignore my question. Now, which floor do you need to get to?" I asked him while he furiously blinked the tears away.

He looked a little less distressed now.

"Anywhere. It doesn't matter," he said in a low voice that painfully reminded me of a younger Henry's. He continued to keep his eyes focused on the ground.

My heart went out to him.

"You know, when I was younger and needed to make a great escape, I realized that the best spot to hide in was sometimes the most obvious one."

He didn't acknowledge me, but I knew he was listening.

"Do you want me to help you hide from your dad? We can hide together. I'm the best at finding hiding spots."

"Really?" he asked doubtfully, looking up at me at last.

I nodded. "When I was seven and mad at my family, I

found such a good hiding spot that neither my mom nor my brother could find me for three hours. Oh, it was splendid."

"Where did you hide?" His voice—boyish, innocent—rang out in the elevator as it continued its descent.

I grinned at that memory. "I was sitting at my table in my room all along. Everyone who came to my room to search for me didn't do more than glance at the empty bed in my room before going away."

He turned and met my gaze. "That doesn't sound like a great spot," he admitted finally. "But at least you had your mom and brother to search for you. If I hid for three hours, no one would even notice."

Oof. Those were deep pains, and for once, I was stumped for a response.

Putting my arm around him, I drew him in for a hug. He didn't resist, but his shoulders trembled while he rested his head on my shoulder.

"It feels like everyone is hiding from me. Mom, Dad … no one's around," he said in a strangled voice.

"Well, how about this? I'll be there for you. The next time your dad's giving you a hard time, you tell him to get Chloe Nichols on the line. I'm his assistant, and that means he gets to call me at all hours of the day and night. So, he'd definitely *not* say no to calling me. I'm one cab ride away from you, so I'll always show up for you. Okay?"

We reached the lobby, and I could feel him nod as he stepped back.

"Besides, I don't want to hide." He looked through the open elevator doors, not making a run for it anymore.

I could hear doors banging shut in the stairwell, some floors above, when he spoke in a soft voice. "I just want to find my mom."

15

SEAN

I finally reached the damn lobby, panting and hoping my assistant had had the sense to stop Lucas. I didn't see the security guard anywhere, so I raced around the lobby, calling loudly for Lucas for a good three minutes. I even searched under the receptionist's desk and behind the extremely large potted plants before I finally heard someone chuckling.

Chloe and Lucas were sitting on the lobby's beige leather couch.

How had I missed that?

I strode over, trying to not seem desperate as I saw my son sitting calmly next to Chloe.

"Well, there you are, Lucas," I said. "And you, Chloe, are clearly incompetent at your job," I said, striding toward them. I'd almost lost Lucas, and I was furious at this woman.

She had sat there for a full five minutes while I ran around the lobby, searching desperately for my son. There was something missing in her brain, and I knew for sure I didn't want her working for me. Forget the alternate job I'd found for her. She wasn't fit to work at Tassater Inc.

I took hold of Lucas, my hands on either side of his arms, as I tried to help him up, but he shook me off and sat back down.

"Are you okay?" I demanded of him.

He turned away, his mouth in a stubborn line.

"He's fine," Chloe said, but I shifted my anger on her.

"He's not fine," I snapped. "You don't know the first thing about my son. He hates being told what to do."

I leaned into her, enunciating each word with precision. "Do you mean to tell me you've been sitting here and sniggering while I've been looking for my son under the receptionist's desk?"

She couldn't resist a smile at that. Her eyes slid sideways to the pots behind me. "And even while you looked under the potted plants too," she muttered, barely concealing a grin.

She must have noticed my anger because she forced herself to focus. "Your son needs more than what you're giving him."

"He has his toys," I said, pointing to the bag that Anne had brought with her. She had hung back, looking mortified, while I lost my temper with Chloe.

"He doesn't need more toys! Toys are a miserable substitute for something Lucas needs more desperately. A parent's time and attention. *Your* time and attention. *Your* love."

"Lucas doesn't want my company. He's told me so himself."

"Well, he's obviously not comfortable enough to tell you the truth. You're always working."

"Let me remind you that you've only been working with me for a day."

"But I've seen your schedule. You work too much!"

"I will not discuss this anymore with you."

"Well, I've only just begun, and I'm not going to stop."

I froze. I wasn't used to hearing anyone speak to me this way.

I took a single menacing step toward Chloe.

"Chloe, listen to me, and listen to me carefully," I said, my voice low but savage. "Your job ends now. You will not work for me for one minute longer."

I broke off when I noticed something odd. Chloe didn't seem to care about what I was saying, but even more strangely, Lucas had a grin on his face.

I stepped back and surveyed that grin.

He was laughing at seeing how worried I was, no doubt.

It made me feel even more irrationally angry with Chloe. It was completely irresponsible on her part to go along with this charade. But that grin ... it was something I hadn't seen on him in a long time.

As I frowned at the two insolent people on the couch, Chloe nudged him, and Lucas nodded back, whispering something.

"What was that?" I asked, my voice echoing in the large and silent lobby.

Lucas frowned at me. "It's a secret," he said, getting up and noticing Anne in the distance. "All right, let's go home," he said with an air of someone wanting to get things over with. He turned to wave at Chloe. "Thanks for the idea," he said and strangely leaned in for a hug, which Chloe gave him willingly.

Wrapping her arms around his small body, she hugged him tight.

How did she get him to hug her willingly?

When he stepped back, she waved at him as he walked out the front doors with Anne. When Anne extended her hand to him on their way out, Lucas took it readily. In a similar situation, Lucas would have refused mine.

I gestured to Anne to go ahead and that I'd follow them in my own car in a few minutes before turning back to Chloe.

"What idea was Lucas talking about?" I asked.

Chloe looked at me for a long moment before standing up. She was so close that I could see her lips trembling with emotion. Unlike most people, Lucas's meltdown had affected her.

"He told me that he felt like everyone was hiding from him. His mom, you ... no one was around." She hesitated. "So, I told him, sometimes, things can be in plain sight before we finally see them. And to test that theory, we decided to wait in plain sight while you—"

"Made a fool of myself, searching for my son under the receptionist's desk?" I growled.

She paused, a coy smile on her lips.

God, she was beautiful.

"He chuckled when you did that," she said, her voice low and her face tilted up to me. "So, now, he thinks his mom must be in plain sight, too, even if he can't see her."

I groaned, putting my hands on my hips. Chloe's response steadied me, even if it didn't help. I looked at the doors through which Lucas had disappeared with Anne, my heart heavy.

"His mom is far," I said, glancing at her. "If you count multiple continents as far."

Chloe's eyes widened, and she winced. "Oops. Sorry."

It wasn't her fault really. She couldn't have known.

"I think a video call with her might be overdue." I sighed.

I wasn't someone who talked about their personal life.

But with Chloe, my guard dropped. I should have resented her for it, but to my surprise, I found that I quite liked it.

I turned to her.

"You calmed him down," I observed.

When would I be able to calm my son down from a meltdown? I had been pushing people away all my life, even the ones who wanted to be around me. And in return, the only person I wanted—my son—didn't want me. It stung, and this incident painfully reminded me of how I'd been ignoring my stepsister's messages to connect. Perhaps it was time I accepted her invitation to talk.

My gaze went to Chloe's hair, shimmering under the lights. She had thick blonde hair, like the warmth of a sunny day, and her side braid from earlier in the morning had come undone. I frowned.

"What were you doing tonight when I asked you to run this errand?" I asked, taking a step closer to her.

16

CHLOE

When Sean asked me that question, the first thought in my mind was wondering what excuse I could come up with.

People had tried to dig out details about Henry in the past, and having had bad experiences every time I confided in someone, I'd learned the hard way not to trust everyone with Henry's health issues. It was the only thing that kept us safe from gossiping tongues and from being the topic of discussion at classic watercooler talk.

I thought back to Henry and his pale, sweating face. Of my hurried call to the doctor's office and my burned chicken in the sink.

I swallowed. "It was just a normal evening. Watching TV," I said.

Something about my response made Sean raise his eyebrows. "So, if you weren't fired, could I trouble you for errands in the evenings?" he pressed.

Wasn't I fired? Was there a chance I could still save my job?

I wanted to refuse his request for my time in the evenings, thinking of how often something unexpected happened with Henry's health or his classes and how little time I got to set things right. Then, I thought about my promise to Lucas. If Lucas ever needed me, I should be around. I'd promised him as much.

"If I weren't fired," I stressed, "it would be no trouble at all." I shut my eyes only briefly as I steeled myself for the coming days.

Sean was trying his best to get rid of me, and I wouldn't give in.

"Well ..." Sean said, stepping even closer to me.

His cologne hit me, all masculine and smoky. I had to look up to see him. His brown eyes were lit up while he observed me with an ease in him I hadn't seen in a while. It reminded me of the man I'd met at the café weeks before. The man I hadn't seen in him all day today.

"Chloe, I apologize. I spoke quite badly to you just now." He paused. "I was too incensed and spoke in a way I shouldn't have. It's my mistake. You're right about one thing though—I need to spend more time with Lucas. I need him to trust me and talk to me, and I don't know how."

I didn't know how either.

"Chloe, I want you to work for me again."

I stared at him in surprise. Was he joking?

But his expression was anything but fake. It was sincere and deep, and as I watched, his Adam's apple bobbed while he waited for my response.

I wanted to work for him, bad temper and all.

"You were great tonight. I've never seen Lucas ease out of a tantrum so quickly."

"Thank you." I drew my gaze away from the base of his throat, realizing I'd been staring at his strong neck. "So, I can still work for you even though I was late tonight?" I asked breathlessly.

He nodded.

"Even though I pledged twenty-five grand to John Keene's son's baseball team?" I continued, pushing my luck. I needed to hear it. It was the only thing that would make this tumultuous night worth it.

Sean looked a bit grim at the reminder and then nodded again. "That's fine," he said. "But that brings me to another question. Why do you want this job so badly?"

Because I'd made a mistake once. A mistake that put Henry in a wheelchair. Losing this job would be a big mistake, and I didn't let myself make mistakes again.

"You asked me that already."

"Yes, and you never really gave me an answer. You're doing the work of someone with far less experience than you—and for a boss like me."

My life revolved around Henry—a continuous cycle of responsibility. Small, manageable tasks that helped me compartmentalize and process things, getting through one difficult day and onto the next. This job was just the same.

I could do this job, if only you'd let me.

I gazed into his eyes, feeling drawn in against my will. Feeling my knees weaken.

"And I am grateful that you gave me the opportunity," I said, not stepping away. "It means a lot to me to have a job at the moment. That's all."

His gaze settled on me for a long time, evaluating. The air felt thick with tension, and he broke it abruptly by looking over at the spot where Lucas had sat, waiting for him. Watching him.

Sean's expression was troubled when he turned back to

me. "You seemed to understand how to talk to Lucas. How to get him to listen to you. How did you do that?"

I considered it. Lucas had seemed so troubled, similar to how a younger Henry had grappled with his emotions. With his sudden loss of mobility, his games, his routine.

"Well, I can understand Lucas's emotions in a way that perhaps you are struggling to. And going by how the nanny couldn't handle him either, I feel like Lucas is aware that everyone around him is on tenterhooks and no one really is comfortable with him, and that frustrates him even more."

Again, very similar to Henry.

Sean drew in a deep breath, tilting his head as he regarded me. "You don't seem to be uncomfortable around him."

I nodded, my cheeks flushing. "That's because Lucas resembles someone I know."

"Do you have a child too, Chloe?"

I drew in a deep breath. "Let's just say, you're not the only one worried about your family."

His gaze went to my ringless finger and then to me. His expression hardened, and he nodded, acknowledging my need to keep my personal life private. "I understand."

I could sense that he was withdrawing. That the possibility of questions I could ask him were now reduced and that I needed to leave. He'd gone cold.

"Is that all, Mr. Tassater?" I asked, getting up.

He gave me a barely perceptible nod. "That will be all, Ms. Nichols."

At the door, I turned around to glance at him. He was standing by the couch, and our gazes locked. His expression matched what I'd seen on him the very first time at the café. Smoldering, intense, but also probing. He was just as handsome at the end of the day as he had been at the beginning. Silent, intense, and misunderstood perhaps.

"Thank you," he said at last. "Rest assured, this will be the last time I trouble you after work, Ms. Nichols."

I had given him many reasons to fire me. Instead of doing that, he had given me my evenings back.

Why did that only increase how much I admired him?

17

CHLOE

Henry recovered from his reaction to the new medicine fairly quickly once he stopped taking it and was able to resume attending his classes within two days.

He hadn't realized I'd gone out that night and was very uneasy when I told him about it later.

"Why would your boss send you on errands at that hour?" he had asked, frustrated, and I'd instantly regretted telling him. Now, he would worry about me. "I don't trust this guy, Chloe."

A few days ago, I might have agreed. But after that night, when I'd seen a different side to Sean, I wasn't so sure. But I'd assured Henry that it wouldn't happen again.

"I'll be at home with you in the evenings, Henry," I'd promised.

I'd picked up his old medicines, paid up, and skipped paying for the PMP certification course. I'd told myself it didn't matter at all. But now, as I sat in our van, waiting to pick up Henry from his late-night club meeting at his college, I wistfully looked at the few students walking across the campus.

Focus, Chloe. Skipping your PMP certification was not a sacrifice at all, I reminded myself, *since you didn't know if you had it in you to get PMP certified anyway, and you're happy to put it off once more.*

But I'd never gone to college, and nights like this—when I faced yet another setback in my career goals—were times when I found myself regretting parts of my life.

I had been eighteen when Dad left us, and I didn't have it in me to care for Henry, earn an income, *and* deal with classes and grades. I took the first job that I could find and made sure we could continue the same basic lifestyle we were used to. And I'd wanted to be cheerful while doing it all. Henry should never suspect I was unhappy. What use was it when he was dealing with his own unhappiness?

It was close to seven at night, and I got out of the van, leaning against the side and looking up at the dark sky.

There was a lot to be thankful for too. Greg, my apartment neighbor, had waved to me today from his kitchen window when I came home at half past five. He hadn't spoken to me yet, but I knew he was grateful for my bringing the trash in on his behalf. Someday, I hoped to be able to invite him over for coffee and cake, but something told me that would take a while.

Sean had made sure I was reimbursed for all my expenses from that night, not even bothering to look at the receipts I'd so carefully collected.

The silence of the night broke with the shrill ring of my phone.

It was from Sean.

"Yes, Mr. Tassater?" I asked, my pulse racing when I answered.

So far, he'd kept his promise to not send me on errands at night. In fact, he had been very reticent the past few days, canceling most of his meetings and preferring to work alone in his office as much as possible.

"Are you busy, Chloe?" he asked, his voice deep and low over the phone.

"Kind of actually. I was just out," I said, hoping to preempt any further errands from him. I needed to get home and keep my promise to Henry that I wouldn't be away at night.

"What are you doing?"

I hesitated as I looked at the college building. "Just waiting for someone."

There was a long pause on the other end of the line.

"I see," he said finally.

I didn't know what he'd made of that, but I found that I didn't want to leave him hanging anymore. I could let him in a little on what my life was like.

"I'm waiting for my brother," I clarified.

I didn't want to keep everything from him. Just the heavy, troublesome bits.

I heard a deep exhale on his end.

"Your brother," he said, and it wasn't much of a question. He seemed to mull over it. "I hadn't pictured you having a brother."

I hadn't known Sean was trying to piece together the world I lived in at all.

"Since we're on the topic of families, I need a favor," he said, his voice sounding rushed. "After seeing how you interacted with Lucas that night, something occurred to me."

As his PA, I was prepared to get calls from him at odd hours, even if he claimed he wouldn't. But I wasn't used to discussing families.

"Can you help me figure Lucas out?" he asked.

I blinked. "Figure him out?"

A seven-year-old? I wasn't sure what deep troubles he thought Lucas was hiding.

Sean let out a deep breath, and I could picture him standing with his hand on his side, brows furrowed and looking lost.

"My ex-wife called me earlier and said she needs Lucas to stay with me for another month."

"Oh."

I hadn't realized the wife was an ex. I felt a sense of spark and hope unfurl in me that had no place doing so.

"Lucas and I don't exactly get along. He ... well, he hates me."

I waited. I knew interpreting a child's behavior was hard, but to assume it equaled hate?

"I sincerely hope that's not true, but I'm listening," I said.

In the distance, I spied Henry wheeling himself out of the college building, and he stopped to scan the surroundings for me. Spotting me, he waved before slowly making his way to me. I waved back.

"If you could help me get along with Lucas," Sean said, exhaling deeply, "well, that would be very much appreciated."

"Me?" I repeated, sounding dumbfounded.

I could picture him nodding.

"We could pretend that you're my friend and get Lucas to join us outdoors."

Show up at places where Sean and his son are in attendance?

"Like parks and ice cream shops?" I asked, and he agreed after a beat.

I considered that. It did help that my evenings were free and Bruce-less, but I also had a younger brother who needed me. In the distance, a classmate caught up to Henry and stopped to have a quick conversation, and he turned his head a few times to make sure I had noticed. I did, and I gave him a thumbs-up from afar to let him know it was okay.

"So, what do you think?" Sean asked, his voice a distant echo.

Help him get along with his son? I wasn't sure how I'd even do that, my recent experience with Lucas notwithstanding.

"Why me?" I asked after a moment.

He grunted in confusion. "What do you mean?"

"Is one incident enough to convince you that I'm the person for the job? I mean, there are a lot of behavioral counselors out there who can help. Professionals."

"I trust you," he said simply, as though that was all there was to it.

I wanted to ask why, and then I realized why. "Is it because it's easier to trust someone whose life you've seen fall apart in front of you?"

He sighed. "You're being dramatic. And having a fiancé stand you up on your wedding day isn't *life falling apart* material."

"I'd argue it is, but let's move on," I said in response.

Most mornings, I'd begin my day by admitting to myself that I was broken, and knowing that my expectations for myself were so low, I found it easier to go through my day. We never expected anything from broken people. Sean didn't know the whole picture; if he did, he would realize just how much my life was fraying at the seams.

Henry's classmate finally left, and he was coming over. I would get another minute with Sean before I had to hang up.

"But you're right. I did see you being vulnerable. And here you are, working with me, even after all the crap I gave you at work. I trust you now, Chloe."

I guessed I should thank him, but it felt like he was painting me as an easy woman. Something I didn't fancy myself being.

"I was vulnerable that day at the café because everything I'd thought was important in my life left me the moment Bruce bailed on me. Just like how Lucas feels abandoned by the mom he's probably lived with forever. Even if she's gone for just a month. So, I'll think about it because I want to help you—or rather, I want to help Lucas."

His voice was wry. "Lucas wins over me, eh?"

I grinned. "Are you jealous, Mr. Tassater?"

"I am conscious of feeling a little let down at the moment."

I laughed. I could picture him in his office, standing by the large, expensive oak table.

"Are you still at work?" I asked.

He had been when I left at five earlier that evening.

"Yes."

He was probably still wearing his suit, his jacket unbuttoned, looking out the windows at the sky. It was dark out, and we were both looking at the same sky.

"Are you looking at the sky?"

"Yes, always the sky."

"What about the skyline?" I asked.

When you worked on the thirty-fifth floor, you had a choice of things to look at beyond a great, expansive sky.

"Never."

"What a pity when you have such a beautiful view," I added, remembering spending early mornings looking out at the view after I placed his breakfast and drink on the table.

"Maybe someone like you might convince me to admire that too."

"Maybe," I said, realizing with a pang of regret that Henry was close to the van already. I'd have to hang up soon. I let out the back ramp for our van and waited. "Could I think about your request for a few days before I give you an answer?"

"Sure. I want to say take as much time as you need, but I only have a month left with Lucas."

"I'll get back to you tomorrow. I find that it is usually best to sleep over things before I decide."

"Are you afraid of being impulsive, Chloe?"

"Very. I can't afford to be."

He was silent. "What happens when you're impulsive, Chloe?" he asked, his voice low.

I didn't speak for a few moments. "I do things that I regret. I decide to marry the wrong man, for example. Or I'd tell—" I bit my lip.

"Me the truth about why you were so flustered that night I needed the Spider-Man figures?" he asked, completing the sentence for me.

I blew out a sharp breath. "You remembered?" I asked finally.

"When it comes to you, I seem to have the sharpest of memories, Chloe."

We were still for a few moments while Henry stopped a few feet away to wave at a friend across the street.

"You know, there's a lot more to you than I imagined when I met you at the café," I muttered.

"You imagined me and my life?" he demanded.

"I tried to," I confessed. "I tried to picture what kind of life someone like you might lead."

"What parts are you disappointed in?" he asked, his voice tinged with urgency, as if that were suddenly all that mattered to him.

"Nothing," I admitted, feeling surprised by my answer. "So far, I've found nothing lacking. And that realization stuns me."

I heard him clear his throat.

"I'm glad to hear that."

To my right, Henry slowly rolled up the back ramp into the van while I waited. Some vans had automated systems with buttons to help a wheelchair in, but ours was manual.

"Oh, and, Ms. Nichols, you don't need to worry about me asking you about why you were flustered that night."

"I don't?" I asked, feeling surprised at this turn of events.

He hummed in assent.

"Because I know you'll tell me the truth someday. When you trust me. Which you will, Chloe. There's no escaping that." And with that, he hung up.

18

SEAN

The large mahogany table gleamed under the lights. I sat at the head of the table, my gaze sweeping the two men and the one woman who were seated around it. The CFO, the head of marketing, and the VP of strategy had just finished discussing budget allocation and potential risks related to our newest initiative to expand into Asia. Everyone was eager to leave, except for Dex Smithson, the head of marketing.

I stared at Dex across the table, and he smiled back at me like he hadn't just asked me for an obscene amount of money.

I'd already pledged support for his wife's charitable cause for the Robin Hood Foundation, but *golf club fund* was his follow-up ask. I'd turned him down once, but given by how he wasn't moving, I had a bad feeling about what was coming next. Everyone knew when Dex started asking for something, his requests never stopped at just one.

A knock sounded on the door, and I looked up as Chloe entered my office.

For the few days that Chloe had been working for me,

I'd seen her busy and occasionally worried while work was slow. She had something else going on in her life. Something that demanded much of her attention, and I had to remind myself that whatever went on in her personal life shouldn't be my concern. Except that I was inordinately interested in all the details of this woman's life. The parts that she would share and the parts that she wouldn't.

Today, however, was one of those days when she was looking happier. She was in navy-blue pants and a ruffled cream-colored blouse that accentuated her cleavage. I swallowed and looked away, but not before I noticed she'd styled her hair in waves and her skin was glowing.

I wanted to pull her to me, to bury my face in her hair and breathe in her scent. I also wanted to punch myself in the face for being weak enough to lust after my assistant. Especially when she was keeping things so professional.

She didn't care one bit about me.

Her head wasn't turned by my excessive wealth or affected charm, unlike others. Damn her.

She shut the door gently behind her before looking pointedly at me. "Mr. Tassater, your Zoom meeting with Mr. Edgar Mercer, the Australian oil baron, is in ten minutes."

I stared at her, feeling at a complete loss of understanding. Oil? We were a tech company. I had no dealings with oil barons, much less ones from Australia.

My CFO and VP of strategy stood up, seizing their opportunity to leave. They shuffled out behind Chloe, the door falling shut behind them. Good for them. Bad for me. Dex was rooted to his chair, looking back at me curiously.

Chloe shifted her weight from one foot to the other. "Whenever you're ready, Mr. Tassater, I'll help you set up the video call with Mr. Mercer."

When I met Chloe's gaze again, perplexed, she blatantly

gave me a cheerful smile and followed it up with a wink and a nod that seemed to imply, *Go with it.*

Was she really kicking Dex Smithson out for me?

Dex looked at Chloe with a grin. He wasn't buying it.

I stood up, pushing my chair back farther than I'd intended to, and extended my hand out to the man. "Yes, I'd completely forgotten about Mr. Mercer for a minute there," I said, my voice firm as I looked at Dex. "We'll have to continue our conversation about golf later. I'm afraid I'm out of time now."

He looked perturbed. "But we never discussed the budget for the marketing department's new team lunch initiative or a possible donation for—"

Chloe all but pushed him out the door, giving him a lengthy explanation about the importance of my upcoming meeting.

When the door fell shut behind Dex, I breathed out a huge sigh of relief while Chloe turned around and gave me another one of her wide smiles.

"I was afraid he'd ask you to invest in his retirement fund next," she said as she walked back to my desk with ease.

I stared at her. "You knew?"

She cocked her head to the side. "That Dex always asks for a minimum of three things when he gets here?" She nodded. "I went to John Keene's son's baseball game yesterday evening, and he mentioned it," she confessed.

"You went where?" I asked and then shook my head. "Of course you did."

She grinned. "I took some photos. They love their new uniforms, and the photos from the game are going on your website for the nonprofit."

"That's overkill. But tell me, how did you know Dex was

here? Weren't you in the meeting down the corridor with the legal team?"

She nodded. "I was. But I saw Dex making his way to your office some minutes later, and I raced out of that room as soon as I could leave."

I appreciated the sentiment and the effort. "Thank you," I said. "I owe you for that."

My hands itched to reach out and stroke her, but I restrained myself. I wanted to focus my attention on her full lips, imagining what they'd taste like. I hated that I was thinking these thoughts around her. Wishing I could kiss her, taste her, and hear her moan under my touch.

She looked at me for a long moment before she spoke again. "By the way, I've thought about what you asked."

I indicated for her to sit.

After my call with Helen, I'd ordered all the Marvel movies for Lucas, only to realize he wanted to watch the movies with my housekeeper, not me.

I'd even gotten him a Spider-Man bouncy castle to play with when nothing else seemed to bridge the gap between us. It was the happiest I'd seen him since having to say goodbye to his mother at the airport, but he still wouldn't look at me.

How could I spend quality time with my son if he kept pushing me away? How did parents make time with their children when their workday was chock-full of meetings and tasks and the child was too cranky at nighttime to care about spending time together?

Chloe was my only hope. The only person I'd seen work well with Lucas, apart from Helen and the nanny. The latter two hadn't been able to help me with Lucas. Anne worked multiple jobs, and Helen had fallen in love and was more interested in her new fiancé at the moment. A new fiancé who would soon be Lucas's step-dad.

A thought flashed in my mind that soon, Lucas would prefer Matt to me. That shouldn't happen. I wouldn't *let* that happen.

So even though I'd gone months without sex, and the universe had delivered the most attractive woman in front of me, I'd ignore every feeling I had for her. Chloe was a woman I couldn't make a move on. Even though she was a woman who made my clothes feel too tight and my skin burn with heat.

I had to because I needed Chloe for something more. I needed to be better than Helen's new man, and I could not ruin that opportunity by sleeping with the only woman who had the power to teach me that.

What would I do if Chloe said no? I thought about what I'd asked her, and I needed to tell her about something else I'd decided to do.

I held up a hand before she could continue. "Before you go on, you should know that I've decided I'll pay you overtime for helping me with Lucas. And of course, I won't attempt to get you fired from your job anymore."

She smiled and nodded. "I've noticed," she said. "It's been a while since I got multiple unreasonable requests in the first hour of my day."

I cringed. "About that …" I drew a deep breath, ready to say the words that I hardly let cross my lips. "I'm sorry."

She smiled widely. "Don't worry. It was fun. And about the overtime"—she exhaled—"it would really help."

I nodded. It was the least I could do for her.

She tapped a finger on the table, thinking. "Though I have a caveat. I can only help you on Thursdays."

I raised an eyebrow, and she didn't offer an explanation beyond that.

"I'll take only Thursdays," I said. I'd get to see her once a week after work to help me bond with Lucas? That was better than nothing. "It's a deal."

Her cheeks flushed, and she smiled, nodding in a way that sent her short blonde hair bouncing on her shoulders. "Now, about Lucas—"

I couldn't wait any longer. "You'll show me how to be less of a grouch?"

She shook her head. "No."

I was confused. "Do you think the grouch is so deep-rooted in me that I can't be saved?"

"Wrong." She leaned forward. "I'm going to help Lucas love the grouch in you."

I thought that was the moment I fell a little bit in love with her.

I sat back. "That's impossible."

"Someone very brilliant once told me that there is no such thing as impossible. That impossible is just an excuse for people who are too scared."

I asked, "Are you going to repeat every line back to me, woman?"

Her sea-blue eyes twinkled outrageously. It was a scandal—that was what it was. Eyes as beautiful as that.

Chloe smiled. "There was a compliment in there for you somewhere, if you care for it. Besides, the name is Chloe. It would help if you could repeat that once in a while."

"I don't have time for trivialities."

"I know. That's what I like about you," she said.

I froze again. Who was this woman who went about confessing her admiration for me like it was a normal thing?

"But my name is one thing that I hope to convince you isn't trivial," she added.

I scoffed. "I meant trivialities such as the compliment, Chloe. Not your name. You, your name, your words, and your body—nothing about you is trivial. A man would be a fool if he thought that," I said with no difficulty. "You help me win the love of my son, and I promise I'll make it worth your time."

She seemed softer around the edges when I said that, and her face glowed even more, if that was possible. She was radiant.

I paused, our eyes holding each other's gaze. In that instant, our warring selves put down their swords, shields, and every bit of armor they possessed. In that instant, we were looking at each other, our souls bared down to their basic levels, naked.

She nodded, her gaze not leaving mine. "I'll do it," she said, extending a hand out.

I stared at the bare, sun-kissed arm for a moment too long before I took her hand in mine. We shook, and I loved the feel of her hand in mine more than I should have. It was soft, quite possibly like the rest of her. Parts of her I could never explore, except in my dreams. Oh, she was a regular appearance in my nightly dreams these days. Lush, sweet, and arousing, in a way that drove me insane. So, in return, *I* drove her insane too.

I'd woken up with an image of my mouth between her thighs while she was lying flat on her back, whimpering. I kissed her inner thighs, dipping down to run my tongue over her clit. She tasted sweet, and I kept up my attentions, stroking her and teasing her while she got breathy, her face flushed and lips parting. Her hands were in my hair, her mouth gasping while she pushed my head further down.

Before long, she had cried out my name while her tense body shuddered with release.

God, what was I doing, having her work for me?

"Why do you want this job anyway?" I blurted out, frustrated. How many more erotic dreams would it take to get her out of my system? "I swear you were doing something else in between all the foolish errands I made up for you."

"Ah." She gave me a gleeful smile, her hand on the table as she stood up and prepared to leave. "Now that you've run out of foolish errands to make up for me, you might find out."

She beamed and turned around, walking away. My gaze went to the smooth curves of her ass before the door fell shut behind her.

Darn it, she was mysterious, too, and my need for her rocketed sky high.

19

CHLOE

The idea that Sean thought nothing about me was trivial gave me a warm feeling that stayed with me all day. I couldn't stop smiling as I went over his words in my mind.

"You, your name, your words, and your body—nothing about you is trivial. A man would be a fool if he thought that."

Wow. No one had ever paid me such a compliment. Compliments had been rare when I was with Bruce. I wasn't even *with* Sean. The idea was ridiculous, but he had made me feel amazing for today and given me the fuel I needed to keep going for the next few days.

Most days, I quietly bore the weight of guilt surrounding Henry's accident. Henry didn't know about it either. It was like a pinprick in my conscience, one I had tried my hardest to get rid of. I usually could ignore those twinges of guilt if I was busy. Running errands, obsessing over Henry's calendar, trying to schedule his physical therapy. Some days, I had fewer things to obsess over, and when time opened up freely, so did my guilt. A stranger's kind word did occasionally make my day better, and to get one from a man as grumpy as Sean, well, its effect quadrupled for me.

In the few days I'd been working for him, I'd noticed that when Sean walked past people at work, they would hold their breath. Once he was out of sight, I'd see people relax, sigh in relief, and crowds disperse. There was a magnetic charm and fear attached to him that fascinated people.

His other request stayed in the back of my mind when I was running between floors to try to get the heads of marketing and sales to agree to a meeting. It stayed with me while I took the subway home and while I cooked dinner for Henry and me.

I spoke to Tess, my childhood friend who lived in Virginia, while I sat on the couch after a comforting meal of spaghetti with meatballs. Henry had gone to his room, and I was yearning to talk to someone.

Tess, a pretty brunette with a never-give-up attitude, had recently gotten engaged. I was itching to find out when she was planning the wedding. Of course, the side effect of her happiness was that she was constantly trying to get me in the dating game too.

When I brought up my previous mistake—ditching Bruce for Henry—she became serious. "I don't want that for you ever again, Chloe," she said, her voice tender. "You, Chloe, deserve something more than just living only for Henry."

I felt hurt. "Tess, I don't just live for Henry. I have my own dreams too," I said, hoping that she wouldn't ask me what they were.

"Forget your dreams. Tell me what you want in a man. I'm sure I could set you up with someone I know."

I laughed. "Tess, my demands are impossible to meet."

"Try me."

I began to protest, but Tess wasn't having it.

"All right," I said, thinking quickly to all the things Bruce hadn't done for me. "Well, I want a man in my life who will take care of me. A man who won't run away when he realizes that Henry is a part of my life. A man who won't think twice about skipping important work meetings to be with me when I need him."

Bruce had once refused to join me to celebrate a pay raise because he wanted to work late.

Tess thought for a bit before she hummed her assent. "That makes sense. I'm surprised you have such a clear vision, Chloe. It's the first step to manifesting."

Tess would not stop talking about *The Secret*, and I'd long stopped arguing with her over it.

"This kind of man doesn't exist," I said wearily.

She gave me a commiserating sigh before she spoke. "You, Chloe, have single-handedly taken care of Henry for ten years now, and in all those years, you've only had one boyfriend. And a jerk at that. I know how amazing you are. I've seen you be strong, compassionate, and resilient. I wish you'd realize that there are better men out there. I know it's only been a few months since your relationship with Bruce ended, but whenever you're ready to date again, I hope you'll remember that there are good men out there. Good men who are worthy of you. Good men who will cherish you and spoil you."

It was one of the last thoughts in my mind before I drifted off to sleep later that night. Going by the way Sean had looked at me earlier that day, with heat and intensity, I wouldn't classify him as a good man. But I couldn't forget his firm grip on my hand while he'd thanked me for agreeing to help him. He couldn't be too bad of a man if he cared so much for his son.

If only my dad had cared about me and Henry half as much as Sean did his son. When I'd seen Sean that night with Lucas, I'd noticed a flash of pain in his eyes when Lucas stormed past him into his office. It wasn't the first time Lucas's words had hurt him, I bet, and it wouldn't be the last. I'd become invested in wanting to help him even before he asked.

When I woke up to a wonderful New York morning—a bright, sunny autumn day—I instantly thought of Central Park and how beautiful it ought to be right now.

That gave me my first idea for Sean and his son. It wasn't a Thursday today, so I couldn't join them, but this was something I was sure Sean could tackle on his own while I kept Henry company at home. Thursdays were my only truly free evenings—days when Henry had a social club that ran late in the evening and I could be out on my own. Thursdays were the days Bruce and I used to go out on dates. The same free days I could offer Sean.

When I got to work, I walked into his office, pausing only for one moment to take him in while he finished his phone call. God, he looked good today. He looked like he had just finished his morning training session at the gym, and his gray suit stretched across his shoulders as he reached for a pen. He hung up the phone and turned to me, a roguish, handsome look on his face when he met my eyes. As though he'd seen my eyes raking over him, taking him in, and enjoyed my scrutiny.

Swallowing, I closed my eyes only briefly before I caught him up about his day. Sean and I would never happen, but in my dreams, I could let loose, couldn't I?

Sean kept his wild, humorous grin on me while I talked,

and he only nodded his acknowledgment at the end to thank me for the update. That was when I brought up the suggestion that he could end his day—or rather evening—by biking through Central Park with his son as a bonding activity.

Sean looked surprised for a minute before he nodded. "You're right; he's been playing indoors at home for too long," he mused, running his thumb over his jaw as his eyes took on a distant look. He looked up, and his eyes cleared up when they met mine. "Thank you, Chloe," he said finally, his voice deep. "That's a great idea."

I nodded and was about to leave when something else struck me. "Do either of you have bikes?" I asked.

The long stare he gave me said it all.

"I'll order them for you," I said with a nod. "Any preferences?" I asked.

His tone was wry. "No tassels on mine, please," he said, and I laughed.

"I can't make any promises," I said, grinning at this moment of humor from him. I hesitated, hand on the door before leaving. "So, you'll let me know how it goes tomorrow?"

He answered my question with a frown. "What do you mean? Aren't you joining us?"

Join them?

Damn, I should have thought it through. I'd already promised Henry I would be at home in the evenings. How could I explain today's absence to him?

"That would take away the father-son bonding that you really need," I said, pushing away the impulsive voice in my brain that said I desperately wanted to join them. But my anxiety ramped up every time I was home late.

He shook his head. "I can't calm him down if he's having

a meltdown. You're the only one who can. I'll need you there."

Lucas had a nanny, which I was about to point out, when Sean added, "What if Lucas hates biking with me? What if I end up making the wrong conversation? You're the bonding coach. I need you there."

I swallowed. The idea of a man like him needing a woman like me sent my mind spinning. But I'd do it. At least for the impulsive woman in me who was desperate for a chance to be carefree for one evening. I'd find a way to make it up to Henry later.

"What time should I be there?" I asked at last.

20

CHLOE

At half past five in the evening, I left home with my old bike. It was a bit rusty, but I'd used a little oil, and you could hardly hear it creaking anymore. I'd told Henry about my task, earning a frown that doubled when he realized it was with Sean. He hated Sean already.

Henry had insisted I shouldn't have to work so hard, and while I loved his sentiment, I didn't tell him the bitter truth. Being paid for overtime would help afford his medicines. I'd led Henry to believe that the medicines were covered under my new employer's health insurance plan, which was a lie.

Tassater Inc. had an abysmal health insurance plan, no better than my previous one. Higher-paid employees at Tassater had access to premium plans and better coverage, but I was not one of them. This was another reason I needed to get my PMP certification and get my career going, but seriously, when did I have the time for it?

I reached Central Park's west entrance and forgot about my worries for a bit when I felt a light breeze around me. It swayed the trees, and the air was cool and refreshing. I found Sean and his son pushing their new bikes across the street from me.

Lucas looked glum, as though he didn't expect this to be any good. I hadn't spent too much time worrying about what I'd do to make Sean get along with Lucas, but now, I was starting to suspect I'd taken my task too lightly.

It was a pleasant summer evening, and we were not the only ones out biking.

"No tassels for you either, I see," Sean announced when he approached me, and I laughed.

Lucas responded to my cheery wave with a short, stiff smile.

"Lucas, this is Chloe. She knows the best bike routes in the park and has very kindly offered to show—"

"You don't need to lie. I know why she's here."

He followed that statement with an accusing glance at his dad. He knew something was up, and I instantly understood that I wasn't Lucas's ally anymore. I was part of the other camp, probably since I'd laughed at his father's tassels joke.

Sean and I met each other's gaze over Lucas's head, and before Sean could correct him, I knelt down to look at Lucas.

"I'll join you guys only if you don't mind, Lucas."

But Lucas was already hopping on his bike and pedaling furiously, as though determined to get away from his father and me.

"Let's go," I said, telling Sean that he had to hurry instead of double-checking the air pressure in my tires.

Ten minutes into our ride, Sean and I were trying our best to catch up to Lucas, who was very good at biking. Darting between paths like he'd been riding in Central Park for all of his seven years.

Then, at one point, he suddenly got frustrated with the bike. Getting off for no apparent reason, he tossed it aside on the ground and stomped off. He found a vacant bench and sat down, kicking a stone listlessly.

"I *hate* this bike," he announced, and I could see Sean not even bother to resist an eye roll at the word *hate*.

I gestured to Sean to follow him, and a second later, he sat down next to Lucas.

"Why?" he asked in an aggressive tone.

It was my turn to try to not roll my eyes. If anyone needed proof of their troubled relationship, their tones were enough.

"Because I saw a girl riding the same bike just now. It's a girl's bike," he said, looking disgusted.

Nothing about the red-and-blue bike said anything about gender—I'd picked it, thinking about his love for Spider-Man—but I could see Sean open his mouth to try to change his mind about that. It was going to be futile.

Ten seconds into Sean giving him an explanation about gender, Lucas got up and strode off, leaving Sean alone on the bench.

Going by Sean's tense set of shoulders, he wasn't happy with how this evening was going.

I hurried over to Sean and pointed to a white ice cream cart in the distance. "How about we try to soften Lucas up with some ice cream?"

"Good idea," Sean said, following my gaze. "I'll get us some cones. You stay with him."

He took ten steps away from me before I called after him, "Do you know his favorite flavor?"

He looked back at me, stumped.

"I'll ask Lucas," I said, and he nodded as I ran up to Lucas, who was kicking stones into the lake.

A minute later, I texted Sean after speaking to Lucas.

Me: *Cookies and cream for Lucas, please.*

Sean: *Thank you. What about you?*

Me: *Butter pecan, please.*

Pocketing my phone, I tried my best to strike up a conversation with Lucas, but I could've attempted to converse with the lake for all the good it did. He was a stark contrast to the boy he'd been that night in the lobby of his father's office. I was about to suggest a game of tossing stones farthest into the lake when I heard footsteps.

I turned around, expecting to see Sean, but saw a dusty-blond-haired man in his early thirties approaching us. He had a young girl by his side, who was probably eight years old. She looked at Lucas closely before registering something and waving at him.

"Lucas, is that you?" she asked.

Lucas looked at her, and I saw a glimmer of interest in his eyes.

"Hi, Brianna," he said at last, half shy.

"Brianna said she recognized you," the father said with a smile at Lucas before turning to me. I definitely saw something that looked like a glimmer of interest in his eyes too. "Brianna said they were in the same class at Preswood Elementary for kindergarten and her first year before we had to move her elsewhere," the man said, and I assumed it was the same school Lucas went to.

Brianna walked up to Lucas, starting a conversation with him easily—a conversation Lucas actually took part in.

"Wow, I haven't heard Lucas talk this much in a while," I muttered more to myself, and Brianna's dad barked out a laugh.

"When they were toddlers, we just wanted peace and

quiet, and now, we can't wait for them to talk to us again, right?" he asked.

I looked at him closely. His blond hair was cut short, and he had a wide smile and hazel eyes that looked at me with fascination.

"Oh, I bet, but Lucas isn't mine," I said. "I'm a ... nanny," I added abruptly, finding a general lack of words in the English language that would adequately describe the job I was doing.

"Oh, I see. Do you live around here?"

"In the neighborhood." I smiled, turning to see that Lucas had searched around for a few flat pebbles and given Brianna one to throw.

They were laughing and talking now, and I let myself relax. Perhaps what Lucas needed was some kid company.

The man followed my gaze. "They're doing just fine," the man said. "I bet Brianna's telling Lucas about her dance school's ballet show at the Gild Gala. I'm Will, by the way," he said, smiling at me.

"I'm Chloe," I said.

"How come I haven't seen you here before?" Will asked.

"Well, I don't really get out—"

"Here you go, Chloe," Sean interrupted, holding out a cone as he stood next to me. His dark brows were furrowed, mouth hard and jaw set.

Intimidation was something Sean did well, I realized. His shoulder touched mine, and I could sense the energy shift and tension rise as Sean looked at Will.

"Will's daughter was Lucas's classmate," I explained, feeling flustered. My gaze fell on the cones in Sean's hands, including the one he was still holding out to me.

He'd chosen pistachio for himself, and he was holding out the butter pecan one for me.

"Here," I said when Lucas and Brianna walked over, gesturing to my ice cream cone. "Do you like butter pecan, Brianna?"

She shook her head. "I like cookies and cream though," she said, looking at the other one hopefully.

"She can have it," Lucas said immediately, and a flash of pride crossed Sean's eyes. "I'll have the butter pecan."

Brianna took the cookies and cream from Lucas happily, and the two kids went back to the edge of the lake, searching for more stones to toss into the water, seeming cheerier.

"Will, this is Sean," I said, realizing the men hadn't been introduced.

Will looked like he wanted to extend his hand to Sean, but one look at Sean, and he seemed to think better of it.

"Sean, Will was just telling me that Brianna's dance school has an upcoming ballet performance at the Gild Gala." I turned to Will. "You must be so proud of her. I loved ballet, too, back when I was a teenager."

Memories of my weekly dance classes and my teacher, Ms. Rimms, who always encouraged me, came to mind.

I'd always wanted to give a performance onstage for as long as I could remember. I had been preparing for the annual *Nutcracker* performance, when Henry's accident happened.

The accident in itself didn't derail my plans. The unexpected events that followed did. Months after Henry's accident and his return home, Dad had left us, never to be heard from again. I never got to dance once more.

"Well, you should come to her ballet show then," Will said instantly.

I bit my lip when I realized that I'd shown too much enthusiasm. I'd been too wistful when I heard him speak about his daughter's love for dance.

"I could get you tickets if you'd give me your num—"

Sean interrupted, taking a step closer to me. "That won't be happening," he said, his voice grim.

His hand went to my waist, fingers brushing the bit of exposed skin above the waistband of my pants. A shiver of longing coursed through me at the touch, but I forced it down. It couldn't mean anything. Sean was doing this to drive Will away.

My face turned red hot with the understanding that I couldn't be setting up dates while I was technically working for my employer.

Will pressed his lips together. "I'm sorry. Are you two together?"

He directed his question at me, and I shook my head slowly, still feeling heady under Sean's insistent touch.

"Oh God, no. Sean is my—"

"Yes, we are," Sean interrupted.

My first thought was that he was doing far too much interrupting for my liking before I registered what he'd said. My jaw dropped.

Will's hazel eyes flicked from me to Sean and then back to me again. I could barely conceal my shock.

"Okay, that's strange—"

"Chloe is my girlfriend," Sean said, his jaw set and eyes intense as he looked at Will.

His arm tightened around my waist, pulling me flush to him. My waist met his torso, his fingers firm as they gripped my bare skin under my blouse. My heart almost did a backflip at the touch. His hold was strong, and my awareness of him had suddenly shot up.

To top it off, he leaned in closer, his breath fanning my cheek. He smelled good by my side with his musky aftershave.

"Sean," I said, trying to focus and forgetting to use his last name, "I'm not—"

He didn't let me finish. He took a step closer to Will, who was looking at him, a bit dumbfounded.

"Leave," Sean said. It was a single word, but it was charged and full of meaning.

Will turned his gaze to me, and when I gave him an expression of apology, he called his daughter.

"Brianna," he shouted, turning on his heel, "we're leaving."

He collected his surprised daughter, who didn't want to leave, but gave in reluctantly, calling out a sad goodbye to Lucas. He looked crestfallen.

Will stopped on his way past me. "The ballet show at the Gild Gala is this Friday at six p.m., if you're interested. I'd love to see you there."

"*Now*," Sean said, his voice intense, and Will flinched.

He turned and walked off, hand tight on Brianna's arm.

I stared wordlessly at their retreating backs before I rounded on Sean. "What *was* that?"

He held his pistachio ice cream cone out to me and looked me in the eye. "I don't tolerate flirting while you're on the job."

"You called me your girlfriend," I pointed out, ignoring the ice cream.

Sean shook his head. "I needed him to know that he was crossing a line, so I had to exaggerate. You are my PA after all."

Before I could retort, we heard a sudden splash. We turned around at the same instant and saw Lucas, empty-handed, hands curled into fists as he stared at the water. The half-eaten ice cream bobbed sadly in the lake.

Darn.

"Lucas, we're so sorry," I said, going over to put my arm around his shoulders.

"Don't touch me," he said, shoving my hand off.

Sean stepped up immediately. "Lucas, you'll apologize or else—"

Lucas faced him, body tense and anger in his tiny, boyish face. "Or else what?" he demanded. "What could be worse than you taking away the only friend I'd made?" His voice was clear and pained before he stalked off.

In the silence that followed, I met Sean's stunned gaze with understanding. Without any encouragement from me, Sean followed him, placing a hand on the boy's shoulder and stopping him.

"Lucas," Sean began, his voice rough, "I'm sorr—"

"You ruined this evening," Lucas said, stomping the ground with his now-dusty black Skechers. "Just like you ruined my life. I hate living with you."

Without missing a beat, Lucas turned to me. "I need to go home now," he said. After a pause, he added, "Please."

I nodded, feeling troubled and looking at Sean, who was still hurting. I reached for his hand to give it a squeeze, to let him know that it was okay. I held his hand for a beat and let go quickly, feeling its absence keenly. But Sean's fingers reached for mine again, curling over mine as we followed Lucas out, and I gave up resisting.

When I looked at him, his gaze was already on me. My breath caught in my chest. His hand was hot against mine, and when he ran his thumb over the back of my hand, the sensation sent tingles all the way up my arm. It made my heart squeeze in my chest.

I wanted to wrap myself around him, kiss him to oblivion and assure him that things would be okay.

I also wanted to soothe that ache of longing between my legs, but I'd think about that later.

Sean caught me looking at him and his mouth curved up a little. His hand tightened over mine as if he never wanted to let go.

He didn't know the real me, just this part of me that he saw at work and bits and pieces outside of work. If he knew the real picture, he'd run, just like how Bruce had left. How others before Bruce had bailed too.

We were silent for a while as Sean trashed his ice cream and let go of my hand. We walked our bikes out of the park. I felt responsible for this mess, and I wanted to make it up to Lucas and Sean. We reached the park's exit, and made our way to the sidewalk, heading to the intersection where I knew we'd have to part ways. I looked at the son-and-father duo, who were stubbornly avoiding each other, wishing I could leave them in better spirits, when I finally got it.

"Hey, Lucas," I said, something occurring to me. "Would you feel better if you got to see Brianna again?"

He snorted. "Dad would never set up a playdate for me with her. Besides, how would you find Brianna? I don't even remember her last name."

I held my breath as Sean turned to me, eyes intense at the memory of Will. "I know how we could meet her again." I faced Lucas. "How would you feel about attending her ballet show at the Gild Gala this Friday night at six?"

I turned my gaze to Sean, noticing how he fought to tone down his disapproval. He was not keen on the idea of running into Will again.

But Lucas was starting to look hopeful. "You think Brianna will be there?" he asked, face upturned and eyes lit up with anticipation.

I nodded, feeling a cold, clammy sensation when I realized that I'd be deserting Henry twice this week. "Her dad told me she would be. Do you want to see her again?"

The ecstatic expression on Lucas's face was the answer we needed.

"It's three days until Friday. Will you come?" he asked me, eagerness in his voice.

I looked at Sean, who gave me a firm nod. I turned and gave Lucas a smile, amused to see his mind ticking furiously. "I will."

"Let's ride back home," he said and hopped on the bike.

I exchanged a look with Sean, who raised his eyebrows in surprise before nodding.

"Thank goodness," I muttered under my breath as we followed Lucas.

"But I still want you to know something," he said. "I won't let Will come within an inch of you."

I gazed up at him, my eyes meeting his deep brown ones. I felt like I was made of liquid when he looked at me like that. "I can live with that."

We walked side by side, our shoulders briefly touching, and Sean didn't pull away. "When Will shows up, I still want to be able to call you my girlfriend, even if we aren't together."

My heart squeezed in my chest, even as I shook my head. I played along with this game where I pretended I had a dating life, like normal people. "Am I really going to have no dating prospects while I'm working for you?"

Sean nodded, his gaze roving over me. There was something different in the way he was looking at me. Something that hadn't been there before. A guarded sense of respect and perhaps even admiration. "You could say that."

"It's going to be a long six months then."

His eyebrows rose a fraction of an inch. "I'll have you

know that most of my PAs haven't lasted longer than four months."

I grinned back at him. "Ah, but I'm not just your PA, am I? As your bonding coach, I might just last longer than six months. And, yes, you can call me your girlfriend at the Gild Gala, if you please. Though"—I chuckled—"that makes me wonder, what do you call the women you really date?"

His intense, probing gaze met mine, and a wave of tingles spread down my arms. His tongue ran over his lower lip as though he was thinking of something dirty, and heat bloomed between my thighs.

"Stick with me long enough, and you'll soon find out."

21

CHLOE

A couple of days passed, days when I simply couldn't get Sean's words out of my mind.

"*Stick with me long enough, and you'll soon find out.*"

Find out what it was like to *be* the woman he was seeing? Or find out based on another woman he would eventually see?

I flushed as I caught myself going over it again. Why had I asked him that ridiculous question? Now, I was picking apart his words, and none of the meanings I came up with could ease the nervousness in my stomach. I wouldn't let anything happen—that much was sure—but the idea that Sean could be interested in me was enough to send flutters going in my heart. Silly, trivial flutters that would amount to nothing.

It had taken me a year of knowing Bruce casually before we dated. I went into that relationship with the knowledge that he knew Henry and Henry's condition well enough and was understanding about how much time went into thinking about solutions to Henry's problems. So, Bruce's words from when he'd broken up with me, reminding me of how I was destined for a miserable life, stung more than it should have.

After Henry had returned home in a wheelchair, our father had vanished abruptly a month later. At eighteen, I'd become responsible for Henry, sacrificing my dreams and my perception of a normal life.

Sean knew *nothing* about how I had become a parent of sorts to Henry. Once he knew how much of my personal time was spent thinking or worrying about Henry, he'd want nothing to do with me.

Dad had been the first man to leave me when I needed him the most, but he wasn't the last. Bruce had followed suit, in spite of my rigorous vetting process. I simply couldn't find a way to have both—a love life and be there for my brother.

During my evening out in Central Park, Henry had been so worried, waiting for ages by the door for me to return. I would never forget that look of relief when I'd come back home at a reasonable hour.

I couldn't bring myself to regret it for too long though. Sean's recent payment had come through, and I'd actually paid off not just the bills for the new meds, but Henry's recent doctor's appointment visit too. For once, my financial situation was not in the forefront of all the things that worried me. It gave me the motivation to tell Henry that I was going out with Sean and Lucas again this week. I told him that, financially, we needed it.

He had tried to be more understanding about it ever since.

In spite of my resolve to keep things strictly businesslike, I couldn't help notice that Sean seemed to be more and more busy as Friday approached. I'd seen him in meetings

—surrounded by people holding computers, showing stock market graphs, and whiteboards with more numbers and calculations than possible—and knew he was up to his eyeballs with work.

Being around him lately was more electrifying than before, as though the two of us knew we were this close to giving in to the sparks between us.

Just looking at him standing by his floor-to-ceiling windows brought to mind dirty images of what he could do to me. I imagined myself naked, breasts pressed against the glass with his fingers in me, and I had to shake myself out of it.

I exhaled and took my third trip to the bathroom in the past hour to splash some water on my face. I needed to calm the heck down.

By Friday morning, when I googled the event and realized just how exclusive this gala was, I started to worry about a totally different problem. I'd already confessed to Sean that it had been years since I had gone to a party, and that was *before* it dawned on me just how selective this party was. I'd never been to an event of this scale. Who would I talk to besides Lucas and Sean? What would I talk about?

By mid-afternoon, I steeled myself, telling myself that I just needed to get through the evening, which was, at max, a few hours long. After all, this event wasn't about me. My job was to make sure Lucas got to meet Brianna. I owed him that much.

Around three p.m., I got a text from Sean when I was down in the lobby, handling the pickup from his dry cleaner for his work suits.

Sean: *What's your favorite color?*

Odd question, I thought, wondering if he expected to be

grilled by Will about my likes and dislikes as a part of the *are you two really dating* test.

Sean: *Also, what size are you in dresses?*

Oh.

I flushed as I considered what he was doing.

That's okay, I texted back hurriedly. *I've got a dress for tonight.*

By dress, I meant the dress I'd gotten for my high school graduation. I hadn't ever worn it, having bought it in a fit of rebellion after dealing with six months of caring for Henry and being abandoned by our dad. I'd never shown up to my graduation since Henry couldn't make it to see me graduate. And what was the point in graduating when there was no one to cheer for you?

It was ten years old, but it would still work.

Sean: *If it were me going to a party after a long time, Chloe, I'd like to make sure I was dressed to kill. So, what color is it?*

You can choose, I texted him back before I hurried home, glad to have wrapped up work early. I wondered how I'd explain to Henry that I'd be out for half the night.

When I walked in, Henry waved to the small wooden table by the front door.

"Someone dropped off a thank-you card for you. It's on the table."

I reached for the card and smiled when I saw it was from Greg, thanking me for bringing the trash bins back last week when it was his turn again. Resolving to take him some cake later on in the week, I turned to Henry, explaining where I'd be that night.

He heard me out, his expression changing to one of curiosity when I finished. "You mean, you're going out on a date?" he asked.

I shook my head. "No, no. I'm just helping this man ... my colleague, out with his son."

I would never date Sean. No man wanted a woman like me, a woman who couldn't think of a life beyond doctor visits, therapy, and financial worries. The past ten years had been filled with that, and the next ten years seemed like they'd be no different. I put up with it because I blamed myself for Henry's accident. My potential partners? They wanted nothing to do with my guilt.

And I was tired of rejection.

I looked at him with some concern as I realized he would be on his own for most of the night. "Is it all right if I go, Henry?"

I could sense his desperate need to hold on to me and the internal fight he put up to not feel this way.

He swallowed. "I've been quite used to having you at home with me all the time."

My heart wrung with ache for him. He was desperate for a sign that I wasn't leaving him, that we weren't growing apart. His voice hung heavy in the air, and I questioned my need to go out. Lucas needed Brianna after all. Not me. I didn't have to show up.

His jaw clenched briefly, his thick brows knitted together in tension. "But seeing you like this, it reminds me that in the past ten years, you've only had one boyfriend. And a jerk at that. You deserve to have dates. You deserve a loving boyfriend and a normal life—" He broke off with a frown.

His gaze went to my dress pants and the black blouse I had on before he spoke, his voice apprehensive.

"Chloe, I've heard of the Gild Gala, and I don't think you can show up in those clothes. And you barely have an hour to get ready. What are you going to wear?"

I stared at Henry, his question ringing in the air, when there was a knock on the door.

22

CHLOE

I jumped, worried that Sean and Lucas were early.

I opened the door and peeked out. A man was walking away, having dropped off a bunch of boxes on the doorstep. I could read the words *Saks Fifth Avenue* on the boxes and realized that Sean had worked his magic again.

"I suspect," I said, picking up the boxes and turning to Henry, "this is what I'm going to wear."

Minutes later, in my room, I undressed and carefully, slowly slipped the blue silk gown on. It was one of the contents of the first box. The second box and third, I noticed, had heels in a couple of sizes. One of them was my size, and it was black Manolo Blahnik stilettos. The fourth box had diamonds—a glittering Chopard string necklace and drop earrings. I gasped as I looked at them in my hands. Real diamonds. Sean was ... out of his mind.

I turned to the mirror, and my jaw dropped at the sight. My ears and neck glittered, and the added height from the stilettos made me look almost regal. As for the dress, the material was soft, and the gown simply cascaded all the way down to my ankles. The halter neckline exposed my shoulders and long, creamy arms. I didn't want to think about how much this dress must have cost in addition to the rest of the outfit. The words *Alexander McQueen* were enough. I turned around, and it swished around me with a delicate sound.

So, this was how the other half lived.

I'd never worn a dress like this before. I'd probably never wear one like this again.

Feeling very conscious about how different I must look, I quickly styled my hair into an updo and put on my makeup before I stepped out.

Henry looked at me from the living room as I approached, and his mouth falling open.

"You look ..." His jaw worked a few times, and he finally gave up. He rolled closer to me. "Who gave this to you?"

"Erm ... just a friend," I said, wondering if Sean could even be slotted into that category.

He was ... friendly perhaps. He had certainly thawed a little in the past few days. I looked through the window out of my apartment just as a sleek black limo pulled up to our curb.

"Bye," I said to Henry in sudden urgency.

I didn't want Sean walking in and asking me questions about Henry. Whether he was friendly or not, certain parts of my life weren't available for him to witness and inspect.

People never did well with the knowledge of Henry's special needs. They fumbled, said the wrong thing, and sometimes, it tapped into a well of anger that Henry usually kept hidden. I hadn't seen one of his angry episodes in a while, but they were always unexpected and volatile.

I got out of the house, shutting the door firmly, and waited to hear the familiar sound of the TV turning on.

In a second, I heard the sports channel come on and

breathed out a tiny exhale. I knew he'd be watching the TV until I came home.

The driver was holding the car door open for Sean, who got out and turned to face me. He stopped all of a sudden, and then he leaned casually against the car as the door fell shut.

He was dressed with a bow tie and a black suit, the fit so close that I could see the fabric move as he leaned off the car when I approached.

He looked sharp, his lips full and brown eyes glinting wickedly. His hair was gelled and drawn into a tight ponytail at the back, and I loved that for a CEO; he had the *don't-care, bad-boy* look that suited him so well.

How was it possible that this powerful, handsome man was here, waiting to pick me up?

"Look at you," he muttered.

His eyes took me in, traveling down my body slowly, and I could see in the upturn of his lips that he approved.

"You look stunning."

Happiness swirled through me at the compliment. It was just three words, but three words I'd treasure forever because they had come from *him*.

"Thank you for the dress," I told him half shyly. I'd never been on the receiving end of such a gift before. "Though I'm not sure it was necessary."

I wanted to tell him it was the closest I'd felt to being cared for in the longest time, but that kind of information wasn't something you shared with an emotionally distant man like him. It felt strangely nice to be on the other side of caring for someone.

"It *is* necessary, and you look great," he said as he took in the navy-blue halter dress that he'd chosen for me. He took a step closer, and I saw his eyes linger on the curve of my neck, where the dress descended sharply into my cleavage. "Will is definitely not getting within a foot of you," he said.

I felt weak with desire at his words. Who cared about Will when a man like Sean was in front of me?

I wanted Sean, his broad shoulders, his wicked smirk and all, even though he was my boss.

If only I could have him.

I swallowed. "You need to promise not to pick a fight with Will today," I said.

"We'll see about that," I heard him mutter as he opened the door for me.

I hesitated for a moment, then took a deep breath and stepped inside.

The car was spacious beyond belief, and I exhaled and stretched my legs out as Sean got in with me. Lucas was dressed smartly, too, in a tux and a bow tie, and he looked so adorable that I wished I could hug him.

"You're looking very handsome, Lucas," I said, smiling at him. "I'm sure Brianna will notice."

He colored, his cheeks going red. "Thank you. I hope so," he said in a low voice before turning to the window. "How much longer before we get there?"

Sean leaned in closer to me while responding to Lucas, and when he was done, he didn't settle back in his seat. If anything, he put his hand on his knee, next to mine, and his fingers lightly grazed me. Lucas slipped his headphones on while I turned to Sean.

When I tried to remove my hand, he lifted a thumb and held my hand in place. The touch was soothing, and my skin heated under his.

"I'm going to do the talking with Will tonight when Lucas meets Brianna," he muttered in a low voice while I turned to him. "If Will so much as looks in your direction, I'm going to kill him."

A shiver ran down to my toes. I noticed his body tense as I angled closer. His lips parted, and he was breathing faster than normal.

Shit.

He was affected by my presence, just like I was with him. The knowledge made my head spin.

In the hazy darkness, I squeezed his hand and let go quickly. He looked like he was barely restraining himself from pulling me to his chest.

"Well, flattering as that statement was, let me remind you that I'm not your woman, and our goal is to help Lucas meet Brianna," I whispered back. "So, no murders tonight, please."

The side of his lips twitched. "You don't object to bloodshed on days Lucas isn't there?" he asked from my right.

I was done with feeling so twisted up around Sean. I was done fighting our attraction. I wanted Sean even if it was a terrible, terrible idea.

"Feel free to vampire your way around town when Lucas isn't around," I said, trying to keep my voice from betraying what I truly felt.

He chuckled while Lucas removed his headphones and pointed to a building we were passing.

"It's The Met, Lucas," Sean said in response to Lucas's question. "Perhaps we'll go there one day together," he said just as the car slowed down to a stop, and we were at Lincoln Center. "Thank you, Chris," he said to our driver.

Chris got out and opened the door while Sean helped me and Lucas out. I stepped out and stared at the breathtaking view in front of me.

The city lights danced in the distance, reflecting off the

tall, glossy skyscrapers towering in the night sky. The air was charged with the energy of New York City, and I couldn't believe I was a part of a luxury party for once. Clutching my year-old purse that had been a purchase from T.J. Maxx, I stood on the bustling street corner as other well-dressed people walked up the steps.

Feeling a bit nervous, I looked at the grand facade of the Lincoln Center. The front of the building was lit up in colors of orange and blue. As the three of us walked in, I saw immense wealth all around.

The men were in dignified tuxedos, and the women were wearing gowns that were similar to mine, helping me blend in. I was one of *them*—the social elite. A world I'd only had glimpses of in TV shows or heard of from second-hand sources at work.

Noticing my expression, Sean switched places with Lucas, standing next to me.

"All okay?" he asked, his eyes taking me in.

My heart was pounding as I tore my attention away from the crowd to focus on him. I felt a calmness spread through me when he met my gaze.

"I didn't know you were expected to wear such clothes here," I muttered, feeling foolish at my naivete and thinking back to what I'd almost worn tonight.

"When you're with me, you don't need to worry about trivialities like that, Chloe," Sean said, taking my hand and walking up the last of the steps. "I'll take care of you."

I closed my eyes, feeling a weight lift off my shoulders. My days had been a constant stream of worrying. If it wasn't about Henry, it was about money and paying for his needs. Someone had told me that I ought to understand my life was not Henry's, but being a caregiver to him since I had been eighteen had solidified my identity into that. I hadn't been *just Chloe* for a long time. A woman who got to indulge in her once-far-off dream of living in a different world. A world where there was time for pleasure every day. It was the difference between expecting to dress up on a Friday night versus considering what movie to pass out to, alone on the couch, by ten at night.

"I love this," I muttered. "If this is a dream, please don't let me wake up."

Sean chuckled as we joined the line of people walking in, just behind Lucas. In the distance, staff in matching attire welcomed the guests, and as we entered the lobby, I heard music fill the space.

Crystal chandeliers bathed the room in a soft, golden glow, and the ceiling seemed to stretch on forever.

The banquet tables, with their crystal stemware and lavish place settings, appeared more like something out of a fairy tale than a dining experience.

Notes from a live piano trio wafted through the air, soulful music that stirred something in me, and I turned and smiled at the pianists. One of the men tilted his head to me in an acknowledging nod. I couldn't help but be captivated by the music. It was a stark contrast to the sounds of my everyday life, a reminder of the beauty and luxury that existed beyond my world.

The lighting was soft, and I looked past the Roman statues that dotted the circular lobby to Sean.

"Do you prefer a signature cocktail, or will champagne do?" he asked.

My mouth fell open a little, and I managed to shut it and simply nod like this was a normal question I got asked at the end of the day. Like I didn't normally decide between a beer or a wine straight out of the bottle.

"Champagne, please," I said and turned to see Lucas scanning the crowd.

"The seats are that way," he said, looking down the short corridor to the open seats. "Do you mind if I go sit down now? I can't wait for it to start."

I nodded just as Sean came back to me in a minute, holding two flutes of amber liquid.

"Lucas has gone to our seats already," I informed him as he handed one to me. "We'll join him in a bit."

"Good," Sean said, standing by my side. "I feel like I need a minute alone with you."

I blushed and regarded him. Back in the car, our flirting had seemed harmless. A response to his possessiveness over me, which had come across as endearing. No romantic partner had demanded my complete attention that way.

Now, in the dim lights, I could see his eyes burn as they took me in. And the best part was that I let myself enjoy it for once. I was tired of being the good girl. I licked my lips as his arm slid around my waist.

I took a sip of my champagne, feeling its sweetness down my throat while his gaze lingered on my lips.

"Did I tell you that since we first met in the café, I've thought of you often?" he murmured, pulling me closer.

The side of my hip met his upper thigh, and I angled my body to him, feeling heat radiate off him.

He did?

"What did you think about?" I asked, not breaking eye contact as I took another sip.

Sean kept running his fingers gently down my arm, and little tingles of anticipation ran through me. His eyes looked intense, and I felt very turned on.

"That instead of stealing your drink, I could have stolen you."

His eyes searched my face while my cheeks flamed. The piano trio played Moonlight Sonata in the background, which was somehow both soothing and seductive.

It's just the night, I told myself. The music, the dress, and the alcohol speaking.

Before we could go further, before Sean could lean in—which he very much looked like he was poised to do, right in the middle of the lobby—we were interrupted.

"Sean, is it not?" asked an older gentleman, looking stately and with a scotch in his hand. He extended his hand out as a glimmer of irritation crossed Sean's face before he shook it. "I'm Ron Gellinger, the host of this event and owner of Faux Industries. Nice to see you here."

Sean nodded, turning to me. "This is Chloe Nichols. She loves dance and was eager to support the art program."

I nodded, feeling both shy and nervous as Mr. Gellinger acknowledged me with a small smile and a nod.

"Did you dance, Ms. Nichols?" he asked, and I nodded.

"Ballet," I said, afraid I sounded like a gushing teenager. "I danced for ten years. An art scholarship in my school helped support my classes, and I'm glad you're doing this. It means so much to the kids, more than we can ever know."

His smile seemed more genuine, and he introduced his wife in a minute—a smaller, cheerier woman who I warmed up to in an instant.

And so the night went.

More men approached Sean, and soon, he was in deep conversation with them, with talk that changed from sports to the stock market and golf, depending on the people he was talking to.

I looked around and saw people looking at Sean Tassater with interest, eager to approach once Ron Gellinger made his exit. This was a gala that was exclusive to the elite,

I realized, since the aim was to raise five million dollars to fund art programs in public schools. An opportunity to give back to the community while encouraging local talent. Sean was popular among this crowd.

As I observed the guests, I couldn't help but overhear snippets of their conversations. Their concerns and interests were worlds apart from my own. Exotic vacations, luxury cars, and high-end fashion brands—topics that seemed entirely foreign to me. In the middle of a conversation about an older man's yacht party near Barbados, I got distracted by the tunes of a once-familiar song. A click-clack of heels followed this tune, and I turned around to find the source of that sound.

I walked a few feet away, and there, off to one side, away from the adults, was a group of girls. They were in intense concentration as one girl demonstrated her ballet dance steps and the others watched. I recognized the steps—a plié and a pirouette.

I stared at these girls from a distance, a faint memory stirring in my heart. I'd loved dancing so much as a child. I'd forgotten this want in the recent past. I hadn't been around younger kids or girls or women with an interest in dancing lately.

"I don't know what comes after this," said the girl who was dancing, extending her hands up. "We learned it yesterday."

"Saut de basque," I whispered, and the girls turned around in surprise, unaware that they were being watched. "I'm sorry," I said. "Don't worry; I won't watch you anymore," I said and turned around.

"She's right," I heard a girl tell the others. "It was saut de basque," she said.

I snuck a glance over my shoulder.

"It's okay; you can watch," the same girl told me before she did the complex jump with a sideways twist.

She landed gracefully on the left foot, completing the turn and maintaining the cross-legged position, and I couldn't help but applaud with exhilaration. It hit me then —a dream I'd once had. A dream of dancing with the New York City Ballet one day, and it was as though someone had bowled over with a substantial punch to my gut.

I'd forgotten my own dreams.

I knew of people who couldn't chase their dreams, of people who had outlandish dreams, but how could someone completely forget the presence of a dream they'd once had?

"I wanted to be a ballet dancer," I confessed to the girls. If no one else, at least some ten-year-old girls in the universe knew about my dreams.

"Why aren't you one today?" one asked confidently.

I began to explain, a trivial justification for my life today, but then I remembered a memory from my high school days. I had left for a dance performance in my local ballet school.

"I had gone to my dance performance against my father's wishes," I began in a hollow voice as they crowded around me. "He didn't want to encourage me to pursue a career he believed wasn't lucrative. Instead, he told me I was supposed to pick up my brother, Henry, from his friend's home and stay home. I refused, wanting to take part in my show. I was the lead performer after all, and what did it matter that Dad didn't understand or didn't want to see it? I sure wasn't going to miss the show I was headlining to pick up Henry."

They nodded.

"Duh," the brown-haired one with a tiara on her head emphatically said.

I could see it in her eyes—the drive to be the best dancer ever.

"Henry understood. He said he'd wait for me at his friend's place, that I could get him after my performance."

I remembered that night. I'd gotten my first and only standing ovation. When I got out, much later than I was supposed to because someone from The Juilliard School had spoken to me about applying for dance school, my head was in the clouds. It was bitterly cold when I stepped out, and I got into the first bus that came along, nervous and shivering with excitement. It didn't matter that we were poor, of limited means. I had a future and hopes and dreams and stars in my eyes.

I had gone straight to Henry's friend's house, and we were walking home together. I'd been so lost in my own world that by the time I noticed the car, it was too late. Henry had been alert, and he'd protected me. Weeks later, when he'd come home, he was in a wheelchair. Indirectly or not, I was responsible.

I stared back at the eager, open faces of the young girls, unable to articulate my thoughts, when Sean came to my side.

"Lucas is missing," he said, his voice rough.

23

CHLOE

Complete and utter silence followed Sean's statement as he continued to tower over me. I turned and ran closer to where Lucas had been sitting, my heart hammering against my chest.

He wasn't there anymore.

Damn.

"Where did he go?" Sean asked, following me, his voice low and still angry.

My heart raced at the sight of the vacant spot where Lucas had just stood.

Where could he have gone? I was right here across from him.

The empty flute of champagne I'd been holding slipped from my hand, falling to the floor. I stepped over it to rush to the spot where Lucas had stood.

"Lucas," I called. Once and then twice.

He couldn't have gone too far. He was a kid. There was no way he would disappear silently like this.

Could he?

My heart beat rapidly while Sean stepped up next to me. His body was rigid and stiff, and he definitely looked angry.

"He's got to be here somewhere. Perhaps he's sulking about not seeing that girl, Brianna. You take the right half of this hall, and I'll take the left," he said, disappearing into the crowd.

I heard him calling for Lucas as he searched.

How was I in this situation again? One that brought back too many feelings—of loss, of emptiness, and a failure to be responsible.

Hoping I wasn't wrong, I scanned the lobby again and again. Elegantly dressed guests descended the grand staircase, their designer gowns and tailored suits glistening under the spotlights, not a worry on their minds. Some of them had children by their side, but none of the children were wearing the dark blue shirt and tux that Lucas was sporting.

In twenty minutes, I'd scoured every bit of the right half of the hall with no Lucas in sight. I ran into Sean, who also had nothing but a look of shock on his face to show for the past twenty minutes of searching.

He gripped my arm, and I met his gaze in fear, feeling like I had completely let him down.

"I'm so sorry," I blurted out.

He shook his head, and his grip on my arm tightened. I could feel the strength in his fingers as he held me, firm but assured.

"Don't apologize. You did nothing wrong. We'll find him, Chloe. There's a floor above that I've not searched yet. I'll meet you back here in fifteen minutes."

For the next fifteen minutes, we raced in a ten-foot radius, searching the lobby, the auditorium, and the restrooms for a sign of Lucas.

Had he run upstairs in his search for Brianna? I climbed to the floor above, panting as I reached the landing and looked at the select few people who were standing around. Still no sign of Lucas or Brianna.

I closed my eyes in regret. Was I not considering the other option? That I'd pushed him too hard. I'd asked too much of him for this father-son bonding event. Just like I'd asked too much of my dad when I told him I wanted to live in the dorm while attending The Juilliard School, leaving him alone with Henry and his health issues.

It was my fault that Henry had suffered in that accident.

Just like it was my fault Lucas was missing.

I didn't hear someone calling my name. Panic and anxiety blended together, overwhelming me. I put my hands on my knees, bent over, and breathed heavily when footsteps rounded on me. Glancing up, I saw Sean—relief, mixed with urgency, on his face.

"I found him," he said.

Lucas was safe.

The sound I made was midway between a sob and a relieved laugh. "You did?" I asked, spinning on my heel to look in the direction Sean was pointing.

"He's at the rooftop terrace, showing Brianna the city lights."

Brianna. City lights. Right.

I exhaled.

"He really is fine?" I asked between deep breaths.

"Are you okay?" Sean asked, looking at me with a frown and taking a protective step closer to me. "You look like you've seen a ghost."

A ghost of regretful memories.

"I'm fine," I lied, straightening up and covering my eyes

with my hand briefly. *I can't be weak here.* "How do we get to him?"

Sean led the way to the elevators, and one of them opened up. Getting in, he pressed the button for the terrace and turned to me as the doors closed shut.

This time, in the privacy of the elevator, there was something more discerning in his gaze as Sean looked at me.

"What happened?" he asked me.

I stared at him. "I almost lost your son," I said, stating the obvious.

"*We* temporarily lost sight of him," he corrected. "But he isn't lost, and you're not solely responsible for him, Chloe. I'm here too. I'm the other responsible adult."

At those words, I wanted to sob into his chest.

Two weeks after the accident, Henry had come home in a wheelchair. A month later, I came home from school to find my dad gone. Just gone. I walked into his room to find the closet empty, his things missing.

I'd spent the next half hour speaking to police officers, convinced we'd been robbed, until I found a note from Dad on my bed. He'd left for good.

He'd left silently and quietly. There was nothing I could do about that.

I'd shredded that letter before Henry could see it, wiped my tears away, and fixed a brave smile on my face ever since.

It was the last time I'd worn my tutu.

Dad had been unable to bear the burden of Henry's care, leaving me, the eighteen-year-old, to take over.

Just like how Bruce had emotionally left me because something about me just gave off the *responsible* vibe and not the *fun, reckless* girlfriend vibe.

If only Dad had stuck around, then I wouldn't have had to be the responsible adult to my younger brother when I was eighteen. I would've been able to follow my dreams, go to dance school, and have a normal experience of dorm life and boy troubles. Instead, all I had were doctor visits, physical therapy appointments, and worries about paying the bills while mothering my brother. I had not relaxed in the past ten years.

"Chloe?" Sean asked, and this time, he took my hand in his. "Are you all right?"

24

CHLOE

I knew he wouldn't let go without something, but I didn't want to let everything out in a momentary lapse of judgment.

"It reminded me of my past," I blurted out, feeling weak. "That's all."

"What did it remind you of?" he asked, sounding frustrated. "I need more than just a generic statement, Chloe. I want an honest answer."

I searched his face, wondering why the man who was so good at intimidating people was concerned about my past.

He was so close that he could put his arm around my waist. The elevator was still riding up, but it could stop at any moment now, and Lucas would see us. I didn't want Lucas to have one more thing to get angry with his dad about.

"It reminded me of my childhood," I said, hoping it would pacify Sean and taking a step away. "About my dad and my brother and—"

Before I could complete that sentence, Sean pulled me to him. I was crushed against his chest, and I realized he was just holding me, hand around my waist, mouth bending down near my ear.

"Did you lose someone, Chloe?"

"No," I said, unable to think with his closeness. "Not exactly." I closed my eyes, squeezing them shut as the memories flooded back in. I was sinking into his chest, his warm embrace weakening my defenses. "I wasn't responsible for a bit, and someone ... suffered."

He held me tighter, hugging me fiercely.

"It's only fifteen minutes, Chloe. We lost sight of him for fifteen minutes, and he's fine." He leaned back and looked at me, scouring my face for signs of worry. "I'm sorry, Chloe," he said. "I'm sorry you had to experience seeing someone suffer."

I looked up at Sean as he ran his fingers up and down my cheek. "Thank you," I said.

He was holding me close, and neither of us felt the need to step away. His arms tightened around my back.

I saw a flicker of a smile on his lips, and it was gone instantly.

"Don't thank me yet. Pretty soon, you'll see the grump that I am, darling."

I leaned into him. "I like him too, by the way."

His expression gave away his surprise.

"Grumpy or not, both sides of you are just fine, Sean."

He leaned in closer, and our foreheads were touching.

"Chloe, if you keep talking like that ..." He broke off. "I'm going to forget that I'm your boss. I'm going to do things that I have no business doing as your boss."

When I looked up, I could see the raw need in his eyes and the restraint he was exercising to hold himself back. I reached up and touched his face, his cheek rough against my palm.

"You're far too good to forget yourself, Sean," I said softly.

He leaned into my palm and closed his eyes before he let out a groan. "You're killing me, Chloe," he muttered.

I wanted to kiss him so badly that I couldn't think straight anymore.

No other man had claimed my thoughts every waking moment the way he had.

I was desperate to feel his lips on mine. I reached out to touch the smooth lapels of his jacket, my heart thundering in my chest when I felt him pull me to him firmly.

His lips were on mine in an instant, his hands cupping my face as he tilted my chin up. His lips moved with expert rhythm over mine, and I closed my eyes, sinking into the heady sensation that took over.

His tongue teased my lips, demanding to be let in.

I opened up to him as I pressed my body against his hard chest. Sean uttered a low moan at the back of his throat as though he was losing his restraint.

The kiss was every pent-up bit of suppressed feeling and passion, all rolled into one, and it quickly turned possessive.

He pushed me against the wall of the elevator, my back hitting the steel handrail. His body was pressing up against me deliciously as he kissed me fiercely.

I whimpered as my hands snaked around his neck, tracing the outlines of his hard shoulders before I pulled him even closer. My body sparked to life, my thighs clenching together as heat pooled between the—

The jarring sound of the elevator doors opening hit me just then, followed by the rush of wind as I abruptly let go of Sean. He froze.

In the distance, I saw a boy, unmistakably Lucas, next to a girl, Brianna.

I felt a rush of emotion when I realized we really hadn't lost him. They were here.

Sean's eyes were on me, and when I looked back at him, he was scanning me, his face inches from mine. The emotion in his eyes took my breath away. Desire.

"They're here," I whispered, and he took a step back.

That gap robbed me of that feeling of security I'd just had with Sean's arms wrapped around me, his warm voice in my ear, and the feeling of being crushed against him.

Sean turned around and took a step toward Lucas when I put a hand out, stopping him.

"Give Lucas a chance to finish his conversation with Brianna," I said, noticing that Lucas was speaking fast. "And could you please not be tough on him about leaving the hall abruptly like he did? Especially not in front of Brianna."

Sean seemed baffled, and then with a second glance at me, he gave in and simply nodded. "Fine, just for today, I'll keep it calm," he muttered.

"Thank you," I said as neither of us moved.

I stayed in place for a moment longer, filled with sadness when I realized Sean also wanted me. An impossible situation—one I hadn't given myself permission to dream of.

"He's coming over," Sean said, and we exchanged a look. "Listen," he said urgently, "I'm sorry about that—"

"We got carried away," I added, feeling ridiculous as I said it.

It hadn't felt wrong. It'd felt so right, but I couldn't bring myself to admit it.

He gave me a long stare that I couldn't quite comprehend. Finally, he ended his inspection with a short nod. "We need to set some boundaries. I'll ensure this won't happen again," he said, sidestepping me.

Cool air engulfed me as I walked out behind Sean.

I turned around, my heart beating rapidly, feeling as though I'd just tripped and fallen into a giant sinkhole. I plastered a smile on my face—a fake smile, which took on an expression of genuine relief when I saw Lucas.

Sean hugged Lucas very briefly, stepping back far too quickly and seeming uncomfortable with his emotions. He cared deeply for Lucas, I realized, but didn't have the ability to show it to him.

Lucas's eyes were shining, and he seemed very happy about his sudden, impromptu disappearance, unaware of the chaos it had created for us.

"I'm glad we found you," I said, giving Lucas a hug in relief. "Brianna," I said, focusing on her, "your dad must be searching for you. Let me take you back to him."

She nodded excitedly. "He's going to be so thrilled that you're here. We were both hoping to see you here."

Over the heads of the two kids, I met Sean's gaze. With heavy-lidded eyes and his jaw clenched, he looked at me for a split second, his face dark before he turned away at the last moment.

"Go ahead," Sean said, leading us back to the elevator. "Lucas and I will wait for you by the piano in the lobby." He barely met my eyes as he spoke, turning to focus on Lucas.

Boundaries. If this was the kind of boundary he was talking about, he sure was following through.

25

CHLOE

Ten minutes later, I met Sean in the lobby as I walked out after speaking with Will and Brianna. Will had been happy to see me, and like us, he had been concerned about Brianna's temporary absence. It was easier to talk to him without Sean glowering by my side, and I left after an interesting conversation with him while Brianna kept craning her neck for a second look at Lucas.

Sean kept his gaze on me as I walked toward him and gave me his arm quietly as he led me down the steps. Lucas was in the waiting car, half asleep in the seat when he noticed us. He waved to us as we approached. I waved back as he made room for us on the seat.

Sean's throat worked, and he gritted the next words out. "Did your meeting with Will go well?"

I flushed and nodded just as I remembered his reaction to it an hour ago. The curt *go ahead*. He was kind enough to offer to drop me home, and I couldn't ignore his question.

"It did," I said breathlessly. Eager to switch topics, I added, "Thank you for a wonderful evening tonight."

Sean simply glowered at me.

"And for being so supportive when we lost sight of Lucas," I added softly. *And for when I was panicking.*

"Are you meeting him again?" Sean asked as though he hadn't heard a word of what I said.

I hesitated. Will had asked, and while I'd wanted to avoid dating at all costs, something had told me I wouldn't be able to get Sean out of my mind unless I dated someone else.

I nodded finally. "He did ask me if I could meet him next Thursday," I added, recalling that Thursdays were my time with Sean and Lucas.

I hadn't given Will an answer yet. I was, frustratingly, hoping against hope for a sign from Sean that I shouldn't.

"Wow, he isn't wasting any time, is he?" Sean said, pulling the door out slightly more so I could get in.

"I haven't answered him yet," I blurted out. "I realized that Thursdays were my days with you."

His gaze roved over my face, and for a long, intense moment, I hoped that he'd demand I honor my obligation to him. Guilt me into skipping my meeting with Will. It wouldn't be the first time I'd be skipping something out of guilt. But it would be the first time I'd be skipping something because I *wanted* the alternative.

"You should meet him," Sean said at last. "We met up twice this week, so I'll take a rain check on next week's meeting."

I should've felt relief, but as I searched his face, my chest hurt. *I would much rather be with you.*

My cheeks flamed with regret, and my throat was tight as I forced my voice to be steady when I thanked him before getting into the car. In a few seconds, Sean followed. Lucas had dozed off, and I clicked his seat belt in place just before the door fell shut and the car began to move.

It was a few minutes before Sean spoke again.

"Where is he taking you?" he asked almost belligerently.

I watched him carefully. "Why?"

For a moment, it seemed like he was going to answer me honestly, but at the last minute, he drew back.

"Never mind. I don't care. It's none of my business."

Things were glaringly complicated between us. He'd made it clear he didn't want to cross any professional boundaries, and as much as I hated that, I had to respect it.

Besides the fact that he was my boss, I also suspected that getting involved with Sean would be a bad idea for other reasons. He was the kind of man who could leave me broken and hurt if I ever gave in to this attraction. I couldn't afford to get emotionally wrecked by him.

The way he had comforted and helped me when I was at my lowest tonight, our freaking kiss, and worse, these feelings, it all seemed to disappear into nothingness. We were back to being strangers.

Our eyes met, and I could feel the intensity in his gaze, as though what I'd said wasn't enough.

He shifted away in his seat, putting more distance between us, and my heart broke.

For the rest of the drive, we stayed like that.

26

SEAN

We'd fucking kissed, and she was ready to set up a date with another man? That thought consumed me all weekend and still wouldn't let go on my drive to work Monday morning.

Only because you'd said the kiss was a mistake.

It *had been* a mistake, but that didn't mean I didn't want to make it again.

I fucking hated the idea of Chloe with another man—someone who could kiss those lips. I wanted no one else but me touching her, but I couldn't pursue her. I couldn't risk ruining what progress we had been making with Lucas.

Lucas had been in much better spirits after the gala. He'd credited Chloe with helping him make a new friend—Brianna. And he was markedly less grumpy around me.

Chloe was definitely working wonders. I gripped the armrest of my seat in frustration. Kissing her nearly undid me. Even if the kiss felt more intimate and passionate than anything I'd ever experienced before.

I'd been craving her for months, and I'd lost all restraint in her presence.

In the fucking elevator.

She wasn't good for me. I was getting increasingly desperate for her, and I hated losing control of myself.

Determined to stop thinking about her, I looked at my phone, where the message from Erin lay unread. I opened it and read it today, feeling sure it would only irritate me further.

It only said that she was planning to visit Mom in a few weeks and hoped to see me, too, if I was in town. The last time I'd seen Mom—at Dad's funeral—she'd mentioned that Erin lived out in Miami.

I wouldn't be meeting Mom. That much was for sure. I wasn't interested in meeting Erin either when she got here. But I could respond to her message.

A familiar flare of irritation coursed through me. Why was I even considering this? I didn't have to be nice to Erin. No one expected me to, and God knew, I didn't care about what people expected of me. But all I knew was when I had heard Chloe talk about her brother, it had hit me that I had a half-sibling, too, out there somewhere. Someone who was interested in knowing me and building a relationship with me based on us having the same mom. When so much of Chloe's conversations had involved references to her brother —references made with love—it'd reminded me of how cold I'd been to Erin's approaches to conversation in the past.

I wouldn't kindle a fling with Chloe. That was given. But I could let her influence me.

Later next week, Erin would be landing in the airport, and I needed to see exactly what kind of a brother I was capable of being.

I kept my distance from Chloe at work, realizing that being around her was changing how I felt.

I had almost convinced myself that I was glad she was going out with Will. She couldn't be anything to me really. She deserved a man who didn't have a reputation for being ruthless.

Not me.

By lunchtime, as I swept past her desk on my way to the elevator, my gaze drifted to her. Her blonde hair caught the lights and shone, and I had another moment of weakness.

She stood up, a lunch bag in hand, and walked over to me.

I could see the curve of her breasts under her blouse and the outline of her hard nipples through the fabric.

Fuck. Either she wasn't wearing a bra or she was wearing something too thin.

I set my jaw as my cock hardened in my pants. I imagined taking her off to the stairwell. I imagined pinning her hands to the wall behind her, her lips parting in a surprised moan, and my lips on every part of her. I would then suck on those pointed nipples through the smooth satin of her silver blouse, licking and biting down on them until she writhed in my arms for release, begging me to make her come. I imagined half the office hearing the sex-crazed noises coming from the stairwell and making guesses about who was in there, having the time of their lives. Because I'd give Chloe that, and nothing less.

My throat worked, and it was a while before I could speak. "Which floor?" I asked finally.

"The lobby, please."

We got into the elevator, and I pressed the button. The doors closed, and I stayed rooted in place, acutely aware of her presence beside me as the elevator began its descent.

There was an edgy guardedness in her expression when she looked up at me. She stared at my lips before looking away. Like she was anxious, but also filled with desire. The anxiety had never been there before. Damn.

I crossed my arms and leaned against the wall, trying to keep our conversation safe. I could see signs of her peanut butter sandwich in her see-through box and felt a stab of frustration that she'd had to make a lunch reservation for me at Balthazar.

"How do you like working here so far? After working for Gary at Mindwell?" I asked, determined to show that we could carry on a normal conversation, like before.

She looked at me and didn't respond for a bit.

The desire in her eyes burned out in a moment, and I felt a sudden disappointment.

When she spoke, she looked and sounded extremely indifferent. "I don't really miss my job at Mindwell," she said at last. "Or Mr. Chalk. He always told me that if shit hit the fan, he'd leave. I saw him do that with his ex-wife during their marriage, and when the business started to fail, he said he had no use for a woman like me."

"Like you?" I couldn't help but ask, feeling enraged on her behalf.

She had a nice voice, feminine and cheery, like a ray of sunlight. Gary must have been a monster of an entirely different sort if he could talk to her like that.

"Yes." Her eyes darted, and she looked away. "When I asked him if I could take time off after my wedding, he responded that if I did, I could forget about getting maternity leave later on. He had no use for people who needed vacations, it seemed."

That jerk. How could Gary treat her like that? If the man were still working for me ... well, he'd been outed, but if he hadn't been, he'd definitely be out the door now. It wasn't fair that Chloe had had to suffer the collateral damage.

"Why didn't you report him?" I asked as we got into the elevator. "To HR?"

She swallowed. "The head of HR was Mr. Chalk's brother. He had been known to stick by Mr. Chalk whenever required."

Damn it.

"Well, I'll have you know that HR doesn't usually work like that," I began when my gaze went to the watch on her hand with a worn-out strap. The glass face had scratches on it, and I wondered why she couldn't afford better things in her life. I looked at her clothes before it struck me that I'd seen this blouse at least three times this week and the skirt at least twice.

"Though I guess you must have a pretty low opinion of HR at the moment," I said when the elevator came to a stop.

I strode out to the lobby with her. Had we really kissed last Friday? I longed to reach out and hold her to me again, but the lobby stretched out before us, the marble floor gleaming. Sunlight filtered in through the glass walls, and the peaceful sound of water trickling into the sculpted fountains met my ears as we walked through the employees standing and talking. People's heads swiveled, and conversations ceased as we went past, only to pick up once we were sufficiently far away. Everyone's eyes tracked the meager lunch box in Chloe's hands before going to her attire, a look of distaste in their gaze.

Damn them.

I walked her to the break room across the lobby. I'd make sure no one so much as looked in her direction on our walk in. Not a word would pass anyone's lips if I could help it. I'd mastered the art of scowling after all. I had a scowl for every occasion, and I knew how to send people scuttling back to their desks. One thing was for sure: I couldn't stand to watch people judge her for her outfit and not show her my support. Not when she'd done enough to show me she was a stellar employee who also did well with my son. The world was usually unfair, but *this* was too much.

If this was how people treated Chloe, what would Will be like?

27

CHLOE

The next week passed by in a blur. At work, Sean still maintained a hefty distance from me. Even if his eyes blazed intensely every time we crossed paths. For my part, the attraction was undeniable. I couldn't stop thinking about our kiss, my skin heating with the memory and my core clenching tight with need.

But he was a mystery. And not just to me, I realized. I accompanied him to one of the lower floors for a meeting, and I saw the chaos he left in his wake when he walked out of the meeting.

When he took off, back into the elevator, alone, cubicles transformed into mini sanctuaries.

"It really was him!"

"I've worked here for five years and never once seen him!"

On Tuesday, Sean took advantage of a light day at work. He canceled his meetings to take Lucas and me to spend the day at the Central Park Zoo.

My pulse pounded in my veins the entire time with how

near Sean was to me. But he was strangely distant, and Lucas was a good buffer for our tension.

I could see that Sean was trying, engaging Lucas in conversation as much as he could.

While being around Sean and not touching him was a new kind of torture, I enjoyed seeing Sean as the dad. He was sincerely trying, and combined with an adorable Lucas, they made a great father-son combination.

Emboldened by the success of that day, Sean took Lucas by himself to the Intrepid Museum the next day. At the end of the day, when Sean brought Lucas back to the office to grab some papers, I asked Lucas about his visit.

He told me it was like stepping into a real-life action movie with aircraft carriers and space shuttles. He also added in a small voice that he wished I could have been there.

So, I still had miles to go with helping Sean bond with him. I kept that bit of information to myself, afraid of ruining Sean's burgeoning optimism about his relationship with his son.

Recently, I'd seen Sean making calls to Lucas from work, checking in with him midday and even asking him if he had ideas for where he wanted to spend the weekend. He'd even go as far as calling him *buddy* every time they spoke.

By the time Thursday rolled around, I tried to push thoughts of Sean out of my mind. I was both nervous and worried about my date. I really needed this date to go well because I really needed to get over Sean.

I wrapped up work quickly, buying myself time to get ready at home before Will showed up. I looked in Sean's office multiple times as the afternoon came to a close, but he firmly stayed out of it all day. I knew his schedule by heart and that he was at work today, but he'd chosen to take most of his meetings at restaurants or conference rooms on other floors. By five o'clock, when I was ready to leave, my heart was heavy as I picked up my bag and took a last look at the empty high-backed office chair in Sean's office.

How had he managed to avoid me all day? How had I not seen him in between meetings, like I usually did? Lately, he had been the only one to know what was happening in my personal life, and I was hoping for a look from him to confirm I was doing the right thing.

Besides, I missed seeing him. His presence and his occasional knowing but intense look, I realized, were a big draw for why I showed up to work eagerly every day.

I took the elevator down and waved to Charles, the security guard, as I walked out of the Tassater building before heading toward the nearest subway station.

An hour later, I was back home. I pushed the door open, expecting to find the house empty when I saw Henry's familiar brown hair and oval face in the kitchen.

"Henry." I smiled as I shut the door.

He turned around from the accessible induction stove, where he had been stir-frying noodles.

"You're on time," he exclaimed as I walked in. "I'm making us dinner. Your favorite—drunken noodles."

It smelled great, and I sniffed it eagerly as I fought against my better instincts. I was very tempted to ditch Will and have dinner with Henry instead. This was familiar and comfortable.

"What about your social club at college?" I asked, setting my bag down.

He waved a hand in the air genially. "A bunch of us decided to ditch the club for today and go out to the mall. I'll take the bus at six. One of my friends, Ronan, will be on the same bus. So, you don't need to drop me today."

"Well," I began, "as it happens, I've got some plans tonight too."

"I know," Henry said, turning the stove off and plating the noodles for him and me. "Your work."

I shook my head as I looked back at him ruefully. "No, not my work. I'm going out with someone."

Henry looked amazed. "Who?" he asked.

"Someone I met at the park," I said with a gentle shrug. "It's just a date," I said, reaching for a fortune cookie and unwrapping it.

Chewing on one half of the cookie, I struggled with my composure. "I could delay my date," I added, but Henry scoffed at the idea.

"What's the need for that?" he asked. "It's been two and a half months since your wedding got called off. You need to meet other people."

Our eyes met over the broken fortune cookie, and I couldn't help but think what might have happened if Bruce hadn't broken things off back then. If the wedding had gone through.

I'd never know.

"Well, it seemed like this was a good opportunity to move on," I said at last. "Will is a nice guy, and this will give me a chance to forget about Bruce." *And more importantly, Sean.*

"Do you like him?" Henry asked, his voice curious.

"It seemed like it was easy to talk to him," I said, choosing my words carefully.

I refrained from telling Henry that he was the most important person to me. I'd done it in the past, and it just irritated him. I shouldn't have to feel that my role as a caretaker was being threatened every time a new person entered our lives. I shouldn't have to feel guilty for letting another person in. But knowing how I should feel and feeling something else entirely was the norm for me.

"But, Henry," I said, measuring my words slowly, "it's just a onetime thing."

Henry said nothing for a moment. "You need to go," he said at last. His voice was firm. "After my accident and after Dad left, well, I didn't expect us to make it this far. Heck, I never thought I'd get to college myself. But look at us; we're marching on. And irrespective of whatever's happened, you shouldn't have to give up fun. I have my life, and you're starting to live yours the way it should be. I'm happy for you. So, go have fun."

He took my untouched plate and dumped the contents into a bowl. "Freeze it," he said, handing the lid and the bowl over to me. "You can eat it sometime later. But go on the date. It's just one night."

I took the bowl in relief, realizing that one night was doable. One date, and then my life would go back to the same old, same old.

Once I stowed the bowl in the fridge, I headed to my room to get ready, my heart heavy. "Are you sure you don't want me to drop you?" I asked from my doorway to my bedroom.

"The bus stop is just down the road, so I'll be fine," he said, but he looked stressed as he thought about it.

I pressed my lips together. Henry loved these occasional evenings where he got to go out with his friends, but it also stressed him out. The uncertainty over getting into the right bus and how the evening would go bothered him.

He rolled away and off to the bathroom, the wheelchair squeaking faintly while his wheels turned.

I took twenty minutes to get ready and was almost done, putting on one last coat of lipstick when the doorbell rang. I turned to the mirror in a hurry, tying my hair up in a quick low knot before rushing out the bedroom door.

When I opened the front door, Will smiled back at me—a pleasant smile that made him look sweet. He was dressed in a short-sleeved white button-down shirt with dark gray trousers. He even had nice dress shoes on, which made me imagine we might be going somewhere mildly fancy. I felt glad that my blue blouse was ironed even if my skirt was a little old.

He was looking over my shoulder when a surprised look came over him. I turned to follow his gaze. Henry was just exiting the bathroom, and one of his wheels had gotten stuck on the edge of the bathroom door, which was trying to fall shut.

My brief look at Will was enough for me to notice the change that had come over him. He looked pale, shifting his weight from one foot to another. His jaw was tight, and beads of sweat shone on his forehead.

When he finally found his tongue, he stumbled over his words. "Oh. He—hey. Hi."

Behind me, Henry cursed. I turned and saw that Henry was not looking up, but pushing himself backward and forward to get unstuck.

"Hang on," I said over my shoulder to Will as I ran back to Henry.

Leaning over, I held the door in place while Henry took his wheelchair back and rolled out and away from the frustrating door. He was panting with the exertion when he let loose a few colorful expletives, glaring at the damn bathroom door.

"Going to the bathroom is already so difficult," he shouted. "The damn door makes it worse."

I mentally cursed the door myself, having seen Henry

struggle with this a few times before. We needed a door that was heavier and one that didn't shut before Henry got a chance to roll out of the bathroom.

"I'm really sorry, Henry. I'll speak to the landlord about it again."

"Don't bother. The bastard does nothing for us. *Nothing.*"

Henry's vehemence wasn't surprising to me. Routines made life easy, and tonight, he was going out—against his routine. He needed to get to the bus on time, and I could see his underlying stress through his anger.

I just made a mental note to be firmer with my landlord next when Henry spoke.

"When is your date getting here?" he asked between deep breaths, looking at me.

I turned back to the front door, ready to make the introductions when I noticed something strange.

The doorway was empty.

"He's out there already," I said, rushing out and grabbing my handbag on my way. "Bye," I called as I shut the door, and Henry waved.

My palms felt clammy as I let go of the door and looked around. I tried to convince myself that Will was just waiting outside, giving us some privacy, but he wasn't in sight.

I stood outside the front door, chest heaving as I looked up and down the road. A few vehicles passed by with drivers I didn't recognize. I saw a row of parked cars on the street and wondered if he was waiting inside one of them.

I shut the door behind me and raced down the street, checking each individual car for a sign of Will. I didn't find him.

I reached the end of the block and looked to my right and left. Apart from a drunk man sitting on the sidewalk in a daze and people lined up outside of a nearby ramen shop, there was nobody I recognized.

Where did Will disappear to? And why?

I reached for my phone and called Will, my heart racing. *Please, oh please, let this not be what I think it is.*

I called him twice, and each time, I got voice mail. Feeling the inevitable sense of despair, I left him a message at last, asking him what was going on in a shaking voice.

Did Will just disappear because he'd been nervous about what he witnessed happening to Henry?

I couldn't help making the obvious connection. Will had reminded me of every single important but unreliable man in my life so far who had been unable to cope with Henry's needs. My dad and Bruce. They'd been the same.

I looked around helplessly when, a second later, I got a call from Henry.

"Hey, did you find him?" Henry asked over the phone.

I bit my lip. "Yes," I lied, determined not to make a big deal of this.

"Great. You guys should have fun. And stay out all night long if you want to. You deserve to relax a bit."

Was my younger brother really telling me to get it on?

"I still don't understand why you went out with a jerk like Bruce. He was horrible to you. I hope the new guy is miles better," he said.

I froze when I heard his words, not wanting to tell him I'd been stood up. "He is," I responded to my brother, feeling my mouth dry up. "I will be back soon," I said and hung up.

Feeling distraught, I sauntered down the desolate sidewalk, determined not to go back for a while. I didn't want Henry to have a clue that I'd been stood up because that would only break me more.

In the end, this was the outcome I was comfortable with

even if I was angry at Will for ditching me. It just confirmed my belief that dating was not for us.

'The Nichols siblings stick together.'

Because the world won't stick by us.

My phone lit up with another text, and a flare of hope surged through me. Was it Will perhaps, texting me with an apology? Even if he did apologize, would I accept it?

28

CHLOE

But the text was not from Henry or Will.

Sean: *I didn't see the weekly operational reports mailed in today. Date night or not, I won't have you slacking off, Ms. Nichols.*

I walked down the street, my cheeks flaming hot with a mix of shame and humiliation.

I'd been stood up in the most humiliating way, and instead of a shoulder to cry on, I got this.

I found a quiet street corner and sat down under a streetlight, red-hot tears rolling down my face.

This was why I didn't go out on dates. This was why meeting Bruce himself had felt like a chance in a million until I saw him for the asshole he was.

Another text popped up.

Sean: *If I don't hear back from you in a minute, I'm calling you.*

I didn't want him to call and hear my voice shake. Just like I didn't want to go back home and let Henry know that my date had left me high and dry.

Chloe: *I mailed them in earlier today, just before I left at five p.m. Could you check your spam folders, please?*

I got a call from him instantly.

I rejected it and looked around for a place to go. There were no bars or cafés nearby, so unless I wanted to keep walking in my high heels, I needed to come up with a better plan fast.

My phone buzzed with another angry text from Sean, no doubt, and I didn't give it a look. I'd done my job, and I didn't want to be troubled by him—especially since he thought I was having the time of my life and that he needed to ruin it for me.

That job is already done. You don't need to do anything here.

I looked up and down the empty street, but I didn't have anywhere else to go, except for home. No one else to call and complain to.

Cars sped by on the road in front of me, a blur in the scene of my life.

A black Rolls-Royce Phantom slowed down next to me. We were on the very edge of New York, a not-very-respectable part of town.

Wondering if someone seedy wanted to approach me, I stood up and turned around, beginning to walk in the direction of my home. I heard footsteps as someone got out of the car, and I hastily rubbed my eyes and continued walking, not looking back. Because my sense of humiliation was long gone, now replaced by a sense of fear.

The footsteps behind me did not falter. If anything, they sped up. Feeling increasingly worried, I reached for my phone just as I turned around to face my presumable attacker.

"I know tae kwon—" I began, but then my words and mouth froze.

On the pavement, I could see the familiar deep blue Tom Ford jacket I'd seen earlier at work. Sean stood in front of me, a look of anger on his face.

Damn it. Did he follow me here just for those ridiculous reports?

"I emailed the reports to you, like I said," I began. "Do I need to show you how to use your email as well?"

He didn't respond, just kept walking closer and closer. The anger on his face was evident.

He stopped when he was right in front of me, mere inches away. "You need to tell me why you're out here, crying, when you're supposed to be on a date."

I laughed a half-maniacal laugh. "Oh, so that's why you followed me? You wanted to ruin that part of my life too? Well, I'll have you know that I managed to do that all by myself. Get back in your flashy car, Sean, and leave. There's nothing left for you to ruin anymore."

I turned away and began walking, but he stretched a hand out and grabbed my wrist, stopping me.

"I didn't come here to ruin anything, Chloe."

I was done listening to his lies. "How did you know I was here anyway?" I asked, trying to wriggle my hand out of his grip.

His grip only became tighter, and he pulled me closer to him.

My body pressed against his, and I was too distraught to care anymore. I could feel every inch of him where his body met mine.

His hard chest, his broad hips, and even his growing erection.

"I came here to check if that jerk Will was treating you right. And going by how upset you look, I was correct. Where did the bastard go?"

"Will was perfect," I lied, no idea why I was defending him.

"Then, why did a perfect date leave you crying on the street out at night?"

"I'm not crying."

"Your eyes are blood red."

My hand was in his, and my body was still flush against his.

I attempted to come up with something. Anything that would help me get away from him instead of recounting my embarrassing date.

"I had to cancel my date," I lied. "I wasn't feeling great."

He leaned in, his lips very close to my cheek. "The idea of you out with Will makes my skin crawl, Chloe."

My breath hitched while his lips hovered just inches above mine. His eyes locked on to my mouth. "Tell me you hated it too," he said while my throat worked.

Sean's driver sat in the car close to us, still in view.

"What if I didn't hate the idea of it?" I asked brazenly.

After all, Sean had told me to go on this date.

I'd *hated* the idea of dressing up for anyone except him.

His dark brown eyes focused on me, his hands brushing up against my waist. He found a strip of bare skin above the waistband of my skirt and settled his fingers on it. The touch sent a jolt through my body, and a small gasp spilled from my lips.

Touch me.

"I think you're lying," he said, teasing a finger on the exposed skin on my hip as he stepped in front of me, blocking us from the driver's view.

My head tipped back. "Sean," I breathed out as his fingers explored my skin, trailing upward slowly.

"Do you know why I think you're lying?" he asked,

watching me carefully. When his hand grazed the hem of my blouse, he froze, his eyes glazing over. "Because everything points to you being desperate for me, Chloe. Me. Not that jerk, Will."

I locked my gaze with his, even as my mouth became slack with desire. "Why don't you find out?" I asked, sounding very unlike myself.

His eyes darkened with a flash of desire. "Get in the car, Chloe, before I lose my mind out here."

I shook my head. "No," I breathed out, stepping in closer to him. "You need to tell me where you were all day today."

He rubbed little circles against my skin with his finger. His touch was scorching hot in contrast to the cool air on my bare skin.

"Were you keeping a lookout for me, Chloe?" he asked, his voice rough.

One finger dipped brazenly under my blue blouse and then another.

"Yes," I breathed out, placing a hand on his chest as cars zoomed past.

His fingers traveled higher up, pulling the blouse up slowly and revealing the bare expanse of my stomach. He kept his gaze on my face, watching me, perhaps for a sign that he should back off.

He stopped his search when his fingers traced the underwire of my bra.

He moved to draw his fingers down, but I gripped his wrist with my other hand, holding him in place.

"Chloe," he said, the word sounding rough.

I reached up to glide my hand over the back of his hand, pressing down on it, taking his fingers up over my bra until they fully cupped my breast.

He must have felt my hardened nipple under his fingers because his jaw clenched suddenly. He could definitely feel that through the sheer lace bra I wore today.

"You know who I thought about when I wore this?" I asked, my voice hoarse when he began to pinch my nipple, teasing it between his fingers.

"Of course, me," he said in that smug voice.

Ugh. The jerk.

I ran my tongue over my upper lip as he gently circled my sensitive peak. The moan of relief I gave was confirmation enough.

"We can't do this," he said, suddenly withdrawing his hand from under my blouse and leaving me empty.

I balked at him, my blouse suddenly loose as cold air rushed in where his warm fingers had been. I wanted more. I wanted to grab his hand and put it back on me, having him touch me in one of the most intimate places, but I would not beg. So, I clenched my thighs and swallowed.

I hate him.

"Will was—"

Sean leaned in closer, crowding me until I was backing up a few steps on the footpath.

"I don't want his name crossing your lips," he growled.

"Or what?" I challenged.

Suddenly, his hand was back on my wrist. "You're coming with me," he ordered as he stepped sideways next to me, leading the way to his car.

I glanced at the black Rolls-Royce and yanked my hand out of his.

"Or you could go back home," he gritted out, turning around to face me.

"No," I said instantly before I could help myself. "I don't

want to go back home. My brother will realize what happened ... and ... I don't want to tell him—"

"The truth," Sean finished for me. "Just like you're plainly hiding the truth from me."

29

CHLOE

I gazed at him, feeling my frustration simmering beneath the surface. The streetlights in the night sky cast a subtle glow, revealing the sharp contours of his features. He was undeniably handsome, the kind of man who turned heads effortlessly. But he was maddeningly vexing. Today, it was the nonchalant aura he wore that left me torn between irritation and fascination.

The sleek black Rolls-Royce started its engine, and Sean put his hands on my shoulders and steered me to the waiting car.

"First, we're going to eat," he said and held the door open for me.

First?

"What's second?" I asked, but he only glowered back at me.

"I'm going to make sure Will's name never crosses your lips ever again."

How exactly?

But the look in Sean's eyes meant he wasn't in the mood to talk anymore. I could still feel the sensation of the tips of his fingers on my breast, out on the street, with cars roaring past us. That memory only made me want to pull him to me again. Not Will. Not any other man out there. Just Sean.

I wanted to lick those lips and hear his voice rumbling over my skin while he whispered dirty secrets to me. None of that was a good idea.

"*Now*, Chloe," he snapped, and I took a deep breath and stepped inside.

The interior was luxurious with leather seating that seemed to hug me as I settled in.

I fixed my eyes on him in the half darkness as he got in next to me.

"I've got a plan that involves feeding you something because I have no doubt that there's no dinner for you at home anyway. That will keep us out for a while. So, you don't have to tell the truth to your brother."

"You're crazy," I said just as my traitorous stomach rumbled.

He smirked while the car began to move.

He reached over and pulled my seat belt out, fixing it in place as he kept his eyes on me. "Would a crazy person be waiting for you outside your home at the time your date was supposed to show up?" he asked, his large body looming over me.

I stared at him, my mouth falling open as he finally sat back down. "You were there?" I asked, my voice hoarse. He was worse than crazy. "You saw Will?"

He didn't bother nodding. "I saw the way he bailed on you, too, getting back in his car and driving off without you. I was so angry that I didn't know if I ought to chase him down first and give him a much-needed kick in his balls or follow you."

I exhaled deeply. I agreed with his sentiment about Will, but this was madness.

"Why did you ask me about those stupid reports then?"

"Because I wanted to hear from you. I gave you an opening to talk to me and tell me something was wrong. Instead, you pushed me away."

He *was* insane if this was how he went about an emotional conversation.

Before I could address that, I looked at the direction we were going in and realized we were heading down to Tribeca.

"Where are we going?" I asked, feeling nervous.

"One of my usual spots—The Hilford."

I gulped. I didn't recognize the name, but if this was anything like Sean's other haunts, I was definitely out of my element here, dressed in a skirt and a blouse. I didn't want Sean to see me like that, even if we could never be anything to each other.

Even though tonight couldn't mean anything.

"Maybe we could do a burger place? Like McDonald's?"

Sean scoffed. "The Hilford makes good burgers, Chloe. You need to trust me more."

It was my turn to snort. "Says the man who camped outside my house to spy on my date."

This time, Sean permitted himself a smile, and I looked away.

My body still tingled from his touch like it never wanted to forget that memory. That wasn't a good sign for a man I only wanted a fling with.

The car glided through the city streets, some of them familiar because we were headed in the same direction as the Tassater offices. I couldn't help but marvel at the stark contrast between my usual commute to work by train, and *this* upscale transportation.

Sean turned to me, his thumb pressing possessively on my chin as he tilted my face up to him.

"Can you tell me why Will changed his mind on your doorstep?" he asked, his voice angry as he rubbed my chin. "You got dressed for him, did your makeup for that jerk. You look more beautiful than ever. Why did Will turn around and walk away?"

I bet Sean couldn't have seen anything of Henry from where he had been watching. I closed my eyes, and a shiver ran through me. How long could I hide the truth?

I opened my mouth to make an excuse for Will, but bit my tongue. Why would I defend the guy who had shamed me? Shamed Henry?

I breathed out as he let go of my chin. My hands were in my lap, and he took them in his, sending heat rushing through me.

"I told you I have a brother, Henry. What I didn't tell you is that he's got some health issues," I said, gingerly toeing the truth of Henry's mobility problems. "For some reason, it put Will off."

Sean's eyes widened, and he cursed under his breath. "He called off the date for that? The arrogant bastard."

"I felt terrible," I said in a hurry, hoping I wouldn't have to go into more details. "Also because Henry is going to ask me how my date went and I don't know how to answer that question."

"Well," he said, his thumb was running in circles on my palm, making my stomach feel floppy, "you don't have to tell Henry that your date bailed on you. You can tell him that you went to a nice place and had a wonderful meal before you politely declined a second date with Will."

He held my gaze for one intense moment, and I flushed at the idea of this being a date. He must have noticed my blush because his face lost its grim look. He reached for my cheek, cupping it with the palm of his hand, with hazy eyes and a delicious smile.

My world seemed to stop spinning when he looked at me like that. Sean and I could never be a couple. So, why was I imagining this to be more than just a dinner? Why did his desire for me feel a little too real?

I expected him to say something, but the car came to a sudden stop.

"We're here," was all he said before pulling his hand away.

My hand went to my cheek, feeling the warmth that he had left before I realized he was still watching me. I blushed even more and pulled my hand away.

"Thank goodness," I muttered.

Sitting next to Sean in the dark interior of his car had felt too intimate. I wanted the safety of sitting across from him at the table, where I could be assured there would be no lingering touches.

I shouldn't have let Sean touch me. And I would not be swayed by his interest in my life either. I knew the man was selfish, and it was just his competitive spirit that had made him follow me and bring me here tonight.

Sean got out and held the door open for me. I got out into the cool night breeze and looked at the building. It was nestled between sleek high-rises, its black exterior giving off a sophisticated vibe. The restaurant must be on one of the upper floors because the first floor housed an upscale furniture store. It had floor-to-ceiling windows, framed in dark, rich wood, and a sleek, charcoal-colored awning extended gracefully over the entrance. If the furniture store was this pretty, what was the restaurant like?

Dad used to work as a HVAC technician, and whenever we had money left after payday, we used to head over to McDonald's for a treat. We had lived a quiet, respectable life, sometimes even heading out to Olive Garden on birthdays. Places like The Hilford had never been in the cards for us.

We got onto the pavement, and Sean noticed my hesitation. "Don't worry. This isn't a real date. I'm just making up for the jerk who stood you up."

His fingers settled on the small of my back as he gently pushed me forward. The touch was warm, sending a spark running through my torso. I hadn't been touched in ages. I wanted to lean into it more. To feel the soft caress of his fingers on my skin and his soothing arms pulling me close.

This isn't a real date.

I cleared my throat and focused on the building in front of me and not the gnawing deep hole of loneliness in me.

A doorman in a crisp uniform opened the door for us, and we stepped into an expansive lobby. Sean led me to the elevator, and when we were in, he pressed the button for the fifteenth floor. He was dressed in a suit that cost more than my month's rent. Nothing about this night seemed real.

When we met each other's gaze, I could see the memory of our kiss from the elevator burning in his stormy brown eyes.

When the doors closed, he banded one arm around my back and pulled me to him, his breath hot and heavy on my eyelids. His knee pushed between my legs to grind against my sex, lifting my butt higher in the process. I arched my back with a whimper while he cupped the curve of my ass.

His fingers trailed down the side of my neck. "Just so you know, tonight I'll feed you first, and then..." I felt my breath freeze in my throat as his fingers snaked down to my cleavage. "I'm going to see what lingerie you chose while thinking of me."

I definitely wanted to see the rest of Sean—including what he was packing under his briefs. But before I could say anything, the doors opened. Sean let go of my waist, and I took a breath and stepped back.

Elevators were never much luck.

Sean took my hand, and giving me a heated look that said we weren't done yet, he led me out.

We stepped into a world of dimly lit chandeliers, soft jazz music, and the clinking of fine china. The maître d', a young woman in a black dress, welcomed Sean by name and led us to a private table at the back. Oversize lanterns hung from the roof, casting a warm glow, and wrought iron accents framed the windows, adding a touch of old-world charm.

"Well, isn't this something?" I said.

Through the window, we had a breathtaking view of the city skyline, including the Hudson River glimmering in the distance.

I took my seat across from Sean and looked out at the twinkling lights of the city on my left. "This is not what I expected, Sean."

"Well," he said, sounding cynical, as usual, "I was certainly not the one you expected to be sitting across from."

I glanced down at my outfit and then at the other patrons in this restaurant. "I meant, this is way fancier than I expected." I hesitated. "After our night at the gala, I didn't think I'd ever get a chance to experience anything as fine as that again. And you've proven me wrong, like always.

"I mean, I know this isn't a date," I added hastily. "But it's nice, being here with you."

Our eyes met over the table, and for a while, it seemed like I couldn't draw myself to look away from his dark brown eyes.

He leaned forward, placing his hands on the table. "Chloe, if this was really a date, I'd have picked you up at your doorstep; I'd have met and spoken to your brother, Henry; and you would definitely not have started the evening off with tears in your eyes."

I inhaled sharply as I considered a real date with Sean. It was shocking—that a man like him could see me as someone sexually attractive. Me—a woman whose schedule had more appointments for her brother than herself.

I shook my head, forcing my daydream out of my mind. This evening was a surprise, but I knew better than to expect good things in my future when my landlord called me names for asking for "a perfectly good door" to be replaced.

The waitress, whose name tag read *Traci*, arrived. She handed us menus. She also offered us an aged red wine from Bordeaux, France, that she said she knew Sean liked.

I watched her leave, wondering how it was that the staff at a restaurant knew Sean and his tastes better than anyone at his company, before I took a sip. It was heavenly; rich, velvety notes hit me, giving me flavors with hints of berries and oak.

My eyes widened, and a subtle smile played on Sean's lips as he asked, "Is it good?"

I nodded. "It's unbelievably sophisticated," I said.

So, this was Sean's taste in things—and perhaps in women too.

Sean handed me the menu, and I ran my eyes over names of dishes I had only heard of in passing. Truffle lobster risotto, sushi with foie gras, a black truffle and gold-leaf pizza ... the list was endless. But it still wasn't enough to distract me from the tall, dark man across my table.

Sean looked at me over his menu, his eyes filled with humor. "Do you still want the burger?"

"I want you. But we have to get through this facade of a dinner before I can have that."

His throat worked, and his tongue whipped out to lick his lower lip.

When Traci came over, Sean rattled off our order, choosing what I should have. I barely cared about eating anymore while Sean's foot teased mine under the table.

"Come over here," Sean said when Traci left, reaching out to pull my chair closer to him.

I shook my head. I'd seen the gleam in his eyes.

Sean placed his hand on the back of my chair and pulled me to him in one swift move so I was next to him instead of across. "It wasn't a request," he breathed into my ear after my chair came to a standstill.

We were so close; my knee touched his. His eyes followed my gaze to where our legs met. Under the white linen tablecloth, he languidly lifted a finger to graze my knee, starting at the edge of my skirt.

He carefully coasted one finger up my inner thigh, reaching my wet underwear unnervingly slowly. I sucked in a breath as I fought every instinct to spread my thighs wide.

My body was hot and needy, and I couldn't focus on anything except his touch, inching closer and closer to my pussy.

"Sean," I gasped, and the look on his face was one of utter admiration.

My hand ran up his arm, feeling the bumps and valleys of his muscles, but I didn't stop him.

Finally, his fingers reached the wet garment under my skirt, and a moan fell from my lips.

"Shh," Sean said soothingly.

I looked up, my heart hammering. We were in a secluded corner at the back, but still in a public place.

I had my back to the window, and the table would shield me from any passing server, but I didn't trust myself to stay quiet.

"Do you want me to touch you?" Sean asked, his fingers pushing my panties aside until he found my wet folds.

My skirt was bunched up at my hips, and I nodded, biting down on my lip.

I was so desperate for him; it was crazy. I leaned back against the chair, spreading my legs on either side of the seat.

"I want you to take me," I said. "To possess me."

His mouth was tight as he slipped one finger in and then the next deep into me, holding my gaze in his. My mouth fell open, and I spread even wider.

"Good girl," he said, his voice rough as he slowly penetrated me with his fingers.

I almost threw my head back as my back arched, wishing I could have him touch me in more places. His fingers felt so good that I slowly ground in place while his fingers fucked me. In the distance, I heard a spoon clatter to the floor and the gentle hum of other patrons' conversations while Sean worked my pussy. The heels of my shoes pressed against the floor as I angled myself so that his fingers touched me *just there*.

My head was spinning with desire, and I wished I could have his cock in me instead of his fingers as he pushed me closer and closer to climax.

"You're beautiful," Sean said, his jaw tight as he pressed the heel of his hand on my clit.

The pressure nearly undid me. And when he circled the heel on my clit, I came undone.

My climax hit me like a truck, a small cry wrenching from my lips before I clamped my hand over my mouth. Wave after wave of pleasure rolled off me. I slumped back in my chair, feeling delirious and happy.

To my utter surprise, when Sean pulled his fingers out, he licked them, keeping his eyes on me. I felt a thrill at knowing he knew what I tasted like.

But more than anything else, Sean's gaze shocked me. He looked wild. He looked like once he'd gotten a taste of me, he was never letting go.

A cough interrupted us, and I turned to see the server who had walked up to our table with a large tray of food. He was looking at us with a bemused expression, as though he'd tried getting our attention before and failed miserably.

"May I place your food on the table?" he asked.

I nodded, removing my hands from the table while Sean looked away. It was one of my clues that he was taken aback with his emotions, like I was.

Had the server seen anything? My face burned while I considered it, but it was impossible. Sean seemed to guess what I was thinking because he shook his head, as though answering my unasked question.

When the server left, I pulled my skirt back down from where it was bunched up around my hips. "That was close," I said, but Sean shook his head.

"No one will see you in a compromising situation unless I permit it," he said, cockiness dripping from him like an arrogant devil. "And I will never allow it."

"You are crazy," I repeated, reaching for my salad.

But he was right. Things had a way of cropping up around Sean only if he wanted them to. Troubles disappeared when he decided he was done with them.

"You make me crazy," he corrected, his voice dropping low, and my pulse quickened.

I exhaled. I wasn't used to trusting the men around me to take control, but I was starting to realize that I could trust Sean.

"Do you come here often, Sean?"

Sean took a sip of his wine before he placed the glass down.

"I end up having a lot of business dinners here, but not dates," he said with a smile. "This is a first."

My cheeks flamed at his allusion to this being a date, but I knew better than to fall for that. This night was a one-off thing. We could never be a couple.

"Is it the first time you've taken another man's date, too, or are you a serial date snatcher?"

He grinned, eyes lifting a little. "If you go out with Will again, I might end up being a serial date snatcher."

I affected a groan as I reached for my napkin, spreading it over my legs. "I'm curious to know who *you* think would pass the worthy-of-me date test then?"

His eyes glinted, as though he was amused by the question too. "I've yet to find that man, Chloe. And I'm not sure what I'll do if I find him."

Our gazes held each other's over the table, a sudden heat in his eyes. He was all kinds of bad for me. There was emotion in his eyes, and if he was thinking what I thought he was, then we were in trouble.

"Now, Chloe, eat," he ordered.

The food had come out with surprising speed, considering how recently we'd placed the order. I had to keep my jaw from falling when I realized that there were multiple courses.

The peach and burrata salad almost looked too pretty to eat. It was followed by a lobster bisque, which had a welcome dash of brandy.

Sean and I chewed slowly, and with each bite, I tasted a world of flavors I had never imagined. Every time I took a bite, I caught Sean looking at me and my expressions.

"Stop it," I said, nudging his leg playfully with mine.

He nudged my leg right back. "I can't wait to see what you'll do when they bring your burger out."

I couldn't believe him. He'd given me the most amazing orgasm in a restaurant, and here he was, joking with me after. As though things like this happened every day.

I'd never had such playfulness in a date before.

When my burger finally arrived, it looked like it belonged in a fancy food magazine.

The bun was shiny and perfectly toasted with these tiny sesame seeds on top that looked like they had been placed with tweezers. The lettuce and tomato were fresh and crisp, not wilted, like I usually got with my regular meals.

When I took a bite, it was like a flavor explosion. I didn't even care that Sean had stopped eating his sushi to view my reaction. The bun was soft and freshly baked, and the burger was juicy in a way that forced me to close my eyes to savor it.

There was a different sauce on it, too, not the usual ketchup and mustard I was used to, but something special—a secret blend of flavors that made the whole thing dance in my mouth. I hadn't had lunch, and this meal was worth the wait, a million times over.

After I had a few bites, I turned my attention to Sean

and saw that he was watching me with a look on his face that I couldn't comprehend.

His brows drew together as he spoke. "Did you have your lunch today, Chloe?" he asked shrewdly.

"Yes," I said, taking a sip of my wine and feeling embarrassed at his observation. *If you counted a packet of honey roasted peanuts as lunch.*

"Liar," he said immediately, and I felt my face go red.

"How did you know? You didn't see me all day today."

"Were you keeping track of my movements today, Chloe?"

Maybe I was.

"Well," I said, "I didn't want to run into you and have you talk me out of seeing Will."

I'd have been better off if I'd listened to Sean in the first place.

He grunted in response. "The next time you skip a meal, I'm having food delivered to your desk."

Well, if it was from places like this, I wouldn't complain. "I guess it's pretty obvious that I don't eat at such restaurants," I said, looking around. "I didn't know food could taste this rich and tender. Did you grow up eating like this, or did you, too, have your first *oh my gosh, this food is exquisite* moment years before?"

"Years before?"

"Yes." I nodded. "When you were normal."

"You mean, not wealthy?" he asked, cocking one beautiful eyebrow up.

"That's the same thing," I corrected.

He grinned. "My dad owned an employee staffing company, and they were famous for treating their employees to luxurious parties."

"That's why you're so comfortable in such a setting," I said, fixing the position of the spoon on my table before uncrossing my legs to look at him. "I don't think I could ever stop looking awed by a place like this."

He inclined his head. "Though your appreciation for this kind of restaurant reminds me that I take this for granted."

I took a bite of my burger and chewed, wondering. "Are you close to your parents?"

Sean twirled his glass of wine with his fingers. "I wasn't. My dad worked a lot, and my mom wasn't around, so as a consequence, I never spent much time with them. And they aren't around to fix things now."

My lips parted. "Oh, I'm sorry," I said, feeling a swell of regret for bringing it up. I usually hated discussing my dad, too, and avoided those conversations at all costs, and here I was, doing the same thing to others.

"Don't be," he said with a curt nod. "But if you're looking for an answer for why it's been so hard for me to bond with my son, it's there."

"I'm not analyzing you," I corrected. "I was just curious—that's all."

We took a few bites before he spoke.

"I've often wondered about this and never had the right moment to ask you. How have you been after the fallout with your ex?" he asked gruffly.

I groaned. "Are we really discussing him? Today, of all days?"

He didn't budge. "Well, I can't escape the fact that I was reminded of that day today. When I wanted to tell off another man for the way he was treating you."

"You were certainly gallant that day."

"Only that day?" Sean cocked an eyebrow.

I laughed. "I've stopped keeping count. How about that for an answer?"

He grinned. "Good save."

"You were very supportive the night of the gala too. I haven't forgotten that."

"You mean, when we almost lost Lucas?"

My mouth went dry as I thought about it. I nodded.

He took a contemplative sip of his drink before he spoke, his voice brusque. "The last time I asked, your answer was very vague, so I'll ask again. Can you tell me why losing Lucas was so scary for you?"

"Wouldn't it be for any caregiver or adult in charge of a kid?" I asked.

"Chloe, you were trembling in my arms within minutes of thinking he was lost."

I thought back to that night. Had I been trembling? The only time I did remember trembling was the night of Henry's accident, and I never revisited those memories. I didn't want to recount those early days in the hospital with Henry and my increasingly distant dad.

"If I had been trembling, it's because my brother is the only person I've got as family. Losing people is one of my many illogical fears." I tried to keep my voice light.

Sean reached out and put his hand on mine on the table. The touch was gentle and supportive, and when I looked at him, his eyes were steady as they looked back at me.

"Chloe, it's my turn to ask about your parents now. And it's time you answer me honestly."

I nodded. He'd seen me vulnerable enough times already. What was one more time?

"My mom died when I was eight," I said, wishing I could get through this part quickly. "And my dad left us some years later."

Sean cursed under his breath. "Really?"

I nodded. "It's just been Henry and me since I was eighteen and he was thirteen. Losing Henry, especially after I lost contact with my dad, is my single greatest fear. And Lucas, even though he isn't Henry, reminds me of Henry, with all his simplicity and innocence."

Sean drew his hand away, and I could feel him glowering. "If anyone deserves to have a personal life now, it's you," he muttered. "How is Henry now?"

I cheered up. "He's doing much better. Thank you for asking. He's attending a community college nearby, and he's made a new friend recently. There's a lot we are thankful for nowadays, including me having a stable job."

And right there was a reason why I should not harbor hopes of meeting Sean alone again like this. We needed Lucas around to stabilize us.

He nodded. "Well, the next time something goes wrong when you're around Lucas, remember, I'm right there with you. You won't have to deal with your fears alone."

I gazed at him in wonder, surprised at his words, when my phone beeped.

30

CHLOE

It was a message from Will, apologizing for his abrupt departure with a lame, *Something came up.*

The jerk.

Something about the way I was looking at my phone tipped Sean off.

"Did Will contact you again?"

When I looked back at him, he had his answer. I didn't even need to nod.

"I assumed the way he'd treated you meant it was the end of Will and you?" he said with a scowl.

I'd thought so too.

I set my phone down on the table. "I don't know what to think about it all actually," I said.

He frowned. "Will is not the right man for you."

I shook my head. "It doesn't matter. The incident with Will reminded me why I never go out on dates anymore," I said. "So, I wouldn't attempt to go out with him again even if you weren't around, making snarky remarks about Will."

His brown eyes held mine.

Long ago, I'd resolved to never make Henry never feel

like he was a burden to me, but I'd partially understood that my partners might not feel the same. It looked like he was a burden to them, and they always left.

He took another bite of his omakase nigiri sushi before speaking.

"What do you mean, you never go out on dates? You were engaged to Bruce until recently."

I spoke slowly. "I never really was in the dating game before, to be honest. Bruce and I, well, it happened organically because we were around each other so often."

Sean raised his eyebrows, and I continued, "With Bruce, it was our connection with Henry that brought us together. Bruce was working at the therapist's office, and we would meet and chat weekly while I waited for Henry's therapy session to be done. It was a year before I agreed to go out with him. He helped Henry a lot with finding appointments on short notice."

Henry had gotten physical therapy, but I didn't clarify that bit to Sean, allowing him to draw his own conclusions.

He leaned forward, his arms on the table. I could smell his aftershave, something I'd become familiar with at work. Sniffing it here, under soft overhead lights, felt different. It made me look at him differently. To take in the fine angles of his face, the broad cheekbones, and the cut of his jaw and wonder why a man like him was single.

"If Henry's recovered, why won't you be back in the dating game again?"

My stomach dropped. Of course, he was asking me if I would date someone else after fingering me in a restaurant. He was a jerk of the highest order.

"You're smart, beautiful, and unbearably cheerful, even around a grump like me."

His abrupt shift took me by surprise. I would be lying if I

said I wasn't a bit smitten by his unexpected compliment, but I reminded myself that it was just that. Empty words that meant nothing. Words people uttered never meant much, and I was used to that, so I shrugged the compliment off. Besides, Sean was giving me such mixed signals that I was confused.

"Henry *has* recovered, but he still needs me. Most people leave when they realize how much time Henry needs from me. Friends, classmates, dates ..." *Even our dad*. I felt embarrassed when I realized the list was longer than I'd previously accounted for.

"So, you're the sole caretaker for Henry, is it?" Sean asked, his eyes shrewd.

I didn't need to nod this time, but the vulnerability in my expression must have been enough because he didn't press for more.

"Let's stop talking about me," I said, taking a sip of my wine and feeling bold enough to ask a question that was on my lips. "Tell me, Sean, why are you still single?"

"Ah, the tables have turned, I see."

I nodded, grinning. "I get to interrogate you about your single status now."

He swallowed his mouthful, staring at his half-eaten plate for a long moment. "Well ..." He paused, and in that instant, I saw a determined look cross his face and knew he didn't want to go there tonight. "In case you haven't noticed, I don't date," he said lightly.

"Well, in case you haven't noticed, women still find you interesting. Quite a few men frowned at you while their dates ogled you when you walked into this restaurant."

He laughed. "I didn't notice." His voice lowered even more. "Perhaps it's because I was looking at you."

I blushed just as the server came up to clear away our empty plates.

"But to answer your question more honestly, my last relationship was over a year and a half ago. With every woman I dated, I'd start seeing too many similarities between her and my ex-wife. I didn't want those reminders, so I decided to keep things simple. Nothing serious, nothing that lasted longer than a month, and only on weekends."

There was more to why he was against love, but he wasn't opening up completely just yet.

"Moving on to lighter topics, how do you feel about dessert?" Sean asked while I stared at the dessert card.

I read the first item—matcha white chocolate mousse with yuzu sorbet—with interest. I had no idea what yuzu was, and I wasn't going to ask. And what was a ganache au chocolat?

Everything looked delicious on it.

I bet Henry would enjoy this place, I thought wistfully.

Something on my face must have given me away because Sean looked up.

"I'll get two of each of the desserts to go," he told the waiter, who nodded.

I looked at him in surprise.

"It's for you to take home," he said in a gruff voice. "You had the look on your face that said you'd feel guilty for eating it alone."

I would.

"You know, I have a theory about why you're single."

He raised his eyebrows. "Really?"

He pretended to not care, but I could see a hint of fear in his eyes. He had dated quite a few women, I was sure, since his divorce. But none of them had lasted because someone had left a very solid, painful mark.

I inhaled. "You know what I think?" I asked quietly. "I think you're a very competitive man. You need to be in control all the time. But you can't control personal relationships, can you? The success of a relationship isn't only on you. They're on both of you. So, you're afraid of long-term relationships because they remind you of the one time you think you lost control. The one time you think you failed."

He shook his head, his expression a mixture of frustration and longing as he looked back at me. "The only thing your psychological skills do is remind me that I made a good choice in finding you to help me repair my relationship with Lucas."

We were just inches away, unable to tear our eyes off one another. Was it just my presence with Lucas that he was grateful for? My stomach bottomed out, and I felt like I could be sick.

I tore my eyes away from him when Traci swung by.

She had brought us six to-go boxes with delicious smells of raspberry, sugar, and chocolate wafting out of them.

I turned to Sean. "Take half of these home," I told him. "I bet Lucas would enjoy them too."

Sean's voice was hoarse. "You never forget our deal with Lucas, do you?" He sounded like he regretted it. "But hold on. Let me ask Traci to divide this up."

Sean spoke a few words to Traci, and I turned around to pick up my jacket when I noticed the tip that Sean had left.

He left a thousand-dollar tip!

Talking with Sean had been so easy that, for the past hour, I had forgotten the vast disparity between our lifestyles. But this was the reality check I'd needed. I didn't do dinners with men like him.

We stepped out into the cool night air, and the city lights twinkled back at me merrily. Sean's hand was on the lower part of my back as the black car pulled up to us. Once again, I couldn't shake the feeling that I didn't want this night to end.

When we walked out to the waiting car, Sean held the door open for me just as Traci came out with brown paper bags. It looked like she was having a hard time speaking as he placed the bags in the car.

"Oh, thank you, Mr. Tassater," she blurted as she turned to him. "That was so very generous of you."

Sean made sure I was fully in the limo before he shut the door and nodded at her. "Take care, Traci," he said before he walked around to the other side and got in next to me.

He looked ahead at Chris, our driver, and said, "Chloe's home, please."

Chris nodded before he pulled the separator up between him and us.

I turned to Sean, forgetting all about the tip. Sean would drop me off at my doorstep like a perfect gentleman. I felt my heart quicken, but for all the wrong reasons. Henry would answer the door—I was sure of it. Sean would see him, and I didn't want the pity and sympathy that would take over him instantly. It would change the way Sean looked at me, and I didn't want that.

"Could you drop me off a few blocks away from my apartment, please?" I asked.

31

CHLOE

"Nonsense," Sean insisted, his jaw set. "In case you forgot, I'm not Will, Chloe. I'll drop you at your doorstep and make sure you're safely inside before I leave."

My heartbeat sped up at the impossible image of Sean and his towering frame in my living room. That lasted for a delicious few seconds before it was replaced by fear. I hadn't prepared Sean for Henry, and I certainly didn't want Henry to witness yet another date of mine stumbling over words when they saw him.

"My brother," I began, only to be interrupted.

"Your brother will not suspect a thing," Sean said. "I remember. I'll tell him you and I had a fabulous night together and that I hope you'll let me take you out again. And when I'm gone, you can explain to him that you felt nothing for me."

His eyes searched me in the dim interior of the car, and when they found mine and held me in a meaningful gaze, I felt my first pang of yearning.

There was no way I could feel nothing for Sean. I felt a

shit ton of things for him, and this hadn't even been a real date. His gaze was raw and probing.

I could go out with you when I was eighty and still feel something stir in my heart when you looked at me like that.

I cleared my throat. "You're right. I'll explain to Henry that I felt nothing special for you," I said, forcing my voice to sound icy cold.

I saw a flicker of vulnerability in his eyes, a weakening that made him resemble a wounded animal for a second, and when it was gone, it was replaced by his usual hard look. We were stubbornly silent for the rest of the ride, and I tried to curb my heart from admitting that it had feelings. It was as if my age-old habit of distancing myself from my emotions was finally broken.

After fifteen minutes, we were back outside my apartment. Sean opened the car door for me, and I got out, legs wobbly, lips pressed shut as he walked me up to the door. The lights in the apartment were off, and I exhaled, relieved that Henry wasn't back yet. I'd managed to get back before he did, just like I'd promised.

I turned around resolutely at the closed door, ready to wave goodbye right here. I looked up at Sean's soft brown eyes and his fine brown hair, steeling myself for an icy good night when Sean took a step forward. His feet were in front of mine, inches away from mine. His body bent closer, his head dipping dangerously lower. Before I knew it, his hands were cradling my face, his breath hot and heavy on my cheek as words rolled off his lips.

"Maybe I should pretend to be Will for just a little longer then," he said, nuzzling my ear.

This was definitely a terrible idea.

His scent—a deeply male, musky cologne—enveloped me, and his closeness sent my head spinning. I didn't know if I would ever get another night like this with Sean dropping me off at the door.

Before I could rationalize, my arms were encircling his neck while my face was tilting up to his.

Reaching up to those lips.

I didn't want him to be anyone else but him. Tall, arrogant, and stubbornly handsome. And my weakness.

"Kiss me, Sean," I whispered, and it was all the invitation he needed.

32

CHLOE

The kiss was urgent and passionate. His lips were soft and warm, and he kissed me like it was all he'd been waiting to do.

His lips pressed against mine gently, pulling and probing until I let out a soft, needy moan. He slipped his tongue into my mouth as my lips parted and my knees weakened. I wrapped my fingers around his neck and angled my head as I opened my mouth deeply, letting him in.

My heart was beating rapidly, and I couldn't think. All my senses were flooded with Sean. He was all I could taste, see, and think of. And as heat bloomed low in my body, I knew it still wasn't enough.

This was definitely a bad idea, but I'd deal with the consequences later. Tonight, I simply wanted to let myself be a fool for him.

He pulled me closer, his hand moving to cup my face roughly.

He was anything but gentle. He was every bit the possessive man I'd asked him to be. His grip on my face was a bit painful, and he pressed my back against the door like he was afraid I'd escape if he let go. I was not escaping from him. There was nothing more I wanted to do than assure him of that.

I could feel his cock hardening in his pants. When I reached out to palm him, he groaned so helplessly, and I loved it.

This time, I wanted all of him bared to all of me. All of him to touch and feel.

"Come in," I gasped as the kiss spiraled out of control and his lips trailed a hot path down my neck.

I unlocked the door, fumbling with the key for only a moment.

"We're alone," I said, flinging my handbag on the couch as Sean closed the door behind me and strode over.

"Good, because I've wanted to do this for far too long," he said, picking me up.

I wrapped my legs around his waist, kissing intensely, pressing hot, firm lips upon his as I pointed to my room.

When he walked to my room, he dropped me on my bed and stood at the foot, taking me in. I noticed that the wounded look in him was fighting to regain control.

I knelt on the bed in front of him, my hands going for his tie. He kept his intense gaze on my face while my hands undid the knot. He wasn't going to forget about my comment about me feeling nothing special for him.

"You don't need to pretend to be Will for me to do this," I said, pulling his tie off. "I don't need to convince Henry that I felt nothing for the man I was with today," I said, taking his jacket off. It fell to the ground next to his tie.

His hand was stroking the side of my neck, eyes half closed while I undid his buttons slowly. I leaned in to trail kisses on his newly exposed chest. He was all hard muscle with a smattering of dark chest hair and warm skin.

"In fact," I breathed out, "I am so turned on by you that I feel like I'll explode from always being close enough, but not with you."

He uttered a short laugh, his fingers raking through my hair as he pulled my head back and looked at me clearly. "Chloe, you have no idea how turned on I've been by you all night."

My hand trailed down his chest to his pants, where I traced his hard length. As I stroked him, he groaned at the touch, leaning into me, his head coming to rest on my shoulder.

"You'll be the death of me, Chloe," he muttered, his breath coming rapidly as I unzipped his pants and pulled them down.

I wrapped my hands around his back, pulling him to me while he stepped out of his pants. "Well, I'll be gentle about it, sweetheart."

33

SEAN

Chloe kissed me back, urgently tugging me closer as we fell into bed together. Her mouth was soft, and her lips parted easily, deepening the kiss. Tendrils of her hair escaped from her updo and framed her beautiful face. My desire for her overwhelmed me. Her and her alone. No other woman came close.

I felt heady with lust as my hands encircled her waist, pulling her as close to me as possible. Her chest was flush against mine, sending sparks through my body. With her, I'd felt more alive in the past month than I'd felt since my teenage years.

I put my arms under her butt and lifted her on top of me.

"There is no way I could feel nothing for you, Sean," she said, cradling my face in her hands. Her cheeks were flushed, and her expression was vulnerable, like she thought I could hurt her with this knowledge.

I kissed her in response—fervent kisses. I'd been wounded more than I'd expected when she said, back in the car, that she felt nothing. I had told myself that it didn't matter—it couldn't matter—but it had hurt. The woman who was part of my erotic dreams every night was not affected by me? Her admission now soothed a tormented emotion that had started in the car.

"Especially when you stood up for me so gallantly after Will bailed," she said between kisses.

"Stop saying his name," I shot back.

I bit her lip in punishment. Unfortunately, she liked it a little too much, going by how she pressed up against me.

I didn't want that blasted man's name crossing her lips ever again, so I pulled her till she was sitting on my cock, trapped in my boxers. She smelled amazing, and I couldn't wait to have my hungry mouth on her soft skin.

I could feel her warmth through the layers of clothes and moved gently until she closed her eyes at the sudden pleasure. I had found the right spot.

"Uff," she murmured, her voice tender as she ground my cock over my boxers.

I sat up, pressing my lips to her neck, biting down gently while she threw her head back.

"It was killing me all day to think about you going out with Will. I couldn't bear to consider how easy it was for him to do what I'd wanted to do all along," I muttered against her skin, my fingers rubbing up and down the sides of her legs.

She arched her back as my lips trailed down her neck to her cleavage to the delicious dip underneath her blouse.

"Like asking you out," I said, my breath hot and heavy against her skin.

Her eyes were misty and gentle, and her hands were working through my hair, weakening me.

"You've been wanting to ask me out?" she asked softly.

A small creak sounded as the bed moved underneath

her, and the two of us froze before I remembered that her brother wasn't here.

"Henry's going to kill me if he finds out I'm doing this with my boss," Chloe said, her eyes widening as she considered the consequences.

"Hey," I said, pulling her face toward me and pressing a kiss on her forehead and her nose and her cheeks. "There's going to be no bad consequences for whatever happens tonight—do you hear me?"

Her expression was tender as she gazed back at me, and then she pulled me to her. My erection was hard and ready, straining against my boxers.

"I'd been waiting for a sight of you all day today," she whispered into my ear while she ground against me eagerly.

I closed my eyes, stifling a groan, while I palmed her stomach. Her skin was smooth, like satin. Just this fleeting touch sent shivers down my back. I'd been aching to reach up to her breasts all through dinner.

"And you denied me what I desperately wanted," she said.

My breath was ragged against her cheek as I looked at her fiercely, remembering why I'd stayed away.

"I don't want you to go out with Will ever again," I growled back, my fingers slipping under her blouse while her breath was on my shoulder, kissing me blindly.

"I won't," she murmured against my chest, and my heart swelled at those words.

Under her blouse, I found the cup of her bra and slipped my fingers under it. She let out a soft moan, her eyes fluttering shut while I thumbed her pointed nipple. Her skin was warm, and her tit was hard.

"Will was just a distraction to get over you," she gasped,

throwing her head back. "I can't think of any other man but you all day long, and it's fucking frustrating."

I used both hands to open the buttons of her blouse, and my gaze was on her cleavage. I was rock hard by the time I reached the last button and leisurely parted the sides of her blouse, revealing a deep beige lace bra that barely concealed much.

"Fuck, Chloe," I muttered, a heady feeling shooting through me. I was a goner.

She was well endowed, her curves barely contained in that slim fabric. I made a low sound of approval before I turned away, hit by a sudden ache.

The fancy underwear meant she'd been hoping for something to happen with Will tonight.

Chloe must have known what was going through my mind because she put her hands on my cheeks and forced me to look into her eyes. "Hey. Will meant nothing to me." She sat up straight and kissed my lower lip seductively. "A distraction to take my mind off you." She kissed my cheeks and my forehead. "I failed at that, obviously."

Chloe should be free to date whoever she wanted. Especially since I was too busy and overwhelmed to have the emotions required for a relationship.

I took my hand and placed my fingers on her barely covered breasts. Her nipples responded to my touch as I ran my fingers over her bra.

I swiped my tongue over my lips as I said, "I'm going to suggest you stop trying to get over me."

"So, we give in, just this once?"

"And get it out of our systems," I said, my voice husky.

"And after tonight, we'll never do this again," she said as she tugged my boxers off and released my cock.

God, when I'd heard her unravel at the restaurant, I

knew I wanted to hear her come again and again. If tonight was our only night together, I'd better make it memorable.

She ran her hands over my length, feeling the smooth skin, and sighed. She made me feel so good; it was more than I could handle. I pushed her back down on the mattress, and dipping my head, I traced her nipple through her bra. Her bra was damp in a minute while she tried to keep her grip on my cock and failed.

"We have to get rid of this," I said, reaching for the straps of her lace bra and pulling them down.

Her plump breasts slid free. My tongue swirled around one of her nipples, gently nipping her rosy tit while she groaned with pleasure. Arching her back, she ran her hands over the back of my head and pulled me in closer, a delicious whimper escaping her.

"Sean," she pleaded in between ragged breaths.

My fingers roamed her waist, desperate to touch more of her and finding only the soft cloth of her skirt.

"Get this damn thing off," I demanded.

She got off the bed and stood up as she reached for the zipper on her skirt. I sat up, watching her in the moonlight that streamed in through the windows. In a second, her skirt and her bra were off, leaving her in her thong.

"Something's off about this picture." I grinned, swinging my legs off the bed, but staying seated on the edge of the mattress as I pulled her to me. I ran my hands over her thighs, stroking her inner thigh, and getting tantalizingly closer to her core, but holding off.

"Sean, don't tease," she muttered, a warning note in her voice as she put her hands on my shoulders.

"Are you reprimanding your boss?" I asked, turning her to the side and spanking her gently on her bottom.

She bit her lip and looked at me, considering the spank. I'd bet she had never had it done to her before.

"Do it again," she demanded in a whisper.

"Hmm, bossy, are we?" I asked.

"I learned it from someone," she added with a cheeky grin, turning around and letting me feel the smooth and soft butt cheek.

I ran my fingers around her bum, and then I brought my hand down with a sudden smack.

She gasped and stifled it as I rubbed her sore spot instantly.

"How was that?"

"I'm still trying to decide," she muttered.

I chuckled, reaching for her panties. I ran the tips of my fingers up and down the length of her thighs as I fought the desire to get inside her.

There will be time for that soon, I reminded myself when I reached her gentle folds underneath her panties.

Moving the underwear aside, I pushed her wet folds apart, marveling at how ready she was and mentally talking myself out of the desire to push my cock in her.

She pulled me closer, her hands around my neck. "Henry could be back anytime. Let's hurry."

My gaze met hers. "Chloe, I need to take care of you first."

She bit her lower lip. "Me?"

I found her instantly more attractive just then, and I pulled her down back on the bed, on top of me as I kissed her soft lips, parting them to plunge my tongue in.

"Yes," I said in between kisses. "Haven't you had a guy take care of you first?" I muttered, and she shook her head ever so slightly.

I shifted, so that she was on the bed and under me

before I brought my finger to her sex. Circling her bud, I built up the kiss while her breaths came in quicker, ragged.

"With Bruce," she gasped, "It was always missionary and nothing else."

I shook my head. "What a selfish asshole," I muttered as I circled my thumb faster while she whimpered, her eyes cloudy.

"You're fucking beautiful, Chloe," I added, sliding a finger inside her folds. "Your hair, your body, your smile—you look like a gorgeous queen, Chloe, and you deserve to be treated like one," I said.

She arched her back, and I reached for her breast, her nipple now a hard peak. I bit down on it just as I added another finger in her, driving them deeper than I ever had before. She twisted her fingers in my hair, panting with need, and began to move on my hand. She parted her legs even wider, and I knew she was close.

"Only when your pleasure is taken care of will I think about mine, Chloe. And when I do, I want to be inside you, to fuck you until you're screaming my name louder than anything else, and I—only I—will be the one who gets to touch you. Not Will, not anyone else—do you understand?" I demanded.

She drew back from the fast-approaching climax to open her eyes and meet my gaze, her lips parted. She nodded faintly.

"Go," I muttered, pressing my thumb down on her swollen clit and driving my fingers deeper and deeper with every plunge. "I want to feel you come, Chloe. I'll take care of you."

I began to suck deeper, pulling at her tit harder while she rode my hand. Pretty soon, she was trembling, calling out my name as she became limp in my arms.

"Oh, Sean," she muttered weakly in the silence with her eyes closed while I grinned.

Pushing a strand of hair off her face, I asked, "Yes, beautiful?"

She opened her eyes instantly at that word, a faint blush creeping across her cheeks. She lifted a hand and cupped the side of my face.

"Yes, that's my name for you," I said.

"Why are we bothering with pet names if this is just a onetime thing?" she asked.

"Because you're far too good for me to be satisfied with just one time. You're the kind of woman a man would want again and again with the intensity of a person craving water in a desert. Until he becomes a slave to you. The kind of woman any sensible guy would stay away from.

"And luckily for you," I continued, trailing kisses on her face, her neck, "I left my senses back at the restaurant we dined at." I planted a kiss in the dip between her breasts.

She laughed, propping herself up on her elbow as she turned to me sideways. "Well, we aren't done yet," she said as she reached for my cock.

It jerked at the touch, and I groaned. Oh, how I'd been craving her touch. She pushed me gently back on the bed and straddled my knees, her hand firm around my hard length.

"Let me—" she began when her expression changed. She froze and looked out the window, where I only saw the inky-black sky. "Did you hear that?" she asked, getting off me.

I felt frustration at the loss of her warmth on me and began shaking my head when I heard it too. Someone was jiggling a key in the apartment's door.

Chloe turned to me, eyes wide. "Henry's back."

I helped her off the bed, and we stood up, finding our clothes scattered at various spots around the bed. She got her panties and skirt on, and I found the bra and the blouse.

"Let me," I said as she reached for them.

She looked surprised and nodded, turning with her back to me. The bedroom door was closed, and I heard someone in the living room while I slipped her bra straps through her arms. Resisting the urge to fondle her heavy breasts, I clipped the hooks on the back and helped her put her blouse back on. When she looked up, her cheeks were crimson, and her expression was flushed.

"Thank you," she muttered, and I nodded.

An odd sound came from the kitchen, the sound of a crash, and Chloe looked surprised.

"Go," I said. "I'll join you in a minute."

34

CHLOE

Feeling concerned, I spun around and opened the door.

Until a few moments ago, I couldn't wait to have Sean be powerless under my touch. To hear him when he came. I wanted him with an intensity that terrified me.

But now, all thoughts about sex fled my mind. Henry was back. I ran out of my bedroom and saw movement in the kitchen.

As I watched, a white kitchen plate went crashing to the ground, breaking into pieces before it was followed by another.

Crash! Crash!

In another moment, clear glasses flew across the room and hit the wall, splintering to pieces.

In the center, Henry sat slumped in his wheelchair. His chest was heaving, his nostrils were flared, and he wore an expression of righteous anger. He moved his wheelchair over the broken pieces and reached for another plate from the counter when I called out to him.

"Henry," I said, stepping over the shards of glass and

ceramics on the floor as I went up to him. I knelt down and put an arm around his shoulders.

He didn't look at me, and I knew instantly this was one of Henry's worst outbursts.

I ran through my mental list of what could have possibly set him off. College ... grades ... classes? Nope. I couldn't think of any reason any of those would upset him so much. But ... was it something to do with his friends perhaps?

It had happened in the past. Henry's accessibility issues meant waiting for the infrequent bus for him to get around instead of the subway, and sometimes, some of his friends "forgot" to invite him to things. It made me mad, but Henry usually put on a brave, understanding front.

"What is it?" I asked, kneeling down to look him in the eye. "Are you okay?"

"No, I'm not okay," he announced, spinning around and staring at the fridge. "I'm stuck and tired of being me."

I followed his gaze and saw a picture on the fridge. A photograph of him with some of his old school friends was taped to it —good friends who had moved out of New York recently.

"Ronan and the others from class went to the mall and asked me to join them. We took the bus, and it was good. No issues there. The problems arose when we got to one of the shops that Ronan wanted to buy a shirt from."

I closed my eyes. I had an idea what could have happened.

"The displays on the rack were too close to one another," Henry explained, confirming what I'd feared. His pupils dilated as his fingers clenched on the next kitchen plate, still whole. "A rack of shirts caught in my wheel, and I tried to maneuver my way past it, but I toppled the entire rack."

It wasn't the first time this had occurred.

I watched, wondering if he was going to fling this plate on the ground too.

"You know what the worst part was?" Henry continued, the knuckles of his hands white as he clenched his fist around the ceramic plate.

The way someone reacted to him, I guessed.

"It was what the saleswoman said," Henry raged. "She spoke to me like I was a freaking five-year-old! *Oh, aren't you clumsy?* She told me I needed to be more careful, but I could see from her face that she was definitely irritated and wanted to say much more."

I hung my head.

"I'm tired of people being condescending to me just because I'm in a damn wheelchair. I'm not even spoken to as an adult!"

He raised his arm, ready to fling this plate on the ground, and I retreated, raising my arm in front of my face when I heard a noise behind us.

When I looked up, I saw a shadow darken the hallway and saw Sean. He had heard everything.

"You'll want to hold off on that," Sean said, looking at Henry as he walked in and pulled me a few steps back. He saw Henry's questioning look. "I don't want the broken pieces to ricochet off the wall and hit your sister," he said, his arm around my waist.

"I'm Will, by the way," he said, extending an arm to the surprised Henry, who took it, shaking it in a stupefied way that told me Henry had completely forgotten about my date. "I was out on a date with Chloe, and I'm just dropping her off."

Henry turned to me. "I'm sorry," he said to me. "I completely forgot about that."

His gaze went to Sean's arm around my waist. I tried to ignore the delicious feeling of Sean's touch and failed.

"Here," Sean said, bending to pick up the broken pieces off the ground. "Let me help."

Surprised, I joined Sean, bending down to pick up something just as he did, and our foreheads bumped lightly into each other.

We laughed, rubbing our heads, as Henry watched on, looking slightly mollified.

"Chloe, I feel terrible," Henry blurted out. "This was your night out, and I ruined it."

I shook my head, but Henry continued to speak. He turned to Sean, who had a questioning look on his face.

"Chloe's not someone with time for a personal life. She works too hard. Whenever she's home late, it's always because she had to work. Her abysmal work hours are the reason she can't complete the PMP certification course, like she wants to." He looked disgusted. "Her new boss is a taskmaster."

I coughed loudly, and Sean turned to me, a look of amusement taking over.

Uh-oh.

"Really?" he asked Henry, narrowly avoiding stepping on one of the broken pieces of a plate. He picked up another broken piece.

Henry rolled over to me on his wheelchair, extending his hand so I would follow him. This time, I gave in, keeping him company in the hallway while I watched Sean in frustration.

Why was my boss cleaning up my floor?

"You must hear Chloe cursing her boss quite often then," Sean added, his eyes full of humor.

The goose. He was deliberately ferreting out juicy details to taunt me with later, no doubt.

"Not really," Henry said as Sean picked up the last few broken pieces of glass from the ground. "Even on that night when I was running a fever, she gave me some meds and ran around the city, looking for some ridiculous Superman figurines for him without a single curse word."

"Spider-Man," Sean corrected immediately, but he gave me a look of surprise.

Henry looked at Sean. "She told you about that, huh?" he said. "Her boss is quite a crazy man. He doesn't believe in letting his employees have a personal life."

"I'm sorry—that you weren't well that night." Sean's shoulders tensed as he walked out of the kitchen. He shot me a quick look that implied he understood me a lot better.

Henry waved a hand in the air genially. "Thank you, but it was a one-off thing. My doctor had changed my meds to a generic one, and I happened to get one of the side effects immediately. Chloe got me on the branded medicine, and her rat of a boss never sent her out on foolish errands at night again."

Another bemused glance from Sean to me. "She told me about the ridiculous boss, but not about your fever that night," he said, a gentler note to his voice. "It almost sounds like you need to confront your lousy boss, Chloe. Put him in his place."

I gave him a small grin. "You mean knock him down a peg or two? I'll give it a shot."

"Chloe never brings up my health issues if she can avoid it," Henry said, gesturing for Sean to sit down, and I watched as I followed them to the living room. "And usually, my health issues don't trouble me much. It's only isolated days like ... well, today." He looked contrite and turned to

Sean. "I'm sorry about tonight. I ... I just got back from a night out with friends, and it had not gone well."

Before Sean could respond, Henry turned to me. "I'm sorry, sis."

I attempted a shrug, but I felt tears prick at my eyes. For a minute back there, Henry's anger had scared me. I hadn't realized how he had been keeping his emotions pent up, and only nights like this were when he let loose.

"It's okay," I said, walking over to him and bending down to give him a hug.

He hugged me back, arms around my shoulders, and as I closed my eyes, he said, "You're trembling."

Sean helped me to the couch while Henry rolled back to the kitchen, where he put the kettle on.

In a minute, Henry made me a cup of chamomile tea while Sean went back to the parked car to grab the box of desserts.

"We've got some pastries here," Sean said.

I walked into the kitchen and dug around for silverware and intact plates, trying to hide my emotions. I wanted to cry. I'd been so close to having the perfect night, and it had been ruined. Just like every other fun bit of my life.

For the next few minutes, Henry dug into the desserts in the living room, and I watched him eat in silence. He'd chosen the ganache au chocolat, and I managed a smile when I saw him close his eyes after the first delicious bite.

I turned to Sean as he stood close to me.

"Don't you want some dessert too?" he asked, but I shook my head.

"I'm not hungry. I'm just ... shocked. I've never seen him this upset before. He's never broken dishes before," I murmured, my voice low while I picked up the broom and swept up the kitchen floor.

Sean's gaze went back to Henry, who was searching for the TV remote, and I held my breath, waiting for the inevitable response that usually followed. A sudden flurry of apologies, followed by a hurried exit. I prepared myself for Henry's crestfallen face when he realized yet another of my acquaintances was beating a hasty retreat.

The TV turned on to one of Henry's favorite soccer games, and he settled in.

Right now would be the time that Sean would make his exit. Polite, but one that clearly showed that he knew where his place was in this scene. Out the door.

"Is that Manchester United?" Sean asked, nodding toward the TV.

Henry nodded.

Sean's gaze fell to the object on the coffee table—a referee whistle, I realized.

"That's a soccer whistle, isn't it?" Sean asked.

What is Sean doing, dragging this moment out?

Henry looked at it and then laughed. "Yes. I don't play soccer anymore, but before my accident, I loved to. I still hope to be a referee someday."

My gaze flicked back to Sean again, but this time, it was just him and his conversation with Henry.

"I've never understood soccer," Sean admitted. "I was a placekicker on our school's football team and failed to understand so many of the rules that I was kicked out soon. The one time I tried to follow soccer, I had to give up when I couldn't understand the offside rule."

Henry laughed at that, but I could see his eyes light up with the challenge. "I could explain it to you if you'd like," he said, pushing his wheelchair back. He turned to me. "If that's okay with you?"

I opened and shut my mouth a few times. Sean had just

witnessed a scene that was worse than the one Will had been a spectator to. And he was choosing to stay put? It was tough on anyone, to be honest, if you just walked in and saw a person having a meltdown over a health condition that was not in their control.

As though confirming my suspicions, Sean answered Henry, "I'd love to hear it."

In a few minutes, Henry and Sean were in a full-blown discussion that involved the saltshaker, a couple of pens, and an action figure from the mantelpiece. There were a lot of questions from Sean and laughter and enthusiasm from Henry as he explained the goals and positions on the field.

I was officially blown away by the scene in my living room.

I watched as Sean shouted, "Offside!" as Henry, the pretend referee, moved his players around their imaginary field on the dining table and signaled for an offside offense by raising his miniature flag.

This was my first glimpse of Sean as someone more than just an arrogant boss. When they were done a few minutes later, Sean ended by inviting Henry over to watch the next soccer game with him that weekend.

Henry was thrilled, but I tried to tamp down the nervousness in my belly. Was it a good idea to see Sean again after tonight?

I watched as Henry waved goodbye to Sean.

I didn't miss the happy look on Henry's face before he disappeared into his bedroom. He had enjoyed the last few minutes, talking soccer with Sean.

Sean turned me around, pulling me to his chest before I had time to blink. I gazed into his beautiful brown eyes for a second before his head dipped and he was kissing my lips. His hand wrapped around my waist, and my legs trembled under his touch. I would never get used to the way my body reacted to his.

His lips were soft, full, and sweet—like sugar. I could never tire of kissing them. We kissed as if we'd been starved for each other for years, and his hand slipped to my butt, giving it a tight squeeze.

I was hopelessly lost to him.

When we finally broke apart, panting, even Sean's eyes were dazed with passion.

His forehead touched mine as we closed our eyes for a moment, leaning against each other to catch our breaths.

I'd been happy to see Henry getting along with Sean, but I didn't want to get my hopes up. I didn't want to imagine Sean and I could get together again.

I couldn't bear to get close to someone else, only to get tossed aside later.

I needed to stop this now, before things got out of hand with Sean.

"What's with that pained look?" Sean asked, biting down playfully on my ear.

I looked up at him, relieved that I didn't have to pretend. "I'm sad our night ended so abruptly. But thank you," I said, recalling Sean's kind offer to Henry. It was more than I'd ever expected. "That was really nice of you."

Sean looked at me long and hard. "You didn't expect me to care about soccer?"

"Well," I said, "no one has shown this much interest in Henry's likes."

Sean shook his head. "That's ridiculous, and it only makes me fearful of the kind of people you've been associating with, Chloe. Henry is fun and smart. He's got a good knack for explaining things. I could see him as a soccer coach someday."

I knew Henry's hopes involved something along those lines, and I was always hesitant to encourage him in case his dreams didn't work out. Henry had never had much success in setting up a wheelchair soccer league, and I didn't want more disappointment for him in the future.

"Besides, I would say tonight deserves a redo, don't you think?" Sean asked. "Especially since you promised to take your boss down a peg or two."

I stared up at him, my mouth falling open. "I knew you wouldn't let it go easily."

"Your words, not mine," Sean said, the edge of his lips tilting up in a smile before he looked serious again. "I understand now, Chloe," he said, and I watched him warily.

"What do you understand?" I asked him, feeling overwhelmed. Just how much had he gotten from this evening's interaction?

"I understand why you don't date," Sean said. "I understand your commitment to Henry. And why you feel like it's impossible to juggle your loyalty to Henry with having a personal life of your own."

I'd always believed Henry was an extension of me. Especially after Dad left us and it was just us against the world. Even though Henry and I were two different people, I was fiercely loyal to him, determined that nothing would come between us.

What had happened with Sean tonight was out of the ordinary, and I knew how to set things right.

"It's okay if you want to cancel our Thursday evening bonding exercises with Lucas," I told him. "I'll find a way to explain it to Lucas—"

"Why would I need to do that?" Sean growled.

I stared at him. "You really mean to continue working with me after what happened between us tonight?"

Sean nodded. "Nothing changes after tonight. I meant what I said about needing you and your help with Lucas. I keep my word, Chloe. Just like I said I would make sure you didn't go without a job."

My breaths came in faster as Sean took a step closer to me. We were next to the doorway, out on the sidewalk, and the night outside was cool and quiet. He was moving in, closer and closer, until I put my hand on his chest, stopping him.

I could spend another night with Sean. What would it matter? We would never get serious. The worst that could happen was this experience would ruin other men for me—because no one else could hold a candle to Sean. Ruining my future love life with anyone else wasn't a problem. Because I was never leaving Henry—ever. So I had nothing to lose by giving Sean another night.

"On one condition," I said.

35

SEAN

"What is it?" I asked, frustrated. I could feel the arousal in my body again, just by standing next to her, and I hated that I had to fight it every time I was around her.

"I'm concerned about—"

"Our professional relationship?" I asked, finding the words bitter on my tongue.

Our jobs had thrown us together, but right now, I hated that it was the one logical reason we shouldn't be together.

"That night when I thought I'd lost Lucas, when you consoled me and held me tight, I knew I was doomed. Because I liked it a lot more than I should have."

"I liked it too." The words slipped out of me automatically. "And in reality, I wanted to do a lot more."

She bit her lip. "After tonight, well, I'll be seeing you at work tomorrow. And outside of work to help you with Lucas. We keep running into each other a lot."

"What's wrong with that?" I growled, suddenly angry that she was threatening to take away what had been the highlight of this week. Seeing her after work.

She gave me a frustrated sigh. "There's plenty wrong with this, and you know it. Even if I desperately want to wave those problems away, I can't."

I reached for her, putting my arms around her back and drawing her closer. Her feet met mine, and she looked up at me, vulnerability written all over her face.

"You're right when you said earlier that I need to be in control, Chloe. And I think I found a way to be in control and for the two of us to still get together."

She raised her eyebrows while I grazed my hands up and down her arms.

I was furious that Will had ever had a chance with her. I was seething at the idea that she would give someone so unworthy of her a shot.

And while she could never be mine, I knew I could do a far better job of worshipping her, both inside the bedroom and out. Even if she wasn't meant for me.

"I know you said you don't date," I began. "That you want to give Henry a lot of your time. As it is, I don't have the emotions for a serious relationship, and you don't have the time for a serious relationship." I looked at her, her gaze curious and waiting. "But what if this was about having fun?"

She frowned. "Fun?" she asked while my hands stopped at her wrists.

I took her palms in mine. "Yes, nothing serious. But we see each other outside of work, when we can. I promise it isn't going to affect our working relationship. And, yes, we can keep it to Thursdays if that's the only day you can give me."

She drew in a deep breath as she considered it, her fingers intertwining with mine. The movement was trusting and comforting, a gesture that said she was in this with me. I was sure she wanted it, too, despite a hundred reasons, not the least of which was her need to give her brother her complete attention. For a brief moment, I felt torn, wishing I could have her complete time and attention before reminding myself this wasn't a competition.

I gave her another kiss, lingering on her soft lips, enjoying the feel of her breath on my skin. Her scent was so seductive that I wished I could stay.

I could see the longing in her eyes, too, but mixed in with some restraint. I ran my thumb down her neck, and she shuddered against me before I reluctantly stepped away.

"You don't need to answer right now. As you know, I'm leaving for DC for the Global Innovation Summit tomorrow morning. Just think about it while I'm away, Chloe."

She hesitated and then nodded. "I'll think about it, Sean."

36

CHLOE

When I woke up the next morning, I felt amazing. It took me a while to place the source of my happiness, and when I realized it was because of Sean, my smile spread even wider. When I made to stand up, I realized the bed was wobbly, leaning to one side. Easing out of bed with as little movement as possible so as to not hit the creaky leg, I stood up and surveyed the wooden frame.

This bed was easily thirty years old.

Thank goodness it hadn't given way last night.

My face flaming red, I walked over to my desk and sat down, trying to think of how I could answer Sean's question. I very much wanted to, but I was reluctant to take my attention away from Henry. The only good thing I could think of was that I didn't have to lie to Sean about my anxiety.

I walked out to the kitchen and made a cup of coffee for myself while noting that Henry was still asleep. I went back to my room, and after shutting the door, I sat down at my desk. Needing to talk this out with someone who wasn't

Henry or Sean, I picked up my phone. In a minute, Tess answered the video call. Going by the brown coffee cup on her counter, she was getting ready for work, just like me. Her hair was in a side part with soft waves, and I noticed a new nose ring on her today.

"You did what?!" she exclaimed when I told her my situation after we'd spent a few minutes chatting about her nose ring—a new gift from her fiancé.

"Tess, I made out with Sean, my boss," I explained, feeling embarrassed.

I leaned forward, noticing Tess's light-green eyes flickering with confusion. I couldn't hide the romantic details of my life from her; the woman knew how much I hated going on dates. She'd been rooting for me to get out there and see someone. I owed her the truth.

"I had a wonderful evening with my boss, and I don't know what to make of it."

Tess swallowed and stared at me.

"Where?" she asked finally, a sudden waver in her tone. The enormity of the situation hadn't escaped her either.

I put my head in my hand. "We started off at a restaurant in Tribeca and ended up at my place," I admitted, feeling ridiculous. "Henry even called my boss a rat to his face. And Sean didn't run for it. He stayed, talked to us, and before he left, he asked me if we could have a not-serious relationship. And I don't know what to think about it."

Why is the one man I feel attracted to the only man I ought to steer clear from?

When I looked up after a brief silence, Tess was taking a sip from her cup, a far-off look in her eyes. "Well, apart from the ridiculous name Henry called your boss last night, what are you worried about?"

My mouth went dry as I considered the possibilities—

my anxiety ramping up every time I considered letting a man into my life, getting fired if Sean and I were found out, losing out on career opportunities because I'd be accused of sleeping with the boss to get ahead.

I took a sip of my coffee. "There's a lot, to be honest."

"I think you should go for it though. If he weren't your boss, would you still want to go out with him?"

I reflected on it, and a newfound sense of relief took over. "Yes," I breathed out.

Tess smiled. "Then, what's holding you back? He's not going to be your boss forever. You said it yourself, right? Amelia will be back at her job. If you and Sean still want to be together after six months, you'll be free to do so."

I blinked. I'd completely forgotten that this was a temporary job.

I'd been up front with Sean—a fling was all I could offer. I had no emotional strength left to ever get serious about a man again. If I had a fling with Sean, it would be easier to make a clean break when I stopped seeing him. Our professional time had a deadline, and once we stopped seeing each other privately, I'd never haunt the same restaurants or the same clubs.

I thought back to the kiss at the doorstep last night. To the way his hand had roamed my back, pulling me to him. And the way my breasts grazed his chest, awakening a desire in me that was so intense that when he pulled away, all I could think of was getting in bed with him again.

I'd felt free, I'd felt relaxed, and more importantly, I'd felt wanted. Romantically, sexually. I hadn't felt wanted that way in ages.

"Thank you," I said, feeling relieved. "That was just the pep talk I needed, Tess."

She gave me a thumbs-up before demanding that I keep her posted and hung up.

Twenty minutes later, I left for work with my heart singing.

I checked my phone for the nth time that day. It was only the first day that Sean had been away from work, and while my day was lighter with fewer tasks, I missed his presence in the office. The gruff voice that became even gruffer when he spoke to me. The way his icy-brown eyes would pause on me before he had to turn to answer his phone. The well-defined jaw that made me compare him to Chris Hemsworth.

When I took the elevator to my floor, I remembered talking to him about his problems with Lucas, but also the way his fingers had grazed over mine while we stood side by side in the elevator.

This is more than missing, I thought, feeling embarrassed as the doors opened and I got out.

I remembered his words from the night before, asking me to go out with him. This turned out to be more than I could have expected—a fling with a man like him. Because I didn't expect anything more from men. Dad had made me suspect that commitment and responsibility weren't a man's forte, and Bruce had confirmed it.

I wasn't just afraid of dating. I was afraid of any kind of relationships, including friendships. I was afraid of asking too much from the people around me. I hated hearing no or being dismissed. Especially when I asked for so little in the first place.

A few hours earlier, Sean had texted me, asking me how I was, and I hadn't responded yet. I was nervous about bringing up the question he'd asked me last night.

I stared at my personal notepad on my work desk. The

first page was my New Year's resolution for this year. There were three things I wanted—to get out of financial debt, to make time for myself to complete the PMP certification course, and to have fun.

Financial, professional, and personal goals. I hadn't done the first two yet, and we were halfway through the year. How about fun? It sounded good.

I responded to Sean, telling him about my day and also slipping in a line that I was looking forward to Friday. The day he'd be back in New York. The day I'd tell him that I was ready for fun.

For the rest of the day, I checked my messages every ten minutes, eager for a message from Sean. It was frustratingly five p.m. before I got an email from Sean.

Sean: *Please have five bouquets of flowers delivered to this address.*

I stared at it, my heart beating rapidly. Was he really having flowers delivered to someone else?

I thought again about that kiss. Was Sean regretting it already? Now that he'd seen how different my life was from normal?

I closed my eyes tight.

There's something wrong with me, I thought as I picked up the phone and made the order for the bouquets.

Who is Sean giving them to?

I looked at the address and realized it was near New Jersey.

I gulped. Did Sean have someone else he was seeing? Was this his breakup routine with her while he got on with me?

I've sent the flowers, I texted him back an hour later. *Anything I should know?*

Feeling my mouth run bitter and dry, I wrapped up work

and took the elevator down to the lobby while I waited for a response from him.

Central Park was in the distance, all lush and green, and the sidewalks were bustling with people getting ready for their runs. I couldn't help but remember the first time Sean and I had met at Central Park with Lucas.

I didn't hear back from Sean for a while after that text. It was after six, and he could have been in meetings with other people, at a bar or something. I wished I could've accompanied him to the conference. At least I could've had a reassuring smile from him to stop my brain from spinning out of control.

The air was crisp while I raced to the subway station, a gentle breeze sweeping around me and the sky clear in the distance.

That evening, when I was at home, I got a response from Sean.

Sean: *Can we talk when I'm back?*

Which meant the answer wasn't pretty.

I groaned and hung my head. I should've known better than to think of dating my boss. He was confident, handsome, moved around in social circles that I had no way of fitting into. Everything I didn't have. Going out with him had been a dream—that was all.

I settled back on the couch and turned the TV on. Henry was in his room, on the phone with the campus safety team about a lack of fire and lockdown drills this semester, and I had no one for company but myself.

The doorbell rang, and I forgot all my worries in excitement.

It's Sean, I told myself, practically bounding to the door before I realized how stupid this was. He was in DC.

When I flung the door open, it definitely wasn't Sean.

My heart sank to my stomach when I saw Will.

He was looking at me, a contrite expression on his face. And he was holding flowers.

37

CHLOE

I stared at Will, my heart beating rapidly. I felt let down. I wanted to see Sean badly. I just realized the full extent of my want right now.

I was still trying to reconcile my disappointment that this wasn't Sean when Will spoke.

"Chloe, I need to talk to you," he said.

I blinked.

Sean was the handsomer, more powerful, and dominating version of Will. Which meant I needed to keep my heart locked up and away before I began anything with Sean.

My body definitely wanted to be back in his arms. I wanted to be touched by Sean and caressed by him. But I sure as hell would not let myself go through heartbreak again.

"Is everything okay?" I asked, taking a step back and looking at Will.

He ran his hand through his hair. "I'm so sorry, Chloe. I thought it would be a good idea to talk to you in person. I want to apologize for the way I behaved last time."

I didn't really care for his apology. The man who had fled at Henry's rightful outburst? Argh. But I did want him to make the effort—to hear him admit that he'd hurt me.

"Well, go on," I said, crossing my arms across my chest.

"I behaved like a fool, leaving you at the doorstep when you were ready for me, and for that, I apologize. I panicked."

He waited, shuffling his feet, as though he wanted me to tell him all was forgiven.

"I'm not good with people who have a temper. When I saw your brother angry and swearing that night, I didn't want to enter that situation. I didn't want to deal with the possibility of his anger directed at me. I was just an accountant, looking for a fun date."

I could feel his earnestness, but I was long past forgiving men for treating me badly. I reached for the door handle, ready to shut the door, when Will stopped me.

"Walk with me, please?" Will asked, placing the bouquet in my hand.

I held it, thinking of the five bouquets of roses and orchids that Sean had ordered for someone else. What an over-the-top romantic gesture that was. I couldn't help but feel envious.

This one felt like it belonged to my world. An apology bouquet that he'd probably bought at the grocery store. A bouquet from someone who ate at the same restaurants I did, who shopped the clearance racks first, and who worried at the thought of the bills at the start of a month.

But Will had abandoned me once already. I had felt like I was drowning in icy-cold waters when I saw the empty doorway on our supposed date night. The bitter taste of being stood up at my doorstep was not something I'd ever forget. I'd had to fight my way back up to normalcy once already when Bruce had abandoned me while I was still in my wedding dress.

Was Sean getting ready to abandon me too? Had he met someone else at the conference—someone who lived in New Jersey? Was that what the five bouquets were about? I'd been so guarded around Sean, showing him very little of my life, and he still behaved so inexplicably. His curt text messages had hurt.

I knew Will's bumbling apologies were a clear sign he'd disappoint me again—and I wouldn't be surprised.

I nodded, swallowing hard. "I can do a short walk around the block," I said.

I grabbed a coat and accompanied Will for a walk.

38

SEAN

I waved goodbye to Tanya at the doorstep and turned and walked down the stairs and into the waiting car.

My time apart from Chloe had been frustratingly empty. I felt a void I couldn't explain. I understood her so much better after our night at her home, and instead of putting an end to our time together, like I had originally planned to, I had asked her for more.

As my car pulled away, I looked back at the red brick building, which was the Beatling Nursing Home for memory care. On the upper-right floor, through the window, I could see a faint image of a woman in white, watching me, and I turned away before Mom could see that I'd seen her. Before she could see my guilt.

Mom.

What would Chloe think of me?

It was partly the reason I hadn't been able to answer her text honestly.

I'd come here to this nursing home to meet with Tanya, the personal caretaker I'd assigned for my mother. Mom was well taken care of. I called Tanya weekly to get updates about my mom's health. This time, Tanya had called me during my conference on Friday to let me know Mom kept asking about my dad.

"She's been demanding to see him," Tanya had explained. "To the point where she tried to make her escape from our facility this past week. Is there anything I can do to calm her down?"

It had been five years since Dad's death, and there was no way I could help Mom. I didn't really want to either—not when the woman had cheated on Dad and broken his heart before leaving us to live with another man.

She'd never paused to consider her son or ex-husband or how heartbroken we were when the one person who had tied us together left.

Thinking back, I could understand leaving a partner, but leaving your kid? Thank goodness Helen hadn't abandoned Lucas. It was why I hadn't fought Lucas's choice to stay with his mom, if that was what he wanted. It was what I'd wanted as a kid and never gotten.

But as I thought of Tanya's question and wondered what I'd do if Mom's next attempt at leaving this facility worked, I remembered an incident from before Mom had left us.

In those days, Dad would always surprise Mom by buying her multiple bouquets of flowers to mark special events. Birthdays, anniversaries, et cetera. Mom loved flowers so much that Dad would joke that our house always smelled as fragrant as a garden in full bloom.

"I think I know what to do," I had told Tanya before texting Chloe. "I'm sending something over for Mom today. Could you please make sure she gets it delivered to her room?"

The flowers had helped, and after my conference was done, I took my private jet over to New Jersey to meet Tanya and get further updates on Mom's health that week.

"She's smiling now," Tanya said when I showed up at the facility, and there was a very pregnant pause, as though Tanya almost wanted to say, *You could go in and see her.*

I never did. I hadn't visited Mom in her room for a few years now, and still, today, I couldn't bring myself to face Mom with a fake smile.

"Back to the airport, sir?" Chris asked while I mused on it.

I shouldn't care about Chloe. I didn't really. It was lust clouding my thoughts. I desperately needed her warm body in my bed. I wanted to bury myself in her, bite down on her neck, and feel her clench around my cock while she came.

I put my head in my hands. I was fucking miserable and didn't know what to do.

Chloe had messed me up more than any other woman in the past.

I had initially planned to fly back to DC. I'd wanted to meet Mark Waldorf, an executive known for his retail brilliance. I'd briefly met him earlier that day and wanted to hear his take on creating unique and immersive customer experiences over dinner or drinks tonight.

But we were closer to New York now, I thought longingly.

Chris could just as well drive me up to Manhattan instead of Teterboro Airport. I could leave the jet in the private hangar. The past two days had been frustrating. I wanted to see Chloe, but I also didn't want to tell her about my mom. Because I knew the truth would be shocking for her to hear. She felt her dad's absence so keenly that she simply couldn't see things from my perspective.

I hated having a past that I couldn't come to terms with. *A normal childhood without complications that asked to be hidden would've been great, Mom and Dad.* Instead, I had a past that Chloe would no doubt balk at if she knew the whole truth about how I avoided my mother.

Thinking about that made me angry. If only I'd had a normal childhood with normal love and affection from my parents, perhaps personal relationships would have been easier for me. Instead, all I had was the feeling I'd been cheated out of something.

Besides, what Chloe and I had was strictly physical. We had both decided that emotions had no place between us. Why was I thinking about coming clean with her about my anger with my mom?

"All okay with Ms. Tassater?" Chris asked quietly as we drove.

I met his gaze in the rearview mirror and nodded. I'd almost forgotten that Chris knew my mother—he'd worked for us when Mom and Dad were still together. Chris knew what life had really been like. He didn't look up to Mom with crazy fervor that some of her old friends did, which was helpful for me. When my first few companies had gone public and I got thrust into a more elite world, Chris was one of the few people I'd thought of when I realized I needed someone I could trust. Just like Chloe now. No matter how briefly I'd known her, I trusted her.

"Yes, Chris. Please take me back to Manhattan," I said, sitting back in my seat, relieved at last. "To Chloe's home."

There was no more conflict in my mind. I'd meet Mark Waldorf later. He could wait. Meeting Chloe couldn't.

I stirred in my seat while Chris drove me, feeling restless. I was back in Manhattan one day earlier than I'd originally planned. The pull to go back to New York, to see Chloe again, was impossible to ignore.

The thing that I couldn't help notice at Chloe's home was how the things she owned were old and faded. The stained couch, wooden chairs with scratches and marks on their legs, and a creaky bed. I had known that Chloe's financial situation wasn't great, but visiting her at her home had really emphasized the fact that we were from entirely different worlds. I now understood her reaction to the venue and the food at the dinner I'd taken her to and the clothes I'd sent her for the gala.

I was starting to feel worried over what I'd asked of her, especially when I thought of how the news and media judged women so harshly if the truth was ever found out. Chloe's professional relationship with me wasn't the best foot to start things off. She needed to stay in her job to make sure she could financially support Henry, which meant we really needed to be discreet about this.

If it hadn't been for the conference and being away from her, I might have backtracked on my proposal to her. But the speed with which I requested Chris to drive to Manhattan told me enough. I couldn't stay away from her.

Chloe and I haven't even started dating yet, I reminded myself.

Why was I so restless to speak with her—face-to-face, where I could see her body shake with laughter or smell her jasmine-tinged perfume? When I had been away, I'd missed that.

My breath caught in my chest. What the fuck was I thinking? I put my head in my hands for a moment and put a stop to my thoughts.

We are still strictly physical, I assured myself.

I called her on the way, partly to convince myself that she wasn't different. What I felt for her wasn't unlike what I'd felt for the women I slept with in the past. But she didn't answer. I waited for ten minutes, and I tried again.

This time, she answered, and before I could say hello, I heard her sobbing into the phone.

39

SEAN

This was not the sound I had expected to hear from her. Heavy, shaking breaths and jumbled words. She wasn't making any sense.

"Chloe, are you okay?" I asked, sitting up in my seat and getting worried.

Chris met my gaze in the rearview mirror, concerned.

"I'm not able to reach Henry," Chloe blurted out between breaths.

"Okay, we'll find him," I said, telling myself that this situation wasn't as bad as I'd thought it was.

"I saw it on the news twenty minutes ago. There's a fire in his college. And I'm afraid Henry is trapped—because why else wouldn't he answer his phone? His wheelchair can't make it if the elevators are shut down—"

"Where are you? Shall I send a cab for you?"

"I'm on my way to his college, but I'm stuck in traffic. I just need to hear from him. It'll be forty-five minutes before I reach the college."

"What's the name of his college?" I asked.

Chloe gave me the name, and I hung up soon after,

giving Chris instructions to drive us to the college. In the meantime, I remembered that I knew someone on the college's Board of Trustees—one of my business partners, Desmond McKinley—and made a quick call. Ten minutes later, I got an update from Desmond.

"It's a fire," he said. "So far, no one's been harmed, but they're evacuating the entire campus while they battle it. They're searching for the young man right now—Henry Nichols, is it?"

"Yes," I said, feeling worried. "I hope he's okay. His sister hasn't been able to reach him."

"Understandable since he is in a wheelchair and has possibly lost access to his phone. I'm disappointed in the college that they wouldn't prioritize taking care of him first. I'll speak to the dean about it once I hear back about Henry."

"Tell them to call Chloe," I said. "I'll give you her number if needed, but she's the one who needs to hear the news first."

There was an interesting grunt from Desmond, and he agreed. "I'll need to hear more about this sibling duo from you later."

Thanking him, I was about to call Chloe when I looked out the window and realized we'd reached the college campus.

Flames burned through the windows of the red five-story building, and smoke billowed in huge clouds from the top of the building. Firefighters fought the fire—battling both the heat and the flames.

I got out of the car, telling Chris to wait for me in the vicinity, when I noticed the slew of fire engines and paramedics on the road.

Hoping no one had gotten hurt, I looked around at the

crowd of students who had taken shelter in the track across from the college. Camera crews rushed around, and young people were on phones, anxious looks on their faces as they spoke. To the side, I could see some people being treated.

Not a single sign of Henry.

I saw a yellow cab arrive, and from it emerged a trembling, shaking, tearstained woman.

My woman.

"Chloe," I called, and she turned.

She had mascara running down her cheeks, and her hair was not brushed, but she was still beautiful. She fixed her bright blue eyes on me while I strode up to her.

"Sean." She uttered my name like a plea for help, and when I reached her, I pulled her to me for a hug.

"They'll find him," I repeated, attempting to lighten my hold on her, but she stepped away. "It'll be okay. I bet you'll get an update soon."

Chloe raced up to the cordoned-off area, and I followed while she tried to find someone who would listen to her, but the police officer ordered her to step back. She didn't obey and seemed to be evaluating the strength of the yellow tape when she began coughing from the smoke.

I gently pulled her back. "He's right, Chloe. We can't have you running into the fire."

When she didn't speak, I tilted her chin up and saw tears streaming down her face. "I can't have anything happen to him," she said, sounding distraught.

"Hey," I said, placing a kiss on her hair. I looked into her eyes. "He's fine. I promise you."

"You don't know that," she said.

Her lips were still pressed together tightly when she stepped back to look at the college. Her eyes were scouring the grounds, the building, and the windows, trying to see if she could spot Henry from down here.

"Don't worry. He'll come out of there in a few minutes and start berating you for worrying over him needlessly," I said, attempting to bring some lightness in my voice.

Her gaze met mine, and I could see how hopeless she felt. She must be exhausted, and I wished I could get her and Henry and take them home right away.

I put my arm around her, and we stood side by side, looking at the building. I hoped no one was in that wing, from which plumes of black smoke surged out wildly. The heat was oppressive, and ash and soot would occasionally drift our way with the wind.

Around us, people were crying, shouting, and sobbing. It was chaotic, and I caught people's guesses for how the fire could have started. Every idea felt extreme, but it seemed the fire alarm had sounded too late, with flames already spreading, fueled by the wind. I tightened my hold around Chloe, wishing I knew if Henry was fine.

"Henry's classes are usually held in the very same wing as the fire," she said, her voice breaking. "I called all his friends on my way here. None of them knew where he was."

Fuck.

I was reminded of how desolate she had been the night Lucas was missing. The night she'd admitted to me how losing Henry was her biggest fear.

She checked her phone again to see if she had heard anything, but a moment later, she tucked it back in her pocket, her body trembling. "How come no one's got any information on him?"

"You look at the bottom two rows of windows," I said, "and I'll keep an eye on the top three."

She flicked her gaze to me in surprise. "You knew—" She

shook her head. "Of course you knew I was hoping for a sight of him through the windows." This time, her expression became determined. "All right, let's keep looking."

"Because standing still and waiting are not things Chloe does," I murmured, gripping her hand and rubbing my thumb over her palm.

Her resolute expression weakened for a minute. "You remember way too many details about me," she said, not taking her eyes off the college building for even a second.

Where was that damn phone call to tell us they'd found him? It had been ten minutes since I'd made that call, and that had been ten minutes of extra stress for Chloe. Just like how stressed she might have been because I hadn't called her for the entire duration of my conference.

"I'm sorry I didn't call you after I left for DC," I said. "I needed some time to think."

She looked at me briefly. "It's okay." After a moment, she wrung her hands, looking miserable. "I need to stop my mind from playing out every worst-case situation possible," she said.

"What did you do while I was away?" I asked, giving her a distraction.

She paused from looking at the college to glance at the assembled students on the track. Still no Henry.

"Will showed up at my doorstep."

Will.

The way that name burned my throat was enough to tell me what I needed to know. I was too far in now. I didn't want that man's name on her lips or that damn man asking for her time after what he did to her.

"I hope you told him to go to hell," I growled out through clenched teeth.

She shook her head, still distracted. Now, my worry for Henry was mixed in with my anger at Will.

I fumed. "Did he explain himself for bailing on you that night on your supposed date?"

She hesitated. "He said he'd had time to think about it and wanted to give the date a second chance."

The jerk. He didn't deserve any more chances from her.

My mouth was dry as I spoke. "I hope you shut the door on his face."

"Well, he had flowers and asked me to go out on a walk with him."

"A walk?" I tried to curb my anger. "Did a walk change your feelings for him?"

She met my gaze, parting her lips to answer when she froze. Her phone was ringing. She brought it to her ear just as my phone buzzed with a text message.

It was a text from Desmond that simply said, *Found him.*

Hearing Chloe's voice in the background rapidly changing notes and going from a low to high pitch, I texted him back a thank-you before pocketing my phone.

She sounded ecstatic when she turned around to look at me. Her eyes were not distraught anymore; they were shining.

"He's okay! That was him on the phone. I spoke to him!" she said, sounding overjoyed, tears of happiness streaming down her face as she hugged me.

I was mad about Will showing up at her apartment, and I needed to make sure that wouldn't happen again. But I would talk to Chloe about him another time.

Her arms went around my back, and I tightened my hold on her. I'd lose her to Henry now, when I desperately wanted this moment to last longer.

"Apparently, he dropped his phone while making his

exit from the classroom. And he remembered that one of his friends was in the restroom and went searching for him. The two of them got locked in the building. They're getting him out in a few minutes. Oh, he's fine, Sean. He's fine," she said, looking up at me.

She rested her head against my chest, and I sucked in a breath. Relief, compounded with her touch, made my cock harden for her again, and I clenched my jaw and swallowed. There would be time for that later. For now, I was glad to hear the ease in her voice.

It only underscored how traumatic this incident must have been for her.

"I've got to tell you this: the dean called me when I was in the cab on my way here," she said, her voice muffled as she spoke into my chest. When she looked up, I could see her searching my eyes for something. "I've never so much as spoken to the man, but he called me and assured me that they were doing everything to find Henry and that they'd keep me posted."

I grunted. "As they should."

"And now, it was the dean again," she added. "Calling me personally to let me know that Henry had been found. He was with Henry and even put Henry on the phone to speak with me as they were getting him out."

Her voice broke. "I haven't been important to a lot of people, Sean. I've felt utterly insignificant and lonely and tired of struggling—just Henry and me for the past ten years. But that moment, after the dean's second call, I felt like Henry and I were not alone anymore. So, thank you."

"If you think you got that special attention because of some strange connection the dean has with me, you're wrong," I said gruffly, deciding to make sure my connection with Desmond and his connection to the dean stayed private. "It was all you, Chloe. You don't need to be connected to someone powerful to matter. You matter. That was it."

Her cheeks glistened with tears as she looked at me, surprised but nodding. "Wow," she said, wiping her cheeks with the back of her hand. "I—I never expected that. I thought you had something to do with it."

I didn't want her ever questioning her worth, so I lied. "Well," I said, running my hands up and down the length of her arms as her body shook with emotion, "I didn't."

"I need to get back to Henry," she said, and I nodded.

All around us, sirens blared, and people cried and hugged loved ones. Our momentary embrace wasn't noticed, but I needed to be careful.

I stroked her hair. "Go," I said, stepping back.

The space between us felt like a mistake, and a longing to fill it up with her embrace again engulfed me.

She looked at me for a moment. "I wish you could come ... but I need to focus on Henry—"

"That's okay," I said, feeling my heart wrench. I couldn't be involved in this part of her life, and I hated it.

My expression must have been pretty obvious because she looked torn. "I'm sorry."

"Chloe ..." I began, unwilling to walk away from her. Unwilling to accept that I needed more of her than just an hour. "Can I see you later tonight?"

40

SEAN

The way she smiled made my heart squeeze with happiness.

"You can," she said softly in a pleased voice.

"But wait," I said, and she paused as she was about to move.

I reached over, rubbing my thumbs over her cheeks, removing traces of her tears. She might not have wanted me to witness her fears and vulnerabilities while she cried over Henry, but I had to do this for her.

"I think Henry wouldn't like to see that you've been crying all this time."

When I removed my thumbs from her cheeks, she gripped my wrist.

"I did think about Will after he came to my apartment," she said, her voice low but sure, as she absently interlinked her fingers with mine. Tingles ran up my arms. "But I realized he was nothing in comparison to you." Her words sounded sincere.

She saw my stunned silence and smiled.

"I was surprised too," she said, as the soft caress of her

fingers against mine stopped. "Walk with me, please? The dean said Henry would be here," she said, turning and leading the way to the ambulance, and I followed her, wishing that I could clasp the hand that had grazed mine as we walked.

If we were strictly physical, what were these emotions doing, taking up space in my heart? I'd never known and felt jealousy, possessiveness, and tenderness at the same time.

And that was my clue that I needed more of her. The clue that should have sent me fleeing the scene. Instead, unable to keep away, I followed.

Henry surprised me even more. I watched from ten feet away, where I wouldn't interfere. My respect for him increased when I noticed that he was calm and even humorous after the ordeal.

He joked about something, and I could see a few people around him crack a smile, and then he took care of Chloe in his own way. He made sure that she had water to drink and that she ate some of the granola bars from his bag before they headed to the bus stop.

Henry proved what I had suspected the last time we met —that he had a solid head on his shoulders.

Chloe looked tired from the last few hours while she waited at the bus stop, her hand resting on the back of Henry's wheelchair. I fought the urge to go over and ask if I could help in any way.

Henry was on the phone, presumably speaking to friends. Going by the number of people who walked up to them, checking on him, clapping him encouragingly on the shoulder, a lot of people cared about him.

When the bus showed up, the bus driver took a few minutes to lower the ramp and buckle Henry in. I walked back to my Rolls-Royce, wishing I were there on that bus, shifting closer and closer to Chloe until my body was flush with hers, instead of being in my car.

But I set my jaw and walked back, asking Chris to follow the bus. Erin was landing later that night, and I'd originally planned to ask Chloe about what I could do for Erin. But I couldn't ask anything of Chloe at this moment, and I certainly couldn't let Chloe go without making sure she really was okay.

Occasionally, while Chris and I followed the bus, I could see Chloe leaning her weary head against the window. That sight tore at something in my chest.

How the fuck was I not able to protect her and Henry? My heart felt like it was being split in two. I was realizing the tight control I tried to maintain around Chloe was weakening.

When the bus stopped outside her apartment, I asked Chris to park a little farther off and walked over after seeing Henry pushing in through the door of their apartment.

"I'll lie down for a bit," I heard him call out.

Chloe turned around, as if she could feel my presence, and smiled when she saw I had followed them home.

She took a quick look through the door before shutting it gently and running over to me. I opened my arms, and she leaned into me, hugging me back hard.

"Thank you," she said while I pulled her into my chest firmly. She clung back, equally desperate, as if fearful that I might just be her imagination. "For everything. Today has been hard in so many ways, but you made it easier. Just by being there. For showing me you have my back."

For a second, my mind went blank, followed by another

blank second and another. It was an odd, weightless feeling, like earning Chloe's complete trust was the greatest milestone I'd ever achieved. As I stood, enveloped by her, her hands wrapped tightly around my back, her breath on my chest, I felt like I had just climbed a mountain and conquered it.

She hesitated for a moment. "Did this change the way you look at me? Running and worrying over Henry—it's not a particularly sexy look on a woman you're considering go—"

"Chloe," I said firmly, determined to make the woman stop. "The only thing this incident has done is make me admire you even more."

She looked nonplussed, and after a few attempts at speaking, she finally said, "That's ... well, good."

My hands ran soothingly up and down her back as her body relaxed against mine. Her heart beating in rhythm against mine.

Her brow creased as she looked at me. "Oh my God. It just hit me. Aren't you supposed to be at your conference? Weren't you supposed to have a meeting with the UK's Secretary of State for Business—"

"Stop," I said, bringing my thumb over her brow, smoothing the crease. She was right. Not just Mark Waldorf, but I'd blown the UK's Secretary of State off too. I'd do damage control later, but now, my time was Chloe's.

She relaxed against my touch, her eyes fluttering closed for a quick second. I could see from her expression that she needed sleep and food, probably in the reverse order.

"Do you have anything for dinner for you and Henry?" I asked, and her eyes opened right away, concern shining through them.

She bit her lip and shook her head. I pulled her to me

and pressed a kiss to the wrinkle in her forehead that had chosen to reappear.

"I'll handle it; don't worry. What do you like?"

"Henry likes Ital—" she began, but I shook my head.

"What do *you* like?" I asked her.

She sighed and closed her eyes. "I hate to be demanding, but since you asked, I ought to let you know that I'd love some pad thai."

"Done," I said, planting another quick kiss, this time on her cheek. "It's not one bit demanding at all."

I wanted to ask her out, to take the next step, but now wasn't the right time.

"Chloe, there's something you should know," I said, speaking fast before I could change my mind. "The flowers I asked you to have deliver for me ... they were for my mom."

Confusion flicked across her face as she tilted her head at me, strands of her blonde hair falling loose from her hair tie.

"When I said earlier that my parents weren't around—well, my dad passed on, but my mom is still alive. But I've distanced myself from her, Chloe, for reasons I'll tell you about later. She brings back too many unhappy memories of my childhood, ones where I was left alone and neglected. It isn't pretty, and someday, I'll give you the entire story. But I want you to know that I'm not harboring thoughts of any other woman except you."

Her lips extended in her signature pretty smile, the genuine one that made my heart swell with happiness. She nodded.

"Thank you for choosing to be honest with me. But also, Sean," she began just as I was about to pull her closer, "I don't want to go so long without hearing from you again."

I loved hearing that it was too long for her because it had been too long for me too.

"When I realized you'd met with Will, I felt even more jealous than I had known I could be. So, I agree," I said gruffly. "It won't happen again."

"You were jealous?" She sounded and looked incredulous. And a teeny, tiny bit pleased, too, if I was reading her correctly.

I nodded. "I'm jealous that you got to spend time with him when it should have been with me. And if I'm being honest, I didn't know I could feel that way." I ran a hand through my dark brown hair as I looked away for a second. "The idea of another man getting you flowers—well, that makes my blood boil. And especially because that man is Will. I hate him for standing you up on your date, and I hate him even more for thinking he could just show up days later and get a second chance with you. You're special, Chloe, and I'm not the only man who sees that."

She reached up and pressed her palm against my cheek. Heat rushed through me.

"Oh, Sean," she whispered, her lips parting as her eyes darted around my face, searching me. She finally took a deep breath and met me at eye level. "When I went for a walk with Will," she began as my throat tightened at her words, "I felt nothing. I was restless, if anything, because he couldn't make me laugh. He didn't infuriate me either, like you do. We talked for an hour, and in that time, I realized I didn't care about him at all. When I'm with you, you draw me out and make me talk about myself—heck, you even make me forget about my troubles. One minute with you is worth more to me than an hour with him. He doesn't compare to you one bit.

"So, my answer to your question from a couple of days

ago is *yes*. I'd love to go out with you, Sean. Even if it's the craziest, stupidest thing to do as your personal assistant—"

My breath caught in my chest at those words.

I cut her words off with a passionate kiss, and her warm, soft lips met mine. A shiver ran down my spine, and I placed my hands on her hips, pressing her body to mine. The kiss intensified, and she parted her lips for me as my tongue stroked hers. I brushed my hands up her arms, finding the base of her neck and tilting her head to deepen the kiss. I wanted to kiss her neck, to move lower, wishing I could get her to a bed and undress her.

A distant noise from her apartment woke us to the notion that we didn't have much time. Henry was calling her name. I lifted my head regretfully, my erection hard and straining against my pants. Chloe took a step back, and I let my arms fall to my sides.

She looked dazed, her cheeks flushed, and her big blue eyes were staring back at me with genuine admiration.

My body felt hot, and my clothes felt too tight. I could see the desire in her eyes, mirroring my own.

"I need to get back," she said regretfully with a look over her shoulder.

"I understand," I said, even as my need for her thrummed in my veins. I wished she didn't have to.

It was better this way though. The two of us were too engrossed in our own lives—her with her brother and me with my decision to never get serious.

I stepped in for a quick goodbye kiss. "I'll see you tomorrow. At work. And if you can slip away from home tomorrow evening ..." I stopped, and Chloe held her breath, lips parting. "I'm taking you out, sweetheart."

The happiness I saw on her face made me feel like I was on top of the world. When I got into my car, the logical part of my brain noted that I wasn't usually this thrilled about seeing a woman again. Something was different this time around.

I had no reason to worry though because she had a life that revolved around her brother. We'd never get too serious about each other, and I preferred the safety net that our busy lives gave us.

All of life was a transaction, I'd realized long ago. With wealth and power, even more so.

Chloe worked well for me. She didn't care about my money or power—that I was confident about. That assurance helped me show her bits of my true self, let me live a life that I would have had if I hadn't built Tassater Inc.

When Dad had drilled into me that loyalty was nonexistent, I'd scoffed at him. Being cheated on by Helen had drilled into me the very words I'd heard at the dinner table from my dad each night, growing up. I'd not only seen Mom leave, but also experienced the heartbreak myself with Helen. I couldn't go down that path again.

Chloe and I would be temporary—that much was sure.

41

SEAN

The penthouse was dimly lit when I got back. I spent the entire drive missing Chloe. I wanted to touch her, kiss her, and to not leave her until my cup of Chloe was full for the day. That cup was disarmingly empty right now.

Tomorrow, I promised as I forced myself to focus on the people in front of me.

Anne, the nanny, had been keeping Lucas company. I could see the bits of craft they'd been working on together —painting a large cardboard dinosaur cutout. Anne stood up when I walked in.

"Thanks, Anne," I said as she made to leave. "I can take it from here," I said, noticing that Lucas stood by the window, arms crossed.

He turned around angrily when he heard my voice. "Where's Chloe, Dad? She promised she'd be here tonight. I want Chloe!"

You and me, both, son.

My mind raced as I tried to come up with something to

soothe him and failed. Being with Chloe had turned my mind to mush.

Giving up, I steeled myself for his anger. "I know, buddy. But Chloe has something important going on. She can't make it tonight."

Lucas shook his head. "She promised she'd spend every Thursday evening with me. What could be more important than me?"

I walked over to him and knelt down next to him. "Chloe has a family too, Lucas. She has a younger brother, Henry. And Henry really needs her today."

The frown disappeared. "I knew she had a brother," he said immediately. It took me by surprise. "Is he okay?" Lucas asked.

I nodded, still next to him. "He's good. They had an issue at his college, and Chloe had to go pick him up. She was quite upset." I hesitated. "She told you about her brother, huh?"

A frown creased his brow. "Yes. About her brother and mother and how they used to play games when they were young." He stared off into the distance. "I wish I had a brother."

Oh boy. I wasn't prepared for this.

"I don't even have grandparents, like everyone else does. I've never met your parents, and Mom's parents live so far off in California that I hardly get to see them. I hate having no family."

I glanced at the clock. It was past Lucas's usual bedtime, but Erin was landing at the airport in an hour.

"You know, I have a way we could fix that," I said gruffly.

It seemed odd, my idea. But seeing Chloe and the bond she shared with Henry had made me wish I had that in my life. The kind that money couldn't buy. The bonds that were built on familiarity and trust and childhood memories.

"Lucas, remember I told you I had a half-sister, your aunt Erin? She's flying in from Miami today. It's her first time in New York."

Lucas raised an eyebrow. "I've never met her before, right?"

I shook my head. "I've been pretty bad at holding on to family in the past," I admitted. "But Chloe has made me want to change. Erin's family too, you know. How about we go welcome her at the airport? It'll be an adventure, just like when Chloe takes you to the park."

His eyes lit up, but the devil in Lucas wasn't going to give in so easily. He crossed his arms tighter. "But, Dad, it's late! I'm supposed to be in bed."

He was always testing me. Trying to make sure I really, really meant my words.

I leaned down. "Just this once, Lucas. Erin's plane lands soon. We'll pick her up, and then you can have a late bedtime. Deal?"

Lucas studied my face, probably searching for sincerity. He leaned in close and whispered, "Dad, I've never seen her before! What if Aunt Erin doesn't recognize us?"

I grinned and reached for the large dinosaur cutout that he'd made and picked up his marker. "Don't worry, Lucas. She'll spot us. Once you write her name on this, we'll be the ones with the best sign in the whole terminal."

Slowly, he nodded. "Okay, but only this once. And if Erin isn't fun, I'm telling her she owes me extra bedtime stories."

I smiled. "Agreed, little man. Let's go meet your aunt."

42

CHLOE

Early the next morning, I woke up to a shrill call on my phone.

I groggily blinked my eyes open. The morning sun was slicing through the curtains and dispelling the warm, gooey thoughts I'd been having. The room swayed, and for a moment, I wondered if I was still dreaming. I'd had dreams of Sean tossing me over his shoulder and whisking me off to a private room, but, no, this wasn't that. This wobbly sensation was all too real.

I swung my legs over the edge of the bed, hazy bits of the fragility of my bed coming to mind. The bed creaked, as though protesting my movement. With a splintering crack, one of the legs detached from the frame. I teetered, arms flailing, trying to regain balance. My shoulder collided with the side table, and I winced, pain radiating through my arm as the side table fell and books and my alarm clock toppled.

I stood up immediately, nursing my bruised shoulder, and surveyed the aftermath. The bed leg lay on the ground, and the bed was a sorry figure, tilting sideways. The side table was fine, but the bruise on my shoulder was dark, and I knew it would be a few days before the pain went away.

And miserably, there wasn't any sign of Sean in the room. I sighed, realizing I'd been dreaming, and gingerly reached for my phone, checking to see whose call I'd missed. It was from Luna Moore, a friend I'd made at work. I called her back, and when she answered, I apologized for missing her call.

"Is Henry fine?" she asked, mentioning that she had seen the news about the fire at his college on the TV yesterday.

"He is, thankfully."

"Oh good," Luna responded. "Because the news article made it seem like he was scarred for life or something."

I ran to my laptop, phone still pressed against my ear as I switched it on. "What newspaper was this?" I asked as I pulled up the search bar. I forgot everything about my bruised shoulder from then on.

I typed in the name of the newspaper she had given me —*The City Observer*—and stared with a sense of doom at the first article that showed up.

Chaos at Hudson Ridge Community College during an emergency lockdown. Drill Coordinator Ian Marcus and Student Leader Henry Nichols failed to prepare the students for an emergency situation.

My heart almost stopped when I reached Henry's name in that sentence.

"God," I muttered, reading the rest of the article quickly.

It wasn't true—Henry had tried his best to get the college's Public Safety Department to conduct safety drills. I'd seen him on many occasions writing letters or speaking on the phone to raise awareness. The rest of the article tried to put the blame on the college for not being up to the mark on the ISO standards for safety, but Henry's name kept coming up in a way that made him seem at fault—Henry didn't take his role seriously and wasn't responding to the calls on the speaker during the actual emergency, adding to the stress of the crisis.

How dare they? He had been locked in the building, and there was no way he could have responded to any call unless someone let him out.

Bristling, I ended the call and dashed out of the room, hoping to find Henry and prepare him for the twisted versions of this article that he might face.

On the way, I passed Henry's room and saw that his computer was on even though he wasn't in there. My heart sank when I saw the same news article about the emergency incident at college on the screen.

Shoot. He was already going to have a hard time getting mentally ready to face college again after yesterday's traumatic event. This was just making it worse and worse for him.

I ran into the living room and saw Henry had rolled over to the window and was looking out. From his posture, I could sense that all was not well with him.

"Henry," I began, walking up slowly to him.

He didn't turn to me for a long moment, and when he did, I could see it in his face.

The broken look. It was there in the set of his jaw and that hopeless look in his eyes.

"I'm sorry," I said, going over and leaning down to put my arm around his shoulders.

He nodded, resting his hand on mine for a second before pulling away.

"How do you feel about lasagna for dinner?" he asked, wheeling himself into the kitchen. "Looks like I'm not going to be student leader much longer, so I'll be home early after all. I'll cook. I need the distraction."

I swallowed and followed him, determined to let him have his way today. "Lasagna sounds lovely," I said, my voice hoarse.

He turned to me, and when he met my gaze, he gave me a small nod. He realized I wasn't going to insist that he fight the administration on this.

"I'm sorry about that article," I said, watching him pull the box of cereal out of the lower drawer and placing it on his lap before reaching for a couple of clean bowls for the two of us. "They're complete idiots."

"Well," Henry said, going over to the table and placing everything on it, "they have all the power, Chloe. We don't. Did you know that *Gallagher News* was going to interview me today for a job once I graduate next month? Articles like that can ruin my job prospects, even before I'm out of college."

He poured out a small portion of cereal for himself—one third of his usual amount—and my usual amount in my bowl. Pouring the milk out into our bowls, he began to eat before gesturing for me to join him.

I sat down across from him just as I got a call from Sean.

I answered it quickly, keeping an eye on Henry, who was still eating absently. I loved hearing from Sean, but right now was not a good time.

"Can I call you back in some bit?" I said when I put the phone to my ear.

I didn't want to give anyone else my attention when Henry was hurting. Besides, part of me wanted to know more about Henry's graduation plans. It was something he'd been very reluctant to speak about, and I wanted to be around in case he finally decided he was ready to talk about it.

Sean paused for a second. "Of course," he said, sounding guarded. "I'm just getting you coffee on my way to work, and I wondered if you'd like breakfast too. Belgian waffles with fresh berries or a pancake soufflé perhaps?"

I stared at the two bowls of Kroger cereal on the table. "Thank you," I said, feeling flustered and almost dropping the phone in my hurry. "But I'm finishing up breakfast here with Henry. Coffee would be lovely though."

"Good. I'll see you soon at work. And, Chloe, in case you haven't heard, *The City Observer* has a slanderous article about yesterday's incident at Henry's college."

"I know," I said, my voice humorless. "It's terrible."

None of my boyfriends have ever kept an eye out for Henry before, I thought before I realized what I'd referred to Sean as. *Why am I thinking of him as my boyfriend?*

"I'll make them pay for it, Chloe. Don't you or Henry worry."

He hung up, and I stared at my phone for a moment before setting it back down on the table. Sean's voice had been filled with a quiet rage, and I *almost* feared for that reporter on the newspaper.

Serves them right.

Henry looked up, his face serene and unchanged. "Does your boss know about the article too?"

He'd obviously seen Sean's name on the caller ID. I nodded, trying to look nonchalant. Thankfully, I hadn't added a photo of Sean to his contact details on my phone. If Sean was going to show up at home again, would I continue to lie about who he really was?

"Could you pass the raisins, please?"

He reached for the box of raisins and checked that we weren't out of it yet before he passed it to me.

"That's odd that he cares," Henry said. "But he's a lot more thoughtful than Dad ever could be. That's obvious."

The spoon of cereal I was lifting to my mouth slipped from my fingers and clattered to the table, splashing milk and cereal outside my bowl. Our eyes met over the table as Henry reached for a paper towel on his right and rolled it over to me. He took another calm spoonful of his cereal.

I caught the paper towel as it neared me and tore off a piece, wiping the mess with more intensity than needed. We never brought up Dad if we could help it. I always thought it was too painful for Henry to hear. But now, I realized it was more painful for me to hear his name being spoken than it was for Henry.

I'd never forget coming home one night after school and realizing Dad had just left.

Even though I'd destroyed Dad's letter, Henry had eventually peeked into Dad's closets while I sat frozen, and discovered they were empty.

"Dad left us," he'd said. "We were too much for him to bear." Henry had sounded more heartbroken than he had the night of his accident.

That was when I lied and told him I'd asked Dad to pay my college tuition because my student loan hadn't been approved. I claimed Dad had left me, and over the next few weeks, I built on that lie, embellishing it until it felt so real that Henry finally believed me.

In reality, I'd felt more empty and alone than ever. I'd tried to wipe all memories of that night from my mind and accept the new normal: I was all alone in caring for Henry now.

Sean hadn't done that.

He'd seen me at one of my lowest moments, and instead of making a run for it, he had actually asked me out.

If that didn't make me feel nervous about the night I had coming up with him, then I didn't know what would.

Henry continued speaking. "Hey, do you want to watch a movie in the evening? Something to take our minds off this mess?"

I stared at him. I was desperate to finally get an evening with Sean. But I also knew I was asking for a lot to leave Henry when he was feeling low like this.

I steeled myself and looked at Henry. "I might not be able to join you for the movie tonight," I said carefully. "I'm going out."

He frowned. "Is this another task for your boss?"

I debated telling him the truth, which was futile when no part of me wanted to talk about the gray line that Sean and I were toeing. Henry wouldn't approve of me having a casual fling with my boss. He was far too logical. Why did I have to come clean to Henry when this was just a fling?

Sean and I would end this soon, and Henry would never need to know.

"Yes," I said. "Just another work thing."

Henry nodded, like he wasn't surprised.

"I'll be back soon though; don't worry," I said.

Henry's phone rang at that instant, and we both jumped before he answered it.

"Yes, it's me," he said into the phone. "Yes," he said, humming in agreement.

I could see his expression change, and in a minute, a look of bewilderment took over. Pressing his head down to keep the phone plastered between his shoulder and his ear, he continued to listen intently.

"Yes, I see. Okay, that's good to know. Bye."

He hung up and turned around. "*The City Observer* just called me to apologize for that article," he said, sounding taken aback. "They've pulled it down, and they're making a new one, which includes an apology as well as correcting the details of their reporting." He stared at me. "Just how well connected is your boss?"

My jaw dropped when I realized what had happened. Sean had used his contacts to make a freaking newspaper issue an apology.

"Very well connected, I guess," I said, feeling breathless.

Just how influential was Sean in this world? Who the heck was this man I was dating?

The care that this man was putting into making my life easier—heck, making Henry's life easier—was astounding. My emotions spiraled out of control, threatening to choke me with their intensity as they took over. Sean had made me feel like I wasn't alone in caring about Henry. He had Henry's back too. I blinked rapidly, trying to stem the tears that had already made my eyes misty.

How nice of Sean to think of this. How had I ever thought he was coldhearted?

I stared when I saw Henry wheeling himself away from the dining table and taking his half-eaten bowl of cereal and dumping the rest of it in the sink.

"What are you doing?" I asked.

"I'd better not be late for class," he said, rolling out of the kitchen and back to his bedroom. "And I've got a meeting in the evening with the Public Safety Department. Sorry, sis, there won't be any lasagna tonight."

Henry was back to normal, thanks to Sean.

I grinned. "Well, there had better be some tomorrow."

43

CHLOE

On my way to the subway station, I got a call from Tess.

"I saw the news. What happened?" she asked, sounding worried.

I filled her in and found it hard to keep Sean out of the story.

"He asked you out?" she squealed.

I couldn't help but blush. "Yes. He might be someone I'm seeing. But I don't know ... it's complicated," I admitted. "Isn't it too soon?" I asked. "After things ended with Bruce?" My voice was half ashamed.

Tess scoffed at that. "Please. It's been months since that jerk left. You definitely need to get over that man. Besides, you're telling me that your boss stayed by your side the entire time yesterday? He sounds more than just any guy, Chloe. He's starting to sound really good to me."

I agreed with that. Apart from being with me yesterday through the whole ordeal, he'd seen me cry, held me, and comforted me. He'd made sure I heard from the dean. No matter how much he denied it, I was sure he'd had a hand in it somehow.

I couldn't believe how comforted that had made me feel, how less alone I'd felt for the first time since taking responsibility for Henry.

I crossed the street at the intersection and hurried across the footpath to the subway entrance down the block. "He's my boss, Tess."

Tess hummed, as though she'd considered this already. "That does make things tough. When you told me about him last time, I initially thought he'd be a good distraction for you … to help you get over Bruce."

I heard her breathe deeply. "But you told me he'd gotten your favorite food for dinner and how he followed you back home to make sure you both got home okay. I'm starting to think he might be more than just a distraction."

I shook my head. "A good distraction," I corrected. That was what Sean and I had decided upon last night.

"Well, if that makes you feel better, sure. But the man saw you and Henry on your bad day, Chloe, and he stayed with you instead of walking away. That's more than what Bruce ever did."

It was more than what Dad had ever done for us, my mind added.

"Thanks, Tess," I said as I hurried down the subway steps. "You're amazing."

She laughed. "Don't I know it?" she joked before hanging up.

Twenty minutes later, I was walking into the Tassater building and taking the elevator to my desk. It was Sean's first day back after his conference, and he had a steady stream of meetings scheduled to make up for his absence in the past few days.

Sean gave me a small smile and I met his brief gaze with my intense one as he walked past me. His stride was confident and never once faltered as he disappeared into his office. I had set out his morning reports by his table, everything but his coffee and breakfast—he had started having breakfast with Lucas at home every day, and what made me happiest was that this had been Sean's idea to spend more time with his son.

My breath left me as I sat outside alone, wondering how it was possible to convey how much his actions from the day before had meant to me and if he'd even understand. Maybe it was better if he didn't know how I felt right now.

It was like I was swept up in a tornado of feelings, and instead of losing steam, they seemed to be building on each other, getting stronger and stronger, until I felt like I was the one who would break.

At ten a.m., when I knew Legal had a morning lull, I pulled out the small strawberry cake from my drawer that I'd picked up on my way to work and the card that I'd bought a few days ago and walked over to the Legal Department on the fifteenth floor. Luna Moore, the contract administrator, looked up when I approached her with the cake and the card.

"Whatever is—" She broke off when a couple of other women next to her began clapping.

"Congratulations!" I said, placing the cake on her table while others looked up, smiling.

I'd made the rounds a few days ago, asking all of them to sign the card, so they knew what was coming next.

"For your promotion to contract manager!" I added.

Luna blushed and then accepted the cake with an embarrassed smile as her colleagues whooped and cheered with applause.

"Your family and friends must be so proud of you," I said as I pulled out a plastic knife and fork for her to take her bite.

Luna had two young kids and also financially supported her mother, so I couldn't have been prouder of her achievements.

"It was tough, but completing the Contract Management Standard Certification really helped me snag that promotion," Luna said, sharing pieces of the cake with her colleagues, who took small pieces back to their desk while Luna took a bite. "Oh my goodness, this is delicious, Chloe," she said, standing up. "Thank you, Chloe. I'm flattered you remembered," she said, walking back with me to the elevator. "Now, I'm a few minutes early to a meeting with your boss. Do you think he'll see me if I show up at 11:58 instead of noon?"

I laughed as I pressed the button for the thirty-fifth floor, where I worked. "I think you'll find he's being very forgiving these days."

Luna shook her head. "I'll believe it when I see it. Last time, he made my colleague go back out of his office and wait because the minute hand on his clock hadn't reached noon."

The elevator doors opened, and I saw Sean standing by my desk. He turned and acknowledged us with a small nod.

When I saw him, my cheeks flamed with the memory of last night.

"Are you here to discuss the meeting with our COO's international contract person?" he asked Luna, and she nodded.

"If it's not too much of a bother," she stammered. "I mean, I know I'm two minutes early—"

He waved her concerns aside and gestured for her to follow him in. "Not a problem at all, Ms. Moore," he said.

Luna turned and gave me a look of utter surprise over her shoulder as she followed him in, and I grinned as I took my seat.

Ten minutes later, when she walked out, she came up to me.

"I can't wait to get back and have more of the cake—if my coworkers left some for me. I'm a bit busy today, but tomorrow, let's go out and grab coffee together." She made to go and then hesitated. She leaned in conspiratorially. "If you need anything from Mr. Tassater today, this is a good time to ask," she said, her voice cheery. "I've never seen him agree to so many of Legal's demands in one go."

I held back a smile and nodded, watching her leave as I felt the tension rise in my belly. It couldn't be what I was thinking, and yet the most obvious answer was that Sean was looking forward to this date just as much as I was.

I walked into his office, closing the door behind me. He was holding a pen over a document, and I remembered how those fingers traced my cheek last night before running over the length of my arm. How those butterfly touches had sent tingles running down my palm and hands.

More than that, I remembered the concern in his eyes while he'd waited with me for news about Henry. No one could fake that.

When he looked up, I noticed a different smile on his face. Not the business smile I'd seen so often before. This one was a teasing smile, just for me. I needed to enjoy this while it lasted. The special looks that were just between us, the ones that sent my cheeks flaming red.

"I've wanted to see you all morning," he said, his voice husky as he got up and walked around the desk to me.

I switched my folder from one hand to another as he approached. Thank goodness Henry would be home late today. Because when Sean looked at me like that, I lost all capacity for rational thoughts.

I wanted to run and jump into his arms and kiss him right there. I also thought ridiculous things, like, *I wish this would never end.*

"Me too," I breathed as he came to a stop inches from me.

He dipped his head and, as though he could read my incendiary thoughts, began to kiss me languidly. Like it was the most normal way to greet his assistant.

I, being the fool I was, kissed him right back.

He pulled my lower lip into his mouth, one arm sneaking across my back and bringing my body flush against his. He tasted so good that I shivered and tilted my head to take him in deeply.

Yes, very good assistant behavior, my brain chided.

His lips devoured mine in a slow, heated kiss. He tasted of mint and longing, and my heart started its drumbeat, warning me I shouldn't get used to this. I ignored it. I was allowed some vices after all.

I slipped my tongue into Sean's mouth, and a low growl sounded from the back of his throat. I held on to his arms as the kiss intensified, and my soft sighs were replaced with a breathless need for him. He cupped my face, kissing me hungrily, and I was incapable of thinking of anything else, of wanting anything else but him.

When we finally came up for air, I sighed with perfect happiness.

"Please greet me like this every day," I said absently before my eyes shot wide open. Sean very well would, and I was afraid he would do it irrespective of who else was in the room. "No, I take that back," I said immediately, but he chuckled, one finger tracing the outline of my cheek as his deep brown eyes looked back at me.

"I told Henry that I'd be out tonight, but I'm also very nervous. I don't know how he's feeling about my absences."

Or perhaps, the truth was, I didn't know how I felt about being away from Henry multiple times this week.

Sean frowned. "He'll be fine. Why wouldn't he?"

I'd never left Henry alone for an entire night in a long time. Sean didn't know the full extent of my anxiety at leaving Henry alone. I didn't correct him. We were just a fling, and he needn't ever know.

"Besides, the last time you and I were together was ... hot. And thinking about where tonight might lead to has gotten me all worked up. So much so in fact that I've messed up quite a few things at work today," I said.

He chuckled and leaned forward. "Given the circumstances, Chloe," he said, his lips hovering above mine for a moment before he closed the gap and kissed me again, "I'd say you are quite forgiven."

When we broke apart, I rested my head on his chest, closing my eyes and enjoying this moment.

"Has Henry gotten over the shock of being trapped in that building and that horrible article?" he asked.

I nodded. "He's recovered. He was laughing and cheerful when I left for work."

He paused. "How about you? How do you feel?"

I exhaled. "I was stressed out for a bit, you know. But being back at work has given me time to feel stable again. For once, my anxiety isn't racing through the roof, replaying the same situation in my mind."

He nodded. "That's good. Do you want to hear something interesting? Last night, Lucas and I were at JFK, meeting my half-sister, Erin, for the very first time."

I was really surprised, and Sean grinned.

"Is it that astonishing when I do something nice, Chloe?" he asked, his eyes full of heat as he tipped my chin up.

"For someone you haven't met? A little," I admitted with a breathy laugh. "How do you feel about her?" I asked.

Sean looked thoughtful. "I liked her. She was quirky and fun. Lucas took to her instantly. She was thrilled to be in New York and also happy that she got to meet Lucas."

He rubbed his hand on his chin, looking a bit worried. "Lucas has another reason to be elated lately, and it doesn't involve Brianna," he said.

I frowned and put my hand on his chest.

"What is it?" I asked.

Sean sighed and leaned against the edge of his table, crossing his hands and looking out the window. "Lucas is happy because his mother is coming back."

Ah. "And you're not happy about having to part with him?" I asked, feeling a flicker of hope for the man he was becoming. Someone who was now attached to his son, who cared for the boy and was not ashamed to show it.

Sean appeared troubled. He straightened up and looked around. "For the past day, we packed up his things so that he could move back in with her—he wants to move out the very night she lands. If that doesn't show you how excited he is to leave me ... well, I don't know what will. Have I not made any progress with my son in the past month at all, Chloe?"

I reached up to put my hands on either side of his face. "Sean, I promise you, you've made amazing progress with Lucas this month. When I spoke to Lucas on the phone one night, I could hear the pride in his voice while he talked about you. You know, he bragged to me that you helped him make a balloon-powered rocket with a straw and a string."

I stepped back, a small smile curving my lips. "And I know for a fact that you've helped Lucas with his homework on the days that you've been in town."

Sean was nuzzling my neck, his breath hot and ragged.

I took his hand in mine. "You're a wonderful dad, Sean," I said as my body came alive under his touch.

He leaned in closer, and I pressed my fingers into his hard, muscular back.

"But for a kid waiting for his mom to come back—especially after he's not seen her for two months? It's something no one can compete with. And parenting is not a competition, Sean. Lucas loves you both."

I broke off as his hands tugged at my hair, pulling my head back and exposing my throat.

"Thank you, Chloe," he said.

He bent his mouth to my neck, grazing it roughly with his lips and giving me a sudden nip. I was already breathing fast, and I yelped in surprise at that bite, but his only response was to widen his lips in a grin. He brought his fingers to my collarbone, teasing me by stroking the heated skin just above the dip of my cleavage.

He took my mouth in a kiss, biting my lower lip gently. The kiss intensified, deeper and deeper, his tongue playing effortlessly with mine until I was breathless. His hands wrapped around my back and pulled me snug to him, and I felt my pulse racing wildly, my heart throbbing against my ribs. The door to his office was closed, but not locked, and I ought to protest when Sean moved his hands down from the back of my head to my front, his fingers slipping expertly to cup one of my breasts through my blouse.

"Oh, Sean," I muttered, feeling both relaxed and intoxicated by the act.

He walked me back to the wall, not breaking the kiss, and I felt like I was living someone else's life. One where I was no longer invisible, but extremely desirable and wanted —by a powerful man like Sean Tassater, no less.

"What is it, baby?" he asked as his fingers moved to undo my blouse's top three buttons. The top of my blouse gave way, revealing my push-up bra, and he wasted no time in pulling it down.

When he moved his mouth to suck my breast, my eyes fluttered shut.

"I've ... wanted you ... so ... badly since you left for the conference," I said, my words coming out in gasps as he sucked my hard nipple with his mouth while I ran my hand through his brown hair.

"Me ... too." The words were fuzzy as he picked up intensity, sucking and pulling as I gasped, my hands tangled in his hair as the intense pleasure built up.

When his free hand moved from fondling my other breast down my stomach to under my skirt, I knew I was a goner.

"Sean," I gasped, wanting him to stop, but also not really wanting this to stop.

I'd never felt so relaxed, and I'd also never felt like I was in extremely capable hands. If anyone could handle giving me an orgasm and making me feel like I was on top of the world, it was Sean.

My nipple was already aching when Sean switched to my other breast. His lips were hot against my skin, and using his other hand, he moved my thighs apart as much as possible, given the pencil skirt I was wearing. Finally, he found my clit. I moaned out loud when he began stroking it gently, back and forth, until I was aching there too.

I heard voices and froze. Someone had stopped by my desk outside Sean's office, and I heard muttering. The way Sean's hand paused told me he'd heard them too.

"Chloe?" I heard someone call, and I recognized Luna's voice.

Sean gripped my hips tight, pinning me against the wall to make sure I understood I wasn't going anywhere until he was done with me.

"Mr. Tassater?" Footsteps came closer to the door.

Shit.

I stared at Sean, eyes wide as he locked his dark gaze with mine. He shook his head slightly, showing that I need not to worry, and pressed a finger to my lips. I could taste my own arousal as someone rapped on Sean's office door. His intense eyes held my gaze as I slowly licked his fingers, one after another, and I felt so turned on. My heart pounded against my rib cage, feeling excitement and anxiety as he got down on his knees.

He pushed the hem of my skirt higher up my hip and swiped my panties aside.

I was wet, and I whimpered when Sean reached in and swiped his tongue over my wet core.

Fuck.

Here I was, pressed up against the wall in Sean's office, with my blouse open, my breasts exposed, and Sean ravaging my body like a beast.

The metal door handle turned, and I was about to push Sean away when it stilled. The handle didn't budge; the door didn't open. Were they outside, listening in?

Sean continued to swipe at my pussy, his tongue doing things that made me feel like I was going to explode.

My muscles clenched as Sean tasted me in gentle flicks of his tongue, and I held my breath, wondering what was happening outside while slowly losing control of my body.

"They're out there," I whispered, hoping against hope that no one would call my phone. Had I brought it in here with me?

My fingers dug into his shoulders as I trembled under his expert moves. My nipples were hard, and I rocked against his mouth, tilting my head back in abandon. This was wild. We could get caught, but the only thing that thought did for me was heighten my arousal.

What the fuck has happened to me? This wasn't what nice girls did.

But I'd long since grown tired of being nice. Nice girls got an impersonal minimum wage paycheck, vacuous performance reviews, and time alone at home. It fucking sucked. I was going to be naughty, and I was going to be darn good at it.

I licked my lips while my hands tugged at his hair, adjusting the position of his tongue on my pussy as he worked me. When he bit down gently, my fingers dug into his shoulders, my body shaking with built-up passion, and I moaned my appreciation. He was so, so good, and I was starting to feel delirious.

I heard the footsteps recede, and soon, my phone began to ring.

On Sean's desk.

My heart jumped into my mouth, but I was not capable of words anymore as Sean kept going. I was torn between my impending release and wanting to silence the damn thing.

He was watching me, eyes alight with mischief, and damn if I didn't love that look on him. He added a thumb to the mix, pressing it over my clit, and I felt so dizzy with pleasure that I grasped the wall behind me helplessly. Under Sean's expert touch and the fear of our passion being discovered by strangers, I was going to come apart at any moment now.

"They're still in the meeting," I heard the voice mutter outside the door as my phone fell silent. "If so, I wouldn't piss off Mr. Tassater. He doesn't like being interrupted."

I felt Sean's lips curve into a grin for a second, pausing cruelly just when I wanted him to pick up the pace. Frustrated, I narrowed my legs around his head, craving his confident touch while a heavy ache built between my legs. He took this order from me—thank goodness.

I was trembling with need while his mouth licked and swirled across my swollen clit. I was arching into him, pressing into his mouth, letting him have all of me, and wishing I could have his bare skin on me when the dam burst. Sweet waves of pleasure cascaded down my body just as I gasped out his name.

My climax tore me apart, as shocking to me as it had been the last time with him. I felt sweet, soothing relief after a tidal wave of emotions, and when I came back down, I continued to feel like I was floating on a cloud while my clit kept throbbing in the aftermath.

There was complete silence outside our door. No one was out there anymore, and I could moan as loudly as I wanted to. I moaned all right.

"Damn, that was amazing."

"How do you feel?" he grunted, his voice husky as he stood up and scooped me into his arms.

I felt like mush as he held me while I looked up at him. I was almost panting with relief and nodded.

"Like I'm on top of the world," I said, my tone feeble as I pushed my hair back.

I hadn't skirted a dangerous workplace liaison before, but it certainly had its appeal.

Besides, this wasn't just any man. It was with someone who, in the past few days, had proven just how much he cared for me.

I wanted Sean. I craved him enough to go through something risky like this and know that he'd have control over the situation, no matter what. He'd take care of me.

He smiled and made sure I was stable before he released his hands from my waist. "I thought you needed it," he said, leaning in and kissing me deeply. When he stepped back, he buttoned my shirt and smoothed my hair. "Especially after the stress of yesterday. But tonight, it's going to be my cock in you."

"I've never looked forward to anything more," I whispered back.

Even after this mind-numbing orgasm, I still wanted more. I wanted *him* in me.

He stopped, focusing on a red mark on my shoulder, noticing it for the first time. He ran his thumb over it, and I winced and pulled away.

Frowning, he asked, "Was I rough with you?" He gently touched the swollen bump.

I angled my head to look at my shoulder and then laughed. Details of the real world were flooding back to my mind after that amazing orgasm. "Oh, this one happened earlier this morning."

"*This one?*" he asked, repeating my blasé tone, flummoxed. "What did you do to get it, Chloe?"

I felt my face turn red.

"Just a little accident when I got out of bed," I said. "I slid out in a hurry, and my shoulder hit my side table."

He considered that. "Is sliding out of your bed a particularly dangerous activity?"

"It is, if you're holding one leg of the bed up with wood glue," I said, finishing buttoning up. "I need to get to the store. I think a metal bracket might work better."

He met my gaze evenly. "I think you're right," he said. "I'll get you that bracket," he added, holding my fingers in his. "You don't need to go to the store."

I looked at him incredulously. "Do you know which store sells metal brackets?"

"You underestimate me, princess."

I grinned. "Yes, handsome."

He bent down for a quick kiss, and when I turned to go, he caught hold of my wrist on my non-bruised arm.

"I just remembered," he said, turning me back from the door. "The last time I spoke with Henry, he mentioned something about you wanting to do a PMP certification course."

"Oh, that?" I laughed. "Henry's being ridiculous. That was a stretch goal for five years down the line."

"Uh-huh. And that notepad on your table has the words *New Year's Resolutions* on it. Why did I see something about completing a PMP certification on it?"

I gave him a guilty smile. "Well, to be honest, I don't have the time to complete it," I said.

"Make it."

I shook my head and stepped away. "I looked up a PMP certification course nearby that runs once a week—the minimum time I could spare to be away from home at nights. And even that class falls on the one night—Sunday

—that Henry has a free evening. With no homework or other obligations. I don't want to leave him alone."

Sean considered that before walking back over to me and wrapping his hands around my waist. "All right then, how about this? You go for the classes, and on those nights, I'll be at home with Henry."

I raised my eyebrows. "Really?"

Sean nodded. "My knowledge of soccer is abysmally low." He gave me a cheeky grin. "But there's one other topic that both Henry and I might know a lot about."

I shook my head. "Don't say it," I said with a groan.

"You," he finished, and leaning in, he placed his lips back on mine.

44

SEAN

When I arrived at Chloe's apartment that night, she opened the door, looking like a million bucks.

She was wearing a sleek crimson dress that hugged her curves just right, subtly revealing her cleavage. The dress paired perfectly with a pair of elegant heels that clicked with determination as she stepped back. Her eyes had a touch of smoky eye shadow, and they sparkled like stars when she met my gaze. Her lips, painted with a hint of rosy gloss, curved into an inviting smile I was familiar with.

My heart did a backflip. I couldn't wait to get her into my arms and hold her there.

The look in her eyes when she saw me gave rise to a terrifying feeling in me. A feeling of wanting time to slow down. I didn't want to think about the day when our time was up. Like when she stopped working for me.

She smiled as I followed her in, shutting the door behind me before I gave her flowers.

"Thank you, Sean," she breathed out as she looked at the lilies. "These are beautiful."

I cradled her face in my hands, my thumb fanning her cheek.

I was so wrong.

Simple things like picking her up for a date made me yearn for more. Made me yearn for things I shouldn't want, like a relationship with no end date.

"*You* are beautiful," I said, pressing my lips to hers.

It felt so right.

Kissing her at her home, at the office, and whenever we were together.

There wasn't any better feeling.

Was it possible to get used to someone and never tire of them?

I swallowed and tried to rein in my thoughts. *What the fuck was I thinking?*

This was just a date, with no expectations of a relationship.

"One of your neighbors waved at me," I said, remembering the slightly plump young man with hazel eyes and short sandy-brown hair.

"That would be Greg," she said, leading me to the living room.

She was wearing a subtle fragrance that reminded me of orchids and jasmine. "I occasionally help him out with bringing the trash bins in when it's his turn. Due to some health issues, he has a hard time leaving his home, but he's making progress. We got him some groceries and cake a few days ago, and he was so touched that he almost wept with happiness."

It was an unusual way of making friends, but with Chloe, I learned things were never the norm.

"You give a lot of people cake," I said, feeling a burst of pride.

How was it that in the midst of her hectic life, she carved out moments of genuine kindness for others?

"And what is this I hear about *The City Observer* offering Henry a job on their team to cover the sports issue in their sister paper?" I asked as she walked over to the kitchen and put the flowers in a vase.

She laughed. "They did," she said as she picked up a soccer ball from the back of the sofa and tossed it to me.

I caught it, surprised, and tossed it back to her, and she set it down, her eyes taking on a distant look.

"Henry said he's taking his time to decide. He's still got four weeks until graduation, and he needs to think hard about what he wants to do next. If he took up that offer though, his office wouldn't be too far from here."

A piece of me didn't like that Henry would continue to be a part of Chloe's life for the foreseeable future. What would happen if I wanted more of Chloe's time than she could give?

"It would be just one bus ride away from home," Chloe continued, filling the water in the vase, oblivious to my thoughts. "And we could still live here and go to work, the two of us, and nothing would change."

Why did I want things to change between her and me? After the conference in DC and staying away from her for a few days, I'd become insatiable with my want for her. I'd had a taste of her at my office—something I'd never thought I'd ever do—and here I was, craving more. Wanting more of her on the same day. It was madness.

I needed to get her to stop painting a picture of her future that was no different from her present. It irritated me that she thought nothing would change. That she *wanted* nothing to change.

"Here's the bracket," I said, handing her the metal

bracket I'd promised earlier in the day, even though I fully knew it was no longer needed. "I picked it out myself from the hardware store down the street from work."

She took it and gave me an exasperated look that said she didn't know whether to laugh or cry. "You're impossible," she said and laughed.

"Come," she said, leading the way to her bedroom.

"What about dinner?" I asked, following her to her room and stopping at the doorway. My cock was already hardening in my pants. The traitor.

It was then that I saw it—the purchase I'd had delivered to her..

A solid four-poster bed occupied the center of her room, complete with a headboard of deep blue velvet with intricate gold embroidery. The frame was made of polished mahogany with rich, dark tones.

At each corner of the bed, slender, gilded posts rose, draped with sheer, flowing white curtains. A solitary floor lamp stood next to the bed, casting a soft, golden light over it. The whole thing looked quite good, to be honest, even if the bed looked strangely shiny and out of place among her other things.

She reached up to give me a kiss, wrapping her arms comfortably around my neck.

I closed my eyes when I met her lips, wishing I could stay like this for a long time, perhaps pulling her to the bed and christening it right away.

Chloe pulled away too damned soon, but before I could fix her back in my arms, I noticed her eyes were shining.

"Thank you for the new bed. You didn't have to."

I caged her back in my arms anyway. She wasn't getting more than a few inches away from me tonight.

"When did they deliver it?" I asked.

"An hour ago. The bed is sturdy *and* pretty. And the men who delivered it assembled it for me before leaving. I'll sleep without a worry tonight." She looked at the tape in her hand. "This is completely unnecessary now."

"Hey, I made you a promise, didn't I?" I asked. "Now, come on. Let's go," I said, leading the way out, determined to get her to the restaurant before my dick took over and demanded I lock the both of us in her room for a couple of nights.

We walked to the waiting car and got in, my arm slipping around her shoulders to pull her to me.

I pressed a kiss to her forehead as the car moved. "You look stunning. I'm not letting another man take a second look at you. You're all mine tonight," I said while she chuckled.

"What'll you do if someone does?" she asked.

"You mean, apart from killing them and leaving them to sit in a pool of their blood?" I asked, cocking my head at her.

Her jaw slackened, and she stared at me, unsure how serious I was. I grinned.

"I might tone it down a notch," I added when her phone rang.

She answered, and it was pretty clear from the questions that it was Henry.

I watched her as she spoke, wondering why I was drawn to this woman in a way I hadn't been to other women in the past.

This time around, it feels different, I thought before I pushed that out of my mind.

When I'd accidentally seen her New Year's resolutions on her notepad earlier, I'd been stunned to know that she was in debt. I'd witnessed my father going through it, and I knew how the thought of money had plagued his every waking hour. Chloe showed me that life could be difficult and you could still smile your way through it. That you could be in situations that tried to break you, but it didn't make you broken. It just made you more beautiful.

"What?" she asked when he said something inaudible. "Oh shoot, was Ronan's music event today? I completely forgot—"

Her expression weakened, and then she shook her head. "I'm sorry. I know you promised him you'd be there, but I still can't be back by nine, Henry."

That seemed to explain a lot to Henry because the questions stopped, and Chloe laughed, looking self-conscious.

Her face glowed at the words, and she nodded. A shy smile took over her face as she considered it.

"Yes," she said, seemingly in response to his question. "Now, let me go, and I promise we'll attend his show next Thursday. And listen, please don't make plans for the weekend of April 18. I'll be out all day that Saturday. Yes, that's three weeks from now."

My mind wandered a bit as I reflected on a message I'd received from Helen. She would land in New York tomorrow, and Lucas was ecstatic about it. It had made me jealous, just like how I was a little jealous of the time and attention Chloe gave her brother, even when I was around.

Chloe finished her call and hung up before turning to me. "Looks like we can't have a repeat date next Thursday." She grinned, leaning into me.

I put my arm around her and drew her closer while she snuggled in. "Well, there are two other Thursdays in this month, so we'll be fine."

45

CHLOE

I looked out the window at the lights as we rode through the city. People walked on footpaths in a mad rush, and I realized this was the third time I was headed somewhere with Sean where I was not racing to make it to the subway.

"Where are we going?" I asked, looking out the window before I turned to Sean.

"I'm taking you to my favorite steak place," he said.

I wondered which one it could be.

The past week, he'd taken quite a few business lunches at Peter Luger Steak House, and I found myself a trifle sad that I was getting the same treatment as his business partners.

I squished that feeling down.

To Sean, everything in life was a business deal, including our little sex-only arrangement. It was what I'd originally wanted, too, so why was I feeling disappointed?

Did I feel anything for him now?

I shouldn't. I didn't ...

But if I were being truly honest with myself, perhaps I

was. I was starting to care about him. And maybe, on that day of the fire, I saw a glimmer of hope that this was something beyond casual.

Silly, foolish me.

I couldn't change Sean. Great, amazing sex didn't mean he had feelings for me.

I looked up when I felt his eyes on me, and for a second, I was stumped. He was giving me a heated but knowing look. It was a look that showed he understood so much more than he let on.

"Didn't I tell you that you don't have to worry when you're with me?" he asked as the car came to a stop.

I flushed. *Thank goodness he can't read my mind*, I thought as he reached for my hand and led me out.

Were we here already?

I looked around in the dark night and realized we were at the tarmac.

My jaw dropped when I realized what we were parked next to.

A sleek, majestic private jet.

"Sean," I gasped as he gave me a wry smile and stepped back to let me have a better look.

"My favorite steak place happens to be in DC," he said.

When I reached up to kiss him, he lifted me up, and I wrapped my legs around his waist before kissing him.

I *was* worth more than his business associates after all.

We spent the most of the one-hour flight to DC snuggling together on the couch while midair. A freaking couch on the plane, complete with blankets and pillows. Sean pulled me onto his lap, his hand tracing the curve of my ass or palming my breasts the entire time. We kissed and kissed some more, in between sipping champagne, with a view of the pink-and-orange sky outside the window. It couldn't have been more perfect. Sean's warm body underneath mine, his voice in my ears, and his kisses on my lips.

We were both breathing fast when the plan began its descent, needing release desperately. His eyes were heavy-lidded as he fingered my nipples through the soft material of my dress, and I moaned.

"You need to be patient," he growled in my ear as the plane made its touchdown.

"You need to teach me," I whispered back, palming his length through his pants.

He'd been hard the entire flight, and I'd partly rejoiced in his misery.

We're in DC, I reflected as the door to the jet opened.

I stood up reluctantly. I'd get some alone time with Sean later, but it would be pure torture to wait.

We had a ride waiting for us on the tarmac as we walked down the steps from the jet, Sean taking my hand in his.

I still couldn't believe we hadn't had to go through security to board a plane. I found myself storing away details of the jet to share with Henry later—like the gold-accented faucets in the bathroom or the pretty spare pajamas they'd stashed in the cabinets for clients—before I realized with a pang that I hadn't been honest with Henry.

He thought I was out with Will, and it was time to come clean with him. Especially since it looked like Sean wasn't leaving anytime soon.

We got into the waiting car, and I relaxed. For a second, I closed my eyes, savoring the smooth, noiseless drive.

And then a thought hit me. *Don't get used to it.*

I opened my eyes to see Sean gazing at me.

"Please tell me you spent the last minute indulging in an erotic fantasy that involved you, me, and at least ten mirrors around us?"

I grinned and sat up. "Save that thought for later," I whispered in his ear. I gestured to the spacious interior of the car. "I feel so comfortable," I told him. "This place has more room than the desk I have at work!"

"Are you taking a dig about your lowly work environment?" he asked, pulling me in closer.

His head bent, and his lips hovered over mine. My breath hitched just as the car came to a stop, but Sean didn't care. His mouth was against mine, the kiss rough, possessive. His tongue reached between the seam of my lips, like it was claiming its rightful place, while his hands caressed my back.

Before I knew it, Sean leaned over and unbuckled my seat belt, pulling me on top of him. I was straddling him, legs on either side of his hips, and I saw stars. My mind spun as I felt Sean's muscular body harden while I wrapped my arms around his neck.

I heard the front door open, and the driver stepped out.

Sean's hands went down to cup my ass. Without warning, he scooted to the edge of the seat and pulled my legs around his waist. I ground over him, and he was positioned so perfectly under me that I felt his hard length throbbing against me. He was more than perfect, and a breathy moan fell from my lips.

I noticed movement on the sidewalk, and I realized there were two valets outside, next to our driver.

"I think there's a growing number of people over there, waiting for us to be done," I said.

"Well, pity for them, I'm not," Sean growled back. "I don't care if the fucking president is outside. I'm taking my time with you."

I ground down on him again, and a groan ripped from his lips.

"No matter how much of you I get, it's never enough."

I wanted to stay here forever, knowing the power I had to make him feel pleasure. I held on to him.

"You feel so good," I sighed as his growing erection rubbed my clit just right.

I was just at the edge, and I couldn't stop.

"The windows are tinted," he reminded me as he helped me take my pleasure.

He pulled the right sleeve of my dress down, exposing my bra. He popped my breast out from the bra, sucking my nipple into his mouth as I ground faster. My breathing turned quick and uneven, and a minute later, I came, calling out Sean's name plainly for all to hear.

When I floated back down from my orgasm, I gazed at Sean. He was wearing a proud smile that told me he'd gotten exactly what he wanted.

I fell on him, feeling like my limbs had turned to jelly. "I can't walk," I sighed as he fixed the bra and the sleeve of my dress back in place. "That was so amazing that I'm pretty sure I can't walk for a while."

"Well then, I'll carry you in," he said, and that was exactly what he did.

He got out of the car and helped me out, and my world literally turned upside down as he flipped me over onto his shoulder without a warning.

"Sean," I said, affronted and mortified as I tried to beat at his back with my fists. I might have swatted at a nonexistent fly for all the difference it made.

The valets on the sidewalk broke into grins while Chris's face remained expressionless as he shut the door behind us.

Does he disapprove, or is he just used to Sean's wild behavior?

Unbothered by any of this, Sean walked into the restaurant.

He's really doing this, isn't he?

Heads turned as we entered the restaurant, and the distance between us and the doors increased as Sean strode over to the host.

The person was speechless for a second, apparently, because it took them a moment to answer him while I used that time to gaze at Sean's firm backside.

"I know you said no man could ever look at me twice. I guess you didn't consider them taking second looks at my ass?"

He surveyed the restaurant. "No man can look at any part of you," he said decisively.

I swiveled my head to see who else was enjoying this spectacle of me upside down. Sure enough, the few people who dared to gaze in our direction quickly turned away when they encountered Sean's scowl.

I grinned. Being with my grumpy, arrogant boss did have its benefits.

We were led to a secluded spot at the back, and when Sean set me down, I sighed.

"This place is beautiful, Sean," I said, taking a seat across from him.

I didn't say what I really wanted to say. I hated seeing the nice things life could offer. Because it meant there was so much I was missing out on. Crumbling sidewalks and broken appliances were all I was familiar with back home.

We ordered drinks—a mint mojito for me and an old-fashioned for Sean—and the waitress left after telling us about the specials, the names of which I couldn't ever pronounce again.

I was so out of my element here.

"Tell me about Henry," Sean said, his gaze cool as he looked at me.

For the next ten minutes, we talked over our drinks, and laughter came easily while I described the hilarious tricks that Henry still played on me on cheerier days.

My nerves eased, and I smiled more genuinely when the waitress arrived to take our order. I didn't care what I ate, so I just told her to choose her favorite meal for me, and she brightened up at that.

"You're adventurous," she said, taking the menu cards back from us. "Don't worry; I'll surprise you," she told me and left.

I laughed and took another sip of my drink. It was delicious and refreshing. "I've never been called adventurous before."

"You canceled an event with Henry to be with me," Sean said, tracing lines on the back of my hand, running down the length of my arm. "That says adventurous to me."

I nodded and gave a tiny shiver. "That felt ... unsettling ... but I want to be with you," I said, looking up and meeting his eyes.

"I'm glad because I definitely wasn't letting you get away tonight," he said while I looked pleased.

I took a sip of my drink. "I think you're changing me, and I like the new Chloe."

Sean laughed. "Just so you know, I liked the old Chloe too. It was the reason I hijacked your date with Will in the first place," he added while I laughed.

He looked at me like I was the most special thing he'd ever laid eyes on. The way he hung on to my every word made my heart flutter. What was this? Even if I wanted to reconsider my stance on relationships, Sean was my boss, and I knew for a fact that he didn't do relationships.

When our food arrived, we dug in slowly.

"Can you tell me something?" Sean asked, a whiff of his

expensive cologne reaching me. His jaw was tight, and his brown eyes were bright. "When you spoke with Henry, you said something about heading out on April 18? Because it's the first warm weekend this month, and I was going to take you sailing with me that weekend."

I froze. Sean was making plans for us. For weeks from now.

This was unexpected.

"I would have loved to, but this is something I can't reschedule." I lifted my chin. "I recently found something out ... something about my dad."

I took another sip of the mojito, the sugar and alcohol making it easier to speak. "For the past ten years, after Dad left, I thought he'd gone to California, where his parents had a home. Well, I googled his name, like I usually do every year around his birthday, and this time, a new social media account popped up."

I swallowed and blurted out the words. "It was on a dating website."

Sean's eyes were intense, and my pulse was thundering as I went on.

"Anyway, without speaking with him, I found out Dad lives in New Jersey. *New Jersey*, Sean. Just an hour's drive away from us. And he couldn't find the time to pop over ..." I shook my head, dispelling the angry thoughts. "Anyway, lately, I've had this idea. Even though he's been out here and not attempted to meet us or find out how we are ..." I held my breath. *Not even on Christmas or Thanksgiving for the past ten years.* "I was hoping he could get over here to see Henry graduate in four weeks. I'm pretty sure Henry would love that."

He leaned forward and grabbed hold of my hand, his fingers squeezing mine. "I think that's a great idea, Chloe. I didn't have the experience you did of growing up with a sibling, but ..."

He sat back, his eyes focusing on the windows next to us as he drew in a deep breath. Something deep and dark resurfaced in his mind because, when he turned to me, his eyes were stormy.

"I'm finally getting used to the idea of accepting Erin. For the past few weeks, I've heard occasionally from Erin and found it hard to ignore the interest with which she asked questions about New York and the life here. I couldn't help myself and asked her if she was considering moving here from Miami."

He reached for his cuff links, fiddling with them before he raised his head and spoke again. "Erin said she was, having looked at renting a storefront to continue her taxidermy business, but it would be another year or two before she could afford it." His eyes cut to me. "It was the first time I had done something genuinely kind, I realized, when I offered to make the down payment for a storefront she liked."

"Oh, Sean," I said.

It was a change for him—I could see that. A wonderful change because if Erin stuck around, it also meant Lucas would have more people to love him.

I ran my hand slowly up and down his arm. "I think what you did was amazing."

The corners of his lips moved up in a small smile. "Erin hasn't accepted—yet. But I can do better by her. Just like I hope you can reach your dad ... and if you need any help, well, I'm here for you. Private investigators included."

I smiled at that. I didn't plan on using a PI—heck, I couldn't afford any—but I was glad for the opening to talk about something else.

"Tell me about Erin," I said, reaching for a second bite.

Sean was silent for a while as he moved his steak around on his plate. "My mom, well, she cheated on my father with another man. When Dad found out, he was devastated. She left us, and I heard later that she had another kid. Erin. Years later, at Dad's funeral, Erin got in touch with me. I was suspicious of her back then and didn't really encourage her. But now, my behavior back then seems repugnant. I'm glad she's giving me another chance."

"What about your mom?"

"Well, she didn't marry Erin's biological father either. She's alone now, well into her seventies. She's not someone I talk about much. I haven't forgiven her for what she did to my father."

"Cheating on him and leaving you?"

"Yes. Dad visibly struggled at his job because of how much the divorce affected him. He ... developed an alcohol problem, which thankfully didn't get out of hand. He recognized it soon enough when I started to hide the bottles from him, and he promised to do better. But I could see how miserable he was without Mom. In addition, he gave up socializing and lost most of his friends. It was like being pushed into a life of isolation. It was hard for him to start over again, to make brand-new friends. When he died at sixty, he had never regained the happiness he had before she left. It was as though Mom had stolen that from him when she cheated on him."

I reached for his hand, and my eyes were moist. "I'm sorry, Sean. That must have been hard to witness."

He nodded. "You know what hurt the most? How nice Dad was. Before he passed away, he asked if I could find it in me to forgive her. He harbored no anger toward her. He always wanted to help people—including the people who had hurt him. I think I'm mad at my mom for hurting him because I've never seen someone so kind ..." He paused. "Until I met you."

I shook my head, blinking away the sadness. "Nonsense," I uttered. "I'm a horrible person. Just you wait and watch."

He laughed, but gave me a look that seemed very intimate. As though he knew me to be better than that.

It made me shiver, these knowing looks, combined with the sparks of attraction between us. I shouldn't feel these things if we were strictly sexual. I couldn't understand why we couldn't keep our hands off each other, why I touched him every chance I got.

I linked my fingers with his while we waited for dessert, staring into his eyes as he opened up more about his childhood. The night was fantastic, and it wasn't because of the private jet or the luxury restaurant.

It was because of Sean.

After dinner, Sean took me for a walk. We had a beautiful view of Arlington Memorial Bridge, all lit up at night, with the Lincoln Memorial and the Washington Monument in the distance. I'd never seen them before, and with Sean, it had happened in a few hours.

It was closer to nine p.m., and the cool breeze gently whipped my hair around as we strolled about like people without a care. Sean's hand was in mine, and all was right in the world.

I remembered the last time I'd felt this light and carefree. It was back in high school, in the days before Henry's accident. Before Dad left us. Now, I was twenty-eight, but I felt like I was much older. I felt like I weighed and considered things more gravely than anyone needed to at twenty-eight.

Who considered tricking their dad into attending his son's graduation ceremony? What kind of woman lied to her brother about their dad's reason for leaving them? And lied about her dating life?

"What are you thinking about?" Sean asked, lifting a wisp of hair and tucking it behind my ear before he turned me around to face him. We were leaning against the railing of the view spot, our coats flapping in the breeze, and except for a younger couple, we were alone. "Is something the matter?" His voice was tender, and the concern in his tone almost did me in.

I blinked rapidly, hoping I wouldn't start bawling right this minute. *Please, let me save it for when I'm home.*

"All evening long, I have been apprehensive. And guilty because I had to turn down Henry's request. But now, I feel like Cinderella," I whispered, looking at him. "Because I've enjoyed this one fabulous night, something I never dreamed about."

He'd shown me a life completely unlike mine, and I was grateful for it. But I also knew that the metaphorical clock would strike twelve soon. I couldn't predict how many dates it would take for Sean to get this fling out of his system, but it didn't stop me from trying to. I felt the onset of abandonment like a nervous itch, the longer I spent time with him. It was hard-wired in me now.

His dark eyes flashed. "It's not just one night, Chloe," he said, running his hand through my hair as he tilted my face up to his.

It wasn't just one night perhaps, but this would end soon, even though I didn't want to think of that. Sean was unpacking my emotions, bit by bit, letting them out of the cage I'd kept them guarded in. And it wasn't just him who had to deal with what came out; I did too.

He bent down, his lips brushing against mine. The strokes were soft, light, teasing. He took his time, savoring me, sending me reeling with sensations.

When we broke apart, my head was spinning. His arms circled my waist, and he held me against him as I rested my head on his chest. How could he kiss me like this and still believe this was only physical? Every time he kissed me, something stirred in my chest. Emotions that I hadn't expected to feel for him. Missing him when he was away, longing to see his smile or the glint in his eye when he passed by my work desk. Anticipation, the buildup, followed by a painfully sweet release, knowing it would be a while before I could be with him again.

I was getting something good in my life, finally, and in my experience, good things never stayed.

If someone good accidentally came my way, they would soon realize how broken I was and leave. Because good attracted more good, whereas broken people attracted the kind of people who could ruin you for life.

Sometimes, I wished it weren't me who lived this life. That I could get to be someone else just for a day. To live the carefree life of a twenty-eight-year-old without having to worry over a younger sibling. And then I'd hate myself for thinking those thoughts when, in reality, I should be fiercely proud of Henry. I'd tell myself not to feel what I was feeling, so often that I'd distance myself from emotions. I'd found happiness in scheduling, in logistics, and conversations that kept uncomfortable emotions out of the way.

But now, I wanted Sean. I wanted the little efforts he went through to make me feel like I was the only person in the world that mattered. Not his things. Just his affection and his time.

The Boss Problem

But from Sean's own words before, he had very little of both to give.

I faked a laugh, sliding my hands up his shoulders and clasping my fingers behind his neck. "I'm used to normal things, Sean. I don't need to feel special."

His eyes flashed with desire. Sean wanted me. That was obvious. I lived for moments like this. Where I felt like I was the only woman in the world and Sean was completely consumed by his lust for me.

"I disagree," he said. "But first, I've got something to show you. Come on."

46

CHLOE

We got out of the car twenty minutes later, outside a piercingly tall steel-and-glass skyscraper. It was now vacant, except for a security guard, who waved us in.

"Special access?" I asked while we crossed the dimly lit lobby to the elevator.

Sean grinned back at me as we waited for the elevator. Once in, he pulled me to him as we rode up.

In an instant, our lips were pressed against each other, yielding to the desire burning inside us. His lips made feathery brushes over mine. Once, twice before he ramped up the intensity.

The elevator doors must have opened again, but Sean had me pressed against the back wall, his kisses intense, because the next thing we knew, we were heading back down.

I burst out laughing while Sean broke off, breathing heavily and staring at the numbers on the control panel as they counted down.

"How the hell did we miss getting out?" he asked,

turning to me after he pressed the button for the rooftop again.

When the elevator rose and finally stopped at the rooftop, he took my hand as he led me out.

In two seconds, my jaw dropped.

We were standing at a beautiful rooftop botanical garden.

The garden was lush and vibrant, filled with a variety of flowers in every shade imaginable—deep crimson roses, delicate white orchids, and vibrant purple lavenders. The air was fragrant with the scent of jasmine and gardenias. It was beyond romantic.

Pathways wound through the garden, lined with soft, velvety moss and sprinkled with petals. Small, discreet lanterns and fairy lights were draped across the trees and shrubs, casting a warm, golden glow that illuminated the flowers and created a magical ambiance. Twinkling lights were also woven into the vines that climbed the trellises. It was like being in a secret, secluded garden.

Off to one side, there was a sheltered seating area with plush, comfortable chairs and a low table, set with crystal glasses and a bottle of champagne. Nearby, a small, trickling fountain added a soothing sound to the background.

Above, the night sky was clear, and the skyline of the city stretched out in the distance. But up here, it was just the two of us in the beauty and tranquility of the garden.

I took a step forward, my jaw dropping as I surveyed the scene. "What is this place?" I breathed out, turning to Sean.

He was drinking me in. "Do you like it?" he asked. "I wasn't sure if you were a flowers-and-gardens kind of woman, but I took a chance."

I wrapped my arms around him, pressing my face to his

chest, my voice wrecked with emotion. "I love it," I said, my voice shaking.

No one had ever done anything this special for me before.

He took me close to the southern edge of the balcony, wrapping his hands around my waist as he stood behind me. "I'm glad you like it," he said, his voice deep and low.

We stayed silent for a while.

Then, he pointed to a building in the distance.

"Down there, you'll see the Kennedy Center. I gave my first piano concert there when I was twelve."

"Let me guess," I said, turning around. "Going by your quest for perfection, you received a standing ovation?"

He chuckled and pressed a delightful kiss to the side of my neck. "The hall was almost empty, and the four people who were there left midway. And they were friends of the family."

"Oh, dear God. How rude," I said, indignant that someone would treat kid Sean like that.

He trailed more kisses down my neck, pulling the sleeve of my dress down my shoulder.

I shivered in anticipation. How would tonight end?

"Sean," I began when his kisses got steamier, his hand on my waist before trailing up slowly to cup my breast.

My head was thrown back, and he was kissing my neck. His hand curved around my back, holding me in place, and he looked very much like he'd soon rip my dress off.

He stopped, and looking at me, he said, "Come here."

He led me by the hand and took me around the side of the balcony, to the northern edge.

"Look," he said, and I turned to see him point to a spot on the rooftop to my right.

My jaw dropped.

In ten feet was a beautiful, pristine white bed with a lacy canopy around the edges. A string of fairy lights encircled the top, and the bed was surrounded by roses.

My hand flew to my mouth, and I turned to him for an explanation.

He smiled. "I had this set up just in case our date went spectacularly well." He broke off and kissed the back of my hand. "Which it has for me at least."

A warm, fluttery feeling swelled up in me. "It's been spectacular for me too," I muttered in a daze.

Was this really happening to me?

"And in that case, well, I knew we couldn't go back to either of our places tonight, and I wasn't ready to take you to just any hotel room—"

I wrapped my arms around his waist, pulling him to me as I hugged him tight. This scene, being with him out here in the gentle breeze, the wine—it already seemed like the best night I'd had in ages. Knowing that Sean had put so much thought into this just brought tears of happiness to my eyes.

I swallowed hard. "Do we keep this ... this relationship only between us? What happens to our jobs if anyone finds out?"

He looked like he hadn't thought that far ahead. "It isn't completely against the rules for us to date each other." His eyes were reading me intently as he spoke.

"Just frowned upon?" I asked.

He nodded.

I considered that, wondering how I felt about it.

"Does it make you uncomfortable, others knowing about us?" he asked.

I nodded.

"If it makes you feel better, we could keep it just between us for now."

I closed my eyes for a moment. "It doesn't necessarily make me feel better. But it's the only solution I can see for the present. And I want to talk about it with you now, before it's too late."

"Regret and you shouldn't have anything to do with each other," he said, taking my hand in his. "But I'll be honest with you, Chloe," he promised. "I'm not looking for a serious relationship, and I'm not sure what this is. But I also know this: I can't resist you. This feels real. More real than anything I've had in a long time, and I'm ready to give it a chance."

"I can't resist you either," I said, clasping my hands around his neck. "But we're going to have to be careful about it. I don't want to be branded as the person sleeping around to get ahead at work."

"You're right; if the news of us seeing each other ever got out, it would unfairly be worse for you than me." His voice was heavy.

When my eyes drifted upward, Sean was looking at me plainly. His face was so rugged in its handsomeness that I felt a tingling in my stomach. I'd never been with such a man before.

"And I still want you, Sean," I said as my legs trembled.

"Are you sure?" he asked.

I answered him with a kiss.

As the kiss deepened, Sean's fingers rose to my shoulders, tugging my dress down. The elastic band of the sleeves gave in to him far too easily. The dress lowered to my waist. Cool air rushed over my bra, and Sean paused, stopping to devour me with his eyes.

His expression was feral, and I knew the dominating man in him had woken up.

"I want all your clothes off," he commanded, a new edge to his voice.

I bit my lip as I considered resisting. It was useless. Tonight, I was going to relish giving up control.

I let my dress fall to the floor. His eyes tracked my lingerie and my belly while I ran my hands over my lace push-up bra. I touched my breasts tantalizingly, inviting him to touch me.

He came closer and hungrily took in my bra and thong. His fingers traced the underside of my bra. The underwire was tight and had been digging painfully into my skin all night long.

"Does this hurt?" he asked, feeling it, and I bit my lip as I nodded.

He reached behind me—to take it off, I assumed—but for an instant, he tightened the clasp, pushing my breasts further up.

I gasped at the sudden pain, and he immediately crushed his lips against mine with a ferocity I had never felt before.

"Sean," I pleaded as he drew the moment out.

Tears pricked the edges of my eyes before he undid the clasp of my bra completely. The pain subsided, and the skimpy garment fell to the floor. In a swift move, he tore off my flimsy thong. It gave way in his hands without a fight.

I stood, completely naked in front of him, as he stepped back and surveyed me.

"Turn around," he ordered, and I did, feeling the intensity of his gaze on my ass.

I spun around to face him, and I noticed he had

unzipped his pants. His pants and briefs fell to the floor, and his cock was out.

It was huge, and he was stroking it while looking at me.

Just seeing him like this made my core ache as a warm spot came to life between my legs.

Also, he had a mad, possessive look in his eyes as he gazed at me, and I knew for sure that tonight would not be enough for us to be satiated with each other.

"Touch yourself," he ordered, and I ran my hands over my breasts, my fingers circling the nipples.

His cock was achingly hard now, and I longed to feel it, to take it in my mouth.

I'd never enjoyed the idea of giving a blow job, but tonight, it was different.

Tonight, I couldn't wait to take him in my mouth and run my tongue over his hard length.

I swiped my tongue over my lip as I approached him. The intense look on his face was now mixed with longing.

Longing for me.

It was *my* lips he wanted on his hard length.

Without another word, I fell to my knees and guided his cock into my mouth.

"Fuck, Chloe," he groaned as my lips touched his smooth skin.

He gripped my hair as I took him in my mouth, gently licking and teasing the tip of his length before I took all of him in, inch by inch.

He was so big; I was close to gagging.

I wrapped my fingers around his base, stroking him as I sucked. It was chill, and I was naked, on my knees, for a man who I'd once thought was an arrogant prick.

How far I'd come.

I swirled my tongue around his cock while I worked my

hands, stroking him. I slowly picked up the pace, and I noticed his balls tightening.

"You're mine, Chloe," he gasped as I licked and sucked him to delirium, pushing him to the edge.

My arousal was not far behind as Sean took charge. He was now fucking my mouth, his hips moving while I sucked.

"Tell me you're all mine."

I nodded, keeping my eyes on him as pressure built in my mouth. I couldn't possibly open my mouth any wider, and it was just barely enough to hold all of him in. I sucked him deeper, loving the groans that fell from his lips. He was desperate for me, and he pumped harder, faster. Until finally, with a guttural groan, he came undone.

He threw his head back, his grip still firm on my hair as he held me in place, and I swallowed. Filling my belly with him as his tense body softened.

"Good girl," he breathed out and looked at me, dazed. "You were beyond good. You were ... fantastic." He stepped out of his briefs and pants, leaving them on the floor, and lifted me up.

Carrying me over to the bed, he set me on it and looked at me deeply, like he could see into the very depths of my soul.

"How did it take me so long to find you?" he asked, settling in on the bed next to me.

I lifted a finger and traced his cheek. "I'm not sure. Looking back, it feels like forever since you were such a dick to me at the café until I saw you again at Tassater."

He chuckled, and slowly, not breaking eye contact with me, he took his jacket off.

"I always act like a dick when I'm attracted to someone," he admitted after a moment.

"Because you hate that you admire someone besides yourself?" I asked in a wry tone.

He threw his head back and laughed. "Touché," he said as he propped his head up on his hand.

"But I haven't seen anyone as beautiful as you," he said, his voice husky as he kissed the side of my neck hungrily. "And I likely never will again," he confessed. "I need to be inside you, Chloe. Now."

His chest was flat against mine, and his fingers found their way down my stomach. My thighs fell apart quite naturally, and Sean's fingers worked my clit, pressing it in gentle circles.

His kisses slid down the front of my neck, slowing down near my chest. He drew one exposed, hardened nipple into his mouth, and I moaned, reaching for his hair.

"Oh, Sean," I muttered, running my fingers through his soft hair, feeling delirious as he circled the pointed peak with his wet tongue.

Waves of pleasure rode down my back and legs with rising intensity. I felt free and alive in ways no other man had ever done to me before. A warm pool of wetness grew between my thighs.

Sean's other hand reached down to stroke my thigh up and down tantalizingly, eliciting a low moan of desire from me. I closed my eyes with a sigh of pleasure, yielding to him completely. The night air, the quiet sounds of traffic, and the stars above—none of them compared to this moment. He could ask anything of me, and I would give it to him. I felt like I was floating on air.

"Do you like this?" he asked, increasing his pressure in his fingers and flicking his tongue over my pointed nipple in circles. Once, twice.

I clutched his hair, pushing his head closer to my breast,

wanting to feel more. In response, he bit down gently on my nipple, making me cry out his name with the jolt of pain before he ran his wet tongue over it again, soothing the ache with his gentle flicks.

It had never been this good with Bruce, and Sean wasn't even in me yet. My climax wasn't too far away, and I clung tight to him.

"More," I gasped, and he pressed down on my clit, sliding a finger in at the same time.

"Sean," I cried, arching my back while he put a second finger in.

I writhed, unable to take it anymore. I was so close.

"I need you," I said desperately.

I ground over his hand, and he rewarded me by plunging his fingers in faster, deeper. With an ease that only he had, he found that sensitive spot inside me, making me moan.

I was trembling, my head thrown back, and like a flash of lightning, my orgasm tore through me. Waves upon waves of pleasure rocked my body while I fisted the sheets hard. Sean's hand slowly stilled, and he looked like he wanted to get up. I wanted to hold him closer, to never let him go.

He lifted his head, and withdrawing his hand, he was on top of me, kissing me again, as though he'd been starved for my touch. He was still in his shirt, and I wished I could feel his warm skin sliding against mine. I wanted all of him against me, bare skin pressed to mine.

I didn't know what was going through me, but I pulled him to me and wrapped my arms around him tightly.

I finally understood what I was afraid of. That he'd go. That he'd leave me.

He was my home, I realized, and I'd never had this feeling before. I'd crossed a boundary I shouldn't have, and I didn't know what to do with this knowledge. I wanted to treasure this moment, and to grip it tight, and never let him be anyone else's.

My hands weakened, and I looked into his beautiful eyes.

I put my face in the crook of his neck, trying to contain my trembling body.

He was handsome, lying on top of me. I could feel the hard planes on his stomach under his shirt and ran my hands over his firm biceps as he placed them on either side of my head. He was, quite simply, perfection from head to toe. I wanted him to be mine and mine alone. I wanted to worship every inch of his body, not just tonight, but forever.

He pressed his forehead against mine. "I can't wait any longer, Chloe," he said, unaware of what had been going through my mind.

I focused on my breath as he pulled his shirt over his head and tossed it aside. I heard the rip of foil as he slipped a condom on before he came back to bed with me.

He placed his body on mine, pinning me down, his lips deliciously close to my ear. He breathed deeply, his lips dipping to nuzzle my cheek. The touch sent a shiver down to my toes.

"I want you, Chloe," he breathed out.

I've wanted you since I met you at the café, I thought, but I only said, "I *need* you, Sean."

He guided his length to my entrance, and I spread my legs, feeling more aroused than ever. I'd never been trembling with desire for Bruce, but I definitely was for Sean.

When Sean, hard and firm, slid in, stretching me from the inside, I bit back a strangled whimper. He moved in slow, intense strokes, his breath ragged as he buried himself to the hilt.

"God," he muttered now that he was fully in me, "you feel really good, Chloe."

I lifted my legs to wrap around his back, pulling him more deeply into me, and he groaned, closing his eyes at the feeling. I needed more, and Sean didn't make me wait.

"You're every bit as delicious as I imagined you to be," he said with a thick thrust.

I closed my eyes as the sensations rolled over me. I felt pleasure and a little pain with every hard plunge.

"You're every bit as perfect as my dreams painted you to be," he said, driving deeper this time.

I moaned when he moved, his angle reaching a tender spot in me.

I put my arms around his neck, pulling him closer for a hot, fervent kiss. "You dreamed of me?" I asked as he pumped into me. Again and again.

Sex with Sean was way different from what I'd had with Bruce. Sean looked me in the eye while making love to me, and I loved it.

"Every. Fucking. Night," he grunted out, punctuating each word with a thrust. His hungry lips were on mine again. "I've dreamed of making love to you more times than I could count. I've jerked off to you in the shower each morning more times that I cared for. Every day I came into work and hated that I was hard for you again. You drove me insane every day, and tonight ..."

I lifted my hips as he sped up. His voice was deliciously hoarse, and I writhed as I waited for him to release my pent-up passion. With Bruce, more often than not, I'd never orgasm. With Sean, he'd made me orgasm two times in twenty minutes.

"Now, it's my turn to drive you insane."

47

SEAN

When we lay back down on the bed, naked and spent, Chloe turned to me.

She was flushed, breathless, and beautiful. I smelled her everywhere, inhaling her intoxicating scent. A totally new sense of longing overtook me. To bury myself in her again.

Chloe rested her head on my shoulder in a simple, trusting movement, and I immediately pulled her closer.

No woman's trust had ever meant as much to me as Chloe's.

She was the first woman I truly cared about. The only woman whose opinions—of me and my choices—mattered.

With every other woman I'd been with, I couldn't care less about what they thought of me.

But Chloe had changed my hard heart, softened me, and brought all my walls down.

For the past few years, I'd been fooling around, dabbling in one-night stands and flings. With Chloe, I was in danger of losing my heart.

I looked at her, her blonde hair spread out on the pillow beneath her, as she put her palm on my cheek.

"Sean, I know this is probably the last thing you want to talk about right now …"

I nuzzled her neck. "Does it involve signing an NDA?" I asked.

She balked. "What? No."

I grinned, running my fingertips along the length of her arm. "I knew that would get you. All right, what is it?"

"You got this beautiful canopy for me. I'm so flattered. I mean, this just elevated the date to something special. Nobody has ever done anything to make me feel so special. I realize this might be common in your circle—"

"It isn't," I said firmly.

We stared at each other.

I wanted her so much. Night after night, exactly like this.

I wanted it so badly that I felt like I'd explode if I couldn't have her again.

I pulled her into my arms and kissed her before saying, "In fact, I've never done this for any other woman, Chloe. I've never had the desire to do anything like this for another woman. This is a first for me too."

She looked me in the eye as I said that, and when she spoke, she said, "I love knowing that. Because it's different for me too. Of course, I feel passion and heady and pure, unadulterated lust for you. But when I'm with you, it feels like it's the first time I've ever been truly intimate with someone."

I groaned and captured her mouth in mine in a ravenous kiss. Her words nearly drove me mad. Add that to how I loved her voice, her smell, her taste, and I wanted to take her deeply. To fuck her hard and to feel her clench around my cock again. Because I couldn't process all the emotions that were sweeping through me anymore.

We were coming up close to the end of her work assignment for me. I didn't want to think about the time I'd walk into work and not find her there. Waiting for me with my coffee and her special smile.

That thought made me feel a strange sort of ache in my rib cage.

I was feeling hot and restless, so I kissed her long and hard, turning over so I was on top of her. In a moment, we were rocking into each other in perfect rhythm.

She was so tender and so sweet that I felt a storm of emotions flood my veins. Something in me had unraveled. My cold heart had finally cracked. I felt my heart pumping wildly, beating for her. Chloe rocked her hips with my rhythm, her blue eyes watching me as her breathing picked up.

Did she know what she had done to me? I fucked her slowly, sensually, enjoying every moment of being in her and the way she reached for me as her climax neared. She lifted her arms, cupping my face as she rose to meet my lips.

We kissed while both of us came apart, exploding into a beautiful, sweet release.

Sleep was heavy, and my eyelids fell shut briefly as we dozed off in each other's arms.

Hours later, in between moments of fistful slumber, her phone rang through the quiet night.

She got up, sitting up and wrapping the blanket around her, before she answered it.

As she spoke gently into the phone, I traced my fingers around her shoulder blades. I frowned when I saw an old bruise on her left shoulder, hoping that I wouldn't see any more bruises now that she had a better bed.

And in a minute, Chloe hung up and turned back to me, disappointment written on her face.

"What is it?" I asked, hoping the answer wouldn't be what I was afraid it was.

She hesitated.

I reached for her waist, wrapping my hand around her and pulling her closer. Her hand went to caress the soft blanket, and she spoke thoughtfully.

"Henry fell off his wheelchair," she said. "He was trying to reach something on the kitchen shelf when he fell." She cursed under her breath. "If only I'd kept it accessible."

I pressed a kiss to her bare upper arm. "Do you have to go? Isn't there a neighbor who could help?"

"Greg—a neighbor—did help. He was out pulling back the trash bins when he heard the shelf fall and rushed over to help. It was Greg on the phone now, too, letting me know what happened. He said Henry was shaken and was wondering when I'd be back. That shelf has been unsteady for a while now, and it's my fault for not having noticed it earlier."

Damn. Her place seemed to be falling apart. I would make sure she got out of there soon.

I'd also requested an exquisite breakfast to be delivered here in the morning. A table and chairs were to be set up on the eastern side, and I'd wanted us to have breakfast with the sunrise.

The look on her face was one of regret. "I'm sorry, but can we go back to New York now, please?" she whispered, placing a kiss on my lips and getting up. "I need to get home."

I nodded even though what I was feeling had nothing to do with being agreeable. "I'll take you home," I said, reaching for my clothes. "It's okay."

My hand was on the small of her back as we made our way down the elevator, and even though I tried to avoid it, our moods were subdued.

I suspected Bruce had left her for the same reason—her role as a caretaker meant she had less to give as a girlfriend. But I hated that I was so conflicted about Chloe's role of being a caretaker. She had no other option, but I wanted more from her and was upset she couldn't give it to me. It felt ridiculous to know she couldn't help something and simultaneously feel frustrated with her for it.

"If Greg helped Henry back on his wheelchair, why do you need to go?" I asked finally, unable to keep the questions off my tongue.

I didn't want to seem irritable at Chloe, but I also needed answers. Was there something I was not getting?

She bit her lip. "Henry's rattled. I'd hate myself if I wasn't there for him right now," she admitted finally, and I stared at her in amazement.

"Why?" I asked as the elevator doors opened in the lobby and we got out.

"I want Henry to know that I'm always there for him. That I'll never leave him like our dad did."

Scenes flashed back into my mind. Her at the café, in her wedding dress, getting dumped over the phone.

"Was that your brother on the phone during your wedding day?" I asked, my voice giving away my utter disbelief. "Was he why you rescheduled your wedding?"

Her gaze stayed on my face, and I could see the vulnerability on hers.

"Yes," she said at last.

Fuck.

This added a whole new dimension to my understanding of Chloe's need to be Henry's caretaker. She didn't just need to be around him all the time; she had decided to not have a life of her own too.

"This is crazy," I said, running my fingers through my hair as we walked out the main doors and into the night, where my car was waiting. "Why are you doing this? I bet Henry doesn't want you to give up your night for him when he's fine. Why don't you give yourself permission to just have fun? To live your life like you should?"

A look of frustration crossed her face as she paused on the steps. "Sean, we can't go there tonight. There simply isn't time to discuss this. Besides, you said it yourself. We wouldn't be serious. We're temporary. What's the need to stay out all night when it's going to end anyway?"

Her questions silenced me.

What had I expected, honestly? That one night would change the way she felt about us?

I was just her boss—someone she hooked up with. And this night meant absolutely nothing more to her.

Even if I felt angry, unhappy, and frustrated about parting with her, even if I brought myself to admit that this hurt, I needed to be sane about this: Chloe wasn't in love with me.

We were nothing more than no-strings-attached sex.

Nothing about us showed signs of us being a couple in the future.

Her brother would always be the most important thing to her. Even if I could start to admit to myself that the mad feeling I felt was something closer to love.

Shaking my head in disappointment, I held open the door to my car. Chloe got in, and I followed, still shocked.

As the car began to move, I turned to her, wishing I could hold her hand in mine and pull her closer. She looked out the window, her chin up and her eyes away from me.

She didn't want me to argue with her, and I knew I couldn't push it.

But I had one last question for her.

"Did you tell Henry that you were out with me tonight? Your boss, Sean, and not Will?"

She turned to me slowly, and I could see the answer in her eyes, even before she shook her head.

Damn.

I'd thought I was the one who had trouble with commitment, the one who had trouble giving time to my partner.

I hadn't realized Chloe would be worse.

48

SEAN

The next two days after my frustrating end to my date involved me working from home.
This was partly because Helen was back. She was staying with us for the night, hoping to introduce Matt to Lucas and for us to get to know one another.

I'd expected it to sting, going out to dinner with Helen, Matt, and Lucas. It was a restaurant just down the street from where I'd taken Chloe to on our first unexpected date. I had looked over my shoulder at The Hilford, wishing I were there again with her, before Lucas called for me to hurry up and join them at their table.

I missed Chloe terribly, but my pride was too strong, and I was too stubborn to ask her how she was doing. Our conversations, when we did have them, had been brusque on my part and professional on hers.

Except for one text she sent me, asking me how I was.

I was too furious with myself to respond reasonably. I cared, dammit, and she had walked out on me.

I was in too deep while she was unaffected.

The other thing that hurt me today was the fact that Lucas chose to sit between his mom and Matt. Not Helen's incessant hugs and kisses to Matt, which I'd come to see as a constant reminder of how easily he fit into their world.

Lucas didn't seem to mind his mother's overbearing affection for her fiancé, I noticed. While I couldn't help but feel Helen's affection should have been focused more on Lucas than Matt at the moment.

I watched Lucas's face light up when he explained to her that he had a new friend now.

"Brianna," I supplied.

"Is that so?" Helen asked, looking from me to Lucas and back at me again. She gave me a funny look, almost as if she didn't expect me to know much about Lucas's friends.

"Dad's the reason I met her," Lucas explained to his mother. "Dad took me biking in Central Park, and it was the best, Mom. Hey, we should do that tomorrow! All of us. It'll be exciting."

She gave me a wary look, and I remembered her dislike for biking.

"We can talk about that once we've taken a look at this," she said, reaching for one of her bags. She pulled out a wrapped present. "I have tons of presents for you—one for each week that I missed you."

We wouldn't be biking tomorrow—I knew that.

Lucas shrieked with excitement and unwrapped his presents—a boomerang, as well as seven other toys that he didn't care for. I saw the warm hug he gave his mother. He didn't care what gifts she got him or if he couldn't go biking, as long as he was with her.

"You've got a look on your face," she muttered to me when Matt stepped out to use the restroom. Lucas was busy with his new toys and wasn't listening.

I felt myself bristle. I wouldn't tolerate her criticisms. "What look?"

"That look you have when you're doing something against your better instinct. Who is she?"

I froze. I'd forgotten how well Helen knew me. "I don't know what you mean."

She snorted. "So, it is definitely a woman then." She was silent for a bit and then snuck another look at me.

"Something's different," she mused as she continued to gaze at me. "You look like you've gone beyond casual hookups and into lovesick territory."

"You're out of your mind," I growled. Surely, I wasn't that obvious.

"Has Lucas met her?"

I took a deep breath. There was no point in arguing anymore. "She's helping me bond with Lucas," I said.

Helen barked out a laugh. "She's one of your nannies?" She didn't wait for an answer. "I hope you haven't been out in public with her. It isn't good for your image or for Lucas to know you're sleeping with the help."

I froze at Helen's vile words. "Don't fucking talk about her that way," I snarled, and Helen's eyes widened in surprise. "I'm crazy about Chloe, and, no, she isn't just a nanny. She's my employee at Tassater—and a very valuable one."

Helen shook her head, biting back a response. Finally, she said, "I hope you know you've crossed a line with dating an employee. She might be good in your bed, but that doesn't mean you need to lose your head over her."

"I haven't lost my head over her," I gritted out and hated the look of relief on her face.

Why shouldn't I lose my head over Chloe, damn it?

Matt was on his way back, and I'd already paid the

check, so I stood up before I slammed my fist into something from frustration.

"I'm leaving," I said shortly to Helen, who didn't look surprised.

Bidding a curt goodbye to Matt and giving Lucas a quick hug, I stepped away. I turned around when I heard Lucas call after me.

"Dad," he said, his gaze meeting mine with a vulnerability I'd never seen before. "You promised me we'd make pizzas sometime."

I had. As I took a more puzzled look at him, I finally understood where he was going with this. My heart swelled.

"Well then, buddy, looks like you're coming home next weekend to make pizza with me."

He gave me a broad smile, and I felt my heartbeat quicken. I ruffled his hair, and then with a curt nod at Helen, I walked away. The last thing I saw before I left was the happiness on Lucas's face as he smiled back at me before it was replaced by a look of pure devotion as he turned to his mother.

It reminded me of the bond between Chloe and Henry. Chloe couldn't get used to leaving Henry alone any more than Lucas could handle his mom being away.

It stung that Chloe couldn't be honest about who I was in her life, but could I really blame her? She'd said it herself that she preferred to keep it quiet. Which included keeping it from Henry. It would take time, but it would get better, and then Chloe would soon trust me that I wasn't here to take her brother away from her. She needed to come around because I was going to fight for her. I wasn't giving up on us.

I reached for my keys and drove to Chloe's. Lucas and Helen were spending the night at Matt's place, and I had my home to myself at last.

When I reached Chloe's street, my heart all but sang out loud.

Parking the car, I reached for my phone and called her as I walked over.

She didn't answer.

I called her again and again.

When she finally answered the call, it was with a frustrated, "What?"

I froze at her tone. "How's Henry?" I asked.

She didn't answer right away, probably caught off guard.

"He's fine," she said at last.

"Was he awake when you reached home at one a.m. after running out on our date?" I asked. I was staring at her apartment door, wishing I could break it down.

"No," she said, after a moment's hesitation.

Great, so she'd run out on me, only to go home to her brother, who had been safe and asleep.

When she didn't speak, I knocked on her door. "Open up," I said.

I heard footsteps, and a moment later, she opened the door a crack. She was breathtakingly beautiful in her gray sweatpants and a beige tank top. Oh, how I wanted her in my arms right away.

"Why are you here?" she demanded, looking frustrated.

She looked over her shoulder quickly, and I realized there was a buzz in the background.

I put a hand on the door, trying to push it open. She stood her ground, not letting me in.

I could hear music and the chatter of voices. Was she having a party?

"What kind of party is this?" I asked, opening the door further as I took a look in.

My eyes roved over the faces of the guests—young kids

in their early twenties, who looked very naive and rather taken aback at my presence here.

"Is he a cop?" someone muttered while I slowly swiveled my gaze to Chloe, eyebrows raised.

She swallowed. "This is Henry's party for his friends," she said, just as Henry came into view.

He pushed his wheelchair over, his face breaking into a grin when he saw me.

"Will, isn't it?" he asked, extending his hand to me. I shook his hand while I gave Chloe a look.

She stared at me for a long, evaluating moment, noticing our handshake and my serious expression before she turned to Henry.

"Actually," she said, taking a deep breath, "this is Sean. Not Will."

Henry's look of shock was plain for everyone to see, and people's eyes were now drawn to this little scene.

But I was too busy savoring those words. Too busy watching Chloe with a feeling of pride surging through me.

She didn't break my gaze as she continued to look at me while she spoke to Henry. "And he is my boss."

Chloe's words were low, but in the sudden silence of the party, with only the dull hum of the music in the background, everyone heard it.

I heard a few gasps and some people mutter from the living room, but I didn't care.

Out of the side of my eyes, I noticed that Henry's jaw had dropped.

"Your boss?" he repeated with a gulp, and I turned to him with a smile.

"Yes," I said, reaching for Chloe's wrist. "And I need a word with Chloe. Alone. Now."

Saying that, I pulled her with me to her bedroom. Giving up, she followed me as I strode up to her room and drew her inside, shutting the door behind her.

I took in her parted lips and the way her wide eyes blazed with fury as she looked back at me.

"What's with the anger?" I grunted out.

She paused before crossing her arms over her chest. "You don't show up for work for a few days. Your emails and texts to me are only about work. Like nothing ever happened between us. And then you have the audacity to show up here? Of course I'm mad."

I leaned in. "Well, what should I assume when you cut our date short after five glorious hours?" I asked.

She didn't move from her spot. Her eyes darted over my face, taking me in.

"It was too much," she said finally.

"The date?" I asked, wondering if the display of my wealth had put her off.

"I didn't trust myself. I'm afraid that if I fell asleep with you, if I woke up with you, if I gave you my nights and days, that I might soon fall in love with you. And I don't want that for myself. I wanted some distance."

My heartbeat picked up. She was feeling something too. And she was scared.

"To be safe from heartbreak?" I asked.

She nodded.

"So, you took the first exit you could?" I asked again.

She was breathing fast, her chest rising and falling rapidly.

"What's your exit plan now?" I asked, stepping closer. One moment later, I was crowding her, breathing in her scent.

Her eyes widened, and she took a step back. "Sean," she whispered in a warning.

"What is it, baby?" I asked, placing a finger on her chin and tipping it up to look directly into her eyes. She couldn't ignore me now.

"I'm afraid," she said, taking another step back.

"Of me?" I asked.

"No." She shook her head, holding my gaze. "Of falling for you."

It was too late for me.

"Go ahead and fall. You're safe with me," I said, wrapping an arm around her waist and drawing her closer to me.

Her soft body pressed against mine, and my own body reacted with a jolt. Her presence drove me crazy. Until now, I'd thought it was lust. But I finally knew better.

"You'll destroy me," she whispered as I rubbed my thumb on the outline of her lips. Tracing those deeply sensual, full lips.

"I'd kill myself before I let anyone destroy you," I whispered. "Including me."

She sucked in a sharp breath, and before I knew it, I was crushing my lips to hers, and she was climbing on top of me. It was madness, how we couldn't keep our hands off each other.

I kissed her lips, her chin, and her neck, biting and sucking at a tender spot while she threw her head back.

"Oh, Sean," she said with a sharp intake of breath while I hitched her legs up around my hips while greedily kissing every part of her that I could.

Her lips parted as I kissed her fervently, desperately.

I needed this woman like I needed air, and I couldn't understand it.

I walked over to her bed and dropped her onto it.

She looked at me with obvious desire and longing before she cast a sideways glance at the bedroom door.

"We can't, Sean. Even if I want to do this so badly, there's no way I could keep quiet—"

I bent down, grazing my fingers down her body as I slowly reached her waistband. I pulled her pajamas off, pressing my lips to her belly. "There's no way in hell I can back off now," I muttered, tossing her pajamas aside as I ran my fingers up and down her newly exposed legs and thighs.

Her muscles clenched as I neared her core. I knelt down by the foot of her bed. I tightened my grip on her legs and pulled her to me.

"Not here, Sean," she begged with another anxious glance at the door. "They'll hear—"

"I need to be with you right now, Chloe," I pointed out, as my tongue found her sweet folds and began to tease her swollen clit. She was wet all right. "I can't wait any longer, Chloe. To taste you, to be in you, to feel you come in my arms. Or else I'll go mad."

She gasped with ecstasy as I pressed down on her clit, and then her eyes fell shut as her lips parted while I circled one thumb on her sensitive core. She trembled, her fingers clutching my hair as I cupped her bottom.

She moaned devastatingly when I tongued her wet folds and circled her clit.

"I need you too," she said breathlessly, her hips rising to meet my mouth better. "But Henry's out there—"

"It's time he hears how much I adore you," I muttered. "Now, stop talking," I ordered as I resumed flicking my tongue over her.

I teased her mercilessly, occasionally using my teeth to graze her clit and hear her gasp in response. I loved every single helpless moan and sharp inhale that came from her lips. I worshipped her over and over, until she came with a cry before covering her mouth with her hand as spasms rocked her body.

When she finally stilled, her breathing calming down, I climbed onto the bed with her.

"I've waited all this time to christen this bed with you," I said huskily, pinning her under me as I took her in my arms.

She came willingly, crushing my lips with hers, the taste of her still on my tongue.

We heard hushed laughter outside and some muttering while we kissed each other hungrily.

"People know what we're doing," she managed to say between ravenous kisses while her hands went on either side of my face.

I lifted my head and looked at her. She looked worried, but I didn't give her much time to think.

"Can they blame me? Everyone could see how sexy you looked in those pajamas. Now, be quiet," I responded before kissing her ferociously again.

I reached for her breasts under her tank top, finding her hard nipples and thumbing them. She moaned in pleasure just as I brought my free hand to her mouth, covering it.

"This is crazy, Sean," she gasped, but she pulled her top off with my help.

I sat up as I hungrily took my suit off. The jacket first, then the shirt, followed by my pants.

In a minute, I brought my hand to my cock. "I don't want a shred of clothing on you," I said, pulling her bra off while she obeyed and raised her hands.

The sight of her full breasts, pink nipples, and svelte figure had me so aroused. I was rock hard.

I climbed on top of her, aligning myself with her pussy before I pushed in. She reached her hands up tenderly for me, and I put my lips to hers while my thrusts were urgent and deep. We kissed, opening our mouths to let our tongues in. She felt so tight and so good as I pushed deeper in her. Her body clenched around my dick, and I nearly came already.

"Fuck, I forgot the condom." I froze, prepared to pull out when she drew me closer to her.

"I'm clean, Sean. And I'm on the pill, so it's okay."

I looked into her eyes. I hadn't been bare with a woman before, and before I could question how I'd let myself come this far, I nodded. I wanted to be with her with nothing separating us. I fucked her slowly, keeping our gazes locked.

"I'm clean too," I said, as I drove deeper into her with each thrust.

My heart was beating wildly, my pulse hammering, and her body was pulsing under mine.

She felt perfect. She was fucking perfect, and I loved possessing her this way.

My body felt tight, my nerves on fire as she clenched around my dick.

"Oh, Chloe," I said, hoarsely while she brought her legs around my thighs, pulling me deeper in her than I had known was possible.

I could feel the convulsions coming, and I knew I was losing control. Going by how tight she was, I had stretched and filled her beyond what she was used to.

I angled my body so that I hit her clit with each greedy thrust, and when she came, she cried out my name wildly and helplessly.

She was delicious when she unraveled, and I crushed my lips to hers to muffle her cry. But it was a second too late. Everyone outside had to have heard her come, and in a second, my body went taut, and I came inside her.

She held me tight while I spilled into her, biting my lip to control a guttural groan that tore from my throat.

In the few breathless moments that followed, we stared into each other's eyes. I leaned forward and kissed her forehead and looked her in the eye.

"You were spectacular," I said.

She looked back at me with undisguised happiness. I'd never seen her this happy and this relaxed.

When I was closer, I could see her eyes were sparkling.

"I thought ..." She trailed off, biting her lip. "I thought I'd disappointed you that night."

"By leaving early," I corrected. "Not with anything else. In fact, with everything else"—I brought her hands to my lips and kissed them—"you have far exceeded expectations."

She sighed with contentment as a rosy blush took over her cheeks.

"Fancy joining the party?" I asked with a wicked grin as I withdrew from her while she put a hand over her mouth, muffling her laugh.

I lay down next to her and stared at the ceiling for a few minutes. I settled her on my shoulder, draping an arm around her waist, and breathed in her scent. I felt strangely calm.

"Lucas is back with his mom," I said, feeling the need to unload all my concerns on her. When I turned, Chloe was watching me intently. "It didn't matter that she got him all the wrong gifts or that she wasn't prioritizing his favorite activities. He loves her."

She smiled and gave me a small, knowing look.

"And I now understand how much you were on tenterhooks that night. Ever since you had turned Henry's request down once already."

"I know," she muttered, looking like she was moments away from starting to tremble.

I was reminding her too much of that night, and she wasn't happy about it.

I pulled her in and gave her a quick kiss.

"I know I pushed you that night to say no to Henry, and you couldn't do it a second time. It'll get better with time, I promise. You won't feel this bad."

"With time?" she asked.

"With our second date, and the third, and the ..."

She cut my words off with a kiss of her own. "You saw me flee from a perfectly orchestrated date, and you still want me for more dates? I can't explain how desirable that makes you seem."

"Don't," I said, breaking apart from her and breathing heavily, my eyes on hers. "I'll insist on taking you again if you keep talking like that."

She grinned and pressed her lips against my parted ones once more.

"You can take me as often as you'd like tonight," she said with a humorous look at the closed door. "There's no way I can go out there and face them now."

The silence in the room was punctuated by a beep as a message lit up Chloe's phone. When she lifted her phone, I noticed it had a wallpaper picture of a woman in her early forties.

She checked the message and set her phone aside, looking conflicted. "Another notification from a recruiter trying to hire me," she muttered.

Our gazes locked, and I knew what neither of us wanted to say out loud. Was our time coming to an end? Would I still see her once she no longer worked for me?

I didn't know the answer to that question myself, so to distract myself, I asked her a completely different question.

"Who's the woman on your phone's lock screen? Is that your mom?" I asked, registering the resemblance between their dimpled smiles.

She nodded as she laid her head on my arm. "Yes, Mom," she muttered, trailing her fingers on my shoulder.

The touch sent tingles up my arm, but for once, I was more curious about the story behind the woman in bed with me than I was in my groin.

"She passed when I was barely eight. She had muscular dystrophy. All I remember was her lying down in bed and not being able to move, until …"

I buried my face in her hair and pressed kisses on her head, her cheek, and her lips. I couldn't imagine having to deal with the process of losing a parent at that age.

"Did you find out anything more about your dad?" I asked, reading from her silence that I was pushing her into uncomfortable territory. "You said you were going to meet him soon."

"Yes," she breathed heavily. "I did. I got his address, and I don't know. I'm debating calling him, and I'm scared. I'm scared that he might say he doesn't want to meet me. That he would laugh at me when I bring up the idea of him coming to Henry's graduation."

I felt an anger bubbling inside me at the idea of Chloe having to doubt her parent's love for her.

"If you need me to accompany you—" I began, and she nodded.

"I know. I'll ask if I need it. But I need to do this on my own. Not even with Henry," she said, her voice faltering. "It's the second secret I've kept from him."

I held her tight. "It'll be the last," I promised.

I thought back to an earlier conversation and realized I hadn't registered some key details back then. "I know I've asked you this before, but when did your dad leave?"

"When I was eighteen," she replied after a minute's hesitation.

I frowned.

"That doesn't make sense," I muttered. "Wasn't that the year he was in the accident?"

She inhaled heavily. "Yes. He left a few months after Henry's diagnosis. When the doctors predicted that he couldn't be mobile again and he'd be confined to a wheelchair, well, my dad said he couldn't take it again."

Again.

"He said he wasn't cut out to be a caretaker for the rest of his life. He didn't want to go through caring for another ... invalid. Like Mom had been before she passed on." Her voice broke. "He actually called Henry that."

"So, he left?" I asked, rubbing my hands over the length of her arms, deciding to take her attention away from this. Wishing I hadn't brought this up when it was still hurtful.

She nodded. "He left. And Henry still doesn't know why."

"What did you tell him?"

"That I wanted Dad to pay for my tuition at The Juilliard School and Dad refused to do so and left in anger. I would rather Henry think Dad left us because of something I did rather than his condition."

So, that was the first secret she'd kept from him.

In the silence, she shifted in her position so that her eyes could face the ceiling. "I still can't get over it. How could it have been that easy for Dad to give up on his family?"

"It shouldn't have been," I said, and I started to feel a

sense of doom for her upcoming visit to her dad. "And you're Henry's sole caretaker?"

She nodded. "Up until he was eighteen. Now that he's an adult, well, I am still involved in his life. I can't imagine it being any other way."

I knew with certainty that Chloe would never give up on Henry.

Looking back, I should have seen that as a warning.

49

SEAN

I took a swing and watched the golf ball fly in the air and bounce on the ground and roll toward the hole.

"Nice shot!" Desmond shouted. "Ouch," he groaned when the ball stopped a mere inch away.

A gentle breeze wafted past me, and I held on to my golf club as I walked over to where Desmond, Jonah, and Alex—my partners from the Lead Capital Group—were standing. The four of us were assembled on the lush green lawn of a private club in the Hamptons. We had a beautiful view of the ocean in the distance and smooth, rolling hills around us. All I found myself thinking about was what Chloe was doing right now.

The past week with Chloe had involved lots and lots of sex, us wearing each other out with how often we were going at it.

Besides the kitchen and the bathroom, we even had a few adventurous moments in the balcony. The only downside was that she still wasn't willing to spend the entire night at my place. She always ran back home, no matter how late the hour.

Someday, I'd get her to stay over with me, but for now, I was willing to wait.

I'd finally attended a longer meeting with my business partners, who had started to complain about my brief appearances at their fortnightly meetings.

Alex took a smooth, calculated swing, and when his ball missed the fairway, landing instead in the sand trap, he just grinned.

"The ball's cursed, I'm telling you," he said while I groaned.

It was easier for Alex to blame the ball than to admit he was off his game today. We all had those days.

"The early morning getting to you?" I asked him while Jonah attempted a shot.

"Not a chance," Alex said.

Jonah's neatly trimmed, precision-cut blond hair barely moved in the breeze as he swung his club.

We watched as his ball veered off course a bit.

I shook my head. "Maybe the green is cursed."

Desmond shot the golf ball just to his right, sending it into the middle of the fairway. He'd set himself up for a good second shot, and he looked just a bit proud.

"Sean's jinxed our game," Jonah insisted, throwing his hands up in the air while Desmond laughed his heart out at the idea.

Jonah's phone rang, and he stepped aside to answer it. Putting it away, he began walking back to us, a frown on his face.

"Giving your team a hard time again?" I asked in a wry voice.

Jonah shook his head. "Don't know what you're on about," he said, pocketing his phone. "I only needed the job done right. How hard can it be to do a bug fix that solves *everything* without breaking five other things?"

I looked through my golf clubs and picked out a seven iron for my next swing. "Well, it depends on how much time you gave them. A week to get it done?"

The three of us stared at Jonah, who took a swing at the ball. The ball sailed gracefully through the air, and it landed on the green and bounced a few times before stopping next to the hole. Jonah always pushed boundaries, and this time, he'd reached the green sooner than expected.

Jonah turned to me. "Fifty minutes," he said finally. "It can't be that hard, really."

Desmond snorted while the rest of us walked over to our golf carts. "If you don't treat them better, you'll lose half your staff soon, Jonah. Good employees are very hard to come by."

Speaking of ...

"I will need to push off soon, guys," I said while the others looked up in surprise.

"An early push-off? Tell me, Sean, who's the new woman?" Desmond asked, a knowing smile on his face.

I groaned. Now that Desmond had found Ava again and was happier than I'd ever seen him, he thought he knew everything about why I wanted to end a game early. It was infuriating.

"A woman?" Jonah demanded, spinning around to face me. "Is she why you skipped last week's meeting?"

I raised my eyebrows as I got into my cart. "I was at last week's meeting," I pointed out. "All ten minutes."

"Perhaps you were physically present, but it sure seemed like you were elsewhere." Jonah walked up to me with a wicked grin.

I grabbed Jonah's head in a mock tussle, and Alex laughed.

"Just for that joke, next time, you're buying lunch," I announced as I let go.

50

SEAN

A couple of happy weeks passed, and I was a frequent visitor at Chloe's apartment. I'd spent two Sundays with Henry while Chloe began her PMP certification course.

Henry had been initially wary of my presence on Sunday evenings, especially since he now knew exactly who I was.

He insisted he was fine to stay alone. Of course he was, but I told him I was here to cook dinner for Chloe so that when she got back, she'd have something to eat and someone to scold.

That got Henry chuckling as he tried to guess what I'd be scolded for. And that had been the start of an easier relationship with Chloe, one where she didn't suspect me of trying to take over her brother's place in her life.

On one of those days, Henry had mentioned Chloe's love for dancing and how she'd given it up after his accident. Once Chloe passed her PMP certification course, I resolved to help her join dance classes again. I wanted to restore everything she'd lost when her father abandoned them, leaving her abruptly in charge at the young age of eighteen.

On my third week, when I showed up early on Sunday evening, hoping for a chance to see Chloe before she left for her class, I was in for a shock.

I found her sobbing in her apartment when I walked in.

"What's the matter?" I asked, rushing to the couch and kneeling down next to her.

Going by the silence in the other rooms and how freely Chloe was crying, I knew Henry had to be out.

"It's Henry's graduation night next week," Chloe sobbed. "I wanted Dad to attend. He should be so proud of Henry. But I caught hold of Dad. He didn't even want to invite me home. We met at a café, and he said he had no interest in coming to see Henry graduate. It was Henry's dream that Dad would show up. And I couldn't make that dream come true."

I drew her into my arms, hugging her to my chest, and felt enraged on her behalf.

"He's an asshole, and I hope you'll cut him out of your life after this incident. And, Chloe," I said, taking her hands in mine, "Henry is much, much stronger than you think he is. Tell him the truth. Tell him your dad said no. He'll take it, and you'll be surprised at how little it will affect him. You are all that matters to Henry. You being there for his graduation night. Nobody else."

She smiled through her tears, and she lay her head on my chest, wiping her tears as she nodded. "That's right."

"Of course I'm right. When have I ever not been?"

She lifted her head and smiled back at me.

I pushed her hair behind her ears and shook my head. "After your experience with jerks like me, I thought you'd be used to your dad's assholey response."

Chloe shook her head. "You aren't like him, Sean—thank goodness. Not one bit. You love your son. You'd do anything for your son—I've seen that."

She wiped her eyes again with the back of her hand and looked around, seeming more composed. "But I'm starting to reconcile with my own pain. Dad won't be a part of my wishes anymore. Just Henry." She turned to me with a wistful smile. "And you," she said, leaning closer to me and pressing her lips against mine.

I understood that with Chloe, this was the best I could get. To be right up there with Henry in her life. It would never be just me, and I was learning to be okay with that.

In a week, her stint as my assistant would be over, and I felt an ache I couldn't explain at the thought of that. I didn't want her to leave.

"I have a request," I said after a while. "If you feel up to it, there's someone in my family who'd love to meet you."

She blinked, her teardrops clinging to her lashes. "Who?"

51

CHLOE

Lucas stood beside me on the balcony, practically bouncing with excitement as I guided his drone through the sky. I was still a bit shaky with the controls. But the way Lucas beamed at me, I was starting to forget about my nerves.

Lucas's eyes were glued on the little whirring machine above us, his face lit up with pure joy. I tried to keep my focus.

"Like this?" I asked, glancing at him for approval.

"Yeah! Just like that!" He grinned, pointing up at the drone as it banked left, swooping in a smooth arc.

I could feel Sean's eyes on us from the living room. Even without looking, I knew he was watching, probably amused by how serious I was taking this.

"You're getting the hang of it," Sean called out, his voice warm.

I shot him a quick smile, my attention still on making sure I didn't crash the thing.

Lucas laughed, and I couldn't help but join in. His joy

was contagious, and I loved how at ease he was around Sean now. There had been a time when he'd been quieter, hanging back, unsure of his Dad. But now, it felt like they'd found their groove.

I stole a glance at Sean, my heart doing that annoying little flutter it always did when I caught him looking at me like that—like I was more than he'd expected. His smile was soft, and there was something in his eyes that made me feel like maybe I was becoming something more.

I turned back to Lucas, who was pointing eagerly at the drone again, shouting instructions, and I couldn't stop smiling.

"Lucas, is it fine if Chloe joins us for dinner?" Sean said, his voice low and smooth as he walked up to us.

His hand grazed the small of my back in a way that sent a subtle thrill through me. His smile lingered just a moment too long, eyes meeting mine with a heat that I felt in every nerve.

Lucas looked up at the two of us with a curious expression on his face before he nodded. "That's fine," he said.

I wasn't sure what to expect from Lucas. Would he like me or treat me with suspicion, like Henry had no doubt done to Sean in the beginning?

Lucas brought his drone down and began packing it up while Sean got the dinner ingredients out. I caught Lucas sneaking glances at us as the three of us worked together on the pizza. Sean stayed close, his touch lingering every chance he got—an arm brushing mine, his fingers grazing my waist, as he helped with the toppings.

"Need a hand, babe?" Sean murmured, his lips so close to my ear that the warmth of his breath sent a shiver down my spine. His hand slid over mine, guiding me as I spread the sauce, his chest brushing against my back, his body heat enveloping me.

I chuckled softly, nudging him playfully. "I've got it," I whispered, but didn't resist the way his hand lingered on my waist, fingers teasing the fabric of my dress.

I could feel Lucas watching us, curiosity flickering in his young eyes, but I couldn't help the magnetic pull between Sean and me.

When Sean stepped onto the balcony to take a call, Lucas quickly leaned in, his voice low, conspiratorial. "Are you Dad's girlfriend?"

I glanced toward Sean, still visible through the glass door, his gaze occasionally drifting to me, even while on the phone, that soft smile never leaving his lips. I wasn't sure what Sean wanted Lucas to know, but I smiled gently.

"Maybe you should ask your dad," I whispered.

Lucas shook his head, mumbling, "Never mind." The disappointment in his voice tugged at my heart as he ran off to use the bathroom.

As soon as Sean returned, his hand was back on me, slipping around my waist as if it belonged there. He pressed a slow, lingering kiss to my temple, his lips trailing just a little too close to my ear. "Missed you," he whispered, his breath hot against my skin.

I laughed softly. "You were gone for five minutes."

"Still too long," he replied, his hand resting on my hip, fingers lightly tracing circles through the fabric.

He let go when we heard Lucas open the bathroom door, and led me to the dining table.

As we sat down for dinner, Sean's attention was laser-focused, never drifting far from me, even as we started eating. Every touch, every glance felt charged, like we were barely keeping ourselves in check.

Lucas, in between bites of pizza, finally broke the silence. "By the way, Dad, Mom's birthday is in two weeks. Can you help me buy her a gift, Dad?"

I saw the flicker of conflict pass through Sean's eyes, just for a moment, before he smoothed it over with a soft smile. "Of course we can," he said, his voice gentle. "That's a great idea, Lucas."

Lucas nodded, visibly relieved, his energy picking up. "I saw this necklace at Macy's that I think Mom would like."

He turned to me shyly. "You'd know the best styles, right? But ... is it okay if, this time, it's just Dad and me going shopping?" His eyes darted between us, hesitant but hopeful.

I glanced at Sean, who was already gazing at me, his hand slipping low on my back, resting just above my hip. His touch was possessive, sending a ripple of warmth through me.

Leaning toward Lucas, I whispered, "Seeing how your dad is practically glowing at the idea, I'd say it's more than okay. It's perfect."

Sean squeezed my waist and leaned in, his lips brushing against the side of my neck, making my breath hitch. "Though girlfriends are usually welcome when men go shopping," he teased, his lips grazing my ear as his voice dropped to a huskier tone, "I'm afraid I'll have to ask you to skip this one, Chloe."

There. It was out in the open now.

Lucas, wide-eyed, looked between us before finally asking the question that had clearly been on his mind. "Is Chloe your girlfriend?"

Sean didn't break eye contact with me, his fingers now tracing soft patterns along my thigh under the table. "She sure as hell is mine," he said, his voice low but firm. Then, as if to prove it, he leaned in, capturing my lips in a slow, deep kiss, one that left me breathless.

His hand stayed at the small of my back, drawing me closer as the kiss lingered longer than necessary. Lucas giggled, pretending to gag, but Sean didn't pull away. His eyes were fixed on me, burning with a hunger that was impossible to miss.

"I'm the luckiest man alive," Sean said softly, his thumb brushing along my jaw as he finally pulled back, though his gaze never wavered.

Lucas, watching us intently, seemed to absorb the shift in his dad's demeanor. "Yeah," he said thoughtfully, "you seem ... different."

Sean grinned, wrapping his arm around me as we settled back in our chairs. The room suddenly felt warmer, more intimate. In that moment, I felt completely wrapped in his love and attention, as if the rest of the world didn't exist.

After dinner, as we cleared the plates, Sean caught my hand, pulling me close, his lips brushing my forehead. "Anne has come over to take care of Lucas for a bit. Are you ready to head out?" he asked in a playful, secretive tone that made my heart skip a beat.

"Where are we going?" I asked, smiling as I looked up at him, already trusting wherever he was leading me.

"You'll see," Sean said with a wink.

We said good night to Lucas. Sean gave him a quick hug, ruffling his hair, before he retreated to his room, his mind buzzing about plans for his mom's birthday, and then we slipped out of the penthouse.

Later, as the car finally came to a stop, Sean hopped out and hurried around to open the door for me. I stepped out, the cool night air brushing my face, and glanced around, curious about our destination. We were in SoHo, and nestled between a vintage bookstore and a cozy coffee shop was Erin's Taxidermy.

Ah, now, I understood.

The storefront had plush velvet curtains framing the dark display windows. Inside, colorful birds were posed mid-flight, their feathers vibrant and delicate. I spotted a few lizards, quickly averting my gaze with a quiet laugh.

"What are we doing here?" I asked, my brow raised, amusement in my voice.

Sean smiled, slipping his arm around my waist. "You'll see. Trust me."

Sean opened the shop's heavy wooden door. A bell chimed as we entered, and the scent of leather and chemicals wafted through the air, creating an atmosphere that was strangely inviting.

"Erin," Sean called out into the empty room, and I looked around, wondering where Erin would pop out from.

I was both nervous and excited to meet her. Sean had met my brother a while ago, and I was aware that today was a big step for him. I'd "officially" met Lucas as Sean's girlfriend, and now, I was meeting his half-sister.

I looked around at the taxidermy animals decorating the space. They were posed artfully, and their glassy eyes seemingly watched over us.

I gulped as I took in the rest of the shop. A life-sized alligator was on display, and I wondered if there were any other stories of odd animals a pet owner wanted to preserve. Off to the side were books on animal and bird anatomy, and the empty shelves had posters of animal skeletons.

"We won't be here long; don't worry," Sean added at my side, a smile on his face as he looked at me.

I nodded. I had just spotted a cobra mount, head raised and its fangs bared, and I had temporarily lost use of my tongue.

Through a side door, a woman hurried in. She had the same striking features as Sean, but with piercing green eyes and raven-black hair in a pixie cut. She wore a folksy blue dress that suited her eclectic style, and she had a smile that was genuine and wide.

Her gaze fell on Sean first before she turned to me.

"Chloe, meet my half-sister, Erin Wallace," Sean said. "Erin, this is Chloe—"

"Nichols, yes, I remember," Erin said, turning warm eyes to me. "He mentions you every time I speak to him, so I've been badgering him to let me meet you. I'm glad we're finally meeting."

"Same here. And your shop looks out of this world. You have a fantastic collection," I said, looking around.

"Erin is obsessed with her job," Sean explained. "She was desperate to show you the shop."

"Do you have pets?" Erin asked me, a hopeful look in her eye.

I opened my mouth to respond when Sean gave Erin a look.

"Erin, I will not have you treating my girlfriend like a potential customer."

"It's a bad habit of mine." She grinned at me with ease. "Come on. I'll give you a tour."

In the next half hour, I saw an otter mount—which she claimed was her best model yet—and an Airedale terrier that looked even more doglike than its photograph, and a grinning hyena with a mischievous appearance.

"How do you like it here so far?" I asked her, remembering that Sean had told me a little about her recent move to New York.

"It's been great. I'm glad I let Sean convince me to move here because I'd been complaining about how lonely I was in Florida."

I angled my head sideways to look at Sean. Did he know how considerate that made him sound?

"When Sean learned that this storefront was available, he sent me a picture of this place and also said that he could help me with a loan for the down payment if I moved here. The location was too good to refuse, even if I haven't been able to pay Sean back as fast as I'd like."

"She's too proud to let me waive it off," Sean said while Erin nodded with an easy laugh.

She turned to me. "So, tell me, how did the two of you meet?"

I grinned. "We met at a café, where I flung a cup of coffee on him, after my fiancé dumped me."

"Over the phone," Sean corrected in a manner that suggested he would never forgive Bruce for it.

"And Sean held me while I sobbed my heart out on the sidewalk."

Erin gave Sean a happy look before nodding at me. "I see that kindness in him all the time, by the way," she added. "Over the past month, he's come over to help me fix things in my shop, and if it's something he can't fix, he makes sure he gets someone who can."

I turned to Sean, amazed at this touching detail of him being a caring elder brother. He gave me an awkward shrug and looked like he wanted to change the subject.

"He's taken great care of me as well," I said warmly. "Though at times, he can be a bit—"

"Of a know-it-all?" Erin asked good-naturedly. "Possessive? Blunt?"

I nodded, giving her a wink while Sean looked taken aback.

"I'm not any of those things," he grunted.

"Don't worry," I said, pulling him close to me and wrapping my arms around him. "Those are the things I love about you."

52

CHLOE

A couple of days after my fun evening with Sean and Erin, I walked back home from the subway station after work.

My week had been going well. Greg had brought the trash bins back this week on his scheduled turn, and a few other friendly neighbors had moved in, making me feel optimistic about finding a community of friends here in our building. I was feeling so good that on my way home, I stopped to get Henry's favorite burger from Shake Shack.

My PMP certification course had been going well, thanks to Sean's support, and I was fairly confident that I could pass the exam and get certified soon. I was glad Sean had pushed me to do this, especially since I was coming up on the deadline to leave my job at Tassater Inc.

I pushed the apartment door open and walked in, putting my handbag down and looking around for a place to hang my keys. The table by the apartment door was a mess, filled with mail that I'd brought in the previous day.

My gaze went to one of the letters that Henry had left on the table. It was addressed to him, and I picked it up, meaning to clean up the place, when my gaze fell on the word *congratulations*.

I froze. Before I could read the rest, I looked up and saw the door to Henry's room open.

He rolled out, humming a tune and looking generally pleased with the world. He stopped when he saw me, his gaze drifting slowly and dramatically to the paper in my hand.

The silence in the room was thick and heavy while I debated what to say.

"Chloe," he said, his voice serious as he wheeled himself over to me.

When he reached me, I held the letter out to him. "What is it?" I asked, my voice trembling because, if Henry was keeping something from me, it must be serious.

"It's just an admission to grad school," he said.

I sat down on the edge of the sofa, feeling like someone had sucked all the air out of me. The bag with the Shake Shack burger fell to the floor.

Had Henry been applying for grad school?

"I did it on a dare," Henry explained. "Ronan dared me to apply because he'd been applying too. I sent it in ages ago and forgot about it until now."

I stared at the envelope, wondering just how much of our future we missed because we never went beyond our comfort zone.

Henry could go to graduate school.

"What is the admission for?" I asked.

The idea did not appeal to me. It would mean a lot of changes for us, and I just wasn't mentally and emotionally ready for it.

"It's a partial scholarship to study chemistry at MIT," he

said. "It's for a five-year master's and PhD program, which is mostly for people who love teaching—"

"But you don't," I interrupted, hating myself as I said those words. "You dislike teaching."

He thought about it for a moment. "I like research," he said. "Chloe, it's MIT."

"What about the job covering sports for the paper?" I asked.

Henry frowned. "I'm inclined to turn it down. It'll involve a fair bit of traveling, and you know I hate any change in my routine."

Even with my reluctant dismissal, pieces of his future life were coming together in my mind, and I didn't like it. I knew the offer from MIT was too good to turn down. If Henry wanted to pursue that—I gulped—then, by extension, I'd be going with him.

It would take some getting used to. Moving to Boston. I'd need to find a job there. We'd need to be in Boston for five years while he completed his PhD.

Tingles ran up my body. My brother had a bright future, and I ought to be proud of him instead of worrying.

"Oh, Henry," I said, running over to him and putting my arms around him for a hug.

I buried my head on his shoulder, inhaling his familiar comforting smell while he patted me on the back. He let me hold him tight for a moment before he looked up at me.

"Can I read the letter?" I asked, and he nodded.

"The first year's tuition is paid for," he said in a minute. "And I'll work hard to get a scholarship in the second year too. And the years after that."

I said nothing, but looked away.

"And there's a grant that's providing me funds for my

living expenses for the first year. We'll obviously need to figure out the living expenses for my second year."

He looked around the apartment. "I know it's a huge change, but we can make it work," he said.

We would leave New York. And therefore ... Sean.

"I'll need to figure out the expenses, of course, but I'm sure I can talk to someone at—"

"Henry, I'm not leaving," I said, my words ringing loud and clear.

He processed that while I looked at the cabinets and the efforts I'd gone through to make sure they were accessible to Henry. So much of our memories were tied up here.

"What do you mean?" he asked, looking confused. "You always said you'd give anything to be able to go back in time and get a college education yourself. It's the easiest way to have access to better jobs and a better life. Those were your words."

I sat down on the nearest chair. "Henry"—my voice was weary—"I promised myself I'd never leave this home."

It was a lie. I didn't want to leave Sean.

"Chloe"—his voice was gentle—"I'm not moving to Boston by myself. You'll join me. I don't want to leave you here. This is the opportunity of a lifetime. How are you not getting this?"

"Why don't you go to Boston alone?" I asked, my voice sounding broken.

He rolled his eyes at that. "Yeah, right," he muttered.

I cringed. I could see it now. I'd let my guilt control my life so much; by being around him every possible minute of my life, I'd taken away his confidence in himself.

"Chloe, do you know how hard it is to get into MIT?"

"Yes, and I'm rightfully proud."

"So, you expect me to go to Boston? All by myself?" he asked, his frustration building.

There had been many arguments between us when it came to his health, but so far, I'd always given in. But this time, I didn't want to give in. I wanted him to follow his dreams alone. Had he never stopped to consider that he could manage just fine, even if those dreams led him away from me?

I was suddenly put on the spot, being made to choose between the two most important people in my life. The answer surprised me.

I was choosing Sean over Henry.

I wasn't ready to tell Henry this just yet. About how strongly I felt for Sean. Sean needed to hear that first.

"Henry, I understand you think you need me around. This is my way of telling you that you don't need anyone anymore. You're very capable of doing things by yourself. Why, just last week, you drove to college."

Of course he hadn't realized that he didn't need me. I couldn't go out on a date without him needing me in the middle of it.

"Boston is five hours from here," he said, cutting me short. "Away from you."

I felt helpless. I didn't know how to make him see sense. He finally had an opening, a chance for a future that would give him a stable, if not stellar, job. Why did he have to insist I be a part of it?

I nodded. "I know," I said quietly. "I can't move there. I'm not leaving this home because this is the place with memories of Mom and Dad," I lied again. "Even if I wanted to, I'm not leaving it. Ever."

That seemed to sting him the most.

"And I can't go without you," he said, looking frustrated.

"I've been naive enough to think that our life would somehow change for the better in the foreseeable future. You know what? It never will. We'll live this life again and again, growing old like this. It's the first time this vision of my future sounds less than appealing to me. I don't want this life ten years from now. Heck, even five years from now. I want more. I want better. And I can't have it."

I agreed. Only the future I saw was different from his. I wanted a family of my own and a brother who wasn't codependent on me. Bruce had warned me about this, and so had Sean, but I could now see it. Henry would never let me go.

"There are many times when I think it's time we face our past and come to terms with it. But we don't need to face our past. We're still living in it," he said, his voice sounding pained. "I'm turning down MIT. So, there."

I stared at him like he was crazy. All I felt was a sort of numbness, one that seemed to spread out to my fingers. Henry would turn down any good thing just to hold tight to me. I didn't know what to do with my life anymore. Apart from a strange desire to run away, away from this apartment, him, and even from Sean, who asked things of me I couldn't seem to give. Like a full night together. We'd been seeing each other for five months now, and I still hadn't spent the night at his place. It was crazy.

His eyes strayed to the takeout bag by my feet, and he looked exasperated. "Let's just have dinner," he said.

I handed it over, and Henry took a look inside.

"Why do you always buy just one?" he asked.

"I buy only one because only you like it. Not me. It's always been about you, Henry. And it doesn't feel right anymore."

At my words, he set his burger back down. I could feel

disappointment radiating from him and felt ashamed. Why was I doing this? Now, Henry wouldn't eat his dinner, and his mood would be ruined. My mood would be ruined. Just when everything was going so well.

"I'm sorry," I added, noticing that his burger lay untouched. I didn't want him to go hungry tonight because of this conversation. "Please eat it, Henry. I'm sorry for being so irritable."

"We're not talking about this again," he said, crumpling the letter of admission up and tossing it in the bin.

Taking his plate, he rolled away to his room, shutting the door, while I stayed alone in the living room.

After a few silent minutes, I made a call to Tess, feeling conflicted. I knew what Sean would say if I were to tell him about this because Sean was biased. Tess was, too, but a little less biased than Sean.

"You know, even if it didn't work out, I'm so proud of you for pushing Henry to do it alone," Tess said quietly after I filled her in. "The old Chloe I knew would have never done that."

"Yes, well ..." I struggled with my emotions for a bit. "There's something to be said for Henry and me being independent, isn't there?"

She chuckled. "Yes, Chloe. Yes. Is this new and improved Chloe all thanks to Sean?" Tess asked after a bit.

"Nonsense," I said immediately, and she laughed.

"Sean's been a good influence on you," she said. "Are the two of you serious? It sure seems like that to me."

I scoffed at that. If there was one thing I could bank on, it was our expectations from our relationship.

Purely physical.

I sat down on the couch, staring at the coffee table. The table where Henry had explained a soccer game to Sean.

Sean had even come to our doorstep to make sure Henry was okay after the college emergency incident. Sean had unyieldingly, patiently been there for me. Right from the day he'd given me a job when there wasn't a position open.

Tess was still talking. "So, have you thought about what it will mean that you won't leave New York for Boston when Sean is still here?"

I took a deep breath and closed my eyes. As the thought hit me, I realized something else.

I didn't want Sean to ever leave me.

The idea was shocking.

We'd decided we weren't going to be in a relationship. I'd wanted exactly that. An emotionless fling. But life, so often, made me feel like I was mountain climbing without a safety harness. And lately, it felt like Sean and I had been mountain climbing together without harnesses, and that felt okay. That felt doable. The mountain conquerable, the safety harnesses unnecessary because we were together.

I was in love with him.

Did I admit this to him? And if I did, what if he just upped and left? What if this was wading into the dangerous territory for him, bringing back memories of his bad relationships? Did I have the courage to be alone, without Sean?

53

SEAN

Chris, my driver, was guiding the sleek black Rolls-Royce through the crowded Manhattan streets. The vehicle glided through the bustling roads lined with towering skyscrapers and a slew of yellow cabs. The traffic was relentless with horns blaring all around us, only intensifying as we approached 59th Street.

"Have I told you that you've been looking better lately?" Chris mentioned as he turned the car smoothly from one lane to another.

I laughed. "Are you talking about the new buzz cut I got?" I asked, running my fingers through my very short hair.

Chloe had been very approving of the new look.

"No. You're happier," Chris said. "And I've seen you with your buzz cut before. Maybe six years ago."

I didn't remember, but Chris had an excellent memory. I latched on to the other bit of information. Happy. I remembered telling Chloe she could be happily single when I met her. What a fool I had been. She made me so happy by being with me. She wasn't meant to be single, and with a woman like her around, neither was I. But Chris and I never discussed such things.

"Thanks," I said. "I hadn't realized it was that obvious. The credit goes to Chloe."

Chris nodded, like it was something he'd known already. "She's great," he said. "Honest and friendly."

That was the shorter version of it. I could add a lot more—gorgeous, made me feel better whenever she was around, mind-blowing in bed—but this wasn't the time for it.

"I've known you for over a decade, and yet I don't know where you got that scar above your eyebrow from," I asked Chris.

He shook his head. "I've been trying to forget about that one. I was riding with my friend who was slightly drunk. He didn't notice the pickup truck sliding to the next lane, and before we knew it, we flipped, the car in the air." He turned the steering wheel as he deftly maneuvered the car to the right. "I was lucky I was wearing my seat belt. Otherwise, I'd have a lot more scars than just this one."

"That must have been traumatic. Did your friend do okay?"

Chris shook his head. "He didn't make it," he said.

Damn. No wonder he's such a stickler about me wearing my seat belt, I mused, looking at Chris with feeling.

Losing people close to us was always a shock, and I hated that so many people around me had been affected by death of their loved ones.

As I looked out, I saw couples walking down the street, crossing the road to Central Park's south entrance. One couple had coffee in hand, a dog in tow, and as I watched, they stopped to share a kiss. A languid, easy kiss in the middle of the street before they resumed walking, the guy's arm around the girl's waist.

I grinned, picturing how wonderful it would feel to do the same with Chloe. *This weekend perhaps*, I noted, planning to pick her up from her home and walking down the street with her, hand in hand. Hopefully, the weather would be good.

It took me a moment to realize I'd never done something remotely similar with Helen.

The realization hit me like a freight train. Had I grown closer to Chloe than I ever had been with Helen?

I closed my eyes with a groan. I was imagining doing couple things and not just with anyone, but with *Chloe*.

My phone rang, and I opened my eyes to answer it when a sudden movement caught my eye.

Out of nowhere, a delivery truck veered into our lane, as though it was oblivious to our presence. Time seemed to slow down as I braced myself for the impending collision. The blare of horns built up around us as Chris swerved sharply, but not enough to completely avoid the massive truck. I felt a sudden jolt as the truck hit the side of our car, tires screeched, and the car began to spin out of control.

The world outside the car window was a blur of flashing lights and frantic faces as adrenaline raced through my veins. My hands reached into space, trying to grip something, while my heart pounded in my chest. The smell of burned rubber filled the air as the car hit a parked green Toyota with less force than I'd have expected before we came to a shuddering halt.

I took a shaky breath before I reached for the man in front of me. "Are you okay?" I asked Chris, who could barely turn with the deployed air bag.

He nodded, his hands trembling as he reached to push the airbag away.

As the dust settled, I glanced through the window to see

the massive truck swerving away, narrowly missing other vehicles. The road was chaotic, and it looked like, apart from us and the parked car, no one else was involved or hurt. For a moment, my world stood still as I realized the gravity of what had just happened.

We'd been inches from disaster.

I ought to be thankful to be alive.

Chris glanced at me through the rearview mirror, a silent understanding passing between us. In light of what we'd just been discussing, this moment felt even scarier. My heart still racing from the adrenaline surge, I closed my eyes and put my head in my hands as the sounds of an approaching fire truck reached us.

Getting out, I helped Chris out just as I stared at the dents in my car and the green Toyota parked on the street.

What if something serious had occurred? What if I'd died?

I haven't told Chloe that I love her.

The thought haunted me all night long, long after the paramedics gave us the go-ahead and we took a cab back home.

54

CHLOE

I walked up to The Regal, a new place that Sean had insisted I meet him at.

It had been a scary week after realizing that he'd been in an accident. He'd taken it easy during my last few days at work with him, and I hadn't seen him at work much, even though we'd met up at home every evening.

I'd had a tough time saying goodbye to some people at Tassater I'd grown close to. I had a couple of job offers in hand, all of which were like the job I had just completed for Sean. I was still hoping to pass my PMP exam, and apply for a different role once I passed.

I'm on my way over, he had texted. *I want you to take a look at this place and let me know what you think. I'll see you there.*

Wondering if this was another of his real estate investment places, I made my way up the sidewalk, slowing down when I reached the entrance. I'd wanted to talk to him, to let him know about Henry's college admission, and the phone had not seemed like a good place for that.

I'd been texting Erin a lot lately, and she had been so much fun to talk to. I loved seeing her and Sean bond with each other. I'd grown so comfortable with her that I realized I'd miss her when things with Sean eventually ended. Her, Lucas, and, of course, my Sean.

There wouldn't be another man like him again. Of that much, I was sure. I was a fool, but a loyal fool, and I would have to pay for the mistakes my dad and I had made. Mistakes that had brought Henry to where he was.

I reached the address Sean had given me. At the apartment, the doorman recognized me.

"You can head on in, ma'am," he said, much to my surprise, and led me to the elevator. "I'll let you in."

"We've never met before," I pointed out, shaking his hand as I introduced myself.

"I'm David," he said. "And Mr. Tassater showed me a picture of you and asked me to make sure you have access."

Stunned, I walked into the elevator, which I noticed was plenty big. I hit the button for the penthouse, and the elevator slowly took me up. When the doors opened, it did so directly to a living room. My mouth fell open when I saw the ten-foot ceiling and the soft orange glow of the setting sun filtering through the floor-to-ceiling windows.

A Banksy painting hung on the wall with its thinker monkey, next to a more peaceful Monet painting of the countryside.

I walked in, my footsteps muffled by the plush beige carpet that covered the large living area.

The room had an open floor plan that led to a gleaming kitchen with shiny stainless steel appliances. Through the window, I could see an expansive view of the New York skyline, its twinkling lights a stark contrast against the darkening sky, and I inhaled sharply. I could never get used to this sight.

The door pushed open behind me, and I turned to see Sean.

55

SEAN

I watched her walk through it all, marveling at the open space and the floor-to-ceiling windows. She could see the city through it, and the sight made her stop and stare unabashedly.

"You're going to love waking up to this view," she said.

She tried to push the curtains aside and failed until I handed her the remote. She raised her eyebrows but tapped a few buttons on the remote until the screens parted, letting the fiery sunshine in.

"Wow, this room faces west, so you're going to have plenty of sunshine when you're back home in the evening. I know how much you like seeing the sun set while having dinner."

"Someone I know taught me that," I teased, holding her hand in mine. Warmth spread through me at the touch. "I've seen you gaze at the sunset for far longer than can be good for your eyes."

She nodded. "I love how everything is dusted golden yellow at sunset. Though sunsets are orange and pink too. I never knew those colors were possible in a setting sky."

Chloe was here, and I was a happy man. My chest felt like it was swelling with joy. She was the only person I'd ever wanted.

Her multihued skirt twirled as she walked round the penthouse, barefoot, but instead of excited, it looked like something troubled her. The delight I'd expected to see didn't show up in her eyes, and her smile never made an appearance.

I watched her for a minute while she pointed out various buildings in the distance and the sparkle of the ocean before I spoke.

"Move in with me, Chloe."

"I bet you can even see the Bank of America Tower—" she said before she turned to me, her mouth falling open. Her blue eyes searched mine. "What did you just say?"

I took her hands in mine, looking at her with the sunny sky in the background. For a second, I wished we were at the point in our relationship where I could even go down on my knee. Heck, she deserved that. But we'd been seeing each other for barely six months, and it would be too soon. To be fair, all signs pointed to us going there eventually, but I also wanted to be careful. To take my time and think things through. To evaluate all the outcomes if I ever went down the Helen route with her and make sure I was okay with it. I wasn't there yet.

This was where I was.

"Let me show you another unit in this building," I said, leading her back to the elevator and down to the first floor.

When we got out into the lobby, I walked up to the first unit on our right, opening the door slowly.

Chloe's mouth dropped open as she gazed at the interior.

It was an accessible apartment unit. "Do you see the wide entryways for all the rooms?"

She nodded, registering where I was going with this.

"Ditto for the entrance and the doorways to the individual rooms in the apartment. There are no steps in this unit; everything fits into one floor with an open floor plan. The bathroom has a roll-in shower with grab bars in multiple places near the shower and the toilet. It also has tons of space, enabling Henry to maneuver a wheelchair."

The kitchen countertops were low. Easy for Henry to access. Including the cabinets at the lower level.

She ran her finger over the marble countertop. "Are you serious?" she asked, sounding awed. "You bought this place?"

I nodded. "Henry can move in here and still be close to you. I knew it's what you'd want."

"Is it what you want?" she asked after a moment.

I breathed in deeply. I needed to be honest with her. "I want whatever makes you happy. If that means you will be with me while being the best sister to Henry, then so be it."

She looked unconvinced, but I took her in my arms and kissed her deeply.

"Move in with me," I repeated, looking at her for a sign of what she was thinking. "I bought this building for us. If Henry doesn't like this unit, he can always choose another one."

She gaped and then looked away. She turned back to me, the shock still evident on her face as I led her to the elevator and back to our penthouse. I got her to sit on the cloud couch at the center of the living space while she continued to look dazed.

"I love you, Chloe. I want to move in here with you. I want to wake up every morning here with you and end my nights looking at you, staring at the setting sun and warning you not to look too hard at it. I want all of you, Chloe—the neurotic, the scatterbrained, the joyful, and the loving sides of you—to move in with me."

It was painful, putting myself out there with an ask that could be turned down. With Chloe, I could've been content to stay in status quo. To date, to see each other in the evenings, and to occasionally take holidays together. We could go on for years doing that, and I suspected Chloe wouldn't complain. She wasn't going to ask me where this was heading or what my plans were.

So, here I was, doing the one thing she'd least expected me to. Surprising her. Competing with the version she had in her mind of me. I was risking it all.

"You can't be serious," she said at last.

I tilted my head to the side. "I'm sorry. What's strange about this? We've known each other for six months now."

"We haven't said *I love you* yet."

"In case you haven't been listening, I just did, Chloe. And I do," I said, getting down on my knees to look at her. "I love you. And I want you to be a part of my world. My day and my nights. Will you?"

56

CHLOE

I bit my lip as I considered Sean's crazy question.

It *was* crazy.

Moving in together when we'd only known each other for six months. But it was a wicked, sending-tingles-up-my-body kind of crazy. The heart-stoppingly-mad-adrenaline-rush crazy.

And it was with Sean. He knew me. He understood not to exclude Henry.

I turned to him, and he was watching me with those earnest, intense eyes. The kind of gaze that left me breathless.

I wanted him. I wanted him with me for every day of the year. Life was glorious when I was with him, whether it was in this penthouse or in my shabby apartment.

And this place definitely had enough room for us. Unlike my apartment.

Here, the elevator opened into a large, airy living room that was furnished in an off-white and cream palette. The entire wall overlooking the street below was made of glass, and a lot of natural light flooded in, making the place seem welcoming. A couple of cloud couches occupied the living area, and a giant TV was fixed to the wall across from it.

The ceiling was so high up; it was as though someone had combined two floors of apartments to make this one. I felt small and trivial until Sean's hand came to my side protectively.

"Why don't we have dinner while you think about it?" he asked, leading me to the kitchen, where I noticed bags of takeout on the expansive kitchen island.

I nodded as I followed him to the sleek kitchen with dark granite countertops.

The kitchen was magnificent.

A large island occupied the center, and a sparkling counter swept around the lengths of the kitchen wall. The fridge was stainless steel, but had a monitor and an LCD screen. The oak wood cabinets that occupied the wall above the counters were classy, and the cabinet handles gleamed.

"Our first meal in what I hope is our new home," he said, stopping by the island.

Our home. I'd never dared to dream of that. But that was the thing with Sean. He gave life to all my impossible dreams.

"Though I'd probably be afraid of eating here and making a mess," I blurted out as I looked around. "Everything looks so shiny and pristine."

Sean laughed and pulled out a pizza from one of the takeout boxes. "Go ahead. Toss one at the wall if that'll make you feel better. This is your home now, Chloe."

Laughing, I put it away and reached for the bag myself.

When I looked at the contents, I turned back to him in surprise. "Did you just order everything on the menu?"

He grinned. "You can tell I'm trying my best to get you to say yes."

"Well, right now, it's a very tempting proposition," I admitted, just as Sean pulled open a bag of beignets, sending a splattering of powdered sugar on my face.

I gasped, stunned. I dipped my hand in the bag of beignets as Sean protested, and then I chased after him through the penthouse, determined to get some on him and his polished suit.

I succeeded. Very well, I might add.

The next hour and a half were spent deliciously getting our bellies filled with the amazing food. And the crazy part?

We didn't even finish our meal.

We forgot about our dinner midway when I discovered the desserts he'd ordered. That was when kissing became more important than eating.

Straddling him, I licked whipped cream off of Sean's nose, and he slowly fed me grapes. Soon, Sean was pushing my dress up to my waist, and I shifted until I could feel his cock straining against his pants. He pulled the straps of my dress down my shoulders.

"Oof," he muttered hopelessly when he noticed I wasn't wearing a bra. "I love this kind of surprise," he groaned, taking in the sight of me sitting topless on him.

He traced the swell of my breasts with his fingers, desire etched over his beautiful features. "Did you plan to fuck me tonight, Chloe?" he asked before he bent forward and took a nipple in his mouth.

I arched my back and moaned while the city of New York twinkled through the glass windows beyond us.

Darkness had set in, and even in a city of millions, it felt like it was just him and me in this world.

"I might have had some plans of that kind," I gasped as he sucked on my hard nipple. I ran my hands through his hair, soon begging him for more.

In minutes, Sean took his pants off, and I slid over his erection, moaning as he claimed me inch by inch.

He stretched me out like no one else had.

I rocked up and down on him while he held my butt, pulling me closer and deeper into him.

Almost immediately, I came apart with a loud cry, my head thrown back while I dug my fingers into his back. Sean followed soon after, pumping his cum into me.

Laughing and spent, we fell into bed, naked, soon after, delaying the inevitable shower while we snuggled.

Our laughter was interrupted by a call, and I sat up, running for the phone.

In a minute, I went back to the bedroom, feeling conflicted.

"Henry wants me back home," I said, sounding dejected.

"Hell no. I'm not going to let you go this time," he said, sitting up. "We will not have a repeat of our previous date night if I can help it."

I stared at my phone, wondering if I had it in me to turn down Henry's request.

"No, Chloe," Sean said even more firmly. "You're not leaving tonight. I need you. I want you here. Ignore Henry's calls for one night. For tonight, I want you to be mine and only mine."

I fought with my first instinct. I fought against the urge to go back to Henry. I had never felt this torn before. I wanted Sean, but I also wanted my brother to trust me. To know that I'd come back.

"Do you want to be here?" he asked while I considered all the possibilities.

I debated his question and finally nodded.

"That does it," he said, settling back down and holding

his arms out for me to join him. "Set your phone aside and go back home tomorrow. Henry isn't hurt, is he?"

I shook my head. "Not hurt. He just doesn't want to be alone."

"After he stays alone for one night, he'll realize it isn't as scary as he thinks it is. He'll be fine."

57

CHLOE

The next morning, after my first full night out, I made my way home in Sean's car, nervous but excited. In my hand, I held the extra key fob to Sean's penthouse. He'd insisted I have them.

Well, not Sean's penthouse, but ours, I corrected immediately.

I'd enjoyed my night with Sean, and I was thrilled at the idea of moving in with him.

Henry had texted and called me a few times throughout the night before giving up. I'd set my phone on silent, and I noticed his missed calls on my ride back home.

I'd need to check with Henry, of course, but going by how the two were getting along, I didn't foresee many problems.

I saw that I could have a normal life, and I could see beyond to weeks and months ahead. And I liked what I saw. Days and evenings filled with Sean, Lucas, and Henry. Not having to pick only one of them, but all of them. I wanted Henry to meet Lucas and to be a part of my weekend mornings with Sean.

When the car dropped me off at home, I all but bounded up the sidewalk to the apartment door, opening it with a flourish.

I was this close to bursting into song when the open door revealed a pale and sleepy-eyed Henry in the hallway.

The happy words on the tip of my lips died when I saw a long and bloody scar on his forehead.

Without thinking, I rushed up to him, dropping my handbag and kneeling down next to him in an instant. "What happened to you?" I asked hoarsely.

"Where were you?" he responded.

Ignoring his question, I looked around the living room.

A heart-shattering mess of broken glass shards took up most of the living room floor. My heart almost stopped at the sight. Had he broken most of the glasses we had?

I turned back to Henry in shock.

"Dad showed up last night," Henry said, looking at me with anger.

I felt faint. "Last night?" I echoed, wondering how I'd missed him. I had left home around six p.m. "When?" I asked.

"At eight p.m. The second time I'd called you last night, and you didn't answer," Henry said, putting his head in his hands and looking distraught. He lifted his head, and there was a new fire in his eyes. "How dare you reach out to him and ask him to show up for my graduation ceremony?"

Oh shit.

"He showed up here, telling me he was planning to be there after all, and I told him to go to hell. I don't want that man anywhere near us," Henry spat. "I hate him for the way he treated us, and how could you find it in your heart to go back to him, Chloe?"

I almost broke down sobbing. Henry was right. The man

had given up his claim on us a long time ago, and only Henry had the clarity to see that. I had been an emotional fool, hoping for a happy-family moment on his graduation night.

The only family we had was each other.

"Did the sight of Dad affect you this much?" I asked, trembling as I looked at the shards of broken glass.

The look Henry gave me was eerie. "No," he said. "But when he told me something you'd been keeping from me, that was when I lost it."

Our gazes locked, and I knew instantly what Henry was talking about.

He knew.

"When I heard it, I got so mad. I couldn't take it anymore. I was holding this glass in my hand, and I flung it at the wall."

My fingers touched his bloody wound. "And a shard ricocheted off the wall and hit you," I finished for him.

"Why did you lie, Chloe?" he asked, his voice sounding strangled. "Why didn't you tell me that the reason Dad left was because of me? Not your stupid college tuition."

My lower lip trembled. "Because I didn't think you could take it," I said finally as Henry's gaze bored into mine. "On top of everything else you were going through, I couldn't trust that—"

"I could handle the truth?" he demanded angrily.

I nodded, finding it impossible to speak for a second. All those emotions were flooding back through me. "You were thirteen, Henry. I couldn't do that to you."

"But what happened when I turned eighteen? Or twenty-one? Heck, I'm twenty-three now, and you still haven't told me the truth. It was him—that man who is biologically our father—who gave me the truth."

I nodded, breaking down in tears. "I'm sorry, Henry. You deserved to know the truth. Just like you deserved to know that I went to visit Dad recently to ask him to show up for your graduation. I made mistakes, over and over again. Not just this, but also for the day you got hit by the car. I hate myself for it, for not being able to protect you from that, and I don't think I can even forgive myself. I'm sorry, Henry. I really, truly am."

He wheeled over to me, and I leaned against him, sobbing on his shoulder while he hugged me tight.

"Hey, hey," he said, wiping my tears off my face. "I don't blame you for the accident. If anything, it was that stupid car that hit me. That driver who was driving high. You have no reason to feel bad about that, Chloe. Do you hear me?"

I raised my head and looked at him through my tear-filled eyes. "It isn't as easy as that to wipe off my guilt, Henry. Believe me, I've been trying."

He laughed a small laugh. "Try harder," he said, resting his head against mine. "I didn't know my sister to be weak enough to give up. The Chloe I knew was strong. She wouldn't let some stupid guilt take control of her life. Who are you, and when can you give me my sister back?"

I laughed, lifting my head and wiping the tears off my cheeks. "I think I last saw that girl ten years ago. She's been missing in spirit ever since."

Henry held my gaze for a long time.

"I'm not going anywhere, Henry. I told you that. You'll always have me, Henry."

I hugged him tight, tears streaming down my face as I saw the scar was three inches long. I needed to get him to a doctor.

He looked at the broken pieces of glass on the floor

while I tried to stand up. When he looked up, his expression was filled with regret.

"I don't know what came over me, Chloe. I did not know what was going on with me—"

"You were terrified, Henry. I promise you, it'll never happen again, Henry. I'm not leaving you again. Now, can we please get to the doctor?"

The silence in the room was thick and heavy while he debated what to say.

Finally, he nodded. "Let's go."

58

SEAN

The past few days had been tough. When Chloe had texted me, letting me know what she saw when she returned home, I'd had a bad feeling.

I was relieved that Henry was fine, but Chloe seemed to partly shut down, refusing to talk for longer than a minute over the phone.

During this, I'd pulled off a major acquisition that I'd long hoped would one day define my legacy.

I'd successfully navigated merging Tassater with Hathwell Textiles. Now, I could expand the Tassater empire into new territories. But when I shook hands with the CEO of Hathwell, rejoicing on our deal and the millions this would bring in to the company, I felt nothing. No joy, no exhilaration, nothing.

When Chloe wasn't with me, my life seemed dull, the happiness ebbing away.

And now?

Work had become completely meaningless when our fate seemed to hang in the balance.

It had been three days since Chloe had spent the night

with me, after we discussed moving in to this new apartment together. I'd finally convinced her to meet me, and she'd agreed to come to the penthouse.

I paced the living room, waiting for her. The place was bare, and a few days ago, I'd imagined how Chloe would like to decorate it. Now, I tried to convince myself that this was still a possibility.

When the elevator doors opened, I watched eagerly, like a starved dog, while Chloe walked in.

Before I'd met her, I thought I was happy. I knew better now. I knew that being with her made me happy beyond my wildest dreams. I'd always wanted to guard myself from falling in love, but now, I embraced it. I was done protecting myself.

"How are you?" was the first question out of my lips when Chloe took a step inside the penthouse.

I'd clocked her somber mood as soon as she walked in. Her blond hair was down to her shoulders, and her expression, when she met my gaze, was one of vulnerability.

The image of her went straight to my heart, and I enveloped her in a hug. She rested her head on my chest briefly, holding me tight.

She smelled sweet and looked so beautiful. The irrational part of me wanted to trace every curve on her body with my lips.

I settled for kissing her.

God, how I'd missed her the past few days.

"I've missed you too," Chloe murmured, leaving her forehead on my chest for a moment before she stepped back.

I took her hand in mine, and she let me, following me back to the couch.

We sat down, and she didn't snuggle up to me like she usually did.

I ran my fingers over the back of her hand, asking her questions about Henry while she answered. I took a clearer view of her as she spoke, noticing she looked a little strained and her voice was unsteady.

Finally, when she finished filling me in, she looked at me. Silence stretched, and the two of us continued to gaze at each other.

She reached into her handbag and drew out the key fob I'd given her days ago. She reached over and put it in my hand.

My heart sank even before she could utter the words.

"Sean," she said, her voice breaking. I could see the pain etched on her features. "It's time we end things."

I stared at the key fob, my heart hammering with the speed of a hundred horses.

"Is this about what happened to Henry?" I asked at last.

"Henry got hurt because I wasn't around. Again. I can't risk that happening in the future."

"So, you can't risk having a love life anymore?"

She nodded. "I tried it. It was wonderful while it lasted, but I don't see us going ahead with this. Not when my responsibility is toward Henry."

I barked a short, bitter laugh. "So, you're breaking up with me? I was afraid of that," I admitted. "Which was why I hoped to convince you we could still make something of the two of us. I thought having you and Henry move in to the same building would give you the best of both worlds. And it would give me what I wanted the most—you."

She looked at me, tears in her eyes. "I never really needed anything from you, Sean, except for *you*. Your time. Your presence. This large penthouse was never one of my expectations from you. Nor your money or things that the money can buy."

She raked her fingers through her hair, looking troubled. "Sean, darling, I've seen you provide for many people—from your son to your half-sister and mom. But I need nothing from you. I don't want this gift of a new penthouse."

I walked over to the windows, looking down at the busy streets below us.

After the scare from a few nights ago, Henry was doing fine. Life should have gone on.

She should have been in love with the idea by now, in love with me, enough that we should be rejoicing. We should be celebrating with laughter, champagne, and sex by that window instead of having a serious discussion.

"Chloe, I love you, and I want to take care of you. This is my way of taking care of you."

"Well, I don't need it, Sean. I'm happy in my apartment."

The words hit me in the gut like a brick.

She hadn't said she loved me. She never had.

Resentment and anger burned in me. She was rejecting me and my gifts.

I turned away. She didn't need me or my money. That much was clear. Call me a caveman, but providing was the role I felt most adept at, most suited to. If she took that role away from me, she left me with nothing. The same feeling I'd felt when my mom left and dad was silent for days on end.

I wanted to rage, to shoot back some of this hurt, to pretend like she didn't matter. Like none of this mattered to me. In reality, I wasn't used to being the one who was hurt. The old Sean would've hurt the woman back. But I couldn't do that to Chloe.

"Chloe, this is me using my resources to take care of the

people I love. Whether it's my son, my half-sister, or you. Providing is my role in relationships. How can I lose you when you're the reason I'm finally on better terms with my family? Give me a chance, Chloe."

"I can't," she said, her voice breaking. "I couldn't take it if anything more happened to Henry. It's hard enough for him already."

"Isn't it hard enough on you too?" I asked, walking up to her and taking her chin in my hand, forcing her to look at me. "To always put yourself last? To put your needs as an afterthought?"

She stared at me, her lower lip shaking. "It's not hard," she said in a tone that made my heart break. "It's not because I've gotten so used to it, Sean. It's normal for me to put my needs last."

I looked at her, feeling devastated and overwhelmed. There were too many emotions swirling in my chest, and I didn't know how to process it. Well, I did. I'd throw money at it, but Chloe had barred me from doing that. So, I was now lost.

She made a strange sound that was halfway between a sob and a sarcastic laugh. "Look at me. I was such a fool for thinking I could have a loving relationship. In reality, I can't. I can't ever know what it is like to truly love someone with all the pain I'm carrying around. With all the guilt I'm carrying around. If I left Henry for you, I'd just add to my guilt. He risked his life to save me, and he took the hit himself. An incident for which he still pays for *every single day*. And then I have the gall to think I can desert him again when our father did it once already. I have nothing left to give, Sean, so please let me go."

How the fuck did one make sense of all these emotions when your hands were tied?

"If I let you go, Chloe, it's giving up. I don't want us to give up. I want to fight for us. Because what I feel with you, for you, is something I thought I'd never experience in my life."

"Don't ask me for that, Sean. Don't ask me for anything more because I have nothing left in me to give you. Nothing."

With that, she grabbed her purse and walked out of our shiny new penthouse.

59

SEAN

Five days had passed, and Chloe hadn't spoken to me at all. I was in my old townhouse, where brightly decorated balloons bobbed in the air, attached to tables covered in vibrant tablecloths. I was devastated after Chloe had rejected me and my offer. I'd thought I'd had the perfect solution. Making space for Henry in my life and having him move in to the same building as us. I'd risked it all to have Chloe in my life and lost. Chloe had chosen Henry over me.

"You know," my ex-wife, Helen, said as we walked up to the doorway of my bedroom, "I was surprised when Lucas insisted on having his eighth birthday party here instead of at my place. Now, I can see why."

I suppressed a laugh. My large bedroom had been transformed into an empty space for bouncy houses. Kids were joyfully bouncing around, giggling and laughing. In the background, hired entertainers, dressed as various superheroes, posed with kids and their parents for photographs.

"I could never compete with this," Helen said, looking around at the dining table behind us, which had a long chocolate fountain with numerous treats that kids would dip into the flowing chocolate. Around it were cupcakes and cookies made by a pastry chef, keeping with the Spider-Man theme. They were delicious.

"You don't need to compete, Helen," I said, leaning against the doorway. "He loves you."

She laughed. "Thank goodness he loves me," she added with a wave of her hand. "I don't have all of this to buy his love."

I frowned, wondering if I was doing that, when a guest tapped Helen on the shoulder. She turned around and began to speak while I watched the kids, still frowning. I felt someone's eyes on me and realized Lucas had been staring at Helen and me in conversation all this time.

I walked into the bedroom, approaching him with some concern. He turned away stubbornly, but I reached out and stopped him.

"Hey," I said. "Is something wrong?" I scanned his expression, which was midway between a frown and a disappointed look.

Lucas's gaze strayed to the door, where some of the guests were still walking in. "Where is Chloe?" he asked. "She promised me she'd be here. Did you fight with her?"

I sighed. "Chloe won't be here today, Lucas. I'm really sorry. But I'm here," I added, holding my arms out for a hug.

He didn't lean in. "Chloe made you a nicer person, Dad. I want her back."

I put my hands down, feeling a heavy weight in my heart. Perhaps Lucas could handle the truth.

"I fought for her, Lucas. I love her deeply and wanted more from her. A proper home and a relationship I could announce to the world. But she ... didn't feel the same."

"Maybe all she needs is some time, Dad. Because she

knows what a wonderful person you are. She told me so herself. She'll come back to you—I'm sure of it. Just like how Mom came back to me."

I knelt down on the ground next to him, trying to process the sudden onslaught of emotions that hit me. "Lucas," I breathed out, pulling him to me for a hug. I ruffled his hair, taken aback at his confidence in me. "Thank you, son. But I hope to prove to you that I can be a nice person even if Chloe isn't around."

He drew back from me stubbornly. "I want Chloe back. She loves spending time with me."

I looked around the room, wishing I could point to everything I'd done to show him how much I cared for him, too, when I remembered Helen's comment. I wasn't buying his love with money. No.

"Lucas," I said looking at him evenly. "I love spending time with you too. If you weren't my son, I wouldn't be who I am today. Instead of being with you on your eighth birthday party, I'd be sipping from a bottle of scotch on the couch, passed out and lost. If I was not your father, I wouldn't end my workday thinking about how to build our next tree house or fly a drone together. I would have spent my evenings setting up more business meetings and being the same miserable person every day. I've changed so much by having you, and you're my biggest source of pride, son. Never ever feel like you are unwanted. You are so much wanted and loved by me and your mom."

I sat down cross-legged next to him, feeling blessed to have this chance, to have his attention on me. How much I'd craved it, having him listen to me, to talk to me, and trust me with what happened to him. It was a privilege, and I'd taken it for granted. Five years from now, I knew I'd be begging for his time and attention, after brushing him off when he'd asked for the same from me.

I put my hands on his shoulders. "I'm sorry, son, that I haven't been a great dad for the first eight years of your life. I promise you, Lucas, that I'll try to be a better dad from here on out."

He gave me a doubtful look, and I shook my head in disbelief.

"Is it so hard to believe that I can be a good dad?"

He gave me a half shrug and an expression that said, *Duh*.

"Well," I said, "how about this? I'll try to be a better person first. Can you believe I can do that?"

He considered that before finally, excruciatingly painfully giving me a single nod. "Okay," he said.

Lucas pointed to the bouncy castle behind us. "Hey, want to go spook the Spider-Man who's walking with his back to us?"

I stood up and gave him my hand. "I can be very quiet," I promised, following him.

60

CHLOE

The sun was streaming through the windows, casting a warm glow on the tiny living room.

Henry rolled backward and forward in his wheelchair restlessly while I sat on the couch, staring at the wall.

It had been a month since I'd ended things with Sean, and I still couldn't stop feeling distraught.

I'd tried to tell myself that I'd done the right thing for Henry. Even so, my heart said losing what I'd had with Sean felt stupid, like I'd made a big mistake. Even learning that I'd passed my PMP exam didn't make me feel better.

I haven't lost anything; I reminded myself.

Henry was still here. I was still here. We had a roof over our heads, a bank account that would pull me along for the next six months even if I didn't find a job, and so much to look forward to with Henry's upcoming graduation party. I hadn't even considered going to the small ceremony that the continuing education program was holding later today for the people who'd gotten their PMP certificate.

None of that seemed to matter when my phone wouldn't light up with Sean's call or text.

The fears of entering a relationship with Sean had been many, and I'd told myself I wouldn't get too consumed by Sean's love. But his love for me had been so quiet, so silent, when it enveloped me in its warmth that I didn't realize how messed up I'd gotten after getting involved with him. I'd realized it only when I was hopelessly in love with Sean.

Every night when I went to sleep on the bed Sean had delivered home for me, I thought of him. Sean had shown me he didn't want to leave me. I didn't scare him off. Henry didn't scare him off. It wasn't a fling at all. It had been a solid relationship, one I shouldn't have had to walk away from.

I watched as Henry rolled down the hallway, briefly glancing at the family photos and personal trinkets decorating the walls. Then, I followed and entered Henry's room after him. It, too, had pictures. An old one of Mom's with me and Henry. In it, I was seven, and we were photographed outside in the snow. Henry was moments away from flinging a snowball at me, and I had a cheeky grin on my face, as though I knew exactly how I was going to dodge that ball. It was twenty-one years ago.

The silence stretched again. Miserably.

"Why does something feel off?" I mused aloud.

He looked confused, but I bit my lip and remained quiet. I couldn't talk about Sean. I wouldn't.

"I passed the PMP exam, but I can't even bring myself to attend the informal certificate-giving ceremony later today. I don't want to do anything, to be honest."

"I'm not surprised you passed. You're nothing but the best at anything you choose to do. But it's definitely been a while since we've been able to celebrate things properly."

Henry rolled himself over to the window, his jaw tight. When he finally turned to me, he looked troubled.

"As a kid," Henry said, "you were always happy, no matter how demanding or unhappy the people around you were. Back then, you used to organize Dad's work schedule so that he could be around to drive Mom to her doctor's appointments, as well as find neighbors to watch over us if needed. You always surprised everyone with how mature and thoughtful you were. And I took your happiness for granted."

Henry's intense gaze was on me. "Do you love him?" he asked out of the blue.

I turned to him in surprise.

Apart from mentioning that we'd broken up, I'd never brought up Sean in the past month because it was too painful to speak his name. Henry had understood my silence on the subject and never pressed me for more.

I considered his question. I thought back to the feelings that had risen in my chest every time I was with Sean. I always felt a bunch of things around him, but one thing was pretty clear: I loved him.

"I did. I mean, I do."

Henry's expression was thoughtful.

I sat down on his bed. "It's been a month since I broke things off with Sean, and for every waking moment, it has felt like I made a horrible, horrible mistake."

The moments stretched, only broken by the distant sound of a church bell ringing.

Eleven a.m.

As a child, Henry had loved early mornings, waking up at six a.m. and rousing the entire household with him. Nowadays, he slept in more because of the side effects of his medicines.

"Henry, I need to be honest with you. When I told you I didn't want to leave this apartment because of memories of Mom and Dad here, I lied. I didn't want to join you in Boston because I didn't want to leave Sean. I love him."

He looked taken aback. "Well, why didn't you just say so?"

I stared at my hands. "Because that was the first time I realized how strongly I felt about him. I didn't know what to do. All I knew was that I didn't want to leave him."

He drew in a deep breath and nodded to himself, like he'd reached some sort of internal decision. "Do you remember, Chloe, in the years after my accident, how much work you took on? Finding a job, accompanying me to my appointments, giving up on your dreams for dance school. At the end of it all, you used to take pride in how strong I was. Those were the words you said so often over the phone whenever people asked you about me."

"I still am proud of you," I responded.

He nodded slowly. "You're my family, Chloe. My person. The one I can always depend on."

That was true.

"Do you think you can depend on me, Chloe?"

I opened my mouth and then struggled for an answer. Of course I could, but I was afraid to. Afraid of asking more from him.

"That's my answer right there," he said after a few moments.

"I don't need to depend on anyone, Henry," I said.

"But I do?" he retorted.

"No." I spoke hastily. "You don't need to depend on anyone either."

"Good, just so we're clear on that." He rolled over to the

table, where he pulled out his crumpled-up college admissions letter.

I frowned. Why was he still holding on to that?

"Because I changed my mind about this," he said. "I'm going."

Stunned, I opened my mouth to let him know what I thought when he spoke again.

"Alone."

I shut my mouth. That had been unexpected.

"You can depend on me, Chloe. Right now. Today. But I can see it isn't something that comes naturally to you. But I think that will change, especially when you see I can depend on myself first. I'm going to MIT, and I'll do it alone."

He gave me an appraising look while I was still speechless.

"Chloe, I know I can't live with you forever," he said at last, interpreting my silence correctly. "And if you love Sean, you need to be with him, not me."

I dragged my gaze up to his, my own eyes feeling heavy and pricking with tears.

"I can't do what Dad did to you," I whispered, my lower lip trembling. That was my worst nightmare.

He shook his head. "You leaving now isn't the same as what Dad did. Dad left mere months after my accident. When I was thirteen. That's not the case anymore. I'm twenty-three. We're both adults now. Both of us need to move on."

I looked at Henry, at his tight jaw.

"I don't need you anymore, Chloe."

His words felt like a dagger to my heart.

For a second, I thought it was all a mistake. Dad's visit had messed with Henry's mind.

I bit back the broken mix of emotions that filled my heart. Anger and frustration flared in me as I looked away.

Henry took my hand in his. The room fell silent for a moment, our emotions heavy in the air.

"Do you really need to be around me all the time, Chloe?" he choked out. "After the night you spent at Sean's and when I lost my temper, couldn't you have talked to me before you ended things with Sean? Couldn't you have trusted that I'd be okay even if I lost my temper? My anger was at Dad's sudden appearance and the secret you'd kept from me and not the fact that you were out of sight and away."

I turned to him, feeling conflicted.

"Chloe, we were young when Mom passed away. That and Dad leaving—it changed my outlook on life. I can't accept that we didn't grow up to be a typical family. If I couldn't have a stable family growing up, then I had nothing else to hold on to. So, every time you try to go away, I tried to hold on to you even more because I was uncertain if I'd lose you too."

"Well, you have me, but I haven't been happy lately," I said when a sudden realization hit me.

I had been caught up in my desire to give Henry a perfect life, but I hadn't considered if I'd filled my cup with love and attention.

I remembered, just then, as a kid, I had hated attention or being admired. It seemed like that hadn't changed since I had grown up. My need to give others my attention always outweighed my desire to receive.

"You know, Chloe, I'm not the only one who had to deal with Dad's absence. Dad abandoned the two of us, pushing you to take on the role of a caretaker. You act like his absence hasn't hurt you, but it has. You're hurt and broken, and Sean was the first man who could make you feel truly loved and happy. It was so clear from the happiness on your face in the past few months that he made you feel love and affection—something you'd been so starved for all these years. Something I couldn't give you—not the way Sean has."

Henry was right.

I was unhappy. I loved Sean, and I was fucking unhappy without him. How the hell had I walked away from him? The man I loved. The man who didn't know I loved him.

I paused, swallowing hard. Going by how I'd told myself all these years that love shouldn't matter and how hopeless I felt about Sean's absence now, I was so wrong.

I had been unhappy at home a lot lately, even before Sean entered my life. And I had been aware of it way before I could articulate it. But that was nothing compared to how miserable I felt without Sean right now, and it had been only a month.

Was Sean unhappy too?

I had spent the past ten years trying to make sure Henry didn't miss Dad for even a single second. I'd tried to be all that Henry needed—a mom, a dad, and a sibling—and it was exhausting.

I couldn't live like this again. Not after I'd seen how easy and enjoyable my life could be with Sean in it. My old life wouldn't do anymore.

Besides, Henry didn't need me to be all of those people. He simply needed me to be happy Chloe.

I'd made a mistake after Sean asked me to move in with him. I had chosen Henry out of guilt, even though my heart wanted Sean. I would not let guilt drive me anymore. I was done. My heart would do all the talking from here on because I was ready to choose to have Sean in my life.

What a fool I'd been by trying to separate my two lives.

"I have something to show you," I said, my voice trembling as I reached for my phone for a photo of me and Sean. It was one of the few we'd taken during our recent stolen dates.

I showed Henry more pictures, feeling embarrassed as I did so because so much had happened without him knowing. My time biking with Lucas and Sean, and my visit to Erin's shop. Why hadn't I shared these tidbits with Henry?

I had never pushed Sean to meet Henry, but Sean had voluntarily done it anyway. He'd gotten to know Henry little by little while I tried my best to keep them away. I had been breaking apart whatever little bond they were building. Looking back, I now felt regret.

We stopped at a picture of Lucas and me flying his drone. Sean had taken the picture, and I was giving Lucas a look of pure happiness.

Henry chuckled and took the phone in his hand for a closer look. "Is that really you?"

I nodded. "And that's Sean's son. And this," I said, scrolling to a picture of Erin, "is Sean's half-sister." I took a deep breath. "I've met Sean's family, Henry. They like me. I want you to meet them too. Will you?"

"I want to," he said firmly.

I walked over to his desk, where I picked up the familiar envelope that Henry had received recently in the mail.

My chest heaved as I took a deep breath. I understood. He was going to Boston, away from me. In my opinion, this was happening too soon. He was asking for too much, too fast. But when was the right time for him to move on, anyway? If not in his twenties, would I feel any better when he was in his thirties? Or his forties?

No, Henry was right.

Staying away from Henry was a risk I'd have to take. A possibility I'd have to face if I truly wanted Sean.

"I know Mom passed away, and we couldn't stop that," I said, realizing what I needed to do. "But there's still a way for you to make the rest of your childhood dreams come true," I said, putting the envelope back in his hands. "I'm glad you're going to accept the admission. I'm glad you're going to grad school, and if research is what your heart wants, I'm happy beyond words that you're following it."

I bent down and hugged him tight, and he hugged me back as tears rolled down my eyes. We were losing our hold on each other, and my familiar emotions were not too far in the recesses of my mind—the hurt, the pain, the guilt. But this time, I was determined to fight them.

My dear, dear brother. I loved him too much, and I was going to miss him so much when he went away.

I pressed a kiss to his head and stood up. His eyes looked misty, too, but he gave me his trademark cheery smile. I walked over to his bedroom door.

I turned around with a last look at Henry.

"The Nichols siblings don't always stick together, Chloe. Because that would mean giving up on our dreams."

I smiled back at him. "And we never give up."

61

CHLOE

In the next hour, I talked to Tess from my room, filling her in on what had happened, before I took a quick shower. I needed to meet Sean, but first, I had to do something else. Something just for me.

I went to my closet and found one of my nicer dresses. Slipping it on and paying attention to my hair and styling it, I stepped out of my room.

When I'd told Henry where I was going, he'd refused to accompany me, telling me he had other ideas. I was disappointed, but I didn't let it change my plans.

Henry stayed in his room, and I knew he could take care of himself for the rest of the evening. He didn't need me anymore.

Before I could step out, there was a knock on the door, and I opened it to find Greg.

"Hello," Greg said, holding out balloons that said *Congrats!*

I could hear the surprise in my voice when I said, "Come on in!"

Greg took one hesitant step in. "I heard Henry was graduating soon ..." His voice trailed off as he stared at me. "Are you headed out somewhere?"

I grinned as I nodded. "Yes. I passed the PMP exam, and there's a small, informal event where I'll finally get my certificate," I announced. "If you'd like to speak to Henry, he's in his room."

Greg gave me a thumbs-up and stepped back, making room for me to walk out the door. "Go, go," he said.

"Bye, Greg. I'll be back soon!" I promised, stepping around him.

"Here," Greg said after a moment's hesitation. He took out one balloon and handed it to me. "I think you deserve it too."

I grinned, taking it. "Thank you."

In my dress and with my balloon in hand, I took the subway to the college where I'd taken my PMP certification course.

I got a few curious looks from the passengers as I got out of the train with my balloon, and as I skipped up the steps into the sunlight, I took a deep breath. I was learning to stand up for myself, and it felt oddly liberating.

It was a few minutes before six p.m. when I finally reached the college auditorium.

About a hundred fold-out chairs occupied the center of the auditorium, almost filled with students and their partners. The auditorium was huge, and I looked around it with some awe. At the far end of the auditorium was the university banner in gold and blue. And a podium for the speakers. My classmates waited in one line, and I walked toward them.

All around me was the excited chatter of my fellow students and their proud families. It was a mid-sized room that the program coordinators had gotten for us and other continuing education students who were here to mingle and meet one last time. Our certificates would be mailed to us, so there really wasn't much to do here, but another classmate had informed me that the dean would still show up and call each of us on the stage briefly just to acknowledge our achievement.

Everyone was all smiles, and I spent the first half an hour laughing and talking just as the lights dimmed and the dean prepared to come onto the stage.

I was still holding on to my balloon when the man I was talking to drew in his breath and asked, "Who is that?"

He inclined his head toward the double doors of the auditorium, and I turned. What I saw made my heart leap. Wearing his trademark frown, one that was not as intense as it had been in the past, Sean swept into the room. Next to him, in his wheelchair, was Henry.

That scoundrel. *This* was what he'd been planning all along.

Henry had a grin on his face as he scanned the room.

Tall and authoritative, Sean stood by the door, and his deep voice reached me as he spoke to some people next to him.

One month—it had only been one month since we had last met, but seeing him here sent me reeling with shock. His face was serious, and he was dressed in his familiar navy-blue suit. I controlled the nerves that spread like fire in my belly.

"No way," I breathed out while people shifted in the line next to me. *What is Sean doing here?*

His deep brown hair was thick and slicked back, and he looked arrestingly handsome. Going by how a few other women were giving him looks over their shoulders, he wasn't missing out on any attention.

He scoured the crowd, his gaze searching, when Henry tapped him on the arm and pointed to a line of students. My line.

I turned around before Sean could spot me, my heart hammering in my chest. To my right, I saw an abrupt movement as the dean finally made an appearance. He walked up to Sean with an outstretched hand, looking surprised by his presence.

Sean gave the dean a brief nod before clapping him on the back and muttering a few words before walking right over to me. The dean stared, open-mouthed, at Sean's back, at his abrupt dismissal as Sean approached me.

He strode up, and his cologne, intense and musky, reached me. The man in front of me coughed and made room as Sean approached.

"Chloe," Sean said when he came to a stop next to me.

I let the balloon go, and it floated up to the roof. "You're here?" I asked, putting my hand out on the wall next to us as I steadied myself.

I'd thought I was prepared to see him, but it still felt unreal. I wasn't seeing things. It really was him.

"Henry told me you passed your exam," he said. He looked around the room decorated in the college's colors. "And that you finally had a reason to celebrate your hard work. So, of course, I'd be here."

I nodded, feeling overwhelmed by his concern for me even though we'd broken up. He truly *was* a good person.

"Thank you, Sean," I said, my hand clasping his. "But ..." I chanced a look at Henry, who stayed back but gave me a cheeky grin. "Did the two of you get here together?"

Sean's face broke into a half smile. "Henry and I took the bus," he said.

The image of Sean on public transportation was too

good to let go. "I'm going to have to see that for myself to believe it," I said, while Sean's eyes lit up.

"You mean you'll spend time with me again?" he asked immediately.

I hesitated, shooting a look around us. It was a fairly noisy environment, but I was still aware of people whispering near us.

"I appreciate you being here, Sean. You didn't have to do this. Supporting me and my success."

"I didn't *have* to, but I *wanted* to. Just like I didn't have to hire you, but I wanted to."

His gaze burned into mine, reminding me of our meeting at Tassater Inc. when his phone beeped. Sean checked it briefly, and when he turned to me, there was an honest to goodness twinkle in his eye.

"Besides, Henry and I are not the only ones supporting you," Sean said, angling his body as he looked back at the doors.

I followed his gaze, and in a moment, I saw two more of my favorite people. Erin and Lucas.

I turned back to Sean, happiness filling my chest, as I understood. Our hands grazed each other's, but neither of us made a move.

"All of us wanted to be here," he said as Erin caught up to us, Lucas by her side. Sean put his arm around either of them before looking at me.

Lucas gestured to Erin. "Have you met my aunt Erin, Chloe? She has a taxidermy shop—did you know that? Her animals are fiercer than if they were real."

"I have," I responded. "She's amazing."

Erin grinned, a bit distracted, as she looked at the groups of families around us. The dean was calling out people's names, and people were strolling up to the stage.

"It's your turn," she said just after the dean called my name.

Breaking off from Sean, I walked up to the stage slowly, hearing the polite applause from the crowd. In a second, however, I heard Lucas's unmistakable voice, joined by Erin and Sean.

"Go, Chloe!" Erin shouted.

"Congratulations!" Lucas shouted.

I saw Sean pumping his fist in the air.

"WAY TO GO, Chloe," he yelled loudly while Henry clapped and cheered next to them, the widest possible smile on his face.

For a moment, I was stumped as I heard Sean and his family cheer and applaud for me.

I'd been so worried on my way here because I had no one in my corner. I'd thought I'd be alone today. But here I was, surrounded by Henry, Sean, and his family, very much not alone and very touched by their love and affection—a love that matched how I felt about them.

My cheeks flushed, and my breath came faster. I shook hands with the dean and walked off the stage. On the other side, I met Sean, Henry and the others who had come over to cheer for me. We found a quiet corner in the room.

"Congratulations, Chloe," Sean said, his voice low. "I always knew you could do it."

His eyes were brimming with pride while Lucas took my hand and gave it a squeeze as Henry looked on in amusement.

"I told Dad you two would make up soon," Lucas said. "I was right, wasn't I? Dad was much happier after he told me we were coming here to meet you."

A look of shock took over Sean's face, and he met my

gaze. The two of us laughed awkwardly while Erin stepped in.

"Lucas, I seem to remember you needed the bathroom," Erin said hastily.

"But I don't need to go to the bathroom," Lucas protested while she pulled him away.

"I think you do," she insisted, while Henry gave us a thumbs up and moved away too.

Their voices faded into the distance while Sean and I looked at each other.

"How are you?" he asked, his gaze roving over my face. "I ... I've tried and failed to not think about you in the past few weeks."

I nodded, feeling my eyes moisten. "I've missed you, Sean." I hesitated. "You're really here for me? Even though we broke up?" I asked.

"Yes, a long time ago, you'd said you skipped your high school graduation because there was no one to cheer for you. Well, this," he said, "is us showing you that you've still got us even if we aren't together and—" Sean broke off, trying to collect himself.

I nodded, feeling my throat dry up. We kept our gaze on each other, and I was painfully aware of how much I'd missed every bit of him.

"Sean," I whispered as people laughed and talked around us, "I'm finally letting Henry go."

He nodded slowly. "He told me."

"I was going to tell you about that too. I wanted to do this one thing first to prove to you and me that I can stand up for myself," I said and hugged him. "I feel horrible that Henry is going away. But it's a small, horrible feeling. Not as big as the horrible feeling I had when I thought I'd lost you."

He smiled that wonderful smile that lit up his face.

"Sean," I said, "seven months ago, when Bruce gave up on me, I decided on a few things. One, I would never find a man who could truly care for me. Well, you proved that wrong when you fixed my bed after you saw my bruises. Two, I decided there was no way I could find a man who wouldn't run when he realized Henry was a part of my life for good. And you didn't run. You wanted him to move into the same building with us. And the last thing I decided was that there was no way I could find a man who could value me higher than his work."

My voice shook. "When you left DC and your meeting with Mark Waldorf to see me, well, I should've known then that you were special.

"I love you, Sean. I'm not perfect. I am nervous and petrified, but I'm here. I'm here to tell you I'm sorry for bailing on our relationship a month ago. That it was foolish of me to run away from you when you were so clearly committed. You're everything I want in a partner, Sean, and I was stupid to not see it earlier. To be scared and push you away. I'm *terrible* at relationships. I worry too much and have spent too long having no strong sense of self. But I love you. So very much. And I want to be with you, if you still want me. I want to keep fighting to be together again. If you'll forgive me and if you'll have me back, I want you. All of you."

Sean had an impossibly hopeless look on his face. "I've wanted you since I saw you at the café for the very first time, Chloe," he said with an unusual tenderness in his voice. "I've thought of you since that day, and weeks later, when I saw you at work, I was determined I wouldn't be around you. Because I knew I couldn't stay away, couldn't resist falling for you if you were around me at work. And that's exactly what happened. I fell for you—hard. A man can't fall out of love easily when that happens. It's been a month since we saw each other, but it might as well have been years. Staying away from you has been the hardest thing I've ever done in my life."

He came in closer and put his arms around my waist, drawing me to him.

I stared up at him, my hands slipping up to his shoulders, meeting at the back of his neck.

His eyes never wavered from mine. "Chloe," he declared, "I couldn't be apart from you if I tried. So, my answer is yes, Chloe." His eyes were soft and loving as he smiled back at me. "I really, really want to get back together with you."

In response, I leaned up and kissed him.

We kissed until I heard a voice say, "See, I knew they'd make up soon!" and we broke apart to see Lucas, Erin, and Henry with bright and cheery smiles as they clapped for us.

Sean extended his arm, and Lucas ran and gave us a giant hug, his arms enveloping his dad and me.

62

CHLOE

I woke just as dawn broke, lying in a bed that was as soft as a cloud. I turned to glimpse the man next to me. A sight I still hadn't gotten used to after a week. When my eyes came to rest on Sean, I noticed he'd awakened earlier than me, and he was lying on his side, propped up on his elbow. Just looking at me.

"How long have you been awake?" I asked, glancing at the clock. It was a little after seven in the morning.

"Not long enough," he said, placing a kiss on my forehead before wrapping an arm around me and pulling me closer.

It had been a magical, busy week. A few days ago, after Henry's graduation ceremony, Sean had suggested we take a quick vacation, just the two of us. I agreed, and we visited the little town of Southampton.

It had been a wonderful three days of lounging about in a luxurious hotel and having nothing but glorious, wonderful sex. We'd had meals at odd hours, stayed up late, and said goodbye to any and every notion of a routine.

Now that we were back in New York, in Sean's old apartment, I considered my options. Most of my things were still in my apartment, and I knew I'd have to go back sometime. It felt strange, waking up in Sean's apartment without having Henry around. I had no idea about Henry's current schedule, but he'd been happy and made an effort to ensure our calls these days focused more on my life and the changes I'd been having than his.

Henry was packing, and soon, our apartment would be empty. That hurt deep, but I knew it was a choice I'd made, and it was the price I had to pay. I'd chosen another life, and our childhood apartment wouldn't be ours anymore.

Sean leaned in, trailing kisses down my neck.

"I have an idea," he said, nuzzling my neck and pulling me closer.

I was in shorts and a tank top, and Sean was wearing nothing but his boxers.

After we came back to his New York apartment, Sean had made sure to introduce me to every nook and corner. We'd made a habit of making sure we had sex everywhere. On the couch while watching TV? Check. On the dining table right before dessert? Check. In the bathroom right after finding a creative way to finish dessert? Check. The kitchen wasn't spared either, and there was an imprint of my hand on the glass cabinet from when Sean had taken me deep on the counter.

Going by the way his lips trailed a path down my face and to my neck, he was getting ready for another amorous adventure. He smelled of his cologne from last night—a hint of citrus and cedarwood. Before his warm lips on my skin could make me catch my breath, something else did. I saw my old black tutu on a hanger in front of the dresser.

"What's that doing here?" I asked, sitting up on my elbows.

I turned to Sean with a questioning look because there was no one else I could accuse. He had a very knowing smile on his face as he reached up and ran his thumb lightly over my lips.

"You're smiling," I noted as I looked at him.

His brown eyes were warm with amusement, a playful expression on his face.

"From now on," he said, kissing my nose, my lips, and my neck, "I'll have you know that whenever I'm smiling, it's completely your fault." He finished up by kissing me on my bare shoulder. His eyes, tender but all knowing. "If there's a question you need to ask, you'd better do it now before I lose myself in you."

I placed a hand on his shoulder to nudge him aside as I got off the foot of the bed and walked toward the tutu. It was old and faded ... but it was mine. My memories were tied up in this smooth fabric. Loss and love intertwined.

"Where did you get it from?" I asked, amazed.

He sat up, swinging his legs off the bed. "During one of my evenings with Henry, I asked him if he knew of any special things from your time dancing, and he said you had this tucked away in your closet somewhere. He said you wore it last when you danced the night of his accident and never again. So, I brought it out."

"But I gave up on ballet a long time ago," I said, running my fingers over the tulle.

"But I remember seeing a rather wistful expression on your face at Brianna's dance performance. So, when I noticed a ballet dance company down the road from my new apartment, I thought of you. You're going to dance again, Chloe. I want you to have everything you've missed in the past ten years."

I walked over to him and cut his words off with a kiss. He

held me tight against him as he kissed back. When we broke apart, I looked up at his warm brown eyes.

"I love you," I said.

His voice lowered. "Move in with me," was all he said as his arms tightened around me.

I inhaled. I wanted to. Ever since that horrible fight, I'd regretted turning him down.

"To your new apartment?" I asked cautiously as my heart thrummed.

He hadn't moved there himself.

He nodded, easing me down gently onto the bed next to him. "Yes. I bought that place for us, and I didn't have the heart to move in there alone. If you don't like that apartment, we can find another one. But move in with me, Chloe. Live with me. It's been only eight months together, but I want to wake up with you and go to bed with you night after night."

All my breath left my lungs as wave after wave of emotion took over me. It took me a while to find my tongue, and when I did, I nodded, blinking back the happy tears.

"I will," I said, my hands brushing up his shoulders and cupping his face.

I loved this man. The way his stubborn expression broke into a smile just for me. The way he reached for my hand every time we walked together. The way he loved me, even when I couldn't.

His eyes lit up at my words, and he bent his head over mine, his mouth soft and warm. He tasted heavenly, his hand sliding up my back and cupping the back of my neck. I reached up to thread my fingers through his hair and angled my face so I could deepen the kiss. When we broke apart, chest heaving, I stared at him. Finding an impossible urge to tease him.

"I don't know about the new apartment though. What if it's too far from my workplace and my next boss has me running errands at all hours of the night?"

He picked me up with a growl and nuzzled my ear. "Then, I'll kill him."

I tut-tutted as I ran my hands through his hair while his lips made their way down my neck. "Behave, Sean. What will Lucas think of his newly changed dad speaking like this?"

"He's taking Brianna out on a date by the time he turns twelve. He'll understand what I mean," Sean said, his lips finding the dip in my cleavage and pulling me back to the bed.

Laying me down, he got on top of me on his knees, looking down with a proud smile.

"You look beautiful," he said.

I savored the sight of him. The fine slope of his nose and his sculpted jaw. His hand slipped under my top, and I closed my eyes while his fingers went up and down my sides.

"But I won't have you running around at night anymore," he murmured. "Not for me or anyone else, for that matter. You've taken care of Henry, and now that he's independent, you need to let me take care of you. So, whether that means watching reality TV for hours after work or having our new cook, Madge, make dinner for us, you can have it."

I closed my eyes at the image of relaxing in the evenings. At the idea of having Madge, his personal chef, handle the housework.

"I like the sound of that very much, Sean. I don't know how I'll ever thank you."

"You're here," he muttered again, bending down to get

on his elbows as he brushed my lips with a light, feathery kiss. "That's all I need."

I stared at him, eyes brimming with happiness. "I can't believe I almost lost you," I whispered.

"It won't happen again," he said, pushing a lock of hair off my face. "I'm happy with you. I'd be a fool to let you leave next time."

He was making sure I was introduced to every part of his life, including his friends and business partners. I'd even met Desmond and his wife, Ava, recently.

"By the way, I had a lovely time with Ava and Desmond yesterday," I said. "Did you know Ava asked me to join her shopping next weekend?"

"Is that so? That's new to me. How do you feel about it?"

"I like her," I said, thinking back to our dinner. "She's very grounded and totally in love with Desmond. I felt comfortable with her in a way I hadn't expected."

"She was Desmond's high school sweetheart. She knows him better than anyone else, and she's a very smart businesswoman herself."

I remembered Ava mentioning her restaurant and resolved to ask her more about it next time.

Sean's gaze turned curious. "How is Henry?"

My eyes dropped to my hands. I was quiet for a moment. "He's busy packing up his things and planning everything out for his PhD program. I'm not one hundred percent happy that he's moving so far away, but it's what he wants."

"I think it's a great sign Henry is going for it. The school has amazing facilities."

Add to that, I didn't have to worry about financing his medicines anymore. Sean had refused to let me worry about that, finding a pharmacy that would deliver his brand-name medicines directly to his home. I'd always worry about

Henry's health, but now, I knew that Sean would have Henry's back even if I couldn't.

I changed the subject, finding it hard to keep talking about Henry. "Lucas should be here soon," I reminded him.

Lucas was going to spend the day with me while Sean was having a busy day.

"And even though I'm not your assistant anymore, I should remind you that you have an event to get to today, even if it is a Sunday."

Tassater Inc.'s foray into Asia had been a success, and they were having a celebratory press conference, where Sean would have to show up.

He was holding me around my waist as he looked at me, drinking me in. "Since you stopped working for me a couple of months ago," he said, trailing kisses on my shoulder and down my arm, "it's my turn to remind you that you need to get dressed for the same event. Lucas *and* you are joining me."

I raised my eyebrows when he looked at me.

He nodded, a smile growing on his face. "All the public events? You're accompanying me from now on, Chloe. You're my girlfriend, and I'm showing you off to the world."

I bit my tongue. I had known we would have this discussion sometime, but I hadn't expected it to be so soon.

I was slowly getting comfortable with the idea of Sean and his world. But a public event?

"I'd love to," I said finally.

Sean wanted to show me and the entire world that he was serious about me. He'd never been photographed with a woman in the years after his divorce. So, this was a big deal.

My fingers found his hand, and I gripped it tight. "Though I don't know—"

"I know what you'll wear," he finished, kissing me again. "It will be delivered to you in a few hours, so perhaps we need to head to the shower soon."

Given my humble background, tongues would go wagging for sure, but I could now shrug and think ... *So what?* I had the best man in the world, a man who truly loved me, and nothing could affect me anymore.

I cupped his face in my hands. "Thank you," I whispered before leaning into his solid wall of a chest and hugging him. "Thank you for giving us another chance. Thank you for loving me. It's been an awesome journey so far, and I'm nervous about what will come next because how do you top this feeling?"

He laughed as he pulled me off the bed and to the bathroom and turned the shower on.

"I think I know how to top this feeling," he said, sliding a strap of my tank top off my shoulder.

He caressed my shoulders before undressing me. I lifted my arms, and in a minute, he took his clothes off as well, and we stepped into the shower.

"I love you," I whispered, and his eyes softened.

He leaned in. "I love you more," he said.

EPILOGUE: CHLOE

Five Years Later

I was standing by the window in our bedroom. The large bedroom was a sanctuary of silk sheets and down pillows. A four-poster bed, its headboard upholstered in velvet, dominated the room. Off to the side was a walk-in closet with a sea of designer gowns and tailored suits.

Ever since I'd passed my PMP certification, I had been working steadily at my career. I'd worked at two companies in the past five years, enjoying my role as a project manager. But I could still not afford this dress or this penthouse if it hadn't been for Sean. He enjoyed spoiling me. Case in point, I was wearing a new dress that Sean had bought for me that was worth a couple of months of my paycheck.

Sean was walking past the room to his private study when he stopped to look at me. I turned, met his gaze, and smiled. He raised his eyebrows in an appreciative gesture as he looked me up and down.

"You still take my breath away, Chloe," he said.

I smiled. "Right back at you, Sean."

He was wearing a sharp, tailored tuxedo that fit him well. Add that to his broad shoulders and the effortless grace in the way he carried himself—well, he ended up looking like he owned the world.

His dark chestnut hair added a touch of rugged charm, and his smile could still melt me.

"I still can't get used to the price tags on these things. This dress is a hundred times more expensive than the ones I'm used to," I protested, but he laughed and put a hand on my back.

"The person wearing the dress is way more precious to me," he responded with a light kiss.

From the living room, I heard a cry as our baby, May, gurgled while playing with Anne. I walked into the expansive living room, where eleven-month-old May played on the carpet. She had Sean's smile, loving and warm, and my blue eyes. She was our darling. At eleven months old, she would crawl like a champ and occasionally stand, no doubt to get more of the view.

Across from her, floor-to-ceiling windows framed a stunning view of the city with its twinkling lights and soaring skyscrapers. Plush sofas occupied the center of the room with silk throw pillows. A grand piano stood against one wall, all polished and gleaming.

"Are you sure she'll be okay?" I asked when Sean stood next to me. "I mean, the show is two hours, and Anne will need to tuck her in tonight by herself."

Sean put his hand on my shoulder before kissing my hair. "Chloe, tonight is your special night. You're dancing for an audience of a hundred. I think May will understand ten years from now why it was important that you couldn't tuck her in one night. If she remembers this incident at all in the first place."

His smile was wry, and I laughed. Of course she wouldn't remember. It would be okay if I missed kissing her good night today.

I leaned against Sean, placing my cheek against his chest. Ballet was irrevocably tied to Henry, and I always wished he was nearer to me. A few weeks ago, he had asked me to come see him graduate from his PhD program.

I'd been so thrilled that I had to sit down and blink back tears of happiness. I'd had a hard time with Henry's absence in the beginning, but over the years, our visits increased, thanks to Sean's private jet. Boston didn't feel that far away anymore.

"Thank you for helping me get back to ballet. Even after we had May and when things got more hectic, you always reminded me to take care of myself too."

His hand swept through my hair, and I felt the warmth of his lips press against my forehead.

"You did the same for me years ago," he murmured. "I have a better relationship with my son because of you. It's made me a better father to both Lucas and May. So, yes, my intelligent, hardworking, and dedicated wife, I'll make sure you never forget to take care of yourself because you do far too much for the people around you. Which is also why we need to leave now."

I walked out of the room with him, stopping to give May a kiss and a hug. May looked up at me with wide eyes, and Anne, our loyal nanny, waved from the doorway.

Together, we stepped out into the night. We got into the waiting limousine, and as we drove toward the Lincoln Center, memories flooded my mind. I had once attended a gala here with Sean, my heart fluttering in a gown he'd gifted me. Now, I was not a spectator, but a performer—a woman who had reclaimed her passion.

Sean held my hand, his thumb tracing circles on my skin. "No one will walk away this time," he said softly as we walked in. "No one will suffer because you took care of yourself."

His confidence anchored me. As we stepped into the Lincoln Center's grand foyer, I glimpsed the chandeliers, their crystals winking like stars.

All around us was the excited chatter of people when Sean gripped my hand tighter, his step faltering. We saw someone come forward from the shadows of the corridor.

"Is that ..." Sean breathed out, and I froze.

Henry was rolling toward us, accompanied by a young woman.

"Henry?" I asked in disbelief.

He nodded. He'd grown leaner, and his face had a mild tan, like he had been spending more time outdoors.

A petite, auburn-haired young woman walked up to us shyly while Henry came closer.

"Gayle, meet my sister, Chloe," Henry said.

Gayle turned to me with a bright smile. There was a definite blush in her cheeks as she shifted her weight from one foot to another.

"Chloe, this is my girlfriend, Gayle."

I knew Henry had been seeing Gayle, but we'd never met before. I could not hide the happiness in my eyes as I gave Gayle a hug and clocked Henry's contented look.

"I figured it was time you both met," was all he said, but I could read him well. I knew he was delighted at us finally meeting.

"I've wanted to meet you for forever," Gayle said. "Henry has always spoken so highly of you."

"Gayle and I were both student leaders, and that's how we met. We've been together for the past year now."

Gayle's eyes were on Henry. "He's amazing. The way he deals with the stubborn admin folks at department offices? He's a great people person and so kind. I'm really lucky to have him in my life."

I didn't know when I started to cry or when Sean's arm went around mine as I wept with happiness.

"Chloe," Henry said, reaching for my hand, "I don't blame you for being so surprised. When you mentioned that you were dancing here tonight in your recent text message, I knew I had to be here. Sean helped us get here in time."

I turned to Sean, who gave me a wicked smile.

"Henry had to be here," he confirmed while Henry nodded.

I stared at them, feeling vulnerable. I couldn't speak. I leaned down and hugged Henry tight. Tears went streaking down my cheeks while his arms went around my back.

"I've missed you so much, Henry."

"Now, go," he said, tilting his head to the stage as the theater hummed with anticipation, the velvet seats filled with eager spectators. "We'll speak more after the show."

The anticipation built within me—a crescendo of happiness, excitement, and thrill. At thirty-three, I felt like the eighteen-year-old me, but wiser, stronger. Tonight, there would be no accidents, no missteps. The stage waited.

Sean gave me a quick kiss and pulled me to him, whispering, "Good luck," before he let me go backstage.

Half an hour later, I stood in the wings, filled with nerves and exhilaration. Fifteen years had passed since I'd last graced a stage, but tonight, under the spotlight, I would reclaim my tiny but meaningful place in the dance world.

My pointe shoes grazed the floor easily with their satin ribbons. The pale blue tutu clung to me like a second skin as the orchestra swelled, the music beautiful and moving. I stepped forward, my breath hitching as the curtain lifted. The audience blurred into a sea of faces, their collective gaze fixed on me. In the past, I'd danced for applause, for pleasing the audience. Now, I would dance for myself.

My feet found their positions, and with my colleagues, I pushed off into the spotlight. The creak of the boards and the hush of the theater were all too familiar.

I glimpsed Sean in the audience. His eyes held a mix of pride and awe, his hands gripping the armrests. He had stood by me during the grueling rehearsals, the late nights, the doubts. His unwavering support fueled me now. And throughout the dance, Sean watched, his eyes never leaving me. He had kept his promise—to support me, to ensure my well-being.

As I twirled, I glimpsed Henry in the front row. Henry's face was a mirror of wonder. He would remember this night—the night his sister finally danced.

As my feet touched down, applause erupted—a thunderstorm of approval. I curtsied, tears blurring my vision. I had danced for love, for loss, for the girl I used to be.

But most of all, I had danced for the man who believed in me—the one who sat in the dimly lit theater, clapping until his palms stung.

Backstage, Sean enveloped me in a hug. "You were incredible, Chloe."

I buried my face in his shoulder, inhaling the scent of his cologne. "Thank you," I whispered. "For being here."

He kissed my temple. "Always."

And in that moment, I knew I had not only reclaimed the stage, but also found my anchor—the one who would applaud my encore, no matter how many years it took.

"I'll dance for you again and again," I said.

OTHER BOOKS BY MEG GARNET

The Billionaire's Proposal
Lucy and Jay's story

The Boss on the Brain
Ava and Desmond's story

ACKNOWLEDGMENTS

Many thanks to Jovana Shirley from Unforeseen Editing for fitting me into her schedule at the last moment and her brilliant work with editing this book. I'm also really grateful to Qamber Designs for the wonderful cover and for being so responsive when I reached out at the last minute. To my writing group friends who kept the inspiration going when the going got tough: thank you! And to you, my reader, without whom I couldn't keep going. Thank you for your support, always.

ABOUT THE AUTHOR

Meg Garnet first started writing romantic fiction when she was just a teenager and completely infatuated with Westlife, the boy-band. She discovered fanfiction and when she was reading and writing them, the world was a wonderful place.

Today, she loves writing books about down-on-their-luck women, the powerful men who fall hopelessly in love with them, and the happiness they find together that turns their worlds around.

You can find her in sunny California where she lives with her husband and toddler. When she's not writing, she's usually exploring local cafes or discovering yet another non-sandy beach.

Join her newsletter for bonus stories and updates.

www.meggarnet.com

Connect with Meg:

Printed in Dunstable, United Kingdom